THE COTILLION
OR
ONE GOOD BULL
IS
HALF THE HERD

THE COTILLION
OR
ONE GOOD BULL IS HALF THE HERD

John Oliver Killens

TRIDENT PRESS | NEW YORK

For my brothers Charles and Richard and my sister Charlie Mae—and all my Brothers and Sisters the world over; and a special appreciation to the Harlem Writers Guild.

Copyright, ©, 1971, by John Oliver Killens
All rights reserved.
No part of this book may be reproduced in any form without permission in writing from the publisher, except by a reviewer who may quote brief passages in a review to be printed in a magazine or newspaper.
SBN: 671-27072-9.
Library of Congress Catalog Card Number: 70-101243.
Published simultaneously in the United States and Canada by Trident Press, a division of Simon & Schuster, Inc., 630 Fifth Avenue, New York, N.Y. 10020.
Printed in the United States of America

FOREWORD

TO WHOM IT MAY CONCERN
(and to all you all who ought to be)

My name is Ben Ali Lumumba, and I'm free, Black and twenty-three. Okay, Lumumba is my given name. Dig. The name I gave myself, that is. My slave name was—well to hell with that. I'm a writer, understand. And I just finished the novel that I'm forewording to you, dear readers. I used to write my novels as I lived them from Rio all the way to Zanzibar. In the oral tradition of my African ancestors. I wrote my novels with my laughter and my tears, with my blood and sweat and years of wondering as I wandered (thanks to Langston) carousing, reading, brawling, learning, looking, drinking, fornicating, from Tashkent to Johannesburg, with all races and religions. I did not discriminate. Right now though, I should state, categorically, I have a tendency to boast and brag, or, in other words, exaggerate, and sometimes I'm a liar, like most men who have been to sea. I was a seaman, see?

Yeah, and like I can lie with the best of them. Which ought to put me in good stead as a writer, right? One has to lie sometimes to get closer to the truth. Check that out. Okay, so after all those years of the seven seas and far-off places in my blood, I was a salty sonofabitch, and I didn't mind dying if dying was all. And here I am back in the Apple, New York City, and my land legs are still a little wobbly, but all that is over now, and I have settled here in this place a few blocks from where my mother birthed me. Dig. I decided to be a writer. What else could I do, sentenced as I was (by me) to dry land for the rest of my young life's duration? I mean, I'd had it, for a time, with that traveling-is-broadening shit. Now I was ready to zero in. Focus, baby. I bought me a typewriter months (or was it years?) ago, brought it to my crib and began to write my first book. Then I started on my second book, after I gave up on my first one. Temporarily. My first book was entitled *All the Way to Timbuktu*, but I laid it aside momentarily till I could learn much more intelligence about the international scene, where things are never ever what they seem. My second book is the one I have just finished, the one I'm introducing with this hellfire introduction to whomsoever it may concern. Dig it.

This book is kind of halfly autobiographical and halfly fiction, all based on facts as I have gathered them. I got my log together, baby, from the natural source, the horse's mouth and his hinder parts. Also from the lips of the sweetest girl on this terrible wonderful earth. Dig it, and like I went to one of them downtown white workshops for a couple of months and got all screwed up with angles of narration, points of view, objectivity, universality, composition, author-intrusion, sentence structure, syntax, first person, second person. I got so screwed up I couldn't unwind myself, for days. I said, to hell with all that! I'm the first, second and third person my own damn self. And I will intrude, protrude, obtrude or exclude my point of view any time it suits my disposition. Dig that. I read all the books on writing. Egri, John Howard Lawson, Percy Lubbeck, McHugh, Reynolds. You name it. I know all about the dialectical approach, character development, cause-and-effect and orchestration, the obligatory scene, crisis, climax, denouement, and resolution. I was uptight with the craft shit. Can you dig it?

I decided to write my book in Afro-Americanese. Black rhythm, baby. Yeah, we got rhythm, brothers, sisters. Black idiom, Black nuances, Black style. Black truths. Black exaggerations. Oh I can use the big Anglo-Saxon words with the best of them, and I used them every now and then for the benefit of those brothers and sisters of the middle-class persuasion who are unduly impressed with the king and queen's faggoty unimaginative English. Nevertheless and basically, this is a Black comedy. I mean a Black black comedy. Dig it. And I meant to do myself some signifying. I meant to let it all hang out.

But now, on with the story. And Black blessings to you all. Right on—

> BEN ALI LUMUMBA
> *son of*
> Harlem, U.S.A.

P.S. But the story is not about me, not really about me, but about a fox named Yoruba.

> B.A.L.

CHAPTER ONE

YORUBA

Hey!
CALL HER YORUBA, RIGHT?
High priestess of the Nation!
You ready for that?
Negritude? Okay?
African queen!
Black and comely was this Harlem princess.
Yoruba, her father named her.
And Yoruba she would always be—praise Allah from whom all blessings flow. Would you believe—GreatGodAlmighty!?
She was Yoruba Evelyn Lovejoy, a working girl that summer, and a queen she was among all working girls. Hell yes! Say it plain —Yoruba! Dig it! And named she was, proudly, from her Georgia father's Black and wondrously angry and terribly frustrated nationalism.
Pure, beautiful, untampered-by-the-white-man Yoruba. Black and princessly Yoruba, as if she'd just got off the boat from Yoruba-land in the western region of the then Nigeria. Sometimes, when her father got into one of his rare and whiskeyed moods, he would trace his father's father's father back to Ogshogbo, then further eastward, to Benin City, then clear across the mighty Niger, at Asaba and Onitsha, south by southeast, by ferry, foot and mammywagon, all the way to Arachuku, that land of fable of the long juju.
Now—she—the girl—Yoruba—walked westward through the jungle to Eighth Avenue and went down into Manhattan's man-made earth and took the "A" Train. Her middle name was Evelyn, the

first syllable pronounced, Britishly, like the woman made from Adam's ribs and like Christmas Eve and the night before the New Year. Spell it E-V-E-L-Y-N—pronounce it Eve-lyn, was her mother's contribution. Her strong, proud, West Indian mother from the small and windward island of Barbados.

The "A" Train almost leaped the tracks, as it thundered underneath the city, reeling and rocking and screeching, like it had blown its natural stack. Winging nonstop from Fifty-ninth all the way to the main stem at One Hundred and Twenty-fifth. Vacuum-packed with perspiring, dehydrated, Black and white humanity of all sizes and denominations. An air-swindled concoction of sound and sweat and soap and perfume and beaucoup talk, Afro-Americanese, West Indianese, Italianese, Jewishese, Puerto-Ricanese, all screwed up with New Yorkese. Africa—Europe—Caribbean. East to West, the twain was met. And it was a mess to listen to. And hot air, baby, by the ton, hot air was blown, stirred together by the whirligig electric fans overhead and shaken up by this St. Vitus-dancing, boogalooing, epileptic "A" Train. Funky Broadway all the time. Funky! Oooh! Yeah! Dig it! Creating one overwhelming impact which rendered Yoruba's senses numb, and the dear child almost senseless. She felt a total assault upon her mouth, nostrils, eyes, ears, throat. Her Black and brown and righteous body. It happened every week-day that memorable summer, after she finished high school and took a job downtown in the garment wilderness.

FIVE P.M. And people erupted out of the monstrous buildings like missiles catapulted from great guns, onto the streets, and flowed in floodtide through the jungle toward those insatiable subways, which, like great carnivorous beasts, starved, and from another age, swallowed men and women whole; then, belching and breaking wind and regurgitating, threw them up again onto the overflowing streets uptown. Every evening it was—

>TAKE THE "A" TRAIN
>Every day. Every day.
>Hurry—Hurry—Hurry—
>TAKE THE "A" TRAIN

She—the girl—Yoruba closed her eyes, as she held onto the subway strap, closed her large eyes, dark and wide ones, and she could hear the Duke of Ellington's immortal music, feel it pouring through her senses like cascades of clear branch water, oooweee! Hear it, feel it, in all its varied and varying movements, in a stormy crescendo now, surging ever onward, upward, swelling, gathering its forces as it went, sweeping all and everything before it, even as the train itself went clackety-clack, slapping the rails with its own peculiar Afro rhythm, amassing speed and sound and frenzy, as it moved toward its conclusion. Destination Harlem. It was the Soul Train. Dig it, mother—brother—sister—

TAKE THE "A" TRAIN

It was no accident, the girl, Yoruba, thought, that a Black man had composed this great song, this tribute to New York's regal train. A train whose soul was as Black and beautiful as burnished ebony. It had rhythm. It had heart. It had Negritude. Right? And it was not the "B" or "G" Train, but the "A" Train.

With her left hand Yoruba clung to the subway strap with a kind of final desperation, as the train roared past the local stop at One Hundred and Third Street, wailing, moaning, groaning, making with the beat and the righteous sounds and taking care of business. At the same time the Black girl jabbed, accidentally-on-purpose, her right elbow into a cushiony overstuffed belly of a fortyish-year-old manchild, who stood behind her much too close to her for comfort (Yoruba's blessed comfort), and was trying his best to maneuver himself into an even cozier situation. She had a violent, well-trained right elbow for mashers. Sometimes she carried a hatpin for such overfriendly straphangers.

The famous train was moving now past the local stop at One Hundred and Sixteenth Street, and braking, shaking, screaming, rocking, screeching like a jet airliner coming in for landing. A case of pure and sweet hysteria. The sound, the smell of burning black-eyed peas and fresh coffee cooking, the shakes, the dance, the rock-the-roll, the sweat, the vacuum-packed homo sapiens were too much for Yoruba sometimes, and today, this day, she knew a giddiness in her head and a feeling like seasickness at rock-bottom in her stomach. She thought she might faint standing up, and she panicked for a moment. She would not faint though, she knew she could not faint, for there was no space for such bourgeois self-indulgences here on this jam-packed subway train.

She was Yoruba (sometimes her father called her Ruba, with affection). Eve and Ruby to her mother. Yo-roo-ba to some. She was a burnished-Black-brown slightly burnt toast of a girl; her skin was like it had been scrubbed with fine stones from the River Niger (her father used to say); scrubbed till her dear dark skin cried out in hurt and protest. She had her mother's thin nose; the tip was turned up ever so slightly like her mother's disposition. She had her father's wide thick curving generous lips, sensitive and sensuous. Life—love—anguish. Her mouth told you so many things. Compassion, tears, laughter. Her mouth was soul music, brothers. Listen to the sounds come out. The bottom lip perhaps slightly smaller than the top. Her eyes were Black on Black. Oooh! so deeply black were they, and wide in the middle and narrow at the outer edges. And slanting like the Orient. The girl thought, here on this train there is no room to faint, as smilingly she remembered an old blues fragment she had heard the great Odetta do the one time Ruba had been down to the Village Gate. She thought:

> AIN'T IT HARD TO STUMBLE
> WHEN YOU GOT NO PLACE TO FALL?

As the train came reeling squealing screaming to a lurching stop, throwing bodies against bodies, in an orgy of crazy off-time dancing, and various and varied familiarities, Yoruba thought she knew how Jonah must have felt in the belly of Moby Dick's great-great-grandpoppa. She thought, Jonah never had it so good. Grandpop's stomach could not possibly have been as congested as the "A" Train. First and foremost, the great train was Billy Strayhorn and Duke Ellington. So it was Blood. Right? It was sound and frenzy, the thunder and the lightning. The train was folks. Right? The train was also happenings. Always and forever happening. Every day—every day. Hurry! Hurry! Hurry!

Halfway between One Hundred and Sixteenth and One Hundred and Twenty-fifth Street, the people fell away from each other, the waves of people parted like the Red Sea must have parted when old Moses waved his famous rod. This time, instead of Moses, here on this train was a tall, powerfully constructed Black woman, weighing in at about two hundred and twenty pounds and nearing forty years of sojourn on this planet. This time, instead of a rod, it was an umbrella that the lady brandished. And she waved it above her head and brought it down again and again upon the blond head of a sawed-off, undernourished, red-faced white man, as she drove him before her, and beat him out of the train onto the platform. She outweighed the pale-faced culprit by seventy pounds or more. A clear-cut case of overmatching, or undermatching, depending on your point of view or how you placed your bets this evening.

As the dangerous and dastardly molester (you ready?) pulled himself, with difficulty, slowly up from the platform, Miss Heavyweight of Nineteen-Sixty-Something shook her umbrella down at him, and told him, with enormous dignity: "I bet you'll think twice about it the next time you git it into your rotten mind to git fresh with a poor helpless Black lady like me, you goddamn no-good peckerwood trash. It's gittin so it ain't safe for a lady to be by herself in broad open daylight. I don't know what's gonna 'come of us poor defenseless womenfolks. I declare before the Lord I don't."

The four-eyed, bug-eyed, cross-eyed desperado looked like an accident on the lookout for a place to make the scene. He mumbled his apologies and dragged himself away down toward the other end of the platform, limping along pathetically, as if his life depended on it. Miss Poor Defenseless Womanhood brandished her umbrella after the hapless hoodlum. Then she turned and walked proudly, and with righteous indignation, up the stairway to the street.

Some of the Black folk (including Yoruba) cracked up with laughter, when a brother amongst them raised his arm and pumped his right fist up and down, and shouted softly: "Black Power, mother! Black Power! Keep the mammy-hunching faith!"

Up topside on the street it was summertime and the breathing was easier than down there in that underworld underneath the city. Are you ready for Yoruba? Yoruba Evelyn Lovejoy? She, the girl, the princess, felt good walking along her street (One Hundred and Twenty-fifth) in the middle September of her eighteenth year, and the dear fox knew she looked good walking; moreover she was a child who loved to walk. She always walked in a hurry, like she was late for an appointment. Long-legged Black girl, she was aware of the men along the main drag and the eyes they had for her and the shaking of their heads in honest admiration. She strolled like she was used to carrying bundles on her lovely head, as if somehow she conjured up from the depths of some dark mysterious whirlpool of sweet remembrance deep inside of her, she called up memories of the roads her great ancestors used to travel on their way to Lagos and Accra. Enugu, Bamako, Ouagadougou. Her distant cousins still strolled down those distant highways. Uhuru! Skin-givers—plank-spankers! Ujamaa!

She was Yoruba and she was pretty poetry set to rhythm. Proud she was and princessly. Her long legs were not skinny, neither were they fat. Slimly round—roundly slim. Her ample hips were built a trifle high up from the sidewalk. That was the only thing. Some of her friends in high school used to call the girl "High Pockets." One old fresh big-head boy always called the child "Long Goodie."

But behind all that and notwithstanding, she was Yoruba of the long strides and the swaying hips and the black heavy hair down to her shoulders, of the dark staring eyes, now laughing, now brimming-full with sorrow. She walked along the street of dreams. Past the Baby Grand Club, where Nipsey Russell used to call the question nightly, before he got "discovered." Walked past Frank's Restaurant, and across Eighth Avenue.

One Hundred and Twenty-fifth Street was also the street of sounds. Magnificent sounds. Jukeboxes all along the main stem blasting out the classics. Blowing love and hate and sorrow. Black classics. Serious music by serious musicians. Max Roach, Ray Charles, Lou Rawls, Etta Jones, Archie Shepp, John Coultrane, horn-blowing horn-blowers. Abbey Lincoln wailing freedom. Nina's Mississippi Goddamn! And always there was the aristocracy. The Duke of Ellington, the Count of Basie and the Earl of Hines, Lester Young, the late lamented President. Yoruba loved the street of sounds. This child dug the aristocracy. And she was an aristocrat. Dig it! She was clean! Black *and* comely! Understand?

The marquee at the Apollo told her James Brown was holding court. And Pigmeat Markham. George Wiltshire—yeah! All right! Well! Folks were lined up almost half the block. New York's riot squad stood at the everloving ready. Three young jiving signifying cats, standing outside the theater away from the line, eyeballed her as she flowed along the main stem. Amongst all these strolling people, she stood out like Lew Alcindor.

As she passed, she heard one of them say, in a kind of singsong, "Hi do, Miss Foxy Youngblood, please m'am!"

Another said, "Walk pretty for the people!"

The third one said, "Lord, make me truly thankful for what I'm about to perceive!"

Yoruba took it all in stride (and this father's child could truly stride). Her head held aloft, she always walked three inches taller than her actual height. (Did you ever dig Miriam, on stage, Makeba?) Yoruba's face did not give away the fact that she had heard the brothers sounding on her, signifying, but all the same she felt a nervous giggle in the bottom of her stomach.

"Walk that walk, Miss Sweet Chocolate Fox!"

"Miss Fine Brown-Black Frame!"

"Come on home, Miss Youngblood!"

Across the street and down the block was the Black and Beautiful Burlesque (the B.B.B. as it was called with fond affection), a famous girlie house, newly founded, where Afro-naturalized Black beauties did a dignified striptease, by the numbers, every day and thrice on Sundays. Long lines of voyeurs clear around the block. And there were pickets picketing pickets picketing pickets, who were picketing. After a while you had to be some kind of a genius to figure who was picketing whom and how come and what for. There was a Black Nationalist group picketing the theater against the whole idea of Black nudity. *"A pure disgrace!"* There was another group of Black picketeers against the admission of white voyeurs.

"Keep the Hunkie's eyes off our Beautiful Black women!"

There was a group of integrated picketeers who came out forthright for integrated burlesque queens. White queens had filed complaints against B.B.B. with the Human Rights Commission. B.B.B. was where the action was, and there were fist fights every other night.

Across Seventh Avenue almost a hundred folks were gathered. In the midst of them a Black man stood on a ladder beside a ragged Star-Spangled Banner, which flapped lifelessly and indifferently in a soft September breeze. A reddish-brown smog hung over the city, ominous and brooding, as if it might fling fire and brimstone down upon the Black and true believers any minute. The man on the ladder was waving his arms back and forth and up and down, as if he were directing traffic. He was working up a perspiration. But Yoruba could not make out what he was saying until she crossed over the beautiful wide parkway of an avenue.

Now she stood on the outskirts of the group of Black folk and half listened to Billy "Bad Mouth" Williams. Self-styled Black nationalist leader. Self-appointed. Self-anointed. Mayor of Black nationalist Harlem. God's and/or Allah's most precious gift to the lucky Harlem masses. Don't take anybody else's word for it. Check it out with Bad Mouth himself. He'd tell you he was the last of the great Black Nationalists. Uncrowned prime minister of the Black government in exile. Hey! There was Garvey, Malcolm, Bad Mouth Williams. After that—well, Armageddon.

Yoruba overheard one man in the crowd running down the action to another. "Bad Mouth's here every damn day the Good Lord sends, running his game, just as often as goose go barefooted. He's the biggest bullshitter on the Avenue."

He was a man of medium height, was Bad Mouth, powerfully gotten together, especially through his massive shoulders. Coal-black was his skin, his eyes aflame like burning coals. And he could talk that talk. He could really blow. He never drew large crowds like Malcolm used to draw. And Yoruba remembered Malcolm. Oh my, yes, yes, yes! Yes! Yes! Yes! Praise Allah—she remembered Malcolm. A Salaam Alaikum! Tall and fire-haired, manhood oozing from every pore of him, fiery in his oratory, lightning fast of wit, uncompromising in his integrity, tough and tender with his people. She remembered Malcolm. She had been helplessly and hopelessly in love with him, like a thousand other girls her age who were of the Black persuasion, and she had cried continuously and for four weeks running after that February Sunday of the fatal infamy.

But like the man said, Bad Mouth was consistent. Every day. Every day. And he was a natural-born champeen at haranguing and cajoling. Yoruba had heard most of his spiel it seemed, a hundred times and more, and in many variations. Bad Mouth could phrase like Louis Armstrong, could orchestrate like Cootie Williams.

"I was born in North Carolina." Bad Mouth paused and let this great revelation sink in. "I lived in a house that I could lay on my pallet and look up through the roof and dig the stars, and look down through the floor and count the chickens. It was built-in ventilation."

Behind this statement came a chuckling kind of laughter from his audience. Yoruba laughed, notwithstanding she had heard it all before. She laughed almost unknowingly.

"We got so damn much fresh air we could hardly catch our breath. Almost choked ourselves to death."

They laughed more loudly now. Warming up. And gathering.

"Go on, Bad Mouth."

"Tell it like it *i-s* is!"

"You oughta be shame of yourself telling them all them bogus lies!"

A four-eyed bearded young man shouted, "Check that shit out, Bad Mouth! Run it down, baby brother! Run it down!"

"Watch your language, young man," another man said to the bearded young man.

"You ain't got nothing to laugh about," Bad Mouth told his audience. "Down home we did at least breathe fresh air, but up here you don't do nothing but fill your lungs with poison. Damn white man so greedy behind them Yankee dollars, he has polluted the air you breathe and poisoned the water you need to drink. Charlie so greedy he'll wipe out his own race including his own self just to make some more of that bread. And you niggers running around here following them hustling preachers teaching you to love the white man. You gon pray for him that spitefully use you."

"Put bad mouth on 'em, Bad Mouth!" one tall, skinny Black cat shouted softly. He sported the baddest Afro-natural hairdo Yoruba had ever seen, standing underneath that wild black bush so thick and so way out the sun could never touch his face, and he was slowly going pale from the lack of sunlight. He wore a truly bad dashiki, long earrings flapping from his hound-dog ears like jingle bells. Everybody on the street knew him to be a plainclothesman in the hire of New York's Finest, even though his clothes were hardly plain. Sometimes he wore a long flowing yellow boubou. He made all the meetings, the greatest shouter in the crowd. Every day. Every day. Old Plainclothes always made the scene.

Bad Mouth continued. "These jackleg preachers telling you when Charlie kick your ass on one cheek, you supposed to turn the other one. You supposed to bend over and to tell him, 'Be my guest.' That's how come some of you walk bent over all the time. You done turned them cheeks so many times you can't hardly sit 'em down to rest."

"Blow, Bad Mouth! Blow, baby! You bad-mouth motherfucker!"

"Rap, brother!"

"Sit down—sit down—you can't sit down—"

Bad Mouth paused and asked his people, "Am I right or wrong?"

"Right!" Plainclothes was jumping up and down. "Rap your Black thing, baby!" He was working himself into a lather. Sometimes he wore a red, black and green African robe, one shoulder bare, the hem of the garment sweeping the street, as if he were from the sanitation department instead of the police.

"Check it, Bad Mouth. Check that shit out!"

"Blow, baby, blow!"

"Do your thing, baby!" The dashiki-ed plainclothesman was screaming now at the top of his voice. Some of the brothers called him Maxwell Smart. Some brothers called him less affectionate names.

"Run it down—run it down!"

"Them hustling preachers telling you to love the man that kicks your Black ass, and you ain't got no better sense than to follow what the hustlers tell you. They the biggest shuckers God ever put breath in."

"Blow, baby, blow!"

"Takes a shucker to know a shucker!" From a lady in the crowd.

"One more time!"

Bad Mouth continued. "I know hustling when I see it. I used to be a hustler my own damn self."

"Used to be?" From a brother in the audience.

"My daddy was a stone hustler. Taught me all the fine points of shucking and hustling. That's right. My daddy was one of them big fat greasy Black and burly chicken-eating Baptist preachers down in Peckerwood, North Carolina."

"Peckerwood, North Carolina? Come on, Bad Mouth!"

One brother in the crowd said, "You a lying ass and a tinkling symbol!"

"That's right," Bad Mouth answered. "That's where my daddy used to preach. That's where I come from. Peckerwood, North Carolina. My daddy was a stone jackleg. Picked cotton all week long and talked shit all day Sunday."

The crowd was laughing now, without restraint. A toothless old lady shouted merrily, "Mind your langwitch, son, else I'll pull you down off that ladder and wash your mouth out with lye soap. Don't think you so big, I won't take you down a peg or two."

"Uh-uh!" From a chuckling brother in the crowd.

"Go on, Mother," Bad Mouth said, good-naturedly. "Go sell your papers on another corner."

"I ain't your mother," the old lady fired right back at Bad Mouth. Both of them were speaking louder now, almost shouting, competing with the fire trucks that came clanging down the avenue past the meeting, piercing eardrums with their sirens blasting. Every evening about this time the fire trucks paid their respects to Bad Mouth's meetings, or to any other meeting on this corner of all corners. The speaker's ladder stood in front of Michaux's famous Black and nationalistic bookstore.

Diagonally across the avenue stood the famous Hotel Theresa, where the great Joe Louis used to hang out in the late thirties and early forties, and where history was made in the early sixties, when Fidel took up lodging there and people stood outside in the chilly rain and shouted:

"Viva Castro!"

"Viva Fidel!"

"I ain't your mother," the old lady repeated, shouting even louder this time. "If your mother hadda brung you up right, I wouldn't have to be putting your backside down this late in life."

"OOOoo-weeeee! You ready for that?"

"Grandma putting old Bad Mouth in the natural dozens—damn!"

"Blow, grandma! Blow, baby!"

"Old Bad Mouth do not play the two-time-sixes!"

"Let him pat his big bad feet then. Miles Davis plays it!"

Everybody was laughing now, including Yoruba. And more folks were gathering now, attracted by the laughter. It was as if Bad Mouth and the old lady had learned their lines and rehearsed them well ahead of time.

Well?

Would you believe?

"Go along, old lady," Bad Mouth said tolerantly. "I want to talk to my people about some serious matters. If you can't listen quietly, get yourself your own corner and draw your own crowd. I pay weekly rent for this here corner."

Yoruba walked away from the gathering crowd, away from the scattered laughter. Behind her she could hear Bad Mouth's froggy voice croaking to his people.

"Black brothers and sisters, it's time we chased the Bible-toting money-changers out of the holy places of our worship. Am I right or wrong? It's time we got some healthy-sized buggy whips and kicked some big fat rusty-dusties and took some names. We got to get our own houses clean before we can worry about taking care of Whitey's. Am I right or wrong?"

Yoruba thought, It's preachers today. Yesterday it was "Negro" leaders. The day before that it was the "white Communist liberals." Tomorrow he would be doing a putdown on something else. The labor movement. The NAACP. The President. It was always something, or somebody. Bad Mouth was the World's champeen putdowner. He'd tell anybody: "Not a living ass is sacred, when Bad Mouth begins to blow. The best you can do is batten down the hatches, send out hurricane warnings and pray to Allah for a rainbow."

Behind her, she could hear him carrying on. "Take this city! Take it! Take it! It belongs to you. And it's just right here for the taking. Between the spooks and the spicks, we can take this valuable piece of real estate known as New York City. All we got to do is get together. But you wanna chase the great and glorious white folks all over the mother-loving suburbs!" He paused. "And you don't want no power. You just want to intergrate."

She walked a few blocks up the avenue, as the applause and laughter ebbed behind her, walked past a half dozen bars and liquor stores, and people, and just about as many funeral parlors and store-front churches, and people, and she turned right off Seventh Avenue into the block where she had spent most of the eighteen years of her life. She, the girl, Yoruba, was, at long last, home.

This evening, somehow, when she reached the block, she felt an overwhelming relief coursing through all of her senses, as if she had been on a long long journey into a foreign land, a hostile country, and now she had come home at last. It was not the first time she had had this feeling after she had spent all day downtown in Manhattan in that jungle that some people called the garment center. Today, as she walked toward the other end of the block, warm memories poured over her with the coolness of a sweet summer shower. And she was a little girl again. Romping up and down the teeming block. Playing stick-ball and skipping rope (double dutch) and hopscotch (potsy) and tag and ten-ten-double-ten and follow-the-leader. Tag was a game that went on and on and on and never ended. Playing with Enrique and Ernie and Claudie and Lloyd and Susan and Cheryl and all the rest of that ragtag group (her mother's term for the gone friends of her yesteryears). All of the times that came back to her now from that faraway age were good times to her. It seemed a million years ago. But Yoruba remembered.

Remembered skinny, big-eyed, snotty-nosed Ernie when they were both about six and seven and eight years old (he was always two or three years older), and they were puppy-lovers, and he, her ragged Black prince, would come and sit on her stoop with her for hours and pick his nose and sometimes suck his thumb, and stare at her in a kind of wordless admiration. His father was a seaman and was away from home much of the time. His mother did days work away up somewhere in the Bronx. Remembered the day she invited Ernie to dinner, much to her mother's great annoyance. She had told Yoruba a million times: "I ain't want you playing with them common low-class Southern niggers on this block, and I particularly ain't want them in my house."

But at the dinner table she pumped the boy with questions like she was from the FBI or something.

"How many rooms in your apartment, Ernest?"

"Two rooms and a bath, Miss Daphne."

"Is that exclusive of a kitchen?"

"Exwho-sive?"

Yoruba's father said, "If you're so interested, why don't you pay Mrs. Billings a visit sometimes? You are the nosiest woman God ever made."

Mrs. Lovejoy ignored her husband, as she had a way of doing—sometimes. "You mean your mother has one room, one kitchen and a bath, ain't you, Ernest?"

"Yessum, that's what I meant to say. And the toilet is down on the next floor. We use it with the Williamses. Sometimes we have to stand in line. Sometimes we have to use the pot."

"Where do you sleep, Ernest?"

He picked his nose and stared at his finger. "With my mother most of the time, excepting when my uncle spends the night, he sleep with Mama, and I sleep on the cot in the kitchen. Course when my daddy is home, he sleep with Mama—"

Ernie was usually a quiet boy, but when he got turned on, it was hard to turn him off again.

During those days, Yoruba's folks were more "well-off" than Ernie's. They afforded all of two rooms and a kitchen. All this and a private bath. The girl slept in the living room on a great Bistro convertible. It was after midnight when she was awakened by her parents' voices from the bedroom. She lay there between sleep and wake trying to get herself together.

Her mother with her clipped British-Barbadian accent. She talked twice as fast as her father.

"One of these days you'll listen to me, damn your Black soul. I tell you a million times these damn low-class darkies on this block is no damn good! Nothing but a bunch of wort'less vagabunds. I ain't blame the white man for not wanting to live around them."

"Shut up, woman," Matt Lovejoy harshly whispered. "You wanna wake up Ruba?"

"That's why I try to teach my daughter to stay away from these wort'less pickaninnies on the block. But the more I try to culturize her, the more you pull the other way. You're enough to vex the devil himself."

She—the girl—Yoruba—sitting up in bed and staring through the darkness toward the bedroom. She had been dreaming, and she had trouble now figuring out whether this was part of the dream or not, or was the dream the real thing and was this a nightmare she had stumbled into? Lie back on your bed and close your eyes and try to catch up with your dream again. Shut out the sound of battle from the other room. Put your fingers in your ears. Still you hear the battle raging.

"Quiet, woman, goddammit! Keep your mouth shut and people'll just think you a fool. Keep opening it and there ain't gon be no doubt about it."

Yoruba pulled the sheet up over her head and tried in vain to shut out the sound of her mother's weeping. "You ain't appreciate me!" Crying—sobbing—choking. "You ain't love me!"

Her father's rough and tender voice. "Come on now, Daphne —come on now. You know better than that. Come on now, lil ole crybaby." In the eyes of Yoruba's imagination, she could see her mother, still shaking with sobs, cuddling up to her father now. "You ain't appreciate nothing I try to do." She had seen it happen before—the times they'd fought in front of her. "Crybaby—crybaby —crybaby." Her mother was in her father's arms now, and Yoruba was wide awake, and it would be hours before she fell asleep again. She would never catch up with her dream. She could not even remember what her dream had been about.

Ernie's mother had died a few years back, and Yoruba had no idea where Ernie was now or whether he was living or dead. Maybe he was at sea like his father used to be most of the time. It seemed centuries ago when they romped innocent and heedless up and down these streets, this turf, this block. And ripped their dresses and tore their pants. And laughed just for the sheer joy that came from laughter. It didn't have to be funny, whatever it was they laughed about. Her mother wanted her to be a lady and never run and sweat and play or swear or rassle with the hoi polloi. "Never get your face dirty. Never ever soil your dresses." But her mother fought a losing battle.

She remembered how she would be playing in the streets with her friends and she would look down the street and see her father turn the corner coming home from work, and she would take off down the block like jet propulsion and race toward him and leap into his arms. It was the happiest moment in the day for both of them. Her father would put her on his shoulders with her legs around his neck and ride her all the way up the block and into the house.

Her mother would scold the two of them. "Take that child from around your neck. How can I ever teach her to be a lady? Both of you're just as common as all the other no-good darkies in this ratty neighborhood."

And it was indeed a ratty neighborhood. The rat inhabitants made their presence felt all over. Always they were in evidence. Walked along the streets, worshiped in the churches, dug the movies in the theaters, especially the cowboy pictures. Put up light housekeeping in the tenements. But refused to chip in on the rent. The rat population was ever on the increase. Wherever people of the neighborhood were, rats were always very close by. They had a fond affection for the folks of Harlem. Notwithstanding, it was a case of unrequited love. Loveless love. Yoruba would always remember her father's desperate lifelong battle with the rodent citizenry. Big rats, little rats, in-between. "There gon be more of them than Black folks one of these days. They gon take over Harlem before we do." He would put down big steel traps all over the apartment and bait the traps with bread or cheese. But these rats were city-slick and hip to everything and everybody. Next morning, the food would be gone, the traps sprung, but not a single rat in any of the deadly traps. Her father tried to figure it out, and after months of great puzzling and frustration, he concluded: "These damn rats so hip they put broom straws in their mouths to spring the traps and get the cheese."

Yoruba remembered sleepless nights, with the sound of rats playing in the kitchen, in the oven, and rattling the pots and pans. Some nights she would awaken and hear them scratching and romping around inside the walls. One night about three o'clock in the morning, a trap went off (bang!) and they all jumped out of bed and her father switched on the lights, and before they could get to the place of execution, bread, rat and trap had already split the scene.

A couple of rats got so bold and familiar, the Lovejoys knew them by sight. They would walk out in broad open daylight. And stake their claims. Her father named them Pretty Boy Floyd and

John Dillinger. He said they had more sense than their namesakes, seeing as how they never got caught.

One night when Yoruba was about five years old, a great big rat got real affectionate and jumped into her bed and bit her on the jaw. Left a scar on her face that was still with her. Her father said it was her tribal mark. People thought it was a birthmark. Said it was her beauty spot. Her father battled the rat for more than half an hour all over the kitchen. Quietly swearing and swinging the broom, he must have struck the rat more than fifty times, blood splattering all over the place, till the rat ran out of steam and let himself get cornered, and Yoruba's father swung away at him till blood flew all over the kitchen floor and all of the poor rat's insides had come outside.

All in all they were good days though, rats and all, the way the girl remembered them. And some days in this new time, she wished desperately she could turn back the clock and be her father's baby again. Dirty-faced, dress-torn, snotty-nosed tomboy. But she could not turn back the clock. She never really wanted to. And she was Yoruba, gentle Yoruba, and she had grown to be a gentlewoman, despite her mother's dedication and determination that this dear child should achieve ladyship. "Lady Eve-lyn."

In front of her house now, three-storied-and-basement brownstone. They lived on the parlor floor. She hoped her father had come home from work by now. Particularly this night, she hoped Matt Lovejoy was already home. She did not feel like facing her mother alone this evening in the very very middle of her eighteenth September.

She turned and stared back down the street past the children skipping rope, playing potsy, a few of them calling playful pleasant motherfuckers, past the winos on a stoop, and the junkies, past the forever double-parked cars, stared longingly toward the corner at the other end of the block trying to look Matt Lovejoy around the corner coming home from work. She felt that if her father did materialize in the deep glow of the Harlem sunset she would break into a run like in the old days when she was six and seven and eight and believed in a jolly, old, fat white man by the name of Santa Claus, and thought the whole wide world was right there on her block in Harlem, and God was great and God was good and everything was for the best, because He worked mysteriously, the Grand Magician of them all. Cars honking, racing motors, fumes belching, children screaming, cursing, squealing, laughing. She stared past the busy intersection clear across Seventh Avenue all the way west to the river where the sun was a blazing disk of fire and washing the streets with a million colors and descending slowly down between the buildings at the very end of the street, down down it was sinking slowly sinking to set afire the Hudson River. Her eyes filled up and almost overflowed at the beauty of the Harlem sunset. The tenements bathed in soft sweet tender shadows now. She took one long last look down toward the other end of her block. Come around the corner, Daddy! Come around the corner! And I will run again to meet you. She turned toward the house. Maybe he was already home. Silently she prayed he was already in the house.

She was in no mood this day to hear her mother carry on and on about the grandest of all the Grand Cotillions. "You are indeed a lucky one, Eve-lyn. And of all the scrumptious places, it will be held downtown at the Waldorf, where few white folks get a chance to go and decidedly no niggers at all. You'll be one of those selected too. The grand magnificent Cotillion. It's everything I've worked to give you, dearie. The opportunity of a lifetime. My own dear baby is going to be a debutante!"

The girl walked wearily up the steps. Suddenly she was of the aged ones. And heavy-limbed. As if great iron weights hung from her arms, her legs. Her body tired; her soul weary; her mind exhausted.

Be home, Daddy!
Be home, Daddy!
Be home, Daddy!
Please!
Be home.

CHAPTER TWO

MATTHEW

Hey!
My man—
Big Matt!
What's happening, dads?
Tired—pooped—dragged—
LAY DOWN MY BURDEN, DOWN BY THE RIVERSIDE and study nothing no damn more was exactly how the man, Matt, felt this Friday evening in a hot New York September.

Matthew Lovejoy closed his eyes, crinkled in the corners now like fallen leaves of early autumn, as he leaned back in his favorite of all favorite chairs. Whew—weeeeeee! *God damn old rose!* Yoruba's father was a coal-black man somewhere in his early fifties. And he was black unwrinkled velvet. He breathed deeply through his large wide nostrils, as all the weariness of the long day's work came down on him—sledgehammer—wham! Sometimes he felt like he'd been working without stopping for the last two hundred years. He thought, maybe I worked way back yonder in slavery time. Maybe I'm the second coming of old Nat Turner and Frederick Douglass put together and multiplied. An angry bulldog in his belly growled like thunder. His feet were bad enough to tote a pistol. They throbbed now like a rotten tooth. All through his limbs he felt a tiredness taking over every marrow every bone every muscle he possessed. But it was a tiredness Matthew welcomed. Sometimes, the wearier he felt the easier it was for him to unwind himself, to realize a kind of complete escape from everything and everybody. Copout was the name of the game. Like the homemade kite he used to have so many Georgia years ago, when he'd let the string out, bit by bit, and every round went higher and higher.

He could sit here right now in this chair-of-chairs with his large handsome head thrown back, his full and thickly shapeful curvy mouth relaxed, his legs his thighs his torso trembling with a kind of sweet exhaustion, and smack his lips, and he could relish his delicious tiredness in his mouth, throughout his face, in his throat, and deep deep down into his belly, deeper in his loins, and even deeper in his bowels, where it was, where it always was and where it always would be. And he could cop out on all the years of his life's great futility. He sometimes thought he felt like Peter at the Sea of Galilee. Master, we fished all night and our nets are empty. Peter must've been a Black frustrated brother. Matthew, himself, had fished ten thousand nights. But now, this night, he could lay down all his burdens down by the riverside and study nothing no damn more.

His chair was one in which he could lean far far back and very easily cop a quick nod, if it came to that. It was a swivel chair, made of leatherette and steel. The bogus leather was loud and bright and claret like a bloody nose. As a boy he'd had a zillion nosebleeds. "Put thick brown paper 'neath your upper lip and press down hard."—"Put a cold key down you back." His great chair was as comfortable as soft shoes were to old folks in the dead of wintertime. So help him Brother Malcolm, he felt good this hot and steamy evening, as he stretched his legs, his arms, and yawned aloud and said, Excuse me, to no one in particular. Tired—tired—sweetly tired. Whipped now past his sweaty socks. Sometimes he would sit here in his chair and sleep-dream with his eyes wide open. Dream of all the gone-days of his yesteryears and of the here-and-now days and of the days that stretched far out ahead. Someday, somehow, sometime, a change was gonna come. Yeah—he was going to overcome. Dream of Africa and all its ancient glory. He'd made his pilgrimage to Timbuktu so many times in so many many of his dreams. He'd entered barefoot at the mosque. He'd studied at the ancient university.

Sometimes he'd get so at home in this chair-of-chairs, he didn't want to give it up, even after it was over. In some ways it was like Aladdin's lamp rolled up in a magic carpet. It was Matt Lovejoy's extra-special juju. All the way from Arachuku.

Way down home where he came from, folks believed religiously in signs and haints and spirits, goofy dust and all that stuff. Working roots and conjure-men. Rabbit feet and black cat bones. Many a girl had sprinkled mojo powder under his steps and put love potions in his food. Then, too, he'd been a natural joiner as a boy. Every time he went to a different church, he got religion all over again, and his sinful soul converted. Each time, he would join right up. From Hardshell Baptist to Holy Rollers to Sanctified and Free From Sin. Tent meetings were his speciality. As a boy he was the shouting kind. Whooped and hollered with the best. All of that was so long ago, so far away in time and space, it seemed to issue forth from dreams he'd dreamed. But everything came back to him when he sank down in his chair-of-chairs and engineered his Great Escape.

His chair was the fourth chair from the entrance in the Jenkins Palace Barbershop. One of the few places in New York where a cat could still get his ears lowered for only six little biddy bits.

Willie Jenkins had already done the major job of shearing Matthew's precious wool and was giving him the finishing touches. And soon Matt would have to give it up (his chair) to another lucky customer. The Palace always did a swinging business, as was to be expected. Your six bits not only got you a haircut, but you also got goo-gobs of philosophical conversation in the bargain. Soul talk, baby brother. And no cover charge. The buzzing of the electric clippers, the talk that went on and on and on from one subject to another (like these cats covered the waterfront). Afro-Caribbean brogues and Afro-Southern accents all mixed up with European-New Yorkese. British subjects and second-class citizens. And like some real heavy Black cats blew their bullshit regularly at the Palace.

This evening, as it usually went down, the dialogue rambled all over the real estate (like Jim Brown on the football field) from one thing to another.

Like sports, Sport.
All right?
Baseball? Ready?
"The Dodgers gon win the pennant and take the World Serious in four straight games."
"Willie Mays the greatest. He the best that ever done it."

"Dig it!"

"Who you humping?"

"Aw, man!"

"I'll take Mickey Mantle any day," the young colored man in the chair next to Matt said importantly. "You see, that's because I'm objective. I'm color-blind. To me, a man is a man is a man."

"And a tom is a tom is a goddamn educated fool!" A brother waiting his turn threw his two cents into the hopper. "Willie can out-hit him and out-field him, out-throw him, and he damn sure can outrun that brittle-ass peckerwood. He done slowed up in his old age, and he can still outrun any of them crackers."

Another brother posed a question. "How come you reckon the Bloods can run so much faster than Whitey? Look at Willie Mays and Willie Davis and Lou Brock and Maury Wills and all them other brothers. Every last one of them can outrun a striped-ass ape behind giving that hairy sucker a handicap."

"Yeah. Like my man Bobby Hayes and Gale Sayers can make a deer look like he walking around with chairs on his head."

"Black peoples foots musta be built different."

Matt Lovejoy made, unsmilingly, his first comment of the evening. When he talked, his lips seemed as if they were curving corners going places with a purpose. "Feet ain't got nothing to do with nothing. Reason them Black cats can run so fast, most of 'em from down home, and they used to hauling ass when the law gets in behind 'em. They used to picking 'em up and putting 'em down. Some of them come from some of them little cracker towns down there so small you can stand in the middle of town and piss clean out to the city limits. They got signs in some of them towns that read: Peckerwoods Read and Walk Fast. Niggers Read and Haul Ass."

"Aw, man!"

"Come on, Matt!"

"That's right. Niggers Read and Run. If You Can't Read, Run Anyhow!"

Well—like how you gon top Matt Lovejoy? Honh?

From sports to religion. Right? Dig it.

A brother said, "To hell with spooks and sports. Handle this one. How many angels can dance on the head of a needle?"

"Depend on what kind of dance them suckers doing."

"*Angels,* baby! Later with that sucker bit. I'm talking about *angels* dancing."

"How 'bout the Watusi?"

"Baby! Later!"

"Funky Broadway!"

"Boogaloo?"

"Is the needle in a haystack? Thatta make a lotta difference. Right?"

"Depend on what kinda needle and what kinda shit they got in that needle."

"Man! Angels, baby! Dig! Ain't no shit with angels."

"Every living thing shits, baby. Even roaches. What goes in, gon come out. Else there gon be some constipated motherfuckers!"

"I mean angels like way up there in Heaven. Them people living up there in the good Lord's pad. That's what I'm talking about." He was working up a fine lather.

"Don't make no never mind who they live with. Don't care if they angels or devils, you got some good shit in that needle, Jim, you can do yourself some dancing."

The educated young man in the chair next to Matthew said, "Brother, you missed the point entirely. Like the other brother was raising a philosophical, I mean, like a metaphysical question, like the scribes and Pharisees used to discuss way back there in olden times."

"You got the right kinda shit in that needle you can raise any kinda damn question you want. You can raise your dear old great departed grandmother from up out of the cemetery."

"Oooooooo-weeeeeeeee!"

"You can raise Jesus Christ, hisself, up from the grave again. Believe me when I say so. Cause if I tell you a grasshopper can pull a plow, don't ask me how, just hitch the motherfucker up."

A pinhead pimply-faced man in the front chair laughed and said, "You know what I heard old Bad Mouth Williams say the other day down at the corner? That sucker said Jesus was a Black man. I mean, like, man! Them Black national cats carry things too damn far."

His barber said, "Don't pay no attention to Bad Mouth. Everybody know Jesus wasn't no Negro. He was a A-rab. That's how come the Jews ain't never cared nothing about the cat."

"A A-rab ain't nothing but a light-complected spook."

"Aw come on, baby. You know Jesus wasn't no spook."

"How come you think they crucifixed that poor sucker?"

"Man, you mean to say all these millions of white folks worshiping a dead nigger, and kicking all the other niggers in the ass? That's some weird muthafucking shit!"

"He was passing, baby, passing! Dig it!"

"He passed all right. I'm hip to that. He faded too. He crapped out like a mother!"

Another waiting customer deepened the dialogue with: "Dig it, J.C. was a club member all right. It figures he had gobs of soul. All that double-talking jive he put down to git around the man, it figures the cat had to be a member. He musta been a stone Blood when you come to think about it."

Matt Lovejoy had hardly said a word since he sank down in his favorite chair. With the shit flying fast and furious, and the fans going, excepting his comment on Black speedsters, he had just sat back and relaxed and listened, and hoped that none flew in his face. He opened his eyes now and a smile played briefly on his face. He said, "Let me run it down for you. Fact of the business, Jesus' mother, Mary, was white. Right? But old Joseph was Black. Yes he was. That's how come they couldn't find no place to stop at in any of them Bethlehem hotels. That's how come there wasn't no place in the inn, cause them peckerwoods couldn't stand to see old Black Joe miscegenating all day and all night with little Miss Mary Anne."

Suddenly, it got so quiet you could have heard a bedbug making water on a snowbank in Siberia. They never knew whether to take old Matt Lovejoy seriously or not. He was always coming out of a weird bag nobody else had ever heard of. Matt continued running down his thing.

"All them Jews were colored in them days. And the white man, talking about the Romans, they had colonialized them, and Jesus was a Black Power man and was trying to freedomize them. That's how come they crucifixed him. A lot of them Jews were toms, and they panicked after Jesus split, and they went off to Europe for two thousand years and miscegenated with them white Europeans and passed on into the white race. That's how come some of them suckers still got kinky hair, I mean till this very day. They ain't nothing but light-complected Negroes passing."

During the time that Matt was running his thing down, his barber had held his mouth wide open and the long straight razor poised above Matt's face. Matt sank back in his chair now and closed his eyes and the man began to scrape his face again.

The barber at the first chair said soberly, "Old J.C. *musta* been a Blood. I'm hip to that. With all that nonviolent jive he was putting down. He must be the cat invented nonviolence."

Laughter in the Palace now, an easy general laughter of agreement, although God and Malcolm only knew what was being agreed to. Maybe that the whole discussion was a bunch of jolly bullshit. But the young man in the chair next to Matt was dead serious all the way. Matt thought, "He's lost his colored sense of humor. That's the danger of the white man's bourgeois education."

A grizzly old-timer, waiting his turn, seated in a chair up against the wall, looking very much like a sepia poor-man's Adlai Stevenson with his legs crossed and two great holes of poverty in the bottom of his shoes, shook his head from side to side. Raggedy-assed was his description, understated. "Don't know what the young folks raising so much hell about. We ain't never made as much progress as we making now. I'm as much a race man as anybody else but after all—"

A hip young dude, process-sharp, do-rag pastel-green and all, seated next to the old man, took a dim view of the old man's outlook. "Pops, you ain't talking no sense at all. Revolution is like a man cunt-hunting. When a woman lets a real horny stud kiss her mouth and feel her leg, that don't satisfy him none at all—not no real man. That just whets his appetite, makes him wanna go whole hog, and settle for nothing but the pure-dee pussy."

The old man pondered the question momentarily, shook his head in awe at all that youthful wisdom.

"Can't argue with that," the old-timer said, amidst the raucous laughter of agreement.

Matt opened his eyes and stared at a sign on the wall in front of him, which read:

IF YOU SO DAMN SMART, WHY AIN'T YOU RICH?

The young educated dude had already been holding forth on the subject of nonviolence. Martin Luther was his main man. After the laughter and the chuckling ebbed, he insisted, "The only way the solution can be solved is through the weapon of love. We have to teach the white man to love us by the example of our undying love for him. Shakespeare said it. 'Love is not love that alters when it alteration finds.' " He was a serious-faced pleasant-looking brown-skinned young dude, rigged out nicely in an inexpensive "mohair" suit. He looked impressive and expensive.

Matt Lovejoy sighed and breathed aloud, and deeply, and inhaled into his mouth and throat the sweet and alcoholic smell of bay rum and hair tonic. He stared at another one of the handwritings on the wall.

REMEMBER THE MISSISSIPPI FLOOD AND DON'T SPIT ON THE FLOOR

The bald-headed barber at the second chair stared at the young philosopher in disbelief. "I wouldn't give a kitty if Snakeshit said it. Eskimos'll be suffering from a heat wave before these hunkies'll love a colored man. And you must be suffering from this here New York heat wave to be talking that kinda stupid crap!"

A skinny little man walked into the barbershop. He sported a handlebar mustache, so bushy it almost hid his face and seemed not to belong to him, like he had lifted it off some other joker. He was so tiny, face and all, his mustache looked like wings. And a good gust of wind would surely put him into orbit. Yet and still, there was about him an air of importance, from the top of his neatly processed head to the tip of his freshly polished shoes. He gleamed and glittered from top to bottom, stem to stern. He was cool in a very very hot September. And when he walked into a place he fell in big and people paid attention.

The barber at the first chair sounded on him. "What was the third one, Good News?"

"Seven," the little man answered.

The barber at the first chair signified. "Doggone, Good News, you don't never bring me nothing but bad news all the time."

One of the waiting customers said, "Doggone my hard luck

time, I watched 'I Spy' the other night and saw them three sevens just as plain as a knot on a old dog's dick. It was on that automobile license tag Bill Cosby was driving. I woke up every morning since then with them sevens on my mind. I started to play 'em too, but I don't never hit nothing except when I dream, and I don't never dream no dreams here lately. And when I do dream here lately, I come up with some real trifling no-count dreams, I mean to tell you." The dreamless dreamer was an elderly white-haired gentleman.

The first barber stared at the dreamer and laughed a short laugh. "Them wet dreams ain't gon never get you nothing, old man. Whatever you don't get while you having one of them kinda dreams, you can forget about it in this life."

The barber at the second chair said, "Damn—Good News, I just missed that number by a cunt's hair, and I started to combinate that mother."

The first barber said, "You miss a cunt that far every time, you'll damn sure go through life a virgin."

"Keep it clean, gennermens," Good News said. "We don't want to give our place a bad reputation, do we?" He answered his own question. "Course we don't. Now then, like tomorrow is another day, and it's time to take care business." Good News whipped out his little book. The little man had a great big voice. A big important voice. It didn't seem to belong to him. He addressed Matt Lovejoy. "My man from Pennsylvania Station. How are the nickel-tippers, brother? And how's Brother Philly Randolph?" Matt smiled and grunted, as the barber scraped around his ear with a long straight razor. And Good News went from person to person with his bad self taking care of business, from barber to barber to the shoeshine man and even to some of the customers. They were his customers too. He began to phrase like the late Sam Cooke. "Get right with old Good News, ladies and gentlemens. Your last clear chance to get in on the Grand American Dream. Get rich overnight. Wake up in the morning in the money. Good news, good news, chariot's already here, brothers, and ain't no needa being left behind. Get on board, this evening, chillun. Cause it's right here for you and if you don't get it, it ain't no fault of mine."

One long lanky fellow in the second chair threw his arms up

toward the ceiling and stretched his body. "Lord have mercy on my soul. If I could hit the numbers for ten thousand dollars just one time, I'd buy me a spank brand-new long white Caddy and get myself a great big beautiful blond bitch and drive all the way to Miami on vacation."

The man in the first chair said dryly, slowly, "Yeah—and like I'd git me a long black Caddy limousine and drive all the way down there just to cry myself a river at your funeral."

The laughter relaxed Matt even further. He could feel unknown tensions easing slowly from his body. Both of his women would be at home already. He hoped it would be peaceful. Tonight. At home. He didn't feel like fussing and fighting about anything, and most particularly he didn't feel like fighting about some stupid cotillion. He'd laid his burden down for tonight and he didn't feel like picking it up again. Ruba would just have to make up her mind one way or the other. He'd tell her. It wasn't up to him, *or* her mother. If she didn't want to be a debutante (he called it debi-tramp) she should just stand right up to her mother and say so. His mind meandered back to the Palace. He was half-tuned in now, and he vaguely heard the young dude next to him still holding forth on nonviolence.

"I don't mean we have to love the white man. I mean like the whole thing is a tactic. You all know what a tactic is? Like the Man outnumbers us ten to one. How you going to be violent against them kind of odds? Right? Tactics, brothers, I'm talking about strategy and tactics. You got to beat this Man with psychological warfare."

Matt half-listened to the serious young man. Matt had heard it all before. New York Negroes were the last of the great bullshit artists, the biggest talkers God ever blew the breath of life into. And he himself could do his share of blowing-in-the-wind, when the mood hit him or the occasion demanded it, but tonight he was in one of his listening moods.

Matt was Georgia-born, came to Harlem in 1928 to make his fortune. He came from a town so small, so far from the last outpost of civilization, the choo-choo train didn't even stop there. They had a sawdust pile down near the tracks. The train came through there once a month. And if somebody had to get off at his hometown, the train would slow up and the passenger would have to jump off into the sawdust pile. He sat there in the barber chair and laughed out loud, remembering. He shook his head and laughed aloud, remembering. His barber stared at him, the razor held aloft again. Matt remembering now, when he came to New York a young and very country feller. His reckless cousin (since dead) and some of his cousin's buddies had met Matt at the bus station. Matt had thought himself to be the sharpest cat that ever put his big feet down in old Manhattan. If you had told him he wasn't sharp, you'd have naturally had to give his ass a whipping. All the way from Plum Nelly, Georgia, on the bus, he'd told himself a hundred times: "Man, you sharp as a wedding dick." He was so sharp, he held his hands out from his sides when he walked, afraid he'd cut himself and bleed to death. Fact of the business though, he looked like he had stolen his baby brother's suit, even though he didn't have a baby brother. He was sticking out all over. His jacket and his trousers were like they were undecided, too long for short and too short for long. Hey! He was sharp! But the thing was he was country sharp. His cousin's buddies laughed at him and named him on the spot "Lil Abner" right there in the Boy's bus station.

When he first came to New York, the city almost scared his britches off. He had never seen so many automobiles in all his life, and up here they had things that rumbled madly underground and sounded off like summer thunder, and streetcars that ran on the ground, and elevated things up in the air. All those tall buildings made his poor head swim. He thought there were more people on one of them thundering subway trains than there were in all of his hometown put together. His cousin told him he used to work up in one of those skyscraper buildings and used to wash his face in the natural clouds every morning. Matt's first job was waiting tables where his cousin worked out in Sheepshead Bay in Brooklyn.

The first time he went down to Times Square, he went with some of his buddies, and as they came up out of the subway, there was an old fat white man standing near the top of the stairway, and he was spieling:

"Razor blades, Shoelaces!" Then he lowered his voice and muttered loud enough to be heard clearly: "*Rubbers!*" He went on: "*Rubbers—rubbers—rubbers!* Don't be caught without your rubbers. Razor blades, shoelaces, *rubbers!*"

Then he walked toward Matt and his cousin and his buddies, chanting softly to them:

>"Wanna white woman?
>Wanna white woman?
>Wanna white woman?"

Matt couldn't believe his ears. Surely he had not heard the man right? But then Matt's cousin answered the man with: "Mister, kindly tell us where your clappy mother is?" Matthew almost put a puddle in his bad bell-bottom trousers.

But where Matt really whooped it up was uptown at the Savoy Ballroom. Stomping at the Savoy. He fell in and out of love (and by the numbers) with each of the dance-for-pay girls. In those days, Matt was so green, his cousin said he smelled like collards. He didn't dance the first night he went stomping at the Savoy. Most of the time, he stood near the bandstand staring at the live musicians, especially at the man who blew the slide trombone. Suddenly, near the end of the evening, he began to jump up and down, pointing at the slide-trombonist, and shouting: "You can't fool me! You can't fool me! You ain't swallowing that thing—*every time!*" Well? Anyhow, that was one of the stories his cousin used to tell on him for a year of months and Sundays.

It was at the Savoy where he first met Daphne Braithwaite, that tall Barbadian beauty. Met her on a Thursday night, which was ladies night, a night when women came in free of charge. It was the night-out for New York's sleep-in "kitchen mechanics." It was a great night for the Harlem lover men. Matt courted Daphne Braithwaite for four long months before he could understand a word she said. With her cheerio and cheery-bye it was as if they spoke a different language, and as a matter of fact they did.

With all the running around Matt did before he met the West Indian beauty, when he got married, he still had most of the money he had come to town with. And after he got married, he settled down and proceeded to make his fortune. He worked like crazy on his first million, and two years later he began to work even harder on his second million. After he had given up on his first one. He opened and closed one business after another during the Great Blow-Out of the late late twenties. With millionaires leaping out of windows, he didn't have a window to leap out of, but he didn't let that discourage him. All of his businesses were on the first floor anyhow. Shoeshine parlor, pool room, several restaurants; he reckoned now, in looking back, that he had been too soft for business. Starving people ate breakfast, lunch and dinner on him like they were visiting relatives—regularly—on "credick." And colored brothers were kind enough to recommend his restaurants to other broke and starving members. He called his last restaurant a "risk to run." And when it closed on him, his books looked good, they looked damn good, and neatly kept. With a thousand and seventy-five dollars and thirty-seven cents in the black and on the credit side. Notwithstanding, it was not the kind of black credit that would ever be converted into green cash.

From a true and firm believer in all the gods in whom we trust in the Great American Dream: "Be ambitious—Work hard—Success is just around the curve—Be prepared when opportunity knocks your door down"—or words to that effect, Matt had taken up the banner of his blackness and carried it unfurled all the way from Garvey to Malcolm. Matt had marched behind every Black man who ever raised his voice in Harlem, including Garvey, Powell, Ben Davis, Paul Robeson, and very very naturally, Brother Malcolm. In the late thirties he took a position at the Pennsylvania Station, and had worn his red cap ever since, even now, as the building gaily toppled down around him, making its merry way for progress. In the early fifties he had saved up a little money, and he decided to give it one more try. Opened up a newsstand up on One Hundred and Forty-fifth Street, but the man he left in charge, while he hustled bags at Penn Station, stole him deaf, blind and crazy. Hustled pot and numbers in the place. After the cops closed him down, Matt gave up forever on free enterprise.

The young educated dude got down from the barber chair next to Matt and gave the barber a dollar and waved at him importantly to keep the change.

"Last of the big goddamn spenders," Matt Lovejoy muttered to himself. Amused.

Big Spender walked over to the clothes rack for his jacket and picked up his attaché case. He turned back to the barber. "The beautiful thing about Reverend King—he got the rich white liberals in his bag. Right? And they like own all the liberal newspapers. *New York Times*—the *Post*. Television stations. Public opinion, baby. He also gets money from them white liberals, to carry out his program. He got them rich Jews on his side too, Jim. That what I'm talking about."

Another youngblood, seated, and waiting his turn, agreed completely with Big Spender. "Yeah. Like I heard my man was getting some real *good* bread out of this Movement hustle, and I say, more power to him. Dig, any time a spook can bullshit a Jew out of some of that green stuff, I say more power to him."

Big Spender said, "I don't mean for himself, man. I mean for the Movement—for the Negro—I mean, the Afro-American people."

"He'd be a damn fool not to be putting some of that bread on his own table, baby. Charity begins at home, Jim. Even the Good Book runs that jive down plain enough for any ass to pick up on."

The bald-headed barber at the second chair said, "I'm with Rev. Luther all the way. He a good man. God-fearing and all that jive. But I just can't see myself letting a paddy beat on me, and I'm just standing around telling the sucker how much I love him. Telling him to be my guest. I believe in a eye for a eye and a tooth for a tooth. That's in the Good Book too. And a head for a head, and some ass for some ass. That's America to me. That's the true Christianity."

Matt stretched and yawned as if it were the last yawn left him on this earth, as the barber took the cloth from over him and around him and waved and shook it with a vengeance, the short hairs flying all over the place like a plague of gnats, a few coming to rest upon Matt's lips. The barber stared at the men seated and waiting like sinners at the mourners' bench. He intoned, "All right —all right. Who's next? You going or you gon get left?" Reminding Matt of sweet sweat and sharp perfume and folks and down home and paper fans waving and body smells like fresh coffee cooking and peanuts roasting, and first Sunday communions. When the pastor finished feeding one group of kneelers with the great Jew's body and his blood, he would singsong in a deep melodious voice to those true believers seated patiently on the front row biding their time to smack their lips on Jesus.

"As these depart, let others come. As these depart, let others come." Like the barker down in the front of the Paramount at show-break time in the old days of the great big orchestras.

Matt stood and stared long and hard at his big head in the mirror. Everything big about his face; large lips, nostrils, eyes, wide forehead. He smiled back at his reflection. "Big, Black and handsome," the Black hatcheck girl at the Savoy used to call him in those gone days that seemed so distant now, and yet so close. Willie Bryant, Al Cooper, Lucky Millinder. Battle of Music. Home of Happy Feet. Jimmy Lunceford. One more time! Matt had been a mean rug-cutter. Chick and Ella—one more time! A tisket, a tasket, she lost her yellow basket!

"Big, Black and handsome!" He wasn't really a big man, excepting his shoulders were like Buddy Young's. Only his head had that enormous look, like his patron saint, Fred Douglass. The top of his head reached no higher than five-feet-ten, even when he needed a haircut. Badly.

The young big-spending philosopher made one last effort to get through the barrier to his "culturally deprived" brethren. "Who said anything about *really* loving the Man? I told you, I'm talking tactics. Strategy and tactics. Psychological warfare. The Man outnumbers you ten to one. Even the President of the United States, and you know he's with the Black man all the way. And a Southerner too. He's one of the greatest Negro leaders the race has ever had. And even he told a group of Afro-Americans that violence in the cities could not be tolerated, and that the demonstrations must remain nonviolent, because the whites outnumber us ten to one. Right? And furthermore, like I say, like Whitey's got all the biggest and the baddest weapons. So it stands to reason. Right? Nonviolence is the only way. It stands to reason."

Matt Lovejoy paid the barber and flicked the fine hairs off his jacket with his fingers. He reached his black hands toward the ceiling and gave out with another yawn, this one louder, more contagious than the others gone before. There was yawning now all over the place. Big ones, small ones, medium sizes. Matt brought his arms down to his sides and started toward the entrance-exit. He stopped and said aloud, to no one in particular:

"I know one thing. It stands to reason, if the rabbits took rock-throwing lessons, there wouldn't be all them many hunters pitching boogie in the forest."

He continued out of the door, leaving the young upset philosopher and the laughter and the "Amens" and the "Tell it like it is!" and the "That's right!" and the odor of hair tonic, the sound of buzzing clippers and the signifying, leaving all that behind him. He went out into the steamy streets, where night was falling with a vengeance, darkly falling, blinking neon lights reminding him of lightning bugs of long ago in Georgia time; a car backfiring, horns honking; falling swiftly was the night; it seemed that he could hear night falling, as Matt Lovejoy set out upon the last lap of his journey home.

He hoped home would be peaceful when he got there. He didn't feel up to the Great Debate tonight. To hell with the Cotillion.

CHAPTER THREE

DAPHNE

But oh my dear, look at the lady's crosses.
"Lord, look at my crosses!"
Yeah—
"You see my crosses, Jesus!"
Okay, Matt had thought a million times before, and even now, this late September evening, as he sat at the dinner table underneath his new haircut, and watched his darling wife go into her daily thing. Yeah—look at the woman's crosses. Would somebody kindly do him a favor and dig her jive crosses? Take a damn good squint at his old lady's everlasting crosses!

Sometimes, even gentle Yoruba would pray, albeit silently: "Yes, dear God, merciful Father, kindly take time out from your busy schedule and observe my darling pious mother's precious crosses."

She was Daphne Doreen Braithwaite Lovejoy. A tall aristocratic woman, who thought that, with a little luck and a slight assist from the Great-One-Up-On-High, she might have been the Queen of England. She surely almost looked the part, as she imagined queens should look. Perhaps a little duskier than ordinary Western queens, but then queens were never ordinary. She certainly was a fine specimen of female pulchritude, Western style, darkly so, extraordinary in all parts of her; slim, majestic, her haughty head eternally in the air as was her slender turned-up nose, as if she were forever sniffing after loftier sterile atmospheres, where folks gave off more heavenly odors than the common folks beneath her. Her mouth, inherited from her father's side, was a thin almost imperceptible slash in the middle of her face; her eyes, so proud and bluish green, could shift from cold blue-ice to flashes of dark, consuming fires. Her eyes were always heavy-laden "heavy-lidded," as if invisible weights were hanging from them, bringing them down. The blue ice was her father's Nordic contribution, she would tell you, proudly. "The fire is the Blackness of my mother's African disposition," she would tell you, not so proudly.

Talk about people having bags, Daphne swore by her bag, of crosses, lived out of her bag, and it contained a million crosses, of all sizes and denominations. One of her favorite crosses was that her family did not appreciate a thing she ever tried to do for them. Like retiring, as she did, from the ranks of the working classes about eleven years ago, so that she could make a happy home for them and send them off to school and work with a hot meal every morning and have one ready for them when they returned. Like joining them to a church way out in Brooklyn in the Crowning Heights, and taking them out there every Sunday she could get the ungrateful ones to go, so they could make the acquaintance of some high-class colored people, and thereby become imbued with some direly needed "couth" by the process of osmosis, all else of her tireless efforts having failed. Miserably?

Because it was perfectly clear to Lady Daphne (a title conferred upon her by husband, Matthew) that her family was uncouth, especially her husband, although it wasn't quite so obvious to Yoruba or Matt. The pastor of the Brooklyn Memorial Episcopal Cathedral (some proper colored members called him Vicar) was Father Madison Mayfair, a bad-walking faggot-acting white man from the wilds of Alabama. Slew-footed, bowlegged, flat-footed, swishing switcher. Ten years before, the church had been white, and as pure and innocent as a virgin's twat rag or a Klansman's bedsheet. But when nice upstanding outstanding understanding colored people of the middle-class persuasion started moving into the neighborhood, the father before Father Mayfair had invited them to join the church (Come on in! Feel right at home. Jesus lives and loves us all!), much to the righteous outrage of the good white middle-class Christian membership. And what began as a slow white trickle away from the church very soon turned into an exodus and ultimately a full-scale disorderly retreat, as the onward Christian soldiers sought the Blessed Saviour in less dark, more illumined quarters. Preferring not to brighten the corner where they were, as they were called upon to do by the blessed Vicar.

A few months later, Father Thatcher himself did a copout, moved on to one of those Bright Mansions Above to see his Master face to face. Some of his colored members thought he had run out on them on purpose. Notwithstanding, Father Madison Mayfair came all the way from the Alabama bush to fill Father Thatcher's shoes, with his big bad flat feet. But look at Daphne's crosses! Did uncouth Matt Lovejoy appreciate efforts to instill him with some "couth"? Hardly! Did Yoruba Evelyn join the choir as her mother had arranged it? Never!

Matt's surly comment was: "All them black damn sheep with a white damn shepherd." And he refused to join the church. "Damn if that don't beat everything. Calling a white man Father in these days and times. Father May-damn-fair! Everybody everywhere else in the world busy as a cat covering up shit trying their best to get rid of all the Great White Fathers, and y'all paying that sissy-ass pimp to help get y'all in the white man's heaven, where they gon have all you Negroes doing days work anyhow. Cooking, scrubbing, and carrying on."

The dark dark fires of Hell built up in poor dear Daphne's eyes. Sometimes her eyes seemed not to match, one blue-green, the other brownish-black. She chipsed (sucked her tongue between her teeth) as only a West Indian woman can chips. "You are a man of magnificent and complacent ignorance, Matthew Lovejoy," she said almost pleasantly, like she was handing out citations for extraordinary excellence. "The nation is working for an integrated society, and our church is a shiny example. The dear Vicar is giving up his entire career as a white man, just to give us an integrated experience. He's the only white person left in the entire congregation. You should get down on your Black knees and thank God for progressive men like Father Mayfair."

But in all his complacent and magnificent ignorance, Matt stubbornly refused to thank God for Father Mayfair. And one of the things he had against the church was the knee-bending bit. The few times he'd been to this very very high Episcopalian church, known by some sophisticated folks as the Cathedral on The Heights, it was the up-and-down genuflecting bit that turned him off. His knees were aching for a week the last time he attended. And he never could get the hang of the kneeling business, up-and-down, whoops, when he was vipping, most of others in church were vopping. He just had no appreciation at all for the sacrifice the holy man was making. "That peckerwood's feet is bad as Jesse James. And the way he switches y'all oughta be calling him *Mother* Mayfair."

Mother Daphne kissed the fingers of her open hand and flung it upward toward the Lord. She chipsed long, loud, significantly. "Look at my crosses!" She turned to Matthew sitting at the kitchen table. "You is the rudest nigger God ever did put down on this sinful earth!"

"All praises to Allah," Matthew dryly answered.

In the first place, Matthew did not appreciate the "indisputable" fact that Daphne Braithwaite had done him one great big favor by marrying him, in the first place. There was the rub. He was an ingrate. Right? Another of her blessed crosses.

A colored girlfriend from one of the Islands had asked her, when Matt had first started coming around: "How you mean—taking up with a man as Black as Matthew?"

Another West Indian beauty told her, "He rather handsome anyhow, even though he is a bit of a tar baby."

Another advised her, "That's right. Get yourself a Black one, dearie. He will worship you for true. Put you on a pedestal, darling. Be your proper slave. He'll wash your drawers and drink the water."

The thing was: He had never even washed Lady Daphne's underthings. Can you dig her crosses!

Daphne Braithwaite Lovejoy was born in Christ Church in Barbados in the West Indies. Some proud Bajuns called it "Little England." Daphne's father was a Scotchman with eleven Black concubines, one of whom was Daphne's lucky mother. Right? The old gentleman was sixty-four by the time Daphne was born and still going strong, full blast, and making heaps of yaller young'uns. Café-au-lait was his style, he was the last of the great baby-makers. He never married any of his African beauties, and they were in constant competition for his favor, and his favors. Sometimes they came to blows over him. Actually. Physically. Sometimes he had two or three of them with child by him, simultaneously. His brother used to tell him: "Angus, you got just as many nigger children as you can shake a dick at." And he would roar with laughter.

Angus Braithwaite was a big important man in Barbados, and, off and on, the moody squire was rather generous to his thirty or forty-five colored children, who proudly took his name. Especially was he generous to those who stayed in Little England, some of whom he sent to study in Big England, and some also of whom he groomed to make up his managerial staff on his sugar plantation and in his rum distillery. Till his dying day, Angus was a gay blade for true. Daphne, herself, had a half-sister still living in Barbados, who was her actual twin, and who issued forth into the world, head first, the same day and the same hour as she, but issued out of a different womb. The Braithwaites were "first family" coloreds in Barbados. Ask Daphne. They were legendary. You've heard of black Irish? Would you believe—black Scotchmen?—All the way. Moreover they were big colored people; indeed they were the biggest family on that small and windward island.

Daphne grew into a long, slim, aristocratic-looking woman, very much aware of her beauty and her claim to aristocracy. Took the thing for granted. Coming as she did from such auspicious beginnings, it was to be expected. If Daphne had not existed, she would have had to be invented. Since she was nine, ten, eleven years old, she had never passed a mirror without staring admiringly into it. Her beauty was also one of her crosses. Every place she got a job, the boss eventually got around to patting her on her wonderful arse and trying to throw her into bed.

She came to the good old USA to make her fortune when she was seventeen years old. Her mother, at the time, was out of favor with her father, and she never forgave her mother for it. Actually her mother didn't understand the limitations of a concubine's prerogatives. In a word, she was a sassy Black woman, gave ol' masser word for word. So off to the good old USA little Daphne did come, where there was Heaven on Earth, and the streets were paved with gold and you could pick money up off the sidewalk. When she reached New York, she walked the streets for a couple of weeks, and she found that one could indeed pick up money out there on the turf, if one gave of one's self, generously, in return. But she loved herself too much for that kind of arrangement. So she got a job as a chambermaid in a downtown hotel in Manhattan.

And she told the other girls with whom she worked, when they complained of the clientele laying hands on them as if they, the clientele, were faith-healers: "It's all in the way you carry yourself, my dears. They ain't dare put their hands on me. They know character and quality when they see it."

One of the girls, a Jamaican, said of her, "She got she nose always stuck up in the air. She must think she shit don't stink. She cleaning up behind these stinking white peoples just like we is. She can go back to that little small island where she really come from."

Then one day a wealthy white gentleman chased her all over his suite. And she reported him to the manager and demanded that he be kicked out of the hotel.

"But Daphne," the manager pleaded. "He didn't do you no harm."

"He insulted me. That's harm enough. I'm a lady."

"True he ran you around the suite, but he didn't catch you, did he? I mean you didn't lose anything by it. Did you?"

"Either he go or I tender my resignation forthwith."

The boss looked dear lovely Daphne over. They were seated in his office. He placed his hand upon her knee—in a kind of fatherly gesture, to be sure. Right? "Now come on, Daphne. We can work this thing out to the satisfaction of all concerned." And squeezed her knee, affectionately.

She stood up quickly. "It's him or I, Mr. Anthony," she insisted proudly.

The next few days were spent looking for another position. She got one doing "days work" up in the Bronx, and from one position to the other, cooking, maiding, she found in each house there was at least one self-anointed faith-healer, sometimes two, Junior and Senior, all hands, and all devout believers in the laying-on of hands. Look at Lady Daphne's crosses! Sometimes she actually wished she were not such a pretty woman. Men, after all, were such filthy animals, all of them, excepting of course, her father in Barbados, who was a gentleman for true. She'd tell the world, "After Angus Braithwaite was created, my dears, they threw away the mold."

When Daphne and Matt got married, she was not the best cook in the world. The first cooking job she got was for a white, cranky, old ill-humored spinster up in the Bronx. The second morning on the job, the lady asked her to prepare oatmeal for breakfast. Daphne got the breakfast together, unhurriedly, with tender loving care. When she took it in to the crochety old woman, the woman took affront and scolded Daphne severely, just because Daphne hadn't known that, customarily, you *cooked* oatmeal before serving it. She had just put it cold into a bowl and poured milk and sugar on it and served it, like corn flakes. Look at the dear girl's crosses! The old woman didn't even have a sense of humor. Sent poor Daphne packing.

Daphne was a slender woman, almost thin, who ate like seven lean years of drought and famine were just around the corner. And food was going swiftly out of style, decidedly. The dear one ate only one meal a day, continuously all day long, always complained about her birdlike appetite and her stomach trouble, never gained a pound, fussed and worried over everything, and slept the sleep of the innocent and the dead.

Yoruba Evelyn was one of her beloved crosses. Came into the house from work that very evening, pecked her devoted mother on the cheek, went into the living room and put some of that ignorant music on the hi-fi, turned it up so high the apartment literally shook (it couldn't stand much shaking as old and shaky as it already was). Ruba knew her mother hated that kind of music. Yes, Daphne hated that ignorant music the girl insisted on bringing into the house. "Calypso, jazz, rock 'n' roll, common nigger music from the streets." She wanted to scream aloud, "Turn the damn thing down!"

Daphne was the kind of proud Carribbean beauty who loftily cherished her British heritage. The only songs that really made her heart leap wildly and warmly wet her eyes with tears were "God Save the Queen" and "Rule Britannia"; and as long as Britannia ruled the waves, though, when challenged by Matthew, Daphne never remembered when Britannia ruled the waves, or precisely which waves Britannia ruled when she certainly ruled them— nevertheless—she was comfortably confident that Britons never would be slaves. It was a source of consolation in these days of strife and strain and race riots and mini-skirts. How Daphne could make such complete identification with Britannia was a mystery to

Matt Lovejoy. But then the poor disadvantaged man had never been a British subject. Right? He had not been born in Little England. Cultural deprivation?

Daphne strutted slowly toward the great noise in the living room. "Turn down the hi-fi, Eve-lyn. I've had the fiercest headache all day long." She stood now in the doorway to the living room. She thought: The girl turned up the hi-fi as high as possible just out of pure spite and meanness, and then went into her bedroom and closed the door behind her. Daphne chipsed and lowered the "noise" and strutted back to the kitchen. Everywhere Daphne went she strutted. Yoruba got her strutting honest. The only difference was—Yoruba strutted hurriedly; Daphne always strutted slowly. Queens were not supposed to hurry. Hurrying was for their attendants. Commoners and such.

She learned to cook through trial and error, first Matthew alone, then he and Yoruba were her patient guinea pigs, Lady Daphne emerging ultimately, undisputed queen of the kitchen, an expert in the culinary arts. Her repertoire became an exciting mixture of Southern and West Indian cuisine. She emerged an expert with pigeon peas and fried chicken (Southern style), coucou with okras, egg bread, eddoes, coconut bread, hush puppies, codfish cakes, conch, hopping johns, fries, black-pudding and souse or Southern chitterlings (either style), corn pones, cassava pones, country biscuits; she was heavy with the spices; chicken-and-rice-curry, collard greens, hamhocks, she learned to do her stuff in the kitchen. Sometimes her speech was like her cooking, a curious mixture of Southern accents and West Indian idioms. Bajun and Jamaican sounds blending and clashing with down-home rhythms. Sometimes Matthew called her, "My little beautiful Savannah Geechie." Sometimes he swore she was from the Sea Islands off the coast of Savannah, Georgia.

Now the three were gathered in the kitchen for their dinner. Yoruba looked up from the table and saw her mother staring at her. Her mother could be warm and tender, but it was the kind of warmth that could suddenly blow up a mighty storm. Sometimes her father called her mother Hurricane Daphne. And when the lady started staring at her crosses—look out!

Daphne smiled benignly at both of them, like the queen conferring knighthood on her lesser subjects. She said softly, sweetly,

"I've got wonderful news for you. Mrs. Patterson called today." There was pure excitement in her voice.

"Which Mrs. Patterson?"

She wouldn't let him dampen her spirit. He knew who Mrs. Patterson was. "Mrs. Patterson is the chairman of the Selection Committee, and it's all been decided for Eve-lyn to participate in the Grand Cotillion. Isn't it splendid? Our daughter will be coming out!"

"Coming out where? To what?" Matt played the whole thing straight-faced. With such magnificent complacency.

"Coming out in society!" Control your disposition, Daphne.

"What society?"

"The first families of Brooklyn!"

Matt said, "But we live in Manhattan. Harlem."

She glanced, almost unknowingly, up toward the kitchen ceiling. Like a conditioned reflex, she started to chips and look at her crosses, but this time she practiced self-restraint. She said cheerfully, patiently, "This is what I've worked for all my life for my baby ever since the day she came into this wicked world. Just think of it! Out of all the girls in Harlem, my baby was one of the ones they picked."

In low key Matt said, "So the Fat Asses picked your baby."

The Lovejoys had discussed the coming Cotillion for months, ever since the Femmes Fatales, a fancy colored women's club in Brooklyn, had decided, out of the piety of their missionary fervor, to do the Grand Cotillion just a little bit different this year. Usually the Femmes Fatales (Matt pronounced it Fems Fat Tails, when he didn't call them straight-out Asses) selected a group of light-skin girls of vowed-for virtue of seventeen or eighteen years of age from among their own, which was to say, their greatest virtues were that they happened to be the daughters of doctors, lawyers, preachers, teachers, number backers, businessmen and postal clerks. But this time they decided to do it differently. It was Mrs. Patterson's idea, bless her heart, and she had to fight like a lady tiger to get it adopted by the group. Some of the Femmes Fatales actually wept bitter tears at the very idea of "carrying integration too far." Others threatened to resign. But between Mrs. Patterson and Beverly Brap-bap, they whipped the others into line. Mississippi-born Beverly Brap-bap was coarse and common, according to the tastes of some of the ladies of the club, but she had more money than all the rest of them put together. Her husband ran a nice, high-class, dignified funeral establishment in Bedford-Stuyvesant. Every body was proud to be handled by Chauncey Brapbap. There was this brightly lighted sign over the entrance of the Brap-bap Funeral Parlor, which read:

> THROUGH THESE PORTALS GO
> THE MOST HANDSOME CORPSES IN THE WORLD
> TO THEIR FINAL RESTING PLACE.

On some of his fans, which he circulated in the colored churches and other varied and sundried respectable places, he had printed:

> YOU'RE IN GOOD HANDS
> WHEN YOU'RE IN BRAP-BAP'S.
> DON'T WORRY ABOUT IT.

On other fans:

> IT'S A PLEASURE TO GO TO HEAVEN
> OR EVEN TO THE OTHER PLACE
> IF BRAP-BAP GETS YOU READY.

In the back of the Brap-bap establishment were the numerous embalming rooms. In the back of the establishment were also some of the finest crap games in the country. If you wandered inadvertently into the wrong room, you might meet all kinds of celebrities, black and white, including mayors, chiefs of police, congressmen, senators, playboys, hustlers—crap-shooters all. Dead or very much alive, Brap-bap did a thriving business.

One night during a stormy session at a Femmes Fatales' meeting, amidst weeping and gnashing of teeth, threats and recriminations, signifying, Beverly Brap-bap took the floor and read the riot act to the ladies. "You bitches better get your asses off your shoulders. First families my royal hindparts! Most of you just one generation off the plantation. Cotton in Mississippi and sugarcane in Trinidad!"

It was Mrs. Patterson's idea, backed vigorously by Beverly Brap-bap, to select at least five girls from the "culturally deprived" of Harlem. A kind of "Operation Upsey-Daisy." Mrs. Patterson was Beverly Brap-bap's opposite, a very proper lady in every aspect, imbued with fierce missionary zeal and devoted Christian spirit.

She was a leading member of Father Mayfair's Brooklyn Memorial Episcopal Cathedral, which was why Yoruba's name was placed into the hopper in the first place. And now, after months of violent debating over the world-shaking question of who the five lucky unfortunates would be, Yoruba Evelyn had emerged one of the chosen.

Daphne looked at her daughter now with open admiration, thinking to herself, she *is* a lovely girl, she *is* a beautiful girl, despite the fact that she inherited her father's color and his looks. The girl's high cheekbones and her slender upturned nose were the only features of her face that wore her mother's stamp of approval. Daphne sweetly remembered now, almost weepingly, how hard she'd worked down through the years to mold her little girl into a thing of beauty and a joy eternal, how she used to make the girl pull her lips in and keep them in when she was a baby, so they would grow thin like hers, and how she used to put clothespins on the baby's nostrils just to pinch them into thin and slender (she used to say "aquiline" till she looked the word up in the dictionary). How she used to keep her away from the beaches and off the streets out of the sunlight, and never ever let the girl drink coffee, which would make her Blacker than she already was. Until Yoruba was sixteen, nobody ever drank coffee in her house excepting her father who was Black and didn't have any better sense than to be damn proud of his Blackness. You thought Daphne's crosses were imaginary? When Daphne thought of how she had striven against all odds, including her very odd husband, to endow this child with the niceties of ladylikeness and the values of the upper classes, preparing her for such a moment as this, which was at long last magnificently here, she had to fight back the tears of joy which stood just out of sight on the other side of her eyes. She stared now, nostalgically, from Matthew to Yoruba Evelyn, her eyes searching eagerly for some expression of the ecstasy she knew they both felt deep deep inside of them, especially Yoruba Evelyn.

The three of them had come a long way together to this historic moment in their lives. As modest as she was, she had to give herself a lot of credit. They had seen hard times, but all the sacrifices had been worth it, if it finally led to this. She remembered when Yoruba was a little baby and they lived in the house a few blocks away, lived in the basement of a brownstone, something like the one they lived in now. Many years ago they had moved up in life, moved a few blocks up the street and from the basement up to the parlor floor. Getting-up-in-the-world was what. The icy cold winters then, when they had to walk around the house with overcoats on, and the baby wore a snowsuit and mittens when she went to bed, all this despite the fact that there was so-called central heating. All day long Daphne had to keep the oven of the kitchen stove lighted. Sometimes it got so cold the rats, teeth chattering to wake the dead, would come out of hiding and sit near the open door of the oven to keep from freezing to death.

Their landlord had been an old man who lived on the top floor of the same brownstone. Trying to buy the house in the twilight of his years. His house had so many mortgages, sometimes he didn't remember how many there were. His mortgages had mortgages had mortgages. A little dried-up hustling-bustling man from Jamaica by way of Panama who talked to himself too much for anybody else's comfort. His wife worked as a charwoman every night in Lower Manhattan. Mr. Deighten Shyler never fixed anything and you never got a straight answer from him in regard to any complaint. He just wanted you to pay the rent, ahead of time if possible, bless his little old pure-and-scheming heart.

Mr. Shyler went past the Lovejoys' basement apartment down to the cellar to monkey with the furnace at least thirty-seven times a day. At seventy-one years, he must have been in good condition. If you asked him why there was no heat in the radiators, he would shake his head tolerantly, and say of the heat: "It goes up, it goes down." And then, philosophically, "What goes up must come down." How was Daphne going to argue with that kind of scientific erudition? Sometimes he would come into the Lovejoys' apartment and spend an hour or so blowing his breath into the radiator valves, which usually left him terribly short of breath and Daphne terribly frightened that he might have a heart attack right then and there. Notwithstanding, his breathing exercises had absolutely no effect on the heat, or lack of it, whichever.

There was the time when Yoruba Evelyn was three years old and had a racking and throat-rattling cold. The doctor had come and gone; the baby's temperature was defying the laws of gravity, had been up for a couple of days and had not come down, Mr. Shyler to the contrary. To make matters worse, not only was there no heat in the house, neither was there any hot water. For hours, desperate Daphne stood near the door inside her apartment (it was a door that opened on the kitchen), stood there listening, waiting in ambush like a guerrilla fighter, to pounce upon Mr. Shyler as he made one of his trips down to the cellar. Finally, her patience was rewarded. Just as he was passing the door, she flung it open and leaped upon him, albeit she leaped ladylike, aristocratically and nonviolently. "I must have some hot water to bathe my baby. She running a fever of a hundred and three. You keep turning the damn furnace off to save some pennies and my baby's life's in jeopardy."

The sweet little much-picked-upon man promised her faithfully that hot water would be forthcoming forthwith. Five minutes later he knocked on the door and when she opened it, there stood Old Faithful with a pot of steaming water in his hands. He had heated it upstairs on his kitchen stove. A man who always kept his promise. "It's good and hot. It's good and hot," he proudly mumbled, as Daphne stood there staring at him, laughing and crying interchangeably. He secretly thought that she had long since lost her marbles.

But all that was behind them. They had overcome. Daphne could even laugh at all those happenings now. This now time was her finest hour, in the words of that grandest of Anglo-Saxons. She looked at her daughter for some sign that she shared this moment with her. The girl was probably so overcome with joy she was afraid to speak for fear she would break down completely.

As a matter of fact, Yoruba Evelyn was so overcome she didn't know what to say. How do you tell your mother you don't want to be a lady? That you would rather be a good Black woman? The truth of the matter, there was this great ambivalence in the girl; forever did the battle rage inside of her between her mother and her father, between ladyship and womanhood. The confrontation black and white. Against her will she did feel a kind of triumph that she had been selected. She, Yoruba Evelyn, was to be a debutante. What was wrong with feeling good about it? Sometimes she felt like shouting: "Will the real Yoruba Evelyn step forward please. And assert yourself?"

Yoruba asked her mother, "How much is it going to cost?"

Her mother said, her dear voice choking with emotion, "Don't you worry your lovely head about that, darling. Me and your daddy will scrape it together, won't we, sweetheart? He's just as pleased about it as you are. He's just tickled to death about it, ain't you, dearie?"

Matt waxed repetitious. "How much?"

Daphne said dreamily, "And to think I could have had any boy in Bimshire to marry, 'deed in Trinidad or Jamaica or anywhere else in those precious islands in the sun. I lived in one place as much as I did another. My father always let us travel. Jamaica was my second home. And I truly would have been living the life. Down there my folks had a staff of servants waiting on them hand and foot. I had my own private maid, my dears, but I was such a spoiled one, and I wanted to see how the other half lived. That's why I came to America." She had changed her reasons for coming to the States so many times, Matt couldn't keep up with them. Indeed, she couldn't keep up with them herself. "And that's why I want things to be different for my baby. Get yourself a man that will give you all the things a lady is supposed to have. Make you feel like Queen Elizabeth."

Sometimes Matt could really be repetitious. "How much, Lady Daphne?"

Daphne almost lost her voice. "Four hundred dollars."

"Four hundred dollars!" From the chorus.

"That's the special bargain price for the five Harlem lucky ones. And that takes care of everything—the practices, the rehearsals, the cosmetologist, the beautician, the dance teacher—"

Matt exploded. "What the hell does Yoruba need with a dance teacher?"

Yoruba could really dance all of the dances being danced plus many that weren't being danced. Years before, when Yoruba was five, her mother had entered her in a contest given by a talent studio, and naturally she had won a chance to attend the Metropolitan Talent School. Every child who entered the contest won, and gained admission to the school, if the parents got up fifteen dollars a month, which meant that there had been children (mostly Black) in the dancing school with two left feet, two right feet and a few with no feet at all, all of whom had a tremendous future, the talent scouts graciously assured their parents. Actually

Yoruba was a damn good dancer, which was probably why she repeated, "Dancing teacher?"

Daphne said, "He is to teach the young ladies how to waltz. In fact, the four hundred dollars include all the expenses, excepting the price of the evening gown, the shoes and earrings." She muttered under her breath again. "And the room in the Waldorf for getting dressed and the party afterward."

Matt said, "You gotta be kidding. Where's all this money coming from? The Ford Foundation?"

"We can afford it," undaunted Daphne insisted. "It's a thing that comes once in lifetime. We'll get the money, even if we have to make a loan at the bank."

Matt said, "Lady Daphne, have you forgot that Ruba is planning to go to Howard University next year? We gon need everything we can steal, beg and borry, and you wanna spend four or five hundred dollars on one damn night. Giving all that money to Mr. Waldorf and all them other white folks."

Daphne clouded up and started suddenly to rain, like in the tropics. Wiped the downpour from her eyes with her apron, and the rain continued. "My baby is not going to Howard University, you hear? She is not going to Howard University!"

They both stared at her speechless.

"She's going to Sarah Lawrence, or maybe Smith, or—or—or Radcliffe. I've been investigating all them schools."

Yoruba smiling sadly at her mother now. "I *am* going to Howard, Mother," she said softly. "That is, if I go to college anywhere."

The storm was building in her mother's face, the fire was smoldering in her eyes, in the thrust-forward of her shoulders. "That's some of your father's ignorant foolishness, but I don't mean for you to get no nigger education. What do you think I've gone deprived and toiled and struggled all these years for?"

Yoruba's face was warm with anger. "All right then, what's the matter with City College? I believe I made the marks."

"Jew school—damn Jew school!"

Yoruba shook her head in anger. "Mother—Mother—Mother."

"Your father would do anything to defeat my purpose. All he do is undermine me."

Matt got up from the table. "What I'm going to do now is go

out here and get myself a drink." He went toward the front door, then turned before he opened it. "Whatever you want to do, Yoruba, your daddy is behind you. From Howard University to that damn Fat Ass Cotillion."

"Fat-tails!" Lady Daphne screamed after him, tears streaming down her face. "Fem Fat-tails! Not Fat-Asses!" As the father continued out of the door.

Daphne's face underwent a swift transformation, as she wiped her eyes and stopped the rain, and her face beamed again with sunlight. Yoruba stared at Daphne unbelievingly. As long as she had known her mother, she couldn't get over the way she could turn it on and off, as if she had an invisible faucet.

Her mother smiled. "Thank God that's settled."

"Nothing is settled, Mother."

"Oh, Eve-lyn, my dear, let us stop fooling with each other. He's gone now. You ain't have to put on an act for your mother's benefit. You know you want to be in the Cotillion. You know you want all the things I want for you. It's just that you feel you have to pretend to understand and sympathize with your ignorant father." She sighed, deep and long. "I don't hold his color against him, Eve-lyn. I just—"

"You hold everybody's color against them, Mother." She walked to the door to the living room. She stared into the room and turned and looked back at her mother. "What did Grandmother Maggie look like, Mother? You have a dozen pictures of Grandfather Angus all over this house but not a single one of my grandmother. Why, Mother? What did she look like?"

"Don't vex me, child. Your grandmammy was a Black woman, a common negra. Not bad-looking for a field negra. But your grandfather was a great, handsome, grand gentleman. He did Maggie a favor to take her out the cane field."

"Mother, you are impossible!"

"Your grandmother was an impudent negra and didn't appreciate what my father was doing for her. He tried to uplift her but she wouldn't be uplifted. She was an ungrateful wretch. Always overstepping the boundaries of her position. That is why he finally had to throw her out. She was a sassy negra. That is why I got disinherited. It was all her fault."

Yoruba was speechless.

"But I don't hold your father's color against him, Eve-lyn. It's just that, just because he was born Black, he insist on living a Black life. He wallows in it like a pig in a pool of mud. All I want is a good life for you." She lifted the apron to her face and blew her nose, unladylike. And went into her thing and turned her faucet on again. "Everybody is against me in this house. Everything I try to do!" She was speaking through her tears. "I'm tired and I'm old and my own husband and my only baby hates me!"

It angered Yoruba to see her mother cry like this. She felt the heat creep through her face and over her shoulders. She figured it was all an act, yet knew it was not all an act—not entirely. Sometimes her mother did feel ganged up on, and unappreciated.

"My poor heart can't stand much more punishment. The doctor told to me to be quiet and not to excite myself over nothing. But what you going to do when all you have in the world is done turned against you." She stared up at the ceiling, the tears in floodtide. "Look at my crosses, Jesus, dear boy-child of the Blessed Virgin! See my crosses! I'm a long ways from my father's house, and in his house there is many mansions, and servants falling over each other to do my family's biddings. But in my own house here in this godless country in this hell of a city, I am treated like a servant. Dear Jesus, what have I done to deserve this? Pass this bitter cup!"

"Stop it, Mother!" Yoruba shouted softly, heatedly.

"I turned my back on my father's house, on all his wealth and riches, gave up everything for this family here. Gave up the easy life for a life of strife and struggling. And all I have to show for it is a good heart done gone bad and broken, so many times by my chosen loved ones, so many times, so many times! And my own baby don't love me! My own baby do not love me!" She was crying now and breathing hard and holding her left breast in the cup of her hands. She sank down into the chair, tried to get up and sank back down again. "Nobody loves me! Nobody loves me!" Gasping for her precious breath. Each breath she took now would surely be her last.

Against her will the tears pushed out of Yoruba's eyes, spilled down her cheeks. She thought her mother was overreacting or just plain acting, and yet—and yet against her will, she watched herself go to her mother and put her arms around her, and now both of them were crying like their lives depended on their tears and sobbing. "I love you, Mother! You know I love you!" Angry with herself for being so susceptible and chicken-hearted.

"No, you don't! No, you don't! Nobody loves me! I'm just an old beatup evil bitch that nobody loves!"

"I love you, Mother! I love you—love you!"

"Everything I try to do to show my love for you, you turn it against me! You and your father! I ain't got a friend in the world! Maybe the Good Lord is punishing me for turning against my father's family in Barbados."

"I love you, Mother, and my father loves you, and I want to be in the Cotillion. I want to be in the Cotillion!"

"You just saying that cause you want me to stop crying—" Her voice broke off again. She wanted insurance against a change of heart—or mind. She wanted guarantees.

"No! No, Mother! No, darling! I want to be in it, because I think it's going to be wonderful! And I appreciate everything you—"

"You're sure you want to be in it—I mean, of your own volition?"

"Of my own volition, Mother." She told herself she was not lying. Just who was she to be scornful of the Grand Cotillion? Out of all the thousands of girls in Harlem she had been one of the five selected. She was proud and grateful. She had something to look forward to.

Daphne wiped her eyes and turned the faucet off again. "All right then, my darling. And you'll be the prettiest lady at the ball."

Yoruba said with firmness, "But next September, I am going to Howard University."

"That's all right," Daphne answered, with a sheepish sly expression. "We'll swim that bridge when we cross that river."

CHAPTER FOUR

LUMUMBA

> "A nigger ain't shit!
> A nigger ain't shit!
> A nigger ain't shit!
> A nigger ain't shit!
> A nigger ain't shit!
> A nigger ain't shit!
> A nigger ain't shit!"

He paused and slowed his tempo almost to a halt, and delivered the next line slowly, pronouncing each word deliberately.

> "A—nigger—ain't—shit!
> But can you dig it?
> The Black man is the hope of humankind."

He bowed, gracefully, smiling through the glistening black bush which sheltered and adorned his face, as the crowd of Bloods exploded now with laughter and a wild applause. The slim, young, bearded man bending regally from his waist, once, twice, thrice, turning, bowing, left, center, right, until he caught Yoruba's eyes. Hold. Turn no more. Zoom in. Bow no more. Focus. Or was it her imagination? Dig. From then on, he rapped, it seemed, to her alone.

He rapped:

> "Time was
> When Blackness was
> The badge of our great shame.
> We wrapped ourselves in snowy blankets.
> We anointed our woolen locks with oil.
> And baked our heads with ignorance.
> And filled our minds with horseshit

In the presence of our enemies.
The white wolf was our Lord and shepherd
And led us gaily to the slaughter—"

In the beginning, when the undernourished-looking young man walked to the center of the stage and opened his mouth and began to rap his warmish cool Black thing through his poetical palaver, there was something vaguely, strangely, even frighteningly familiar about his royal, fine, brown-blackness. The way he walked? Or was it his voice, all soft-and-Southern-sweetness like Willie Mays's everlasting Alaga syrup thick-and-cold-in-the-middle-of-winter, all mixed up somehow with definite New York phrasing, down-South up-South clashing and blending? Was it the sledgehammer-hard, bitter-gleaming ebony of his eyes, large and wide, burning coals, flashing fire sometimes like lighted lanterns? Then lighting up a different way with acid humor, angry laughter. Even though Yoruba had heard him introduced, the name hadn't meant a thing to her.

He rapped:

"Okay, Snakeshit was right.
There is a tide in men's affairs.
We are the ocean and the tide.
And we must take it in our stride.
The waters are polluted now.
For centuries polluted now.
The flood is here—and everywhere
We Black folks are the cleansing flood.
And we are men, not motherfuckas.
Screwed without enjoyment all these centuries,
Mother Africa doesn't need her sons to do it to her.
She's got a royal screwing all these Western decades.
Of our colonial degradation,
While we looked on and masturbated
The great orgy went on and on in the missionary fashion.
Okay, Snakeshit was right—"

The texture of his voice, his mannerisms got to the girl somehow, stirred something deep down in the bowels of her, where the very quick was quickest. She had known somebody like him somewhere sometime in the eighteen years of her sojourn on this Mother Earth. He, slim-waisted and of the middle heights and masculine and deep in voice, in the Robeson and Marshall style, like some trousered fellows these days definitely were not. There was something about him conjuring up some long forgotten incident, not quite forgotten actually, but badly remembered was more where it was at. Really!

"Rap, you fine Black rapping rapper!" A youngblood sister shouted. And so he did. He rapped:

> "It's here, my brothers, here, here, here!
> Not in Paris or in Rome.
> Not in Denmark or in Sweden.
> The fight is right back here at home.
> But they all tripped off to Europe,
> Where things were nice and fine.
> You could get your fill of pussy,
> But no jobs were for your kind.
> If you can make it just on pussy,
> Run to Europe very fast.
> But if you can't live on straight-haired cunt alone,
> That's gon be your fat Black ass!"

He paused, smiled, and then continued.

> "You gon sure lose weight,
> My brother."

Feet-stomping, riotous laughter, mad applause.
"Teach!" . . . "Teach!"
"Let it all hang out!"

Before he'd opened his fine, fat, shapeful mouth, she, the girl, Yoruba, had known what he would sound like. Weird? Oooooh! Somebody she had known in high school maybe? At work? At the Sunday school camp that crazy summer long ago? Who? What? When? Where? Maybe she had met him in a dream somewhere sometime (she was a dreamy girl), and there he was right here in the actual altogether in the très hip Café Uptown Society of the hip Black people, where the KKK (Kool Krazy Kats) got together and got themselves together and rapped and blew each other's minds, and some say they blew other things and sundry. Yeah. Yoruba wouldn't know about those other things, especially the sundries, but she dug the poetry and the bullshit sessions, she herself, Yoruba, having aspirations in poetical directions. Dig it.

Who was this fine wailing cat? Delivering his poetic thing in the 'Roi-Jones-Dante-Graham-Archie-Shepp-Askia-Muhammed-Touré fashion, shoulders hunched forward into the storm, head dancing side to side, Afro-life-style, body rocking with the rhythm of a down-home Baptist preacher. Declaiming at its natural best. When Malinda sings, she just spreads her mouth and hollers. Did you ever see Mahalia do her thing? Raymond Charles got a woman way over town. She, the girl, Yoruba, trying desperately now to put this manchild here in time and place and circumstance. Why did this fine one keep eluding her? Her memory tried to seize him, hold him. Like trying to hold a snowball at high noon in the middle of Sahara. Ending his old fine poetic thing as he did:

"Oh what a grand and glorious thing,
To make a poet Black
And with so much to sing
Singing wild Black notes of
Love and hate and revolution."

Dig it! He, with the sparse glistening beard covering the lower portion of his face like the black mask of a stickup man. This child, Yoruba, was a cheap drunk, could get high and soaring into orbit off of Coca-Cola and Black poeting happenings. Shake it all together. Moon girl. Dig it! He with the fierce and heavy eyebrows joining over the bridge of his nose in a kind of Black and groovy fellowship. Brotherhood of Blackness. Yeah! The meaning of his familiarity lurked now just around the corners of the eyes of dear Yoruba's mind. She sipped her Coke and was all eyes and ears and anxious feelings. Perspiration pouring now from all the silent secret places. It was the weirdest thing. She felt somehow that he was deliberately playing hide-and-seek with her remembrance, peeping around the corners of her recollection, then ducking quickly out of sight again, never letting her memory get one good look. Peek-a-boo was the name of the game. Ring-a-levio. He, with the wild and woolly African bush atop his head so way out it made Rap Brown resemble Mister Clean.

And now it must be said, through those large dark eyes that belonged to the girl, Yoruba, that the cat on stage was clean. Not clean like Mister TV Clean, but handsome clean, hip clean, fine clean. Clean clean. Black clean. In his rainbow-colored dashiki and all up tight, but not uptight, in his hip-hugging East Indian slacks.

Dig the cool one now, taking his last bow to the wild applause of the Admiration Fellowship, and putting on his dark crazy glasses and almost breaking his ass falling off the stage, but he didn't lose his cool. Not this great dude. Now he walked his Afro-American walk, masculine-like Africa, limp-stride, limp-stride, limp-stride, rock-roll, rock-roll. Jazz, swing, rhythm-and-blues, all there in his crazy walk. A stone-pure act of Black defiance. He seemed to be heading straight for Yoruba's lonely and forsaken table. Or was it strictly her imagination? She knew this, she had never seen him before, and it was crazy how the idea of familiarity fought this realization of reality. Yet she knew him knew him had to know him. Dig the girl Yoruba's confusion when the cool clean cat stumbled as he neared her table, he and his dark glasses in this dark room with all his dark brothers and sisters. With the dark-sweet smell of Eastern incense in the atmosphere, which was everywhere. Cool he was, even as he felt his way, his hand before him now like a blind man. He sat down heavily in the other chair at her table against the wall. Dig it. He was cool but never ever cold.

Sat there in a deafening roar of silence staring at her through his stupid blinders, with his wide and fluoroscopic eyes. Staring through the confused girlchild, disrobing her, psychologically, physically, everyotherkindofwayly, laying the fine fox naked with his X-ray eyes. She did not hear another word from the rapping stage, as the next poet went into his thing. Finally Mister Fine Black Clean with the blinders broke the roaring silence. "Do you mind if I sit here a moment?" It was a voice unlike the one he'd read his poetry with. All his Blackness seemed to vanish in the darkness of the Dark.

His voice this time was thin and reedier than before, like a Georgia peckerwood who had graduated from Harvard and done a stretch in Hollywood. It rubbed her the wrong way, like scraping broken bottles on a Southern railroad track. Or a Northern one, whichever. He had turned her on before. Now he definitely turned her off. She thought, Who are you Mr. Blind Man, with your phoney British accent? Good-bye, Mr. Chips, good-bye. Get lost. Split.

But two could play the blasé game, she thought, although it was not her stick. Definitely it was not Yoruba's stick. She said, "Like I heard somebody say one time, it's a free country, and the chairs sure don't have my name on them." And sipped her suddenly tasteless Coke. And told lies to herself, like: I don't like him. Like he's a real out-to-lunch character. A stone phony-baloney. I never saw him before and if I see him again a hundred years from now, it'll be two hundred years too soon. And besides, her mother had always taught her never to pick up with strange men. And this one was Mr. Strange, himself, in person. OOoooh! Later!

He smiled and motioned importantly for the waiter. "*Garçon, s'il vous plaît—*" And turned to her again. "Would you have something a little more potent with me, Miss—Miss—Miss?"

She said, "No, kind sir. I'll stick with Coke. And pay my own way, thank you very much." He was bugging her more than ever now with his jive accent—internationale. Well, like the lady said, the supersophisticated bit was not her stick-of-tea! Actually, she was the kind of New York girl that people thought was long ago extinct, she was the last of the provincials. A New York unsophisticate, a modern contradiction in terms. Take Yoruba downtown Manhattan on a dark smoggy day and you could lose her easily. And if you took her across one of those bridges to Brooklyn, you'd better attach her to a Seeing Eye dog, or she would never get back home in one piece. All of her eighteen years she had been out of Manhattan very few times. You could count them on your fingertips. Never across the George Washington Bridge. Never through the Holland or the Lincoln Tunnel. Once she took a trip up the Hudson River to Bear Mountain on a church picnic, and the child thought she had been abroad. When she first got the job down in the garment center she got lost every day between the Man's job and the subway. Had she led a sheltered life? Would you believe?

"Oh," the poet said, in accents phonier by the second, "the little pretty petite bourgeois really believes that things go better with Coke—or is milady in and of the Pepsi generation?" Turning now to the waiter again, his black glasses perched atop his maddening Afro. "Will you bring the lady another Coke, *s'il vous plaît*, and bring me a bit of cream sherry of your very oldest bestest vintage?"

If he wanted to play the supersophisticated bit, she could dig it, and she knew where it was coming from. Two could play the game. In the words of Godfrey Cambridge, she could make a statement. Her father didn't raise any backward young'uns.

He smiled patronizingly. "My name is Ben Ali Lumumba."

She could not believe this was the same man who had blown her natural mind a few moments before with his poetry and his Afro-and-poetic rhythms. In a word, he had come on strong with his mucho Black and beautiful thing. But this sudden change he had gone through was strictly Mr. Charlie Hyde. The sweet and unspoiled child of Harlem mustered all the disdain she was able to call upon and smiled and said, "My name is Sheba Cleopatra."

He threw back his head and laughed. The man brought the drinks, merci. Mr. Sophisticated of Nineteen Sixty Something said, "Yeah, like I can dig it, but what was the lady's slave name?"

The lady countered with: "I never was a slave."

He brought his blinders back over his eyes. He combed his fine black bush deliberately, ritualistically. She watched him with a put-on bored expression. What effect was this supposed to have on her? He stared and smiled at her again, and said, "You're still a slave." His accent decidedly British now. "That's what America is, a glorified slavocracy. It should be renamed Chuck's Plantation."

She said, "And I imagine you're a British subject. How else could you have cultivated such an accent?"

"Negative," Mr. Super Clean answered. "I just happen to be an earth traveler, citizen of the universe. Japan, Africa, Hong Kong, South America, Tashkent, Timbuktu, Rome, London. Like Lady Day, I've covered the waterfronts, all the way to Zanzibar and back." He paused and sipped his wine and asked, "Where have you traveled?"

She said, "Down to the garment center and back to a Hundred and Twenty-ninth Street."

He fluoroscoped her with his eyes gone coal-black now. Hard, shiny anthracite. He laughed softly, as if to himself, at first. Then the laughter came rich and creamy from his mouth in loud hahas, his upper teeth large and white and gleaming like a toothpaste ad. His teeth were tiny in the lower berth. He seemed completely unaware that others turned to stare at him. So cool and cocksure of himself. He was oblivious to the angry shhs aimed at him from the unwashed at the other tables. He was he. And that was that. But who he? Yoruba wondered.

He stopped laughing and sipped his wine again. "Mark this night, my Queen of Sheba. And mark my word. I am going to be a great writer one of these days. As soon as I get myself together." His mood had changed again. Taking himself very serious now. Reflective. Eyes darkened to black on black inside of black. Wherever did the white go? He shook his head from side to side. "Oh I don't mean that jive I just read. That's for the birds, the Black ones I mean. All you got to do for this crowd here is call whitey a bunch of mother-humpers and say that Black is beautiful, and like you got it made. But I'm going to get myself together one day real soon, little baby sister. And then you'll see some writing written. Believe me when I tell you. That's why I've been to all those places. Cairo, Mexico, Brazil. I've just got to find myself. Got to get my thing together."

She stared at him, suddenly all wise and everything, with her sheltered eighteen New York years. And said, "You're really trying to escape yourself. You were together with yourself when you were up on that stage doing your thing. But as soon as you put on those dumb glasses and sat at this table, you became somebody else." The wise words tumbling from her mouth surprising even her this time. She was not one easy with the fixed opinions. But she heard herself go on and on to her own amazement. She said, "You're with yourself wherever you are, if you're together. You could be together with yourself right here at this table at this moment, that is, if you would give yourself a chance and get rid of all that excess baggage, all those phony-baloney other people you've picked up on your way around the world."

He did a down-the-hatch with the rest of his wine. And made fierce dark narrowing eyes at Yoruba, and said, respectfully, "OOooh! You sure know what to say, Madame Philosopher." Quietly. Smilingly. He shook his head from side to side, no longer smiling. "I've put on so many masks, sometimes I don't know who I am." He sounded now like she had known he'd sound before he'd sounded. Sounded real good to her happy ears.

"Let's blow," he said.

"Blow?" she said. All of her defenses going up again. How had she let them down so easily? All the danger signals flashing now. The girl had had one grand affair which had led her almost to the brink. It was her last affair. It was her first one too. In her senior year in high school, there was this boy who hung around the school grounds and knew all the answers. "Drop out of school," he'd told her. "It ain't relevant to the Black experience. Read Fanon and Mao and all them people." Tall, handsome, seemingly mature Black man, glib of tongue as if it had been lubricated. His mouth was perpetual motion. Listen to the words come out. "I got your education, Sister Yoruba. You just let this proud Black man take care business." For three whole months she had been under Jaja Okwu's (born Bobby Jack Sampson) spell. Under the mesmerization of the torrents of words that were forever flowing from his lips like he had dysentery of the mouth. The furtive hours planning, stealing around, making chances to meet the Glib One in all the out-of-the-way places. She shivered at the shame of it. Her mother and father mustn't know. Mustn't ever even suspect. They would never understand. The first time in all her life she ever played hookey. This girl who was in love with school. The torrid love scenes that always came up short of the actual act of intimacy. Then the fundamental confrontation. Finally she and Big Talker up in his shabby room where he was supposed to spring the coup de grace. He was to cut her long black shoulder-length locks. He'd been a barber in his time and he would give her the cleanest coolest Afro-naturale that had ever been naturalized. Ultimate salvation for her Black and tarnished soul. The quiet desperate wrestling match, the softly spoken oaths. He was too arrogant to fight for what was already his by the divine right of his selfdom. Finally: "What is it, bitch, you're so protective over? Don't hand me that cherry shit. Ain't no seventeen-year-old cherries in this Harlem jungle, baby." She adjusting her clothing, her eyes in floodtide, overflowing. The walls of his pitiful pad plastered all over with *Playboy* Bunnies of the Month. "That's the trouble with you Black bourgeois wenches. You don't wanna get up offa nothing. You think your poontang made of gold or something. If you going to be my baby, sister, you going to have to get out there on the block and sell it, while I'm organizing the revolution." She found out later, there were other hustlers around the Black Movement, thugs and hoodlums who had skimmed through a few books and memorized a few catch phrases, bought a few dashikis, put their do-rags in hiding for a season, washed the process out of their hair, changed their names, got themselves a niche or corner and gone into the business of Black Nationalism. They saw the Movement as a hustle, and a mighty fine one. But they were not the Movement. Not even were they of the Movement. They had been pimps before and were still pimps. And they were not the Movement. She must make herself remember that they were not the Movement.

She stared at the poet, shook her head. "Blow? Oh no!" she mumbled, sadly.

Lumumba said, "I mean—let's split."

"Oh," she said.

"I'll walk you over to 'Twenty-ninth Street."

Ben Ali Lumumba walked quietly now beside the girl, as they both drank in the Sunday evening happenings like wine of the very best and oldest vintage. Horns honking, sirens blasting, children playing, laughing, squealing, dig it, one of New York's Finest exchanging pleasantries with a lady of the avenues, three dudes nodding on a stoop, up above a bar some Holy Rollers doing their thing with tambourines and drums calling up dreams of Africa, old and new ones, and some cat blowing his natural wig on a saxophone for Jesus. Were you there when they nailed him? THE CHURCH OF THE LIVING CHRIST WITHOUT CONTROVERSY is where it was at. Dig it. Neon blinkers, Hustleville, African boutiques, Gypsy tearooms, change your luck and get your fortune told. Wilt's Paradise. Everybody doing the Uptown-lowdown.

Home, the young man thought. Home, dig it. Harlem. YMCA, Countee Cullen Library. Cockroaches. Schomburg. Love. Langston Hughes. Jesse B. Simple. Race riots. Pot. Laughter. Adam. Horsing around. Rats. Tears. Apollo. Hate. Blacks. Sounds. Folks. Funeral parlors. Liquor stores. Jackie Robinson. *Amsterdam News*. Jones. Wine. Jews. Mitchell. Turf. Hustlers. True believers. Hardworkingmotherfuckers. Pimps. Pussy. Whores. Church. Charley. Home!

"Dig," Lumumba said to Sheba. "Observe the guardian of law and order, blond hair and blue eyes, Mick, dig him consorting with the dusky lady of the very oldest profession. She smiles, he smiles. The deal is made and he escorts her up the steps to the place of assignation. Payola taken out in trade. Integration, little Sheba."

She wished he hadn't broken the sweet and awful Harlem silence they had shared between them. She had eyes. Didn't need him to spell things out for her. But he loved the music of his voice.

"Follow the noble one in blue after he leaves the fair Black maiden of the boulevard and dig him saunter down the avenue and get his Sunday payoff from the junkman and the policy director. Portrait of a crime-fighter. Keeper of the frame."

He took her hand now as they strolled down Seventh Avenue. "Cognize the fine brown Black leggy sister in her natural state of being underneath that clean Afro in the hip-squeezing mini-skirt strolling with the great cool stud in the mighty fine dashiki with the do-rag tied around the bright lavender process which adorns his loverly head. Purple hair and bright dashiki. You have got to have heaps of soul to dig it. Ooooh!"

He laughed quietly and she found herself laughing with him. "Now then, take notice of the cat in the flaming yellow El Dorado, making careful preparations to do his beddie-bye. Now I lay me down to cop nod, and does he bug the white man and the Black petit bourgeois. Why, they ask, does he not use his money to buy a home? But who is to judge which makes more sense, to get in hock for a home or for an El Dorado? You see, our driving-man has not committed himself to the Boy's system. (We do not call Whitey the Man no more.) At a moment's notice, our El Dorado man can put distance between him and Charlie in his all-purpose mobile housing unit, but you can't make no getaway with one of them brownstone houses on your back."

She laughed.

He squeezed her hand and said, "And who is to say which makes more sense, a brownstone or a Cadillac? They both are monuments to all them bourgeois insecurities."

He went on and on and on, as she thought to herself, Why am I walking down this street with this strange and moody man whom I had not known existed two or three hours ago, and feeling at home in this place alongside him strolling like I have never strolled with any man before? What do I know about this Blood? That he is able to get up before a group of hip young Bloods, and read some jive Black poetry that, for all I know, might have been written by someone else? Perhaps I'm the kind that attracts his kind. And perhaps also vice versa. He might be hustler, junkie, pimp, agent, thief. I need to have my head examined.

Now they stood in front of her house, and she looked up into his face, sometimes humorous, sometimes angry, but a good face notwithstanding, handsome in a careless, don't-care way. She thought, he probably never looks into a mirror. She knew that no matter who he was or what he was, she wanted to see him again, she did not want this night to be the end of it. She felt this crazy curiosity about this manchild. And she had never been this curious in regard to any other.

She said, "Where are you from?"

He said, "Especially from all over."

Lumumba prided himself on being the most hip of all the cats in the whole, wide, man-made jungle of cats, but this little fox had his natural teeth on edge. Her eyes were hardly nervous, but somehow you could tell that they were busybodies. Dig it. This mother's daughter was altogether all together. She was boss. Would you believe? Maybe even she had soul? The kind of wide staring eyes that seemed to be staring directly at you and looking shyly away from you at the self-same time. When he had sat down at her table in the café, he had thought her eyes were surely crossed. But now he knew that they were not. They were just so damn intense was what. And they were eyes that he remembered from some far-off place in time and space. Was it in Bamako or Calibar? Enugu or Ouagadougou?

She said, "I mean—where were you born?" Her heart went boom boom in her breast. Boom. Boom. Boom. Boom! She thought her dear heart would explode.

His heart went bam. Bam. Bam. Bam. Bam. He laughed a short laugh. "Harlem, USA, little Sheba."

"And how did you come to do all that traveling?"

"I figured I wouldn't make a good soldier doing my thing for Uncle Sam in Vietnam. I was sure I wouldn't look good in khaki. And then again, you could get hurt messing around like that. Behind which, I wasn't mad with them Viet people. So dig, I went to sea to see what I could see." He added, "Like my father did before me. I've been back here a few weeks now, and you'd better believe I'm still at sea. You see?" The girl was not, definitely she was not cross-eyed. Not in the very slightest. But them there eyes!

There was this strangely pleasant uneasiness growing inside of Yoruba now, similar to the feeling she'd known when he was rapping at the Café Uptown. Fresh bubbles of sweat broke out all over her body, and crawling now, like an army on the march. She was conscious of her heavy breathing. "What was your slave name, Mr. Lumumba?"

He half mumbled, "Ernest Walter Billings. I used to live right on this street right up the block—a million years ago."

The girl felt weak with pleasure, frightened somehow with delight, as she stared through the million years at the young man's face, stared through to the thing that had made her feel a kinship to him, an uncertain certainty that she had known him all along. Her memory desperately fashioning from his now bewhiskered face the sweet face of his boyish yesteryears. She had the picture now, of the little skinny boy, snotty nose and all, who used to romp with her up and down these crazy streets. No! No! Then quietly—No. No. She began to laugh and shake her head. "It can't be! It can't be true! It can't be true!" She did not realize she was talking aloud.

He seized her roughly by the arms. "What can't be?" the boy demanded.

She said, "I'm Yoruba! I'm Yoruba! Don't you recognize me?" Softly shouting.

The cool one did not dig at first. But then he took her in his arms. "Yoruba! My Yoruba! Ruba Evelyn. Ruba Evelyn."

Dig it!

CHAPTER FIVE

FIRST INSTRUCTIONS, ON THE RITES OF LADYSHIP

At Pattersons.
In the Crowning Heights.
A stone's throw from Bed-Stuy.
Would you believe—a cocktail à la Molotov?
Brooklyn Borough.
County of Kings.
Churches, Ebbetts Field, Trees, Jackie Robinson, Dodger Fans.
Black mansions—above the hoi polloi.
Only the dead know.
At Pattersons.
A cannon's roar from Brownsville.
She, the girl, Yoruba, was in another country.
It's a real corny bit, Yoruba thought, like "Two Different Worlds" and "The Other Side of the Tracks." The scene was strictly soap opera of the afternoon variety. As she sat there in the Pattersons' living room, she could hardly believe that this was also a part of the Black and beautiful experience. Everything so white and proper here in this pretty prissy place.

Her mother had told her there would be days like this, had earnestly prepared her for them, but, for the last fifteen or eighteen months, she had lived a life, whenever she was outside her home, or away from school, or job, in a world of total Blackness, where the competition went on and on, never ending, to determine the World Individual Champeenship of Blackness. Everything was Black and hip and soul and together and cool and down and clean and funky. Many Blacks worked overtime at getting blacker. They bought sunlamps. Flocked to the beaches, even in winter. Integrated the Icebergs, sued the Polar Bears for membership, and all the other hot-natured Caucasian organizations that go ocean-swimming when the snow is high up to the ass. Coney Island was these Black ones' January rendezvous. The World Series of Blackness was played every hour every day every week to see who was the very Blackest of the Black. African robes, dashikis, African and Arabic names, naturals, Afros, Muslimization, fetish worshipers, true-believing sacrificers, violence-for-the-pure-and-lovely-sake-of violence-worshipers, Yoruba temples, Yoruba priests and priestesses, governments-in-exile, Hausa-and-Swahili-talkers, boubous, no-pork eaters, Maoists, kosher-blessed-by-black-assed-rabbis, Fanon quoters, leadership threateners, Malcolmites, tribalites and internecine tribal warfare (Black unity, baby!), militancy competitors, bathless funkies, sepia hippies, Allah-worshipers. Black! Say it loud! Brothers! Sisters! Ebony! Black-and-tan fantasy, prophesized decades ago by the Duke of Ellington.

In Yoruba's now world, Black was the "in thing" and the "end thing." Alpha and Omega, or words in Swahili to that effect. She had gone all the way with the Black thing, except that she had not cut off the long black stuff that crowned her head with shining glory and spilled down to her shoulders in sweet black cascades, and, unlike some (not all) of her Black (in quotes) brethren, she still showered every morning. She worshiped cleanliness like a fetish. Bourgeois? And she worked regularly for a living, which was known, by some, to be unhip.

There were cats who had skimmed through Malcolm's book and deliberately got themselves arrested for hustling pot and heroin, did a stretch in Sing Sing and came out and knighted themselves as the Black shining prince, Premier-of-the-Black-government-in-exile, and announced themselves as Malcolm's Second Coming. Interlopers, imposters, pretenders-to-the-throne of Brother Malcolm's dignity.

Yoruba had been to Black happenings where the brothers and the sisters of the darkest complexions did violent putdowns on those unfortunates of the lighter hues, all in the spirit of Black unity. She had even caught herself at evil moments, bugging her own mother because her mother's color had suddenly become unstylish, as if her mother had ordered her pigmentation COD from Macy's. "You ought to get out in the sun more often, Mother. You don't want to be mistaken for a hunkie, when the real stuff hits the air-conditioner." Instantly Yoruba would realize what she was doing to her mother, a vicious thing, and feel guilty at the doing of it. But in the social sphere in which Yoruba circulated, it was the blacker the berries the rarer and more exquisite the wines (cats were brewing black champagne), and your light skin was a natural drag. Everything was topsy-turvy compared with what it used to be. The world was turning upside down, the bottom coming to the top, and erupting like Mount Etna.

Some in-a-hurry free-wheeling freely enterprising cats of Harlem, in the spirit of Black Power, had opened up a Boutique-Afrique selling nylon Afro wigs, rabbit feet, blackening powders and blackening creams made primarily from minstrel lampblack. Talismans and amulets, voodoo essence, mojo mumblings, incense and God-and-or-Allah knows what else. These hustling cats did a swinging business. Every day in the week and Sundays too, grim-faced happy people, hell-bent for their soul's salvation, formed unsmiling lines more than a block long outside this Black and Beautiful Shop, which was the name of the game, and also was the name of the shop. Say it loud! Sometimes even frantic hunkies made the everloving scene. Everybody wanted to be saved. Black was a big and booming business. Would you believe—you could get real comfortable in your little old loverly Black thing? It was a trip. And you could outright lose perspective. But at Pattersons. In the Crowning Heights. Of the Brooklyn Borough. In the County of the Kings. In black mansions here below. It was different. And it was another country, darling, with appropriate apologies. It was the real world, dads. Believe it.

Yoruba and the other lucky girls (five in all), representing the "culturally deprived" unfortunates of Harlem, were respectfully in attendance at the First-Thursday-Evening Instructions. A kind of preliminary introduction into the Holy Rites of Ladyship. It was a great thing if you could dig it and if you knew where it was coming from. There were thirty girls in all, including the twenty-five hifaluting girls from Brooklyn's high society. They were the children of Frazier's Black Bourgeoisie and Hare's Black Anglo-Saxons. "Big niggers," as their parents sometimes called themselves. Affectionately?

Crowded into the Patterson living room, which was already

crowded with bookcases containing bric-a-brac and very few books (the first families did very little reading. Anti-intellectual). No eggheads here in any great numbers. Balling was these people's style. The room was also crowded with two large sofas and three easy chairs and pictures on the wall from Gimbels, of trees and woods and apples and oranges and streams and horses too; no images of human beings adorned these hallowed walls. And three fat table lamps and three giant floor lamps and two and a half cocktail tables and knickknacks and thingamajigs all over the place.

A mess of pennants and banners on the walls of the foyer from Yale and Harvard and Princeton and Fisk and Farmers Market, Hollywood, and Yellowstone. And Alpha and Omega and A.K.A. and Delta. And also in attendance here were five society matrons including, of course, Mrs. Patterson, herself, Mrs. Downjohn and Mrs. Brasswork and the one-and-only Beverly Brap-bap.

Prissy proper Mrs. Patterson's husband was an everyday plain-talking dude, who despised affectations and pretensions, and was proprietor of a kosher butcher shop for colored Jews and Muslims and a motley assortment of other persuasions and denominations. A shrewd, hard-working, coal-black man with soft eyes like a friendly-hearted Irish setter, he moonlighted on the night shift at the Brooklyn Main Post Office. And on Sundays he sold real estate. A triple-threat man with a hobby, right? In his spare time he was an avid chippie-chaser. "Good old-and-aged whiskey and good young-and-tender pussy" was his avowed philosophy. And he lived by it, religiously. A man who had the courage of his convictions and the stamina to execute them. Some of his drinking buddies called him "Wild Turkey"; others called him "Old Granddad." An elder in the Episcopalian church, he was, by nature, a foot-stomping, feet-washing Hardshell Baptist. But in important matters like those of religious piety, he went along with the Missus. The house and the church were her acknowledged jurisdictions. Jacob Patterson was the money-maker.

So this is high society, she, the girl, Yoruba, thought.

"All right, girls," Mrs. Patterson chirped. She was birdlike all the way. A tall, skinny, thin-legged mama, aquiline and eagle-beaked and owl-eyed. There was enough powder and bleaching cream and other ingredients on her face to bake a three-layer cake, that is, if you told the generous-hearted woman you were coming.

She is probably a good-looking, good-hearted woman underneath, Yoruba thought. If you were ever able to penetrate that monumental superficial cosmetological superstructure.

It was seven o'clock P.M. and the chimes from Father Mayfair's Episcopal Cathedral on the Heights down at the other end of the block pealed into the room with "Let the Lower Lights be Burning," soft and sweet like playing for a heavenly glee club. Mrs. Prissy Patterson stopped to listen. She shook her head and wiped her eyes, as a beam was sent across her wave length. She smiled in pure aesthetic ecstasy. As Yoruba stared into Mrs. Patterson's rapturous face, and listened to the blessed chimes, she thought of her mother and how excited she had been when the chimes were first instituted. "Oh how wonderful it must be to be awakened every morning by such heavenly music! It's worth the forty or fifty thousand dollars you'd have to pay for a house in that blessed neighborhood." Everybody did not share Mrs. Patterson's and Mrs. Lovejoy's raptures for the holy chimes. One dissenter was Mr. Patterson. Especially did he not appreciate those heavenly chimes at six o'clock of a Sunday morning when he had just gotten to bed at five A.M. and was in that land beyond the river known as Hangoverville. The trustees of the church sent out a lovely letter to the neighborhood telling the lucky people of the neighborhood how much they, the beautiful people, themselves, adored the chimes, and asking them to make contributions to the chimes' sweet maintenance. This pushed Jake Patterson to the breaking point. One Sunday morning, six o'clockish, D.P.T.—Dues Payment Time—Jake was in bed with his head already "tore up" from the Saturday night happenings. The saintly chimes boomed into his bedroom and bombs exploded in his head. It felt to him like the clumsy IRT subway train was thundering through his tender sensitivities and jet airliners crashing on the airstrip of his brain, and devils on roller skates were tap-dancing on the innermost layer of his skull, to the tune of "Pass Me Not, Oh Gentle Saviour." He got painfully out of bed, his wife beside him gone for a time into the land of sweet oblivion, snoring gently like a hog-calling expert, a profession her down-home grandfather used to pursue, before he went to meet his Maker. Jake Patterson crossed the room (boom! boom! went the chimes inside his head) and put on his bathrobe. He stumbled around the room (bang! bang! boom! boom!), cursing softly to himself, the goddamn motherfucking chimes, the cocksucking preacher, the church, some religions, all religions. He went quietly down the stairs and out into the streets where the dawn was slowly breaking all over the city. He walked the streets for almost an hour looking for members of the Brown Tigers or the Black Lion Tamers. He wanted to pay them to blow up the goddamn church, chimes and all. But he walked and sought in vain. Back to the house he came, cursing the no-good somebitchingchickenshit black-ass Tiger Tamers. It's seven A.M. and the chimes are going off again. He goes around the side of his house and collects some old Cutty Sark bottles, fills them with gasoline from his Hog, gets a long, roof-reaching ladder from his garage and proceeds down the street to the church. Puts the ladder up against the church and starts up the ladder with his cocktails à la Molotov and a pocketful of matches. And a lighted cigar in his mouth. Sweating, cursing, stoned for days. Puffing on his El Producto. Gasoline from his El Dorado dripping from the Cutty bottles, cigar ashes dropping. Slipping, spitting, swearing, sweating. Halfway up the ladder, he is accosted by two policemen, friends of his, who bring him laughingly home, him cursing for all he is worth, calling God and the Devil's choicest of damnations down upon the church, the chimes, the police, people in general, Black folks in particular, and so forth and so on. It was the scandal of the year, of the neighborhood and church.

Now, this evening, at the First Instructions, Mrs. Patterson sat there carried away by the heavenly chimes into another world where all was peace and beauty and in a continual state of heavenly rapture. As the chimes softly died away she came back from her celestial trip. She shook her head as if suddenly awakened from a dream of purest ecstasy. "Well—" the lady said. "Where were we? Oh yes. Now, then, girls, this is just a get-acquainted meeting. The girls from Brooklyn already know each other. They travel in the same circles." Mrs. Patterson had a teeth-setting-on-edge habit of repeating the last part of her sentences. "Travel in the same circles." Sometimes even the entire sentence.

Darkly visaged, cleanly chiseled Charlene Robinson, one of the lucky Harlem unfortunates, leaned toward Yoruba and whispered out loud (she always whispered loudly). "Dig. These chicks over here go around in circles. But they look like squares to me."

Mrs. Patterson continued, in her singsong, breathless voice. "First of all, we don't want you people from Harlem segregating yourselves. Segregating yourselves. All of you over there sitting together. Let us start off on the right foot. On the right foot." She rolled her rrr's all over the place, like she had marbles in her mouth, and her dear tongue was on roller skates. "Now ladies, let us change places and mingle with one another, shall we? Mingle with one another, shall we?"

The young, innocent, nubile ladies, a couple of them pimply-faced, stared across the room at one another. Immobile, hostile and suspicious. "All right, ladies, don't be bashful. Don't be bashful."

Finally they got to their feet, almost simultaneously, and it was so crowded in this living room they stumbled over one another, jockeying for position the better for the darling dears to mingle. The sound of walking across the expensive, deeply piled wall-to-wall carpeting was like a host of hip ones boogalooing on a floor covered with soda crackers. Not that the floor was actually covered with soda crackers. Perish the dusty-throated thought. The thing was: all that expensive carpeting was covered with a transparent plastic covering, as was everything else in the Pattersons' expensive domicile, including the goose-feathered couches and the easy chairs à la Louis Quinze, and the silken drapes, the cocktail tables, and the lamps and the Gimbelish pictures on the wall. And even those fabulous aquamarine toilet seats were covered with transparent plastic. Everything crunched and crackled when you touched it. Cold and unpleasant was the plastic to those with hot and gentle buttocks. And it could bite, without provocation, into your tender bottom-most. It could really prove distressing. Notwithstanding, the plastic kept everything clean, untouched and pretty. A couple of girls slid and stumbled on this slick surface, even as they mingled. One of them slipped and fell upon her round little nonplastic backside. It was hot and steamy outside on the streets of Brooklyn in the Crowning of Heights, but the air-conditioning inside the Pattersons had everybody sniffling and sneezing.

These high-society people really have everything their hearts desire, Yoruba thought. Even if they do have very little heart. So much display of comfort made the girl downright uncomfortable.

The girls now, standing around staring at each other, like prizefighters sparring for an opening. Looking curiously at each other as if one group or the other were creatures from another planet. Right? One light-skinned red-headed girl reached out and touched Yoruba on the face as if she thought the black would come off onto her delicate pinkies. Okay. Yoruba reached out and repaid the girl the compliment. Charlene Robinson popped her fingers and went temporarily into a kind of Funky Broadway routine. "If you want me to mingle, like give me some of that mingling music. Ooooh! Sock it to me!"

Mrs. Patterson went into her song again. "All right then. You may take your seats now." All of them went back to the very seats they previously occupied. "We just wanted you girls from Harlem to feel at home. We are all equals here. We do not discriminate. Do not discriminate. There is no distinction for the reason of race, religion or previous condition of servitude. Previous condition of servitude."

Yoruba did, as did some of the others. Looked around her in search of at least one of Mr. Charlie Peckerwood's daughters. Mrs. Patterson had to be kidding. Had to be kidding. She stared at Mrs. Patterson to see if the lady's tongue was dug deep deep down into her rosy cheeks. One or two of the girls were what would be considered white of color, true. But there was no question about them being colored, Negro, Black, African-American. Was there? Right? Most were light-brown skin, high yaller, café-au-lait, just about Yoruba's mother's color. Only one other girl was as brunette and as swarthy as Yoruba. Charlene Robinson was her name. Of the Harlem contingent. There was this copper-colored girl with eyes of almond shapes who smiled at Yoruba now and then, a warm and friendly smile; her name was Pamela Jefferson. She was of the famous Crowning Heights blue-blood Jeffersons.

The young ladies were seated again. Mrs. Patterson went on and on, in her breathless bubbly fashion. "Now, just a wee-wee bit of orientation. The Femmes Fatales is a social club, a social club. But we have always been more than just a social club—more than just a social club."

"Some of these fems got some real fat tails all right," Charlene whispered to Yoruba, loudly, in her style which was sarcastic, in every aspect, as a little, short, rotunda-bottomed, overfed, good-natured lady bounced dancingly into the room underneath her orange-colored wig (it seemed to have been scalped from some poor and unsuspecting poodle), crunching and crackling over the carpeting, with a tray of goodies, cookies and such, as in came another lady behind her with cups of steaming tea. The two of them began to pass them out, much to Mrs. Patterson's chagrin, the girls losing interest for the moment in the orientation, so intent were they now in going for the tea and goodies. Mrs. Patterson waiting, patiently impatient. Smiling her plastic smile with all thirty-two in gleaming evidence, the very best that money could buy. Mrs. Patterson cleared her smiling throat.

"Girls—now, girls—ladies—let us contin—now young ladies—" But the fight was on in earnest now for the goodies, and the girls from Harlem were giving a good account of themselves, outnumbered as they were twenty-five to five, not to give the impression that the Crowning Heights socialites were any pantywaisted slouches. It was all good clean fun in the spirit of the American Way of Rugged Individualism, and God help the drag-asses, or immortal words to that effect.

"Now, girls—now, girls! Oh dear! Oh dear! That's just what the Cotillion is all about—to—to—to teach you how to be a—oh dear! Oh dear! That's exactly what they say about us!"

The goodies vanished, the battle subsided, law and order restored, flushed young perspiring faces and labored breathing returned to normal, Mrs. Patterson continued in that breathless manner of hers which was her trademark and her calling card. She seemed always to have just finished doing a couple of hours of roadwork, running uphill all the way.

"Girls—young ladies, as we were saying, the Femmes Fatales has always been more than just a social club. More than a social club. We have always been civic-minded and interested in helping in the uplift of our fellowman, those less fortunate than ourselves. Those less fortunate than ourselves. To brighten darkened corners wherever they may be. Our annual Grand Cotillion has always been for charity. We make a contribution every year to send some unfortunate girl to college, and we always pick the girl who is the most deserving without regard to race, or religion, or previous condition of servitude. Previous condition of servitude."

Yoruba thought, She likes to say "previous condition of servitude." Her mother must have been a slave.

She could not believe her ears, when she heard Mrs. Brap-bap say, clearly and distinctly, "Sheee-it!" And the freshly nubile girls giggled and the breathless face of Mrs. Patterson turned a rosy sunset-red as she became more breathless than ever.

"Only last year, the fortunate young lady who won the scholarship was a Jewess. Was a Jewess."

She's gotta be kidding. Gotta be kidding, Yoruba thought.

"My ass! My royal hindparts!" was Mrs. Brap-bap's interjection.

"This year we decided to go one step further. One step further. We decided to integrate the debutantes. Integrate the debutantes."

"Sheee-it!" was Mrs. Brap-bap's contribution.

The giggling debutantes looked around at each other with deep suspicion in their innocent, sweet, flushed faces. Pam Jefferson smiled at Yoruba, and shrugged. Integrate the debutantes. Integrate the debutantes. One of the girls burped, loudly, nervously, marvelously. Who among them was the interloper? Which one was the integrator? Who was passing, and for what?

"We decided to go beyond the boundaries of the socially elite of Brooklyn's famous first families and to choose some of our ladies from the ranks of the culturally deprived of Harlem. The culturally deprived of Harlem."

"My fine Black ass!" Mrs. Brap-bap commented with the deepest of Black feelings.

Mrs. Patterson paused, staring at her vulgar echo now, as she pictured Mrs. Brap-bap. Smiling deprecatingly at the chubby-wubby lady. Then back to the young debutantes. "We are very proud of our Harlem choices." Then she called on each of the Harlem girls to stand and give her name and her parents' names and parents' qualifications and pedigrees and their occupations.

A tapioca-colored girl with mini-skirt up to her navel and a blond wig to her shoulders said, "My name is Pamela La-Smythe. I am a graduate of the New Lincoln School."

Charlene whispered loudly to Yoruba, "Her daddy was named Smith when he went into the army. Came out La-Smythe. Dig it."

"What does your father do, Pamela?" Mrs. Patterson asked.

"My mother teaches at a nursery in Harlem."

"And your father?"

The dear girl almost lost her voice. Shakily she whispered, "He's a maintenance engineer."

Yoruba stared at the trembly-legged girl with the deepest soul-felt sympathy. Some of the girls giggled, some of the ladies cleared their throats significantly. Signifyingly. Everybody at the Pattersons knew that "maintenance engineer" in Afro-Americanese meant simply that Pamela's father was a janitor. But Yoruba didn't giggle. She remembered when she had felt ashamed of her own father's occupation, even as she had loved him more than any other person.

One of the ladies, Mrs. Downjohn, from the Committee, whispered loudly, "Well, at least she's pretty to look at, and she's the right color. I mean, that compensates for something."

Yoruba said, and proudly, "I'm Yoruba Evelyn Lovejoy. My mother is a housewife, and my father is a redcap at the Pennsylvania Station."

The same lady from the Committee said, "Well! We are becoming democratic, aren't we?"

Charlene Robinson said loud and clear, "I am Charlene Daisy Robinson. And my father is a bookmaker."

Mrs. Antoinette Brasswork said, "How wonderful! You mean he is a publisher."

"No m'am. Not that."

Mrs. Downjohn bubbled over. "Oh my! Don't tell me your father is a celebrated author!"

"No m'am. I mean he makes book for the numbers racket."

"Well! I never!"

Most of them were shocked at first, and speechless. Then Annie Brasswork whispered loudly to another woman, "How *did* those two Black ones get in without a writ of habeas corpus?" She usually spoke in legalistic terms.

Girls and ladies now, they all began to talk at once. Integration with white folks, yes, even with Jews and Jewesses, but to integrate with Black nobodies, this was carrying things too far. Janitors and redcaps and black skin—well!

"Too much deliberate speed was what!" Mrs. Brasswork interjected.

Mrs. Brap-bap took the floor. "All right! All right! That'll be enough of that. How come the girls from Harlem have to give their pedigrees and the Crowning Heights girls don't have to, honh? I thought we said there would be no discrimination. Okay, so what is all this signifying about the numbers racket? Tell it like it is. One of the big members in our club used to be a Harlem madam. My husband, Mr. Brap-bap, himself, is in the—well—but that's besides the point. And it ain't nobody's business if he—And I can buy and sell most of you prissy-assed wenches. I mean, let's don't look down on each other. And don't get me started reading pedigrees, cause I can read quite a few of the sisters of the Femmes Fatales."

Pam Jefferson shouted, "Let it all hang out, Miz Brap-bap!"

"Now—now—now—" Mrs. Patterson said, completely out of breath now, and panting, uphill all the way. "Remember we are all ladies and we must always be ladylike." She took a deep breath. "Now then, all of you young ladies have been thoroughly investigated, and you all have passed with flying colors. Flying colors. Your records are pure and white and spotless. There are no black marks in your record. Nothing black at all. Nothing black at all. You are all virgins and you must remain white and spotless and virginal until the Grand Cotillion is over. Until the Grand Cotillion is over."

"Then every man for himself," Charlene Robinson, of the Harlem contingent, mumbled.

Mrs. Brap-bap amplified, in serious and solemn tones. She broke it down: "In other words, girls, keep your little fat hot tails cool as a cucumber and your drawers dry as a chip, you steamy-tail hussies. Last year two of the first-family girls came up with blessed events and a whole lot less than nine months after the Grand Cotillion. So don't play stink finger with the boys, cause if they feel your thigh, they'll want to go up high, as the saying goes. Cherish your cherry, if you still got one. It's the only one you'll ever own. Time enough after the Cotillion to let nature take its course."

The daughters of the first families giggled nervously. The Harlem ladies laughed aloud.

Charlene said, "Amen! Rap your fine Black thing, Sister Brap-bap!"

"Let it all hang out!" From Pam Jefferson.

And even shy Yoruba shouted, "Tell it like it is!"

And she, the girl, Yoruba, smilingly, was at long last in society. High above the unwashed masses.

Mother! Mother! Pin a rose on me. We are in society.

CHAPTER SIX

INSTRUCTIONS IN LADYSHIP, CONTINUED

Seasick on dry land.
Shipwrecked on Manhattan Island.
His stomach was a sinking ship, replete with scurrying rats and all.
His bowels in a revolution.
Asshole squeamish. A barrel of cockroaches in a DDT airraid.
Strung out—for days.
Absentminded—without leave.
Rocks in his bed.
Bats in his head.

As hip as he was, as mature as he was, far beyond his actual age. He, who had been in hurricanes, typhoons, monsoons. He, who had sailed the seven oceans, had seen them wild and raging, mad and frothing, oftentimes heaving up their great white foam. He, the man, Lumumba, who had ridden out many a storm. As cosmopolitan and international, as world-traveled as he definitely was, the ship-jumpin'est dude that ever shaped up and shipped out, it made no sense at all for him to let this little old, fine Harlem society-conscious, Cotillion-participating, hair-cooking broad get him so hung up he could not get his thing together. Put his ship completely off its course. Okay. All right. He was just letting that childhood days-of-yore bullshit get his head all messed up, was what. Lumumba loves nostalgia, right?

The thing was, Ben Ali was madly, unreservedly, uncompromisingly in love. Had ever been, eternally. Dig it. In love passionately, entirely, all the way, to the Philippines and back, by way of Timbuktu. In love, oh my yes, and with no holds barred. All was fair, and all that jive, when Lumumba fell in love. Most of all, and everlastingly, he was in love with womankind. Even as a little lad, Ben Ali was love-addicted. Had a tonsillectomy on his fifth birthday and fell wildly in love with his nurse at the Harlem Hospital. Fell in love by the numbers with teacher after teacher, year to year, in the days he did his stretch in public school. Show him a woman who looked good to him, and there he went again, falling head-over-heels (on his ass, actually) from Hong Kong to Honolulu. All colors and denominations. He did not discriminate. Hold it! Don't put that lie out on the kid. Say it plain. In things of love he was old-fashioned. He did not work both sides of the street. No he-ing and he-ing, or me-ing and me-ing, just he-ing and she-ing was his style. Ambivalence was not his stick. He did not go along with those fashionable fetish woman-haters of the decade, who were forever putting down the Matriarchy. He would say to these so-called sex revolutionists, "Fuck the Matriarchy!" And he would try to do precisely that, to the extent of his capacity. Ben Ali was a serious lad, loyal to his dedications. One of his favorite LPs was Dionne Warwick chirping "What the World Needs Now Is Love Sweet Love," and Lord knows he tried to do his part to fill the poor world's greatest need all over this unhappy earth. "Help the Needy!" was his motto. Say it plain. He was lover-man, incarnate. And every new love affair was the real thing, this time! Yeah! This was different. But now, this time right now, this was really different. For he had always been in love with her, as long as he remembered love. She was extra-extra-special. She, Yoruba, was the Queen of Foxes. She was the foxiest of all the foxy foxes in the whole realm of Foxarchy. And he wanted her for his one and only foxhole.

They had seen each other several times, since he met her at the Uptown happening. And she had played it cool, real cool, ice-cold cool, "menthol-cool," in the words of Dante Graham. Every time he saw her, he would enter his impressions in his diary when he got back to his lonely room. A diary he had kept religiously, ever since he went to sea, when he was seventeen, and the year was very very nice. In his log, of her, he wrote:

> She is as nervous as an alley cat and four times as suspicious, and yet, I, the hip one, know that this chick is no alley cat. And she is not the purring housebroken kind of kitten, and will not soon be

stroked into submission. Won't go nowhere near my pious crib. Okay, I'm hip, she likes to be around me, near me, but at the same time, she always keeps her distance. A bird of paradise forever poised for sudden flight. So finely feathered. Magnificently plumaged. Stay away closer seems to be the name of the game. And every time I've mentioned dropping by my crib to dig my etchings (no jive, I've really done myself some etching from Zanzibar to Bamako) or to read some of my poetry, she throws up all of her defenses. Conditioned reflex. Yeah, believe it. She has no trust in me at all. And yet, I know the fine fox is trustworthy. Dig it. I can't even get the chick to have one martini or a little old jive-ass glass of sherry. Loosen up! Baby! Lumumba wouldn't harm you for nothing in the world. And wouldn't let nobody else in this wide world harm you. Why can't you see that I'm a one-woman man?

There she is, Yoruba, relaxed one moment, jumpy the next, lovely of the loveliest, foxier by far than all my recollections. And believe me, baby, female recollections this hip one *has* collected. But Yoruba remains everlastingly an unadulterated Coke-sipper. How do you like them juicy mangos? Like, can you dig my great frustrations?

But everything would be different from now on, he told himself. Tonight, in the real cool cool of the late late, the enterings in his log book would be entirely different. Her tender heart might be put away, wrapped in dry ice for a season, and even for a reason, but he would surely melt her down tonight. With his own unfaked enthusiasm. He had just this day received the offer of a contract from a big publishing house to do a book about his travels. *From Harlem All the Way to Timbuktu.* Dig it! Ain't that good news? How could she resist such good news? Full speed ahead with the wind at their backs, the storm behind them for a time. We must take the tide together, baby. Blow, sweet trade winds!

They had dinner in a little restaurant downtown near the garment district. He, Ben Ali Lumumba (*né* Ernest Walter Billings), the last of the big damn spenders. He had waited for her and met her as she came out of one of those ancient garment structures. He, all smiles, skinning his jaws from ear to ear, and she all serious, her face a mask of wonderment. What does it mean, this moody man so vastly different on this October night? Her eyes were always asking questions.

Now they sat there in the Way-Out Restaurant. She had called her mother and told her she would not be home for dinner. What? Why? Where? The questions poured from Lady Daphne. "I've already made dinner—It's dangerous in the garment district after dark—What will your father think? Be home by eight o'clock—Remember, you're a debutante!" And so forth and so on. Hurricane Daphne. Well, she would face that storm again later in the evening. Meanwhile—

"You've got to have a real drink with me tonight, even if it's only just for old times' sake. This is a special occasion. Things will not go better with Coke. And the Pepsi generation is a natural drag."

She had heard him laugh before but had hardly ever seen him smile. It was a new experience for her. Arousing all her deep suspicions. "What's the grand occasion?"

He took the letter from the publishers from his pocket and handed it to her. With a customary flourish. This hip one flourished everything.

She read the letter hurriedly and did not get the drift, at first. She had to read it several times, before the smog of New York lifted and her eyes were opened to the actual happening. "You!" she said, quietly excited. "This letter is about you!"

He laughed. "I'm hip," he said. "Could be that's why it's addressed to me."

She smiled the loveliest smile he'd ever known it was possible to smile. She reached across the table and kissed him fully on the mouth. "A thousand dollars!" she said. "In advance! A thousand dollars—"

"It ain't that much bread," the hip one said. "No big deal, but—" She felt the grin behind his placid face. All right, cool one.

"It's wonderful, Ben Ali. And I didn't even know you were serious—I mean reading poetry at the Uptown is fine, I mean it's boss, great, but—"

"But you didn't think anybody else would take me serious—not to the tune of a thousand bucks—"

She said, "Oh, Ben Ali Lumumba, I—I—I don't know what I mean. I'm just so happy for you—and—and—and just a little jealous too—you see, I didn't tell you, but I've always wanted to be a writer myself—"

He said, "So be one already. We could stand two writers in the fam-bu-lee."

She laughed. "I'll take you up on that offer of a real drink this time, that is, if it's still open."

He stared at her. "I don't know if it is or not. I don't know about you." Then he laughed and waved for the waiter. "What'll you have, Miss Debutante of Nineteen Sixty Something?"

"You're the master, Master. Anything you say."

The smile wiped from his face, momentarily. "Be careful how you commit yourself. Nobody deserves that much trust from you." He reached across the table and took her hands in his and squeezed them as if he would break every knuckle in them. She had to say, "You're hurting me."

They laughed and talked through dinner. The Way-Out Restaurant was a happening, and it was so way-out it almost never got back in. It was as busy as a Black Power conference, at the Harlem Hilton. The food was good, and the price was right, comparatively speaking. Way-Out was a hybrid, born of the sexual revolution, right? A funky, orgiastic copulation of cabaret and restaurant and coffee house making it flamboyantly, situated on the upper outskirts of the Village where the dark and light folk met in an atmosphere of semidarkness. Psychedelic happenings adorned the walls. Cats came there some special nights to do their things and plunk guitars and howl sad songs of happy times and great-gittin-up-mornings. And sweetly spoke of hate and love and revolution, like proper bourgeois rebels that they were. Every funky bourgeois son and daughter.

Bloods came over to their table from moment to moment, each of them giving Ben Ali their version of the Black-handshake-of-brotherhood. A creative combination of hand-grip, Indian-wrestle, chest-pounding, hand-grip, again, finger snapping. Depending on what Black neighborhood a cat hailed from in the Harlems of the USA, from the basic, you went off in all directions, grabbing the forearm, grabbing the shoulder, heel-kicking, ass-bumping. Some cats did it by the numbers. They did audibles. One—Two—Three—Four—Five—Six! Lumumba told one of the Bloods, a heavily bearded one with eyes like they belonged to a mucho sly mongoose; hair sprouting uninhibited out of his nostrils and dipping down into his mustache at the edge of the wild black bush. He told this very bushy cat, "Brother, we got to get ourselves a quicker handshake. Whitey be kicking our heads in while we still going through the ritual. Spank-the-plank and gimme-some-skin might be the best bet after all. The way the brothers do it in Tashkent. You can do it on the run, or while reaching for your razor." All the brothers eyed Yoruba.

After dinner they caught a cab and went uptown, stopped in Wilt's for another drink, she felt good good good, his eyes forever watchful of her, her own eyes ever widening, all the suspicion gone forever now, no more nervousness, he was the master, Master, whatever he said was where it was at—and always was at and always would be—was the way she wanted it on this October night. Fool! She let down all her guards that night, she wanted him to be the guard in whom she put her trust. He was not like other men, definitely not like other men, she told herself, neither was he like some of the hustling types she'd seen working the avenue. Purse-snatching pimps, gamers of the boulevards. He was not like that at all. Let go! Let yourself go. Unwind. Live. He is here and you are here. Put your living in his hands this night, let him be the shepherd, and how can he be the wolf? Can the shepherd also be the wolf? Simultaneously?

Out on the street now, strolling with the other strollers, Eastside, Westside, New York is a strolling town. "Where are we going now, Ben Ali?"

He loved the way she pronounced his newly-for-her-discovered name. She ran the first and middle names together and they came boogalooing off her lips, "Benali." Benahlie—Benaly—Benalee! "Well," he said. "The evening's still in swaddling clothes. Right? The sea is sweet and soft tonight. We might set sail down to the Africa Room or drop anchor at the Waldorf Room of Empire. On the other hand, we could lower the mizzenmast and make for shore and storm the Village Gate."

"You're the captain of the ship," she answered.

She was all eyes when she laughed like this, glowing now with happiness, clear and black and all engulfing. She, stopping amidst the flowing strollers and turning toward him, magnificent from stem to stern, she was, her bow was open to the sea. And unprotected. With Captain Lumumba mastering this ship, she had worries none at all. Yoruba was unsinkable.

His eyes, usually strong and penetrating, were not up to the eyes she had for him this night. Hers were an ocean full of feeling. Deeper even. He looked away for fear of drowning. He, who had been at sea so young so long and was seaworthy, but was not immune to seasickness, had this awful fear of drowning. Sea of life, sea of love. Save the man from sinking down. Come on, man. Get your thing together. The lady already told you you're the master, Master. You're the captain of the ship.

"On the other hand," Lumumba said, "we might just remain in port this time and make it to the Captain's Quarters and have an evening of refinement. Poetry readings and etchings on exhibit and all that jive, a kind of soirée uptown la-de-da set. Tea for two, and whatnot."

She stopped strolling and he stopped again, and she turned toward him, and there was this flicker of a moment when contentment vanished from her eyes, there was this tick-tock of a doubt when the smile wiped from her face, the slightest quiver of her lower mouth, eyes all pain, then like the sharp prick of a hypodermic, come and gone the selfsame instant. The smile broke over her face again, the tide of doubt receding swiftly almost as if it never knew existence. "You're the captain, Cap'n." She mimicked Godfrey Cambridge's Gitlow in Ossie Davis's *Purlie Victorious*. And they continued strolling toward the Captain's Quarters.

At the Captain's Quarters. She, the girl, Yoruba, more effervescent than the wine Lumumba served her. One large, wide, all-purpose room, stacked with books along the walls from floor to ceiling, of all sizes and denominations. Du Bois, Baldwin, Spengler, Jones, Marx, Engels, Malcolm, Freud, Franklin, Bennett, Giovanni, Frazier, Hare, Douglass, Fair, Mitchell, Randall, Wright, Fanon, Hamilton, Ellison, Williams, Killens. Hundreds of books! Her eyes gone wild with staring at the titles.

"You mean you've read all these books?" She was awestruck by such erudition.

He laughed. "Can't tell you no lies, Miss Sheba. I just skim through superficially like a rock skipping over the water's surface and never plunging to the deep. Learn a few hip phrases and become an expert. Talk that talk with the hippest of the hip. Like cats flying over Africa for a couple of weeks and coming back reluctantly and writing a big fat book. In other words, my real name ain't Lumumba. My name is Captain Phony, and the last name is Baloney. Dig it."

Notwithstanding, he did not really want her to dig it, or in any ways believe it. Wanted her to protest, almost violently. Behind his statement she was silent and he hadn't wanted silence from her. Her eyes wide, dark, intelligent, she let it all sink into her, tasting the words with her intelligence, like savoring an ice cream cone, she let it all soak into her, absorbing every aspect of the meaning of it. He had not meant to be taken so seriously. Finally she said, "Everybody is a little phony."

He said, "Maybe I'm a great big phony."

She said, simply, "You are not a great big phony." As if that was the end of that. Settled forever and a couple of centuries beyond.

Her large wide eyes were all-encompassing now. She walked around his room inspecting everything. The alcove in the corner where he did his cooking, his homemade desk with Ashanti stool before the window with the bamboo drapes. His sofa bed was up against the opposite wall. She walked back to Lumumba and sat beside him on the sofa. Her eyes moved like sensitive gentle fingers over Lumumba's room, tasting and caressing anything and everything.

"It's lovely," she said. "I love the way you have everything arranged. I like the bamboo things at the window and all."

He said, "I'm glad."

She said, "I like your taste. I mean, you keep the place so neat and clean." Everything looked like it had shaped up for inspection, excepting the busy clutter on his desk. "I mean, it's like a woman took care of the place."

He laughed. "My mother believed religiously that Godliness came after cleanliness. I mean, she worked all her adult life cleaning up for white folks. Days work. General cleaning. If work ever killed anybody, it damn sure killed Mama Hester. And she didn't believe in no double standards. If she kept the white man's house spotless, she didn't mean to keep her house no less spotless. It was like a fetish with her. Every Saturday morning she'd work me and her both near about to death. She used to say, 'We don't clean up for no company. We keep things neat and clean for us. That's self-respect,' she used to say. You could've always eaten right off the floor. Why even the rats preferred our place to most because it was so neat and clean. We housed and fed the great rats of twentieth-century distinction. King and queen rats of the tribe."

Yoruba laughed. "I remember your mother," she said. And then she got very quiet.

"Yeah," he said.

And he got up and put Hugh Masakela on his hi-fi record player, and he read poetry to her, and she dug his etchings and drank his wine, impressed she was by everything, books and poetry, and his etchings, most of them sketches of Africa reminding her of Tom Feelings and Elton Fax, but having a special feeling all his own. It seemed he talked a million words a minute. It seemed his dear glib tongue was jet-propelled. How could his mind keep up the pace?

He warned her, too. "Don't ever trust a cat who talks too much or talks too fast. My dad used to say anybody who talks too much a mile a minute got to be lying some of the time, maybe even most of the time. It stands to reason."

She laughed. Was it possible he didn't realize how much he talked and at such speed? She said, "Of course, there are exceptions to the rule. Or should I say 'present company excepted'?"

He opened his mouth to give her an answer, stopped, closed his mouth, a questioning smile moved over his face. Quizzical now, and hesitant. Was the joke, in fact, on him? He laughed. "Present company always excepted."

She laughed at him and said, "Okay. All right. You win."

They talked nostalgically about the Days of Snotty Noses, of the street that once was theirs by right of occupancy, the good old times of Puppy Love. He took her by the hand and they walked together backward, kicking over garbage cans of memories, playing potsy with the olden times, knocking on the creaking doors of all their crazy yesteryears. They grew old as they remembered. And she, the girl, Yoruba, was the most nostalgic of the two.

She told Lumumba about Mr. Shyler, the fabulous legendary poor downtrodden landlord of her babyhood. When she was two and three and four years old, and the Lovejoys had lived in the basement of an aging brownstone, and the landlord had lived on the top floor. The house was like the landlord, old and creaking, full of ancient musty odors, in desperate need of overhauling, everything out of order, going leisurely to pot and smelling like too many pots.

"He was like the old woman that lived in the shoe," Yoruba told Lumumba. "He had so many mortgages he didn't know what to do." She laughed, remembering.

Lumumba laughed and stretched comfortably out on the couch, his shoes off now, his head in dear Yoruba's lap.

She reminisced about the time Mr. Shyler tried to fix their toilet himself and ended up splitting it half-in-two, so that it could not be used. When you flushed it, you had to run for higher ground, because it flooded the whole apartment. Every other day, the little old landlord promised her mother he was going to have a new bowl put in, and by a real and registered plumber. Months went by, during which time the Lovejoys had to jump the fence and use their neighbors' toilets. Finally Yoruba's father grabbed the bull by the horn (by the balls, Lumumba thought, albeit silently) and had a new one put in by an honest-to-goodness plumber. Rent day came, and that evening Mr. Shyler knocked on the kitchen door and asked politely for his rent. Her father told the landlord, quietly, he was taking the toilet expenses out of the rent and handed him the plumber's bill. Mr. Shyler stared at the bill as if it were a house rat that surely would bite off his hand. Then he came into the kitchen and sat down at the table. Shaking his head from side to side. "No—no, mawn, you can't do that. I want my rent, every penny of it." After bickering back and forth for more than a half an hour, during which time Lady Daphne called him, among other things, a damn West Indian Jew, the dear little misunderstood man said, sincerely, "I wanna be fair and square. I'll tell you what I'll do you."

Matthew said, "Yeah?"

The little old landlord said, "We'll split the toilet bill three ways."

"Three ways?" Matt whispered, in pure, divine astonishment.

"Three ways," the little old man repeated, fairly, squarely, proud, sincerely. "Split it between you, Mr. Lovejoy, and you, Mrs. Lovejoy, and me, I'll take the third part of it." He counted on the tip of his wrinkled brownies. "That make three ways, don't it?"

Matt was speechless.

Dauntless Daphne said quietly, "How come we ain't include Eve-lyn and the kitty cat and make it a five-way split? Make it easier on everybody."

Mr. Shyler looked at four-year-old Yoruba seated at the table, her mouth ajar. He glanced around him till he spotted the black cat lazing in the corner near the stove. He smiled stingily. "It's all right with me, Mrs. Lovejoy, but I don't see how you gwine make it legal binding on the cat, even if he do agree to the bargain."

Both of them were laughing now, Yoruba and Ben Ali. The wine, the moment, the first time they had ever been alone together, the sweet taste of nostalgia, the tensions oozing out of them, but never really leaving them. She, the girl, Yoruba, ever mindful of his head in her lap, and the laughter making her lap more sensitive even as it helped relax her. At the same time making her more mindful that he was a man and she a woman, boy with girl. He turned his head in her lap, and she felt the movement to the quickest quick of her. She took his head in her hands, and he misunderstood, thinking she was ready now. For whatever he was ready for. For love's sweet everlasting trip. He reached up for her to put his arms around her neck. But she laughed a nervous laugh, and moved quickly out from under him. "I want a glass of water." His head fell back on the couch. She said, "I haven't finished telling you about Mr. Shyler. Or maybe I'm boring you."

He said sheepishly, "Of course not." And he was not lying, altogether. It was just that he found that his attention span was very limited this night, when other things were on his mind, especially with his head in her lap, which was a dangerous place for his head to be. It was difficult to focus on other than the girl's sweet lap.

She said, "Mr. Shyler is kind of a legendary folk-figure in the Lovejoy family." She sat back on the sofa now, but when he went to lay his head in her lap again, he missed the target, because her lap had moved. This child was fast afoot and quick alap. He sat up and stared at her, no longer smiling. Frustration! But she forced a smile.

She sat on his Ashanti stool near him seated on the sofa. Her heart pounding now, her breathing coming fast and labored, as if she had walked to the top of the Empire State. He rose and came to her and tried to share the stool with her, but the three-legged stool was also swift afoot and moved right out from under him and his backside hit the floor, undignifiedly. When he tried again, the dear girl moved away and sat back on the couch again. "Don't you want to hear anymore about dear Mister silly Mister scheming Mister Shyler? Poor man, he's been dead more than ten years now."

Lumumba said, "I'm just dying for it. I can't stand the tension."

She stared at him. She said, "Okay." And she told him about the first time her father had fallen back in the payment of the rent. Her father told Mr. Shyler he expected a check in the mail in four or five days. He had a sick and accident policy and had been off work for more than a week with influenza. It was in the days before viruses were invented, or, at least, before they became so popular. Two days after the rent was due, her father was served with a summons to show cause why he should not vacate the premises for nonpayment of his rent. Well! Lady Daphne really got busy. She bugged Attorney Williamson who belonged to her church; she flirted with him, cajoled him, jujued him, flattered him, called upon his Christian spirit, till finally the beleaguered gentleman told her to go down to the Department of Housing and find out if there were any recorded violations and to check with the rent control board and find out how much rent they were supposed to be paying. Well, my dear, my Captain, she found that there were seventeen recorded violations and that for more than two years they had been paying fifteen dollars per month rent above the legal amount. Lady Daphne gave all this information with duly certified copies of violations and affidavits of the legal rent to the lawyer. And one fine spring Friday morning they all found themselves in court. Here was the classic non-example of the landlord-tenant relationship. Mr. Shyler stood there before the judge, hat in hand. He was his very own and only lawyer with a damn fool as a client, as the saying goes. There were Big Matt and Lady Daphne and Yoruba fully represented by the very dapper and most proper and progressive attorney Major Williamson. Four against one.

Lumumba laughed and rose and stretched and went and sat near Yoruba on the couch again. He said, "It's enough to make you lose faith in the capitalistic system. Behind this happening, how could you ever believe that justice always would emerge triumphant?" He put his arm around her waist.

"Okay," Yoruba said, "but let me finish." And she continued.

Attorney Williamson said, importantly, "May it please the court, my client pleads seventeen violations and twenty-seven months of overcharging of rent. And we enter these two duly certified documents as exhibit A and B, and we thereby rest our case."

It was about eleven thirty in the A.M. and the judge dreamed impatiently of getting away from the city for the weekend, to the golf links, maybe, or some other place, anywhere else excepting this place, and here was this simple stupid landlord-tenant case between "niggers" holding him up. Who ever heard of a landlord in court without legal representation facing a tenant duly represented? "Niggers always get things bass-ackwards," his honor seemed to be thinking. He stared at the documents handed to him by the proud and pompous Black attorney, and then he looked down from his august perch, impatiently, and growled at Mr. Shyler. What have you got to say for yourself?"

Mr. Shyler shifted his weight from one foot to the other and his beat-up hat from one hand to the other. He seemed to get smaller by the second. He mumbled incoherently.

The judge looked at his watch. "On second thought," Lumumba suggested, "most likely the good judge had a date, away from the city and his wife and kids, with his young mistress for a weekend in the Catskills."

"Speak up, Mr.—what-is-your-name—Mr. Shyster, is it? What about these violations?"

Mr. Shyler spoke barely above a whisper. "I need my rent so I can take care of the violations, Judge, your Honor, please sir."

His Honor blew his nose and snorted, growling: "Why have you overcharged these people?"

Mr. Shyler's voice got smaller and smaller in direct proportions to his body shrinkage. "I-I-I-I thought you could charge them anything you wanted to charge them long as everybody was in happy agreement. This is a free country, ain't it, Judge, your Honor, please sir?"

His Honor blew his nose again. And turned to the defendants. "Here's my decision. You, Mr. Lovely (is it?), can pay the rent in escrow to the Housing Authority, Mr. Shyster not to get a single cent of it until he gets rid of every one of those violations, and even so, you're not to pay a penny over the certified amount. Now —as to the two years overcharge, you would have to bring a different kind of action against Mr. Shyster." He turned again to the steadily shrinking landlord. "Do you understand what I'm saying and what your obligations are?"

Mr. Shyler whispered, "Yes sir, Judge, your Honor, please sir. But I sure could use that money they gon put in scarecrow."

At this point, the very liberal, generous-hearted Attorney Williamson stepped forward toward the bench. "Your Honor, my client does not seek to drive Mr. Shyster into bankruptcy. We know he's trying to buy this house of his in the twilight of his life. We're entirely sympathetic. And we are willing to pay the prescribed rent, if Mr. Shyster solemnly promises before your Honor to take care of the violations forthwith."

His Honor turned again to the swiftly disappearing landlord. "Well?"

The little man mumbled, "I solemnly promise, Judge, your Honor, please sir, so help me God."

The next evening Yoruba's father met Mr. Shyler in the hall and handed him the prescribed amount of monthly rent. Mr. Shyler counted it slowly and carefully and looked up into Matthew's face. "Where my other fifteen dollars?"

Her father just stared at him at first. Surely he had not heard the little man properly. Sometimes Mr. Shyler mumbled badly in his mustache, and whistled through his four black teeth, the only ones left in his mouth. "What did you say?"

This time Mr. Shyler spoke very clearly. "Where the rest of my rent money?"

Her father exercised admirable control. "Mr. Shyler, didn't you hear the judge say, I mean, don't you know I don't have to pay you a penny till you get rid of these violations? And never ever a single cent over what you got in your hands right now? Not to mention getting back all that two-year overcharge. You heard the judge—"

Mr. Shyler handed the money back to her father, mumbling, "That judge don't know my business." And went for two more days before he came back for the rent, minus the fifteen dollars overcharge.

"That judge don't know my business!" Lumumba repeated after Yoruba, and he started laughing. "Yoruba!" he shouted. "You got to be putting me on." He laughed some more. "That judge do not know my business!" He was laughing now without control. "You ought to write a book about old Mr. Shyster." And he laughed and took her in his arms and held her close to him and kissed her hard, and felt her trembling in his arms.

She pulled away from him and sat on his Ashanti stool again. "Now you talk to me," she told him. "Tell me all about yourself, and everything, the places you have been, and everything, your books and stuff. How're you going to write your story?"

He said, "Okay, all right, you win." He was a man who loved to talk. And he talked with her about his books, about Africa, Asia, the Caribbean, Europe, South America, the Movement. "Everything depends on the Black brothers and sisters in the Movement right here in the USA. We're the hippest Black folks in the world. We're the hippest, purest, beautifullest, most dedicated, most disunited, most together, most opportunistic, most naïve, most corrupt, most humanistic on this planet. If we don't get our thing together, you can forget it. The Black folks of the world are lost. Even China. It's okay to wear boubous and dashikis and change your name and all that jive. And Afros. Dig it. I got a closet full of African identity, like authentic from the source and jive. But most of the Black hip people up to now have been only *acting* Black. That ain't nothing new. We're a nation of Black actors. Always have been. Now it's time for some Black doers. But doing Black is another level altogether. We've always had great Black actors all the way back to Ira Aldridge all the way up to Sidney Poitier. We've entertained the world for centuries. Now exorcise the gods to issue forth Black doers doing Black. Let the conjure-man get busy. We Black USA-ans are the people where it's at." He paused. They were aware again of the music filling the room with sweet and terrifying sounds.

The Americanization of Ooga Booga, Hugh Masakela blowing his thing, soaring higher than the moon, the high priest calling the brothers and sisters back to the Nation.

And he talked on and on eternally, as she watched the words flow from his mouth. She, the girl, Yoruba, was on a trip now. She was seasick over words. Tripped and word-drunk on Lumumba's mighty Ship of Glib, which did not run on steam or the Grace of God or diesel or horsepower or nuclear power, but word power, a steady heady flow of the thing that was always with God, in the beginning.

She got up and went into her dance. She whirled and danced and whirled and danced, she did her African number by the numbers, all her inhibitions, even those Lady Daphne instilled, gone with the selfhoodship of the words and music. Whirling, dancing, swiveling, pirouetting, gyrating, Africa calling, reclaiming her own, her very very very own. Lumumba calling. She danced until the things inside her head began to dance and spin and the couch came up, it seemed, to take her, as she fell into Ben Ali's arms. He took her strongly, gently, his muscled arms around her waist, and kissed her firmly, softly, mouth to mouth. A strange kind of loving-God was conjure-man Lumumba. She felt a tingling, unfamiliar, run the length of her body down her spine to the very very tip of her tippy toes. The baby hair at the back of her neck bristled like the wind was blowing through it. It seemed the couch was moving underneath her. She knew the calm strength of his arms about her. He was her Captain and they were in the Captain's Quarters. She felt like shouting, "You're the pilot, Pilot!" She tripped up over her metaphors, confused her Captain with her conjure-man. Her arms tightened around his neck in a pure unconscious act of simple desperation. She was drowning deep at sea and he was the last straw of her sweet salvation. Save me, Captain Conjureman! Take me! Save me! Exorcise me! It was as if he had a hundred hands, and she trembled as she felt his hands all over her. Her mother had warned her of these kinds of situations, and suddenly she grew rigid in her Captain's arms; her own arms collapsed from around his neck. And his strong arms relaxed their hold.

She fell away from him and began to sob.

"What's the matter with you?"

She went into his arms again. "Nothing! Nothing, Ben Ali! You're the Captain!" Smiling in the midst of tears. And she tried with all her might to recapture the sweetness of the other moment for him, for her, for them, but she tried in vain. It was all in her imagination, but no less real; it was as if her mother stood tall and awesome in the room, stood above them like a queenly accusation. She, the girl, Yoruba, knew her mother's words by heart. She heard them now just as clearly as she felt her mother's presence. "Listen, child. I going give you some intelligent advice. Men is no good, dearie. Specially nigger men. They ain't mean a woman no good. After they get their satisfaction, they ready to throw you to the dogs, and they all come sniffing around in heat after the hapless wanton bitch!"

Yoruba closed her eyes as if to shut out the sighted sound of her mother's all-pervasive presence. She went further into Ben Ali's arms. Save me, Captain! Save me! Take me! Exorcise my evil spirits! Cast them out! And he tried his damnedest to save her, take her, exorcise her. Wild he was with this terrible desire to be her one and only Captain. But Lady Daphne was, after all, a queen and of a strong and queenly presence, and queens were not to be denied. Gods and captains and conjure-men were always flunkies for her majesties. Jesters at the queenly court. By divine right. It was ever thus. And now, against her will, Yoruba remembered when she was twelve and thirteen years of age, and her mother would take her to the doctor, though she knew no pain or ailment, and without her father's knowledge. Every other month her mother took her and watched while the doctor examined her, not even trusting the highly respectable grizzly old bewhiskered lip-quivering half-deaf man from the then British Guiana. It was a mother-daughter thing, her mother warned her, and her father was not to be involved in the knowledge of it. Much much later Yoruba understood that her mother was checking out her virginity. "Your mother mean you nothing but good tidings, Eve-lyn. One of these days you will be thankful to me."

She tried hard, for Lumumba, but she knew it was no good now. It was as if she were making love with her lover in her mother's presence with her mother as a chaperone and supervisor. Candleholder? She pulled away from Ben Ali and sat up and arranged her skirt. She hated herself now. Felt an ugliness that was unfamiliar to her. Her face, her mouth, her throat, her eyes, her soul exuded ugliness.

He said, "What in the hell's the matter with you?" He had lost his vaunted cool, he, the hippest of the hip ones.

"Okay," she said, bitterly, "something's the matter with me, is it? Just because I don't run and jump in bed with every Tom, Dick and Hair-ree?" It was as if her mother were a ventriloquist and threw her voice all the way into the Captain's Quarters from a Hundred and Twenty-ninth Street. As if her mother had managed somehow to get inside Yoruba's skin. She even talked with a Bajun accent. She saw the pure hurt in Lumumba's eyes and wanted to cry out that this was not her speaking.

"Thank you very much. However, I'm neither Tom, Dick or Harry. The name is Ben Ali Lumumba, *né* Ernest Walter Billings."

"You men are all the same," she said, wondering why she said it. Not even wanting to believe it. "You're all after one thing from a woman. You don't love them—don't respect them."

"Well—well—well—" the Captain said, hating the whole situation, wondering how and why the ship had suddenly foundered. "I never thought of you as just another woman, Anne, Sylvia or Josephine, but only as Yoruba, something very extra-special, very sacred, but now we see what a fool a cat can make of himself when he sets foot on dry land. I guess I've been at sea too long, and it seems as if I'm still at sea. Okay. I guess that sums it up for tonight and all the other nights. We'll get you a cab and send you off to mama and papa."

She started to cry again and she went to him. "Be kind and gentle to me, Ben Ali. Have patience with me. Please have patience!"

He did not put his arms around her. He said dryly, "Okay. Patience is its own reward."

She pleaded. "Don't be angry with me. Please!"

He said, "What's with angry? I'm as happy as a faggot in a Boy Scout camp."

She laughed a laugh that wasn't good, trying to pretend that he really meant to make a funny. "Don't call a cab," she said. "Please walk me home."

He said, "Okay. All right. You win. The game is over now, called on account of sudden darkness. And we will walk the good queen home. We will be her honor guard."

The hurt was in her wide eyes now. He knew it, saw it. She shook her head in deep denial. "It isn't a game with me, Ben Ali. And I don't want it ended when it's just beginning. It's just that you have to have a little patience with me. I'm not used to—I'm afraid—I act sophisticated, I talk like I know everything, but—I'm just a small-town girl—Manhattan—I mean—I mean, Harlem—I haven't traveled like you have—I—"

"Forget it! It's all my fault. A clear case of mistaken identity. I thought you were one of them rare Black chicks who knew her beauty, could see it even in Harlem mud puddles and dishwater reflections."

She said, "Am I truly beautiful, Lumumba?" Her eyes, large, wide, bleary, with a million questions. Some that never would be answered.

He talked on, as if he hadn't heard her question. "*I am Black and comely, O you daughters of the Western World.* That is how I cased your attitude. Thought you took your loveliness for granted." His voice hardened, deliberately. "There you sit now in all your 'nigger' ugliness. I wouldn't want to make love with you now even if you wanted me to." He paused, stared at her, shook his head, in sorrow. "How can you really love me anyhow, and at the same time feel ugly and unworthy of my love? I mean, how can you ever believe that I love you unless you love your lovely self?"

She looked at him. "I don't know, Ben Ali! I don't know what's the matter with me. You'll just have to have a—"

He said, "All right already." Deliberate, and gruffly spoken. And took her out of the door and down the stair, leaving his hi-fi going strong with the high priest Masakela.

They stood for more than a half an hour on the stoop outside the brownstone where she lived, even though she knew somehow that her mother was doing sentry duty behind the curtains at the living-room window. They, Yoruba and Lumumba, discussed the whole thing in a passionate heat, and as they parted, he took her into his arms and kissed her fully on the mouth. Long, hard, strong, with all those promises to keep.

Promise, promised, promising.

Before the door had closed behind her, her mother went into her bag of crosses, and came out instantly with: "Lord, look at my weary crosses!"

The girl broke into furious laughter. "Okay, Mary's boychild, will you kindly dig my mother's crosses?" She stared at her mother, still laughing, and imagined her mother bound from head to foot with crosses, large ones, man-sized, one on her back, one on her sagging breasts, skinny long ones on each side, one atop her head. She had never spoken to her mother like this, derisively. This child had always been respectful.

Lady Daphne said, "Don't you dare to laugh at me, you brazen hussy. Coming in here all times of night like some common nigger woman off the streets."

"But that's all we are, Mother. Just common niggers, as you love to call us, off the street. What makes us so different from all the other common niggers?"

"After all I done to make a lady out of you, you standing out there carrying on with that woolly-head nigger man look like he just got captured in the jungles of Africa."

She laughed again at her mother. "Oh, but he was not. He's from the same jungles I'm from, right here in Harlem."

"I should have bought me a pistol and blowed his few brains out the first time I see him bring you to the door."

"Not you, Mother. You're a devout believer in nonviolence."

"That's the only way you can deal with savages. Shoot them down."

"I'm tired, Mother. I had a hard day at the job, but I had a very pleasant evening, that is, until you spoiled it."

Her mother screamed, "Who is that African? Who is that woolly-head African? I told you I wanted you to marry a fair-skin colored man, so your children will be lighter than you and have a better chance in life. You're an American!"

"I have no plans for getting married, Mother. Not for this year or the next."

"You have no marriage plans for getting?" Her mother screeched.

Yoruba had to laugh this time. "You're right on target, Mother. I have no marriage plans for getting."

"So you just sleeping around, living in sin. And they picked you for a debutante?"

"Are you accusing me?" She laughed. "Are you going to bring your darling American daughter up on charges before the Cotillion Selections Committee?"

Her mother took her seriously. "No, child, no! I wouldn't dream of turning you in! I'm your mother through thin and thick!"

Yoruba said, "And do they have a mother-confessor on the Committee? And should I go and make a full confession?"

All the arrogance in her mother's eyes, in the turn-up of her nose, in the set of her mouth, turned to horror. Suddenly she looked like an old woman, sagging with the weight of years piling up on her thin shoulders. All at once Yoruba realized her mother possessed no sense of humor. The hard life of great expectations and colossal disappointments had left her humorless. She started to say "I'm only joking, Mother." But the devil in her kept her mouth unopened. She blamed her mother for spoiling her evening with Captain Conjurer and yet there was this terrible ambivalence. She was also grateful to her mother for preventing her from turning a corner in her very sheltered life. She, the girl, Yoruba, had lived in a Harlem shelter, and she wasn't certain she was ready to make the break out of this holy place of refuge. She wasn't sure the Captain was her Captain. Her Black shining prince, her Black knight, piloting his ship instead of riding a great steed. He might turn out to be a pirate. Her mother knew more than she knew. Her mother had lived longer. Had lived longer, yes, the devil told her, and had more time to learn more stupidness.

Her mother said, "I'll make a pot of tea, come. And we can discuss this thing like intelligent people. Come. Like mother and daughter, not like cats and dogs." She turned and moved heavily toward the kitchen, the strut no longer in her walk.

They sat sipping tea and munching homemade coconut bread. Her mother was a muncher from way back. Munched all day and half the night.

"Now," her mother said, breathing heavily, "I should have had a talk with you the first night I saw you out front with that African."

"Mother—"

Her mother, strong of voice, gaining strength now by the moment. "I've always talked with you, mother to daughter, ever since the curse came on you. I told you what a woman's lot was. I brought you up to be a lady. I told you men was no good. A lady just tolerates them as a necessary evil, a lesser of two evils. Matrimony or spinstershiphood. A real lady gets no pleasure out of sex. If you're a real lady, you do like the dear Queen, you consider your choice for a husband very carefully and then make the best deal you can."

Daphne's eyes were shining brightly now with tears of nostalgia and regret, at squandered opportunities, as she saw it now, and her life's colossal waste of time. She took the girl's hand in her hand. "Oh my dear, all the chances I threw away—all the handsome ones were at my beck and calling. Cream of the crop. All I had to do was snap my fingers and they come running. Don't know what to say they wouldn't do just to get my hands in matrimonial relativity. Their hearts was quick to all my charms. But I was so lighthearted and a little fickle-headed, I suspect." She gave her eyes the back of her hand. "Can't you see what I'm trying to tell you?" She blew her nose.

Yoruba's eyes were filling now and spilling down her cheeks. "Mother—Mother—"

"I made a mistake and that's why I don't want you to make the same stupid mistake and get yourself tied to some common ordinary negra."

"Say something about love, Mother."

"How you mean, love?" her mother answered spitefully. "Love is what exist between a mother and her daughter. Between men and women, there is only respect, that is, if you fortunately inclined. Otherwise, there is lust and lust alone, and only the man gets anything out of it. A woman who is happy over sex is nothing but a whore."

She, the girl, Yoruba, stared at her mother in amazement. She shook her head. "It seems to me you got it backwards. It seems to me the woman who does not enjoy sex is the prostitute. She's participating solely for the money arrangement. She—she—she's a businesswoman."

Her mother ignored Yoruba's discourse on the wherefores and the whereases of prostitution, as she had a way of doing when she had no ready answer.

Matthew was awakened by the voices coming from the kitchen. He got up and made it up the hall and stood in the doorway unnoticed.

Lady Daphne said, "Now, you simply must not see that boy again. You're a debutante now. You're a queen and he's a commoner, so to speak. You understand, don't you, Eve-lyn?"

"Like John Henry said, 'A man ain't nothing but a man.'" Matthew's drowsy contribution from the doorway.

Lady Daphne said, "I wish you wouldn't interrupt us when we are talking serious women-talk. We're discussing intelligence."

"You want a cup of tea, Father?" Yoruba said.

Lady Daphne turned to Matthew. "While you sleeping, your daughter was out gallivanting with every Tom, Dick and Hair-ree."

"His name is Ben Ali Lumumba, slave name Ernest Walter Billings. Grew up on this same street with me."

Matthew laughed. "You don't mean little biddy old snotty-nose Ernie?"

"The same," she said. "He's a grown man now, and his nose no longer snotty."

"Where that boy been all this time?"

"He went to sea when he was seventeen."

Lady Daphne said, "See what you done? Your daughter ready to throw herself away on some no-count seaman. It's all your fault. I told you not to let him in my house ever since that little nigger was eight or nine years old."

"I bet he grew into a fine young man," her father said, his eyes filled up now with the good old days that never were. "You tell him to drop around to see us sometime."

Lady Daphne said, with finality, "I don't want that kind never in no house of mine. He don't got no education or no refining qualities."

"One thing sure, Lady Daphne," Matt Lovejoy said, "you ain't too old for your wants to hurt you. You ain't that old yet, I don't reckon." He didn't raise his voice above its normal tone, but Yoruba could feel the heat. "And if I invite somebody to my house, they better be treated with respect." He turned to Yoruba again. "I sure be glad to see old Ernest. Whatchoo say his name is now? Lumumba?" He laughed and laughed and laughed and laughed.

Miss Daphne said, "I will not have that kind of nigger in my house."

Matthew stared at his wife and said, "One man just as good as another. Sometimes he's a damn sight better."

Yoruba Evelyn looked from her mother to her father, laughter softly bubbling out of her now like an overheated percolator. Her mother stared at her in wonder. What in the devil was she laughing at? She looked from Yoruba to Matthew and back to Yoruba again. She felt all alone and conspired against. Husband and daughter were against her. The Lord was punishing her for forsaking her dear father and his family and coming to this Godless country. And moving in with "niggers." Consorting with a "nigger" man. She was the prodigal daughter. But, unlike the son, she could not go home again. This place was her home now in this wicked city of Babylon. She loved these people, she told herself; she loved them, even felt compassion for them, and she had to make them understand.

"One man just as good as another. Sometimes he's a damn sight better." Big Matt was famous with his daughter for such down-home bits of mother wit. Another one of his goodies was: "Things can't git no worse, but they damn sure can git worser."

The girl began to laugh now, loudly, gales of laughter issuing forth in great volumes, tears spilling down her face. As if the devil himself, invisible, were goosing her, her mother thought.

It *was* a distinct possibility, her darling mother thought.

CHAPTER SEVEN

PREPARATIONS

Wonth—Two—Free
Wonth—Two—Free
Wonth—Two—Free
Wonth—Two—Free

Yoruba was up to her sweet dark cheeks in preparations for the Grand Cotillion.

Wonth—Two—Free
Wonth—Two—Free

There were, of course, the dance instructions, the most important dance instructions, which were conducted in a loft somewhere in mid-Manhattan not far from the famous center of garments. A big, wide, stable of a place, it looked like it might have been inhabited by a cavalry of Revolutionary horses way back when. And the smell still lingered, stubbornly. Tired horses. Sweating, snorting, urinating. Say it plain. The place was funky. And in an unhip fashion yet.

Wonth—Two—Free

The dance instructor was a nice, old, friendly looking white man, who lisped flamboyantly, whose teeth bucked like a wild mustang, whose eyes were forever crossing over one another, colliding sometimes, his nostrils flaring when excited somewhat like a neighing horse. His face was mostly downward cast, long and dropping away unceremoniously from a sparse and stingy forehead. He reminded her of horses. Prancing horses. And he always seemed to have to go. Yoruba fondly thought of him as "Prancer."

"Wonth, two, free—Wonth, two, free—(bouncing, flouncing all the while) Wonth, two, free—" She, the girl, Yoruba, thought, as she bouncingly Wonth-two-freed along with the other girls, she thought: Maybe he's the reincarnation of the old cherry-tree-chopper's horse! He certainly was a horsey one. Of the nightmare variety. She had seen one or two horses in her life's brief time, and they had been old beaten-down nags, one jump ahead of the scrap heap, dragging some wagon of junk around and impolitely constructing small dung heaps all over Harlem. The only horses she had known up close, or close up, whichever, were television stars like Silver and Black Beauty years ago when she was young and believed religiously in television. Prancer had been a great dancer in his day, but his day was in the twilight time, his jumping up and down was over, and he was put out to pasture, in the teaching field.

"Wonth, two, free—Now, ladieth, jutht remember—Wonth, two, free—the walth is the—Wonth, two, free—take the chewing gum out of your—Wonth, two, free—the walth is the very key to royalty and ladyship—Wonth, two, free—gentility—Wonth, two, free—" Waving his hands and bouncing up and down like he had to make wee-wee instantly. "Wonth, two, free—it is the danth of queens and kings and barons and—Wonth, two, free—all the other people of the leisured clathses—Wonth, two, free—you learn the walth and all other cultural things—wonth, two, free—will be added unto thee —Wonth, two, free—wonth, two, free—Oh dear me! Thath not quite it—Wonth, two, free—You are Funking Broadway—that is not the walth, chérie—Wonth, two, free—Mith La-hyphenated-Thmythe—Wonth, two, free—Pleath, thtop chewing the walth— Thaths not it! You're Funking Broadway every time!"

Some of the queenly ones were doubled up in laughter now, in a most unqueenly attitude. "Wonth, two, free!—Oh dear me! Thaths not it at all!" The dear instructor pranced around and stomped his big unlikely feet, which were a contradiction to his gentle voice. "Wonth, two, free! All right! Let uth thtop for a brief moment, and let uth get ourthelves together. Now then, we can do the walth, if only we think pothitively, I know we can, we are the proud producth of Wethtern Thivilithation, of which the walth ith ith thining thymbol. Learn the walth and it will open up all the doorth of thivilithed thothiety to you." He patted his meager forehead daintily with his filthy handkerchief, perspiration pouring from his horse's face. He stared from one to the other of them now as if he suspected them of engaging in one colossal, very dark conspiracy against him. "I refuth to believe that color or rathe hath anything to do with it." He stomped his big feet, each one in its turn. "I will not believe the bigoth. Therefore I know you can learn to walth." He was Lizzie in a tizzie, now. His dear cool had deserted him. "Now, thall we try again? Mith Fothter, we are ready now." Miss Foster was his most worthy assistant. Tiny, dried-up, bug-eyed spinster, who could have stood in as an understudy for Woody-the-Woodpecker in her younger days. She manhandled the piano like in the old days (which were her young days) of the nickelodeon. She was all hands and seemed to have them in a great supply. Bomma lomma—Bomma lomma. Bomma lomma. Bomma lomma. Otherwise, she had a lot of personality, personally speaking, from the standpoint of her inner pulchritude, which nobody ever penetrated, which was their loss and her deep sorrow.

Okay?

"Now then," the dance instructor lisped, " 'The Blue Danube'— 'The Blue Danube'—Wonth, two, free—Wonth, two, free—You can do it, if you try—If you try—If you try—Wonth, two, free—You are not from Africa—You are proud Americanth—Wonth, two, free— Producth of a great thivilithation—If you try—Now you thay it after me—We can do it if we try—if we try—if we try—if we try. We are proud Americanth. We can do it if we try—Wonth, two, free—Wonth, two, free—

In the poetic words of Brap-bap, Charlene Robinson said, "Sheee-it! Ain't this a bitch!" And continued to do her individual thing. Some of the ladies began to chant, "We can do it if we try— Wonth, two, free—We are proud Americans—Wonth, two, free— if we try—if we try—" Notwithstanding the sweet and patriotic sentiment of the lyric, the dance they danced to the famouth "Blue Danube" was a conglomeration of Mashed Potato, fugue, calypso, Funky Broadway, High Life, Boogaloo, Watusi, Blackbottom, Ball-the-Jack, Charleston, Mess Around and every other kind of dance excepting the one the darling man was teaching them. Each gentle lady was going for herself, doing her natural thing.

Yoruba said to her new friend, Pamela Jefferson, "How come a white dance instructor? It doesn't make sense."

Pam laughed. "Who's worried about making sense? All they want is for us to be like Mister Charlie's chillun."

"Oh my God!" Mr. Phil Potts, the Prancer, exclaimed. "You're not even Funking Broadway anymore! Mith Lovejoy, will you thtep forward, pleath?"

"Who? Me? What did I do?"

"Yeth, my dear. Pleath thtep forward." His fickle eyes followed Yoruba as the girl stepped forward, wondering what she had done to be singled out for ridicule. "Now," he said, "girlth, obtherve how Mith Lovejoy moves. Thuch grath, thuch charm."

When she stood a couple of feet away from Mr. Phil Potts (you know what some of the naughty girls had already nicknamed him, behind his back), Mr. P. Potts said, "Now, girlth, every young lady can move with the grath and charm of Mith Lovejoy. It is thomething that comes from practith and from thpethal training. Mith Lovejoy obviouthly attended finithing thchool."

Chuckling, giggling, open laughter from the darling nubile innocents.

"Mith Lovejoy, did you go to finithing thchool?"

All right, Yoruba thought, she would go along with the program, momentarily. For laughs. She said, "Yes sir, indeed I did. I certainly matriculated." She imagined herself, Miss Lutiebelle Gussie Mae Jenkins of *Purlie Victorious* fame. It was her favorite Broadway play. It was her only Broadway play.

"There you are, girlth! I knew it! I knew it!" He was in a frenzy of excitement. "Now then, tell uth the name of your finithing thchool." He pranced. He horsed around, triumphant. He had won the race at Churchill Downs.

She said decorously, "They finished me at P.S. 999, known by some as Ignorance High, and when I finished, I was indeedly finished."

He laughed politely along with the girls, then coughed fitfully. His eyes colliding more than ever. "Very well, a clear-cut cathe of thimple noncommunication. But that jutht proves my point even more though. If you can walth like that without attending finithing thchool, then there ith hope for all of uth. Now then, Mith Lovejoy, may I make an example of you?"

She stared.

"Oh dear, I mean, I thould like to illuthtrate with you." He took her hand. "Thall we danth thith one, milady?"

She curtsied, and he took her into his arms. "Mith Foster—'The Blue Danube'." And they began to do the waltz. "Wonth, two, free—Wonth, two, free—" Her mother had prepared her for these kinds of moments years ago. The waltz, the one-step, two-step. When she was a tot her mother taught her. The two of them would dance together. The dear sweet girl remembered now, when she was a little girl and her parents used to take her with them to the West Indian jump-up parties. Lady Daphne would never do the common jump-up dances. Only the sedate white folks' proper one-steps and the like. But her father would jump-up like a true West Indian. People used to laugh and say, "Which one of they is from the Islands?" Matt was a proper Calypsonian when it came to doing calypso and meringue and all the other "native" dances. But the waltz and the one-step and the two-step were Lady Daphne's favorities, and she spent many hours dancing them with her little girl in the kitchen on One Hundred and Twenty-ninth Street, as the hip-and-funky-oriented rats stood by and watched with genuine amazement. One, two, three—one, two, three—

"Wonth, two, free—Wonth, two, free—" The dance teacher's breath smelled somewhat like his new nickname. His entire being exuded an odor that was a mixture of sweat and over-sweet perfume and alcohol, like if you sprayed a lathered horse with a Paris Evening or a Chanel Number Five.

Mr. Piss Potts was the kind of dance instructor who could no longer follow his own instructions. Couldn't practice what he preached. Like a five-by-five basketball coach teaching rebounds to Wilt Chamberlain. He danced like he had four left feet, hands and all. Yoruba felt pawed at and stampeded; it was like a girlie wrestling match to dance the waltz with Mr. Potts. He, stumbling all over her, his big left feet upon her feet (the dear man had seen better dancing days), his whiskeyed breath enough itself to knock her off her feet, and his mouth forever open—Wonth, two, free—a cesspool of assorted stench—Wonth, two, free—and pouring forth its lively fumes. But for all that, he was a nice man who meant well, even if he did so poorly.

Then Miss Annie Foster, Mr. P. Potts's most worthy assistant, taught the girls how to walk like ladies, queenly. Can you dig? With books atop their lovely heads they tipped softly across the floor and curtsied. With Miss Annie leading the way, notwithstanding, the dear, sweet, pale-faced woman never quite made it across the floor without her own book leaping devilishly from her wig-topped noggin, cone-shaped as it was like the pyramids of Egypt and the white tents of the Klan. Her head was not constructed for shipping things atop. And some of the naughty girls had no better upbringing than to laugh, and loudly, at the lady, who after all was there, unselfishly, to teach them things for their own good. Right? To teach these uncouth darlings couth was what. And like Mr. P. Potts, she was possessed of the zeal that is traditional with missionaries. The ladies of the darker hue should have been more grateful. Right? Here she was, giving her very all, chisel-chinned and bow-of-legs, her bottom built so close to the earth she literally bounced along; she had to be the pure-in-heart. In point of fact, it was the easiest lesson for the girls. And they should have been more grateful for the lady's sacrifices. A nice white lady who couldn't walk herself the queenly walk, but struggled valiantly to teach it to them. Indeed, they should have been more grateful. And several of them were. Three, in fact. Including Yoruba and La-Smythe. They taught Miss Annie how to walk that walk. Almost.

"But Miss Annie gets paid for learning," Lumumba chided Yoruba. "A kind of on-the-job training." They were having dinner one rare evening.

"Yeah," she said, "but it was funny, I mean, how *we* learned so easily."

"After all," Lumumba told her, "it's your African heritage. You oughta see them fine black chicks strolling down them dusty roads with the whole damn marketplace on top their lovely heads in Bamako and Ouagadougou."

She laughed and held his hand and squeezed it. "Some people name-drop, but you country-drop and city-drop and continent-drop, and especially you Africa-drop."

Her father laughed when he heard about Miss Annie and the preparation happenings. "You oughta seed your grandma strut down them roads in Georgia with them white folks' clothes on top her head when she took them to the white folks' house, after she done washed and ironed them. Every Saddy she would take them. That lady could do herself some strutting."

It was a busy time. The cosmetologist was a proper-talking woman who taught them the proper use of cosmetology, what else? She also taught the ladies how to sit, how to stand; it was like being a baby all over again. How to curtsey, how to sip their tea, and all the other white and cultured graces. Likewise how to walk, again. (There was overlapping of jurisdictions.) It was a clear-cut case of overteach. She taught them how to use their rouge and lipstick, and especially she taught them how to put a kind of white lipstick down the middle of their mostly wide and flaring noses to give illusions of Caucasian slenderness. How to be pretty white ladies underneath their colored skins was what was being striven for. And valiantly. Bicycles or roller skates would have come in very handy, so busy were these innocent lovely debutantes, and especially on Thursdays, when it was back to Mr. P. Potts and his lady, back to the cosmetologists and so forth and so on. And on and on and out of breath and on and on.

There was the get-together merry-go-round of teas each week from one house to another of the future debutantes, and the competition was cutthroat among the proud, insecure mothers to see who could put on the grandest dog, or words to that effect.

Brap-bap said, "They put on Rockefeller airs with Jones and Jackson pocketbooks."

They made it back one more time to the lovely Pattersons. And one of the dear young debbies (Deborah was her Christian name) was bitten on the cheek of her innocent little plumpish bottom by a snag in the plastic of the toilet seat, as the dear sweet one sat pleasantly and dreamily wee-weeing. She leaped from the stool as if a snake had bitten her, wet her precious panties, jumped, seeking refuge, into the green and sunken bath, which was also plastic-covered. Thrashing around a desperate moment in the plastic. Then from the vantage point of the sunken tub, she peered around the bathroom looking vainly for the fanged and vicious culprit. Finding nothing, she stepped out of the tub, put her panties in her pocketbook, got herself together and returned to the party with a kind of nervous dignity, her dear cheeks none the worse for wear and tear, the dear girl thought. Nevertheless, it was a distressing experience, especially when she tripped back, bare-assed, to the living room and plopped back down on the plastic-covered sofa. When she got up again, she left a red stain on the plastic.

Dowdy Mrs. Downjohn of the Femmes Fatales Committee huskily whispered to the poor girl, loud and clear, for everyone, with ears, to hear. "My dear child, you are menstruating." Mrs. Downjohn's voice was a mixture of glad tidings and terrible embarrassment, as if she could not really make up her mind which attitude was more appropriate.

Darling dimpled Deborah stared at the dumpy gentlewoman. "Huh?"

"The curse is on you." She sounded like she was born with laryngitis.

Now the girl stared at Mrs. Downjohn. "Who? Honh? What?" As if the dowdy little woman was a soothsayer, saying sooth.

"Your period has begun. Your monthly—"

"No, m'am." She smiled a nervous dimpled smile.

Yoruba felt her face go hot with compassion and embarrassment. Poor Deborah!

Mrs. Patterson said, "It's a blessing that my couch was covered."

The Lord works mysteriously.

Mrs. Brap-bap shook hands with the flustered girl. "'Congratulations. You made it one more time. It ain't nothing to be ashamed of. And it's a bloody good thing, I mean to tell you, at your age and situation, it ain't no kind of curse, it's a bloody blessing in disguise." She turned around to the now furiously giggling debutantes. "What's the big joke all about? All of y'all be laughing out your other mouth, if y'all can't make the bloody scene."

Duly-dimpled Deborah stood there, staring stupidly; then she looked back at the place her backside had just vacated, and she understood. She said, flush-faced and flustered, "I don't have the rag on, Mrs. Brap-bap."

Mrs. Brap-bap said, "I'm hip."

The girl said, "What I mean is, I'm not ministrating."

Mrs. Brap-bap said, "It's all right, dear. You're old enough."

The fainthearted girl perspired and persisted. "It's not that at all, what I mean is—"

"What is it?" Mrs. Downjohn asked, closing her eyes to shut out the terrifying answer, keeping her ears wide open, like a Labrador retriever, nostrils flaring. Breathing heavy with excitement. And the greatest expectations.

"Something bit me in the toilet."

"Something bit you in the toilet?"

Ladies shouldn't giggle like the debutantes were giggling now.

"Yes, m'am. I think it was the toilet seat."

First the roar of deafening silence.

Then some damn uncouth fool giggled, causing the entire group to erupt into loud and raucous laughter, which was admittedly unseemly for such ultra-proper maidens. And dear Deborah flipped her billy-dip. She ran around shouting, "Take it off! Take it off! Take it all off!" And ripping plastic from the couches, from the draperies, from the chairs and from the hassocks, shouting, "Take it off! Take it off! Let it all hang out!"

Okay?

At Pattersons. In the Crown of Heavenly Heights.

Then there was the soirée at the Jeffersons.

Yoruba and Pam Jefferson had become real tight. Had met in town for dinner once, and laughed and talked about Cotillion preparations. Some of the other Crowning Heights girls took a dim view of their budding friendship. Most of them would have nothing to do with Yoruba and the other "culturally deprived" from Harlem. At rehearsals, the young ladies from the Heights would gravitate toward one another and look down their protuberances at the "uncouth ones," and talk about this boy and the other one and what they did the night before. About Yoruba, one of them said, "Humph! She's trying to get in with our crowd!"

Debutante Brenda Brasswork, of the Crowning Heights Brassworks, agreed enthusiastically. "Yeah! Who does that Black one think she is?"

Silken-haired Brenda, as the saying goes, was mucho light and damn near white, though she'd never been accused of being "quite bright."

The Jeffs put on a different dog. Pamela Jefferson was a sweet-faced, copper-colored girl with eyes that always seemed to be poking loads of fun at you, and everybody else, for that matter. Her mother, Zenith, taught school at Brooklyn College, and thought the whole Cotillion bit was one big good black joke, which she went along with, strictly for the laughs, or maybe for a book she was putting together; she taught the English language. And spoke Afro-Americanese. Pamela's father was a damn good divorce lawyer who dabbled in politics and civil rights and artistic endeavors in his spare time, which was very spare. The Jeffersons were one of the really big first families of Brooklyn—from way back. And everybody knew it. Everybody also knew they lived in a grand old mansion on President Street and that they gave the best parties of any of the great Black first families. These were the real "Black Irish," some said facetiously; others said seriously. Believing it.

Black movie stars, Black athletes and all other kinds of Black leaders and celebrities came to the Jefferson home to party. Like the lady said, the Jeffersons' tea was different from the other teas. First of all, the house was differently decorated. Right? Large, wide, spacious, high-ceilinged rooms. No plastic coverings in sight. No treacherous toilet seats. Second of all, original paintings on the wall of Black happenings by Black artists. Okay? There was even one of Malcolm. Third of all, it was the first home in which Yoruba saw more books than were in Lumumba's pad. Fourth of all, instead of serving tea, the Jeffersons served cocktails. And lastly, fifthly, but not leastly, the Jeffersons dressed in dungarees. Can you dig it? Everybody else was dressed in cocktail dresses, though they did not expect to be served cocktails, nor did they expect the Jeffersons to play jazz and rhythm-and-blues and other uncouth types of music on the finest stereo system Yoruba had ever heard, or even imagined. The Jeffersons had other kinds of funny, uncouth, nasty idiosyncrasies, like sitting on the thickly carpeted floor and laughing loudly like colored people, and doing things they felt like doing, and talking like only colored people had a way of talking. Speaking Afro-Americanese and all that uncouth shit.

Pam Jefferson's mother asked Charlene's mother, "Do you dig Ray Charles?"

Charlene's mother answered, in a vague and horrifying mixture of assorted and affected accents: "Oi don't like jazz, blues, spearchals and that kind of common averday music. Oi prefer the clausics. Oi like Chopping."

Mrs. Jefferson said, "I'm hip. Everybody like chopping. You have to eat to live, but I thought we were discussing music."

"Chopping!" Mrs. Robinson repeated softly, desperately, breaking into a sweat. "He's a great European musician. He lives in Paris." Could she be wrong about this too? Why was Mrs. Jefferson staring at her as if she were a total idiot? Mrs. Brap-bap saved the day, so to speak. "She means Chopin," she explained to Mrs. Jefferson. Then to Mrs. Robinson she said, "Honey, you can't even pronounce him, let alone appreciate him."

When Yoruba and her mother first arrived, Lady Daphne stared aghast at the happenings. She whispered to Yoruba, "Look! Look! They're sitting on the floor! Sitting on the people's pretty carpet! Negras won't do right no matter what you try to do to uplift them. I'll bet anything they from Harlem."

"It's all right, Mother. They're just making themselves at home."

"There's such a thing as carrying things too far."

"It's their home, Mother. That's Pamela and Mrs. Jefferson. They're getting up now to welcome you."

"Well, how was I to know? They look like common ordinary negras."

Okay?

None of the ladies took cocktails at first, excepting, of course, the one and only Beverly Brap-bap and those sophisticated Jefferson people. Most of them just stood around looking stiff and acting stiffly. Then Mrs. Robinson took a drink after the musical dissertation with Jefferson and Brap-bap. Then another lady took a sip, just to be sociable and so as not to offend the hostesses. Then another and another and another. Gradually people began to loosen up and be just who they really were. Excepting Daphne Lovejoy, who refused to be who she really was, possibly because she did not actually know who she really was. It could be a problem when you had pretended all these years.

Jethro Jefferson, Pam's father, came home from the office. He was a long, tall drink of Scotch-and-water, and the girls and ladies were all eyes, he was that tall and Black and handsome, as was the man who came with him, who was a colored movie star. All the ladies oohed and ahed. One of them lost her cool completely. Her feet literally left the floor, defied the laws of gravity, as she leaped about like a grasshopper.

"It's him! It's him!" Mrs. Brasswork shouted. "I can't believe it! I can't believe it! I can't believe it!" Her daughter, Brenda Brasswork, tried to calm her. "Mother! Please! You're making a fool of yourself!" But she kept leaping about like crazy. "I can't believe it! Can't believe it!"

Zenith Jefferson put drinks into the newcomers' hands and took them around and introduced them to the ladies. It was said that a couple of these fancy colored matrons put little puddles in their panties as they met the famous movie star, who shall be nameless at this point. Suffice to say now, he was really big.

After the introductions, Jet Jefferson and his daughter started to do a bad Watusi, and the movie star followed suit, dancing with Yoruba Evelyn. Movie Star would never win a dancing contest, but it mattered little to Yoruba. He was graceful even dancing badly. And he kept up a deep-voiced chatter (he of the deep and lovely voice), telling her how elegant she was and how exquisitely she danced that dance. He asked her questions, but she could not remember how she answered them. "What are you studying in school?" . . . "Are you an artist? Actress? This stupid Cotillion is not for you," he whispered softly. She remembered every word he said. But remembered saying nothing in return. The other ladies got so upset, they started dancing with each other. When Movie Star and Yoruba finished dancing, he said, "Thank you, my lovely lady." And took her hand and kissed it gently.

Brenda Brasswork went around all evening looking mean and mumbling to herself. "Who does she think she is? Dancing with the movie star. Who does that Black bitch think she is? Play with a dog he'll lick you in the mouth."

Now they all surrounded Movie Star, some of them speechless, others taken suddenly with dysentery at the mouth. It must be said, he was a charmer.

When the din subsided, Mrs. Brap-bap asked him, "Why don't you play in some kind of pictures about the Black Experience?"

He stared at her. "That's a good question, madam. That's a very good question."

Daphne Lovejoy said, "She was only kidding. Heh—heh—heh."

Yoruba was shocked at her mother's behavior.

"I am not kidding," Mrs. Brap-bap insisted. "Why do you always play in all them shucking and jiving moving pictures?"

"She's only kidding," Daphne assured him. "Your movies is wonderful!"

All other activity had come to a screeching halt, even including the stereo, as if it too wanted to dig the happenings, the Great Debate. Yoruba could do nothing but stare at her mother. Her mother had not been inside a movie house since she could remember. She always said the seats were not far enough apart or her legs were too long and she got cramps when she sat cramped too long. It was the same excuse she gave, in all her piety, when she didn't feel like going to church. Her legs, her long thin legs, her darling legs, her everlasting aching legs.

Matt Lovejoy figured Daphne *should* have aching legs, as much as she stood on them in the department stores of Manhattan. She was a champeen window-shopper and department-store browser. Sometimes she even ventured as far as Abraham & Straus over in Brooklyn and Alexander's away up in the Bronx. But Macy's was her natural habitat. She browsed so much at Macy's and bought so little, they had a store dick whose instructions were—"Whenever that tall colored lady comes into the store forget everything and everybody else and concentrate on her alone—from the time she sets foot in the store till the minute she leaves." And Lady Daphne would lead the detective dude, unknowingly, a dusty road from floor to floor, up escalator, down elevator, and so on and so forth. But suddenly she had become a film critic, to Yoruba's astonishment.

Mrs. Brap-bap said, "I do not know this lady" (referring to our Blessed Lady of the Bimshires), "and I am not kidding, and you are a great actor, no doubt about it, but the movies you play in are strictly jive, and why don't you do something about it?"

Big-Time Movie Star said, "Madam, I—"

But he didn't finish, because Lady Daphne had taken up the cudgel and she would not let this vulgar Southern nigra woman best her. This nonviolent Christian lady from the Island of the Barbados would hold the cudgel to the end and bat Mrs. Brap-bap on the head with it, if it came to that. "The educated intelligent colored people is with you one hundred percent—"

"How would you know?" Mrs. Brap-bap asked indignantly.

"And likewise the common Black people, they is also with you too. You are making splendid artistic endeavorings. The Black people is not going to picket your pictures. And us colored people is giving you our unadulterated support."

"That's very nice to know, madam, however—"

"So you just go right ahead and make whatever pictures you want to make—It's a free country—"

"But that is precisely the problem, madam. I wish very much to make the pictures I would like to make. Mrs. Brap-bap is exactly right. She—"

"Exactly right?"

"Exactly," Movie Star replied. "She makes the same valid criticism every time we meet. And she isn't kidding. The only problem, she hasn't convinced her husband to go into film productions and leave the dead to bury the dead."

Lady Daphne's thin slash of mouth dropped. Her lips worked soundlessly for a moment. Then the words formed. "Wulla—Wulla—Wulla—" Then she said, "You mean you've met her before? You acquainted with Mrs. Grab-bag?"

"Certainly, madam. We're lovers from way back," Big-Time said jestingly. He took Mrs. Brap-bap into his arms, and you could almost hear the old girl purring. "My wife and her husband have an understanding. That's why you criticize me so severely, isn't it, darling? You want me to be the absolutely greatest, don't you? Excellence is your goal for me." And he kissed her soundly, fully, on the mouth.

The other ladies oohed and ahed. Orgasms can be achieved by vicarious experiences. It was a put-on that Mrs. Brap-bap and Movie Star always put on whenever they met, wherever they met. The love affair was all in fun. But lacking a sense of humor, which should have been her heritage as a colored woman, Lady

Daphne took the whole thing at face value, and she fainted standing up, notwithstanding she fainted with enormous dignity. Can you dig it?

The days went by, the weeks the months the planning and the preparations. The cold sharp breath of winter breathed upon the neck of fall. The rains came, the leaves fell turning golden brown, some trees seemed to have struck fire with the fall-time happenings. Burn, baby! Then came the quiet of the snow. Law-and-order was the thing in winter. Wars were fought all over the earth. Men died for freedom and democracy and Blackness and liberation and communism and socialism and capitalism. Planes crashed, automobiles collided, casualties soared, especially on holidays. Some men just lay in bed and died, mundanely, and without imagination. Through it all the girls prepared for the Grand Cotillion. It was indeed a tribute to their singlefulness-of-purpose. She, the girl, Yoruba, was so busy with the "preparations" she had no time for Lumumba, and saw very little of him, much to her mother's deep delight.

The dancing lessons went apace. Being conscientious, Mr. P. Potts, the Prancer, always called the roll. The very first day, some sweet little mischievous debutante prankster wrote, in addition to her own name, "Hortense Horsecollar" on the attendance sheet. Every Thursday without fail, old Piss Potts, the Prancer, would call for Hortense somewhere near the middle of the roll call. "Hortense Horsecollar—" Clearly and distinctly. The first time he called her name, one of the girls said, "Mr. P. Potts, Hortense's mother told me to tell you that Hortense had to go to her grandmama's funeral down in Chittling Switch, Louisiana." "Oh dear me!" Mr. P. Potts said sympathetically. "That ith too bad. We can't bear to mith these practithes if we're going to be ready to danth in the Cotillion. Can we?" "No sir, Mr. P. Potts." The next Thursday it was another excuse, and another and another. Till one Thursday he brought his big feet down. "Now where ith that young lady?" But this time none of the girls had ever heard of Hortense Horsecollar. "Hortense Horsecollar? You got to be kidding, Mr. P. Potts," Charlene said. "Hortense Horsecollar? That sounds like Horace Horsecollar's old lady. How could that horsey one be a debutante?" Then and there he went to the phone, fled from the giggling girls, to check Hortense out with Mrs. "Prissy" Patterson, who confirmed the girls' suspicions. "Hortense Horsecollar? Mr. Potts, you certainly have to be tiddly-winking."

Okay?

A person with less dedication and missionary fervor would have thrown up his hands then and there. But not Mr. P. Potts. He was a liberal integrationist from his tender heart, a man bent on doing good and bringing culture to the culturally deprived. A Christian-hearted true-believer in the brotherhood of man, and likewise the sisterhood, for that matter. If all Christians were like Mr. P. Potts, the world would be entirely different. Understand?

Notwithstanding, the girls and the boy escorts, who now attended, learned doggedly to waltz, not-again-withstanding they waltzed with a distinctly different idiom that was definitely un-European. They did their own three-quarter time which was African-influenced. They also learned the schottische and the minuet. One evening Mr. Philip Potts asked Yoruba to stay after class.

They sat now in his cubbyhole of an office, the walls were covered top to bottom with pictures of boys and girls in varied and varying stages of dishabille. The floor was cluttered with books and scripts and magazines and whatever else his cubbyhole was cluttered with. Yoruba sat across from her fickle-eyed dance instructor. He blinked his eyes like William Buckley. She sat there amid the clutter without the slightest aprehension, for after all he was not the type to play the role of wolfman, right? If I was a boy, she thought, then I really would have cause to worry. But after all, it's fairly obvious that—

"You're probably wondering why I asked you to thtay the while?"

"Well, you might say I am wondering, yes."

"You have a great future ahead of you, Mith Lovejoy. May I call you Yoruba? It'th thuch a charming and exotic name."

"Yes."

"Thank you very much." He reached into one of his desk drawers and took a bottle of whiskey and poured some in a paper cup. "You don't drink, do you, Mith—I mean, do you, Yoruba?

Well, of courth you don't. What a lovely name—Yoruba Lovejoy."

"Thank you very much."

"I have had my eyeth on you thince the very firth day. You have a tremendouth creative talent. Do you thing?"

"What?"

"Do you thing?"

"I'm not quite sure I—"

"Thing!" he chirped. "Contralto, alto, thoprano."

"Oh!"

"Do you thing?" He threw his head back and blasted at the ceiling with an aria from something or the other.

She stared at him in openmouthed amazement.

"Do you thing, Yoruba?"

She said, "Not exactly, I mean, of course—" She thought, all of us colored people can thing. Even Thidney Poitier.

"Yeth indeed, Mith Lovejoy, Yoruba, that ith—you are truly gifted. Well of courth, the other girlth are gifted altho. They're pretty in a kind of ruthleth callouth way, they're bubbling clumthily over into womanhood thestfully and all that thort of rot, but you—you're altogether different—You know what I mean?"

He stared at her and a great and deep compassion for her and all the underprivileged throughout the earth began to build inside of him and finally to overflow. He wiped his eyes shamefacedly. A man of tender sensitivities.

He repeated, "You know what I mean?"

"No sir." She almost said, "No thir." She wondered at his tears. He was such a sweet man, this conscientious softhearted one, serious and sincere beyond imagination. She was almost moved to tears herself. She thought: If all the world were like Mr. P. Potts, how very different men would be!

He poured himself another drink. "My cold ith getting villainouth. Athian flu ith making the rounds, you know. Damn Chineeth probably thent it over here." He laughed, he-he-he-he, and took another drink. It was more a giggle than a laugh.

"Mr. Potts, I have another appointment. I mean, I'm in a kind of hurry—" She hated to be mean to one so tenderhearted.

"Of courth—of courth, my dear. A girl like you, your age, and all that kind of rot, you're obviouthly in a hurry. Now then. Tell me, what are you planning to do with your lovely thelf, in thith life, I mean, career-withe, I mean with your inherent creativity—Did you thay you were a thinger?"

His eyes were crossing over each other, as if they had been waiting for the red light to change and finally concluded that it never would. His eyes were lit with red all right. And crossing over and back again, flitting over back and forth, as if they could not make up their mind. He got up and came around the desk and stood beside her, and put his arm carelessly around her shoulders. In a gesture of pure and unadulterated fatherliness.

"You were meant to be an artitht, my dear, and Uncle Potty ith going to thee to it. Let uth thay, I want to be your godfather. Do you have one? I thuthpect not. Now let me thee, you did thay you were a thinger, didn't you?" He put his hand gently upon her neck. "Now then, let uth have it from the larynth. Let uth hear the lovelieth thound you ever made."

"This, I mean, sir—Mr. P. Potts—I mean—"

"Now—now—" he tut-tutted. "None of that girlith nonthenth. Thith ith all for art'th own prethious thake and abtholutely for no other reason. Now then let me have a thound from here. Beautiful thound, come forward inthantly, pleath. The lovely lady ith in a hurry and tho am I."

She thought, Why not humor the poor man and get it over with. No need to start a scene. Surely one with wrists so limp could not mean me any harm. He's just a queer one like some artists are. And much much queerer than most. And more compassionate.

So she gave out soft and clear with her best soprano thing.

He cleared his throat. "Not bad—not bad at all." His eyes were crossing fiercely now, and red like lanterns, as if a flame were burning in them. His hand descended gently now almost unnoticed and came to rest upon the space between her budding breasts. "Now then, dareth one of all, let uth have it from the diaphragm. Thweetly from the diaphragm."

This is carrying things a bit too far, she thought. But surely one as sweet and queer as he could mean no harm, she told herself. She started to move away, when suddenly the queer sweet one grabbed the nipple of her breast, and she went over backward in her chair, so taken aback was innocent Yoruba. Her shoe toe came into sharp contact with his chin and a couple of teeth leaped gaily from his mouth onto the floor. Undaunted he pursued the lass, face claret, and not from wine this time.

"Let me have it from your diaphragm!" he shouted as he pounced upon her. But he had lost all sense of direction, because the place he tried to kiss her was far beneath her diaphragm. Unless here again it was a case of noncommunication. There are diaphragms and diaphragms. Tears crisscrossed down his cross-eyed face.

"Mr. Potts!" the dear girl screamed as she kicked and scrambled. "Mr. P. Potts!"

"Don't deny me! Don't deny me!" he pleaded pitifully. "You can thave me from thith dethperate thnakepit of ambivalenth. I can be a man! I know I can, and only you can help me find the way. Pleath my deareth darling, help me!"

She scrambled from beneath him as he pleaded like a maniac. "Help me! Help me! Don't deny me. Find compathum in your heart of hearth to help me! And we can help each other!"

"Help each other!"

"Yeth! Yeth! Help each other. We are both unloved! Both dethpithed! Both unloved!" He had read all the good books he could lay his hands on on the color question. He had pondered the question, fretted over it, day and night, thought about it pro and con. Dreamed it. And had come to the conclusion that, since the books clearly proved beyond a reasonable doubt that Black men did not, could not, love Black women, then it was up to men like him to fill the gap. His own problems with white women proved the other question, that white women had no eyes for white men, sexually, that is. Now he felt somehow a martyr in the present situation. Literature vindicated him. He was a missionary all the way.

He chased her around the cubbyhole. He hemmed her in a corner. He grabbed her and began to slobber over her, his mouth bleeding; his liquored-bloody breath almost did her in, but she got strength from some unknown source inside of her, and she reached out and took a vase nearby and broke it over poor Mr. P. Potts's sweaty cranium. But the queer little dear kept coming on. His head bloodied but unbowed. She made it out of the office door and he chased her across the studio, pleading pitfully all the while. "Dear Black beauty, you're my lath clear chance! Thave me! Thave me! Only a lovely one like you can thave me!" She could still hear him as she ran down the seven flights of stairs to the nighttime streets below. Stumbling along in disarray, weeping all the while, she made it to the subway and rode all the way to Harlem. She cleaned herself up in the ladies room, and got herself together. Then she made it to Lumumba's crib and into the Captain's arms.

Now there in the Captain Quarters on his couch in his arms, she felt safe and sheltered from the raging storm outside. All the way uptown she told herself that she must get to him, to her Captain, and nothing could harm her, if she could just get to him in time all would be all right with her and she would be secure. She burrowed her head into the fold of his arms, leaning heavily on his chest. Safe! Safe! Safe! Safe in the arms of Ben Ali!

"What's the matter? What happened?"

"If you hadn't been at home I don't know what I would have done. I don't know what I would have done!"

"What happened, baby? What's the matter?"

Burrowing deeper into all of him. Laughing now. "All the way uptown, I told myself, if I can just make it to the Captain's Quarters, everything will be all right. If I can just make it there, no harm can come to me. But-but-but, what if you had been out. What if you had had somebody else with you?" She, now laughing, crying, laughing. The safer she felt, the more she cried for the joy of feeling safe.

"Well—well—well," Lumumba said. "They say that God is good and looks out for the innocent. Now I did start to go out tonight, but something kept me here, and I just sat around listening to the righteous sounds and did some more work on the book and waited for the princess to come and let me know she still thought of me sometime. Mental telepathy and whatnot."

She said, "I would have just died if you hadn't been home. I believed I would have killed myself."

He said, "A lovely one like you does not just die. A fox like you will never kill herself. Maybe you would have been a little disappointed that I wasn't thoughtful enough to be here in the Captain's Quarters when you finally got around to thinking of me in the context of your busy debutanty schedule. Now then tell me what happened to make you think of Captain Lumumba."

How could she tell him about the little cross-eyed fairy godfather dance teacher, who wanted her to be his mammy? And he a mammy-lover. Lumumba would probably go downtown and beat the white off the faggot, maybe kill him, and get into worlds of trouble he would not get out of in a lifetime. He had always fought her battles for her up and down the block when they were children, in the far-off time. If a bully picked on her, he had to deal with her skinny Black Knight. She couldn't tell her father either and for the same reason. "Nothing happened," she said. "It was just that all of a sudden all of the world was such a sad and lonely place, a stormy raging sea, and I just felt so tossed about, and I just realized how much I missed the Captain, and I just had to see him."

He said, "Okay. All right. You win. God save the Queen. Captain Lumumba at your service, your royal of all highnesses." And took her into his arms again and kissed her deeply and profoundly.

He kissed her eyes, each in their own dark turn. "My Yoruba! Black and beautiful Yoruba! How many times did I walk the roads of Yoruba—land in faraway Abeokuta—Ibadan—" He kissed her mouth again. "And thought of you, sweet Yoruba—looked for you in the soft eyes of Yoruba women—" He kissed her cheeks. "All dressed they were in blue they were—Soft blue dresses." He kissed the corners of her mouth. "The way they walked—great-goda'mighty! The way they walked!" He kissed her ears. And he turned her on with talk and kisses. "But it was always you—you—Yoruba—you—you! I thought of, always looked for, you—Sometimes, I remembered you as you used to be at six, seven, eight years old—And yet I looked for you, the woman you, in Benin City, as if a miracle could happen."

When she was with her Captain, she needed no strong drinks, or pot, to turn her on; he could take her on a trip with words, set her sailing out to sea, with verbs and nouns and adjectives. He kissed her on her lips again, and she felt rivulets of sweetest feelings run the course of her entire being. And she held on to him, in a kind of desperation now, the sea was really choppy, and she'd never learned to swim. Now she felt the Captain's gentle hands all over her, talking all the while, "You, Yoruba, you, Yoruba," all the private secret places of her, tenderly did he explore. She thought she heard herself screaming, but not a sound came forth. Save me, Captain! Save me! Save me from sinking down.

She felt herself being lifted gently firmly from the sea into the Captain's arms. He laid her on the Captain's bunk, the couch. She felt herself as in a dream being dispossessed of her underthings, she thought she hoped she mouthed a feeble protest. When he laid her back upon the couch, she thought that she would truly sink this time as the great awful terrible wonderful waves washed over her, gaining force each time, and she reached up to him. Save me! Save me! Take me! Take me! And he took her, and they rode the waves together, moving ever toward the shore, they took the mighty waves together. Higher! Higher! Higher! Painful, painful, was this first ride for her, blood and pain and joyous feelings, all converging as they rode the swells like great surf-riders.

But being one who naturally knew the ocean, he was the Captain and seaworthy, and, of course, he reached the shore ahead of her, as she thrashed amongst the waves, heaving, sighing, breathing heavy, in all her inexperience, in an awful desperation, thought the world was lost forever; so he stayed the tides for moments, long and agonizing moments, and came back to bring her with him. She, floundering and faltering, thinking: I can't make it! I'll never make it! I'll die here among the waves, amidst the blood and sweat and tears! Weeping now in great frustration. But the Captain firm and gentle, tough and tender all the way. He, the wise and patient Captain, whispering: "Take it easy, I'm here with you. Wouldn't leave you for the world." They began again together. He, her one and only Captain, kissed her eyes, salty-sweet with tears, kissed her trembly vacillating lips. No! No! Yes! Yes! Let us try another time another day. Never ever again! His dear sophisticated tongue caressed her ears, "Shh—be quiet—" tongued deliciously her breasts, her darling bellybutton, her tippy-toes atingle now, his sensitive fingers, touching everything now, like a great maestro conjuring exquisite music from a masterpiece of instrument, all the secret private only-for-him places, touching all and tuning up and turning on. A symphony of feelings, an ebony rhapsody, "Oh yes! Yes! Yes! Lumumba!" Softly whispering to her, "Take it easy! Take it easy! Take it easy! My Yoruba!" She, the girl, Yoruba, thinking, Can I? Can I? Will I ever? I can't! I can't! I can't! We can—we can—As they stroked for shore again. Slower, slower was the painful rhythm. Oh yes we can—Oh yes we can—We must—We must—You see—my lovely queen—we did —Yes, but—yes, but—I understand, my darling Ruba, it will never be like this again—You'll see—next time we'll really make the shore together—together—together—always together. Without pain we'll make the shore.

Now they lay there panting in the sweet smell of the salty sea, the salty bloody smell the virgin soil of love had made. Lay there where the blessed beachhead was established, as the ebbing tide receded. Lay there basking 'neath a rainbow at the end of love's horizon which was also the beginning.

Now the Captain's eyes surveyed the lovely landscape, as the dear princess slept serenely on the Captain's bunk—breathing softly, fearing nothing with the Captain's arms embracing her. He had pulled back all the covers without the dear queen's knowledge. She only half heard him now as his voice began to bring her back from her exquisite slumber. She, the girl, Yoruba, was in that never-ever land between sleep and wake like the moments in between moon-down and sunrise, when the dogs begin to move around and the chicks begin to stir out in the sticks, just before the city lights go off. The newsboy and the milkman's time.

She heard Lumumba as if from far away, coming closer, fading further, now closer, now further. "Your breasts are like what? Plump cupcakes with darksweet rare grapes at the center. Or are they cone-shaped honeycombs tipped with wild sweet muscadines. Your hips so darkly round and black and brown, a million shades, and sweetly slim. The sweet slope of your stomach around your sunken bellybutton. Your hair so dark and shortly cropped and pubic and shining blue-black triangle of our love—the pubic hair is the loveliest dearest most exquisite hair in all the world, there is no hair like this, there never was." He laughed. "They should cover up the tophead hair of womankind and let the lovely hair of maidenhead be brought to light."

When she awakened fully, the modest child let out a squeal of very deep embarrassment. She quickly reached for the Captain's bedsheet and covered her embarrassment. The Captain laughed and laughed and laughed. Until she slapped the Captain's face.

They say we always hurt the ones we love.

CHAPTER EIGHT

"EENIE, MEENIE"

Eenie, Meenie, Minie, Moe—
Who will take her to the show?
To the Grand Cotillion Ball?

There was this list the Committee gave to the girls to choose their escorts from. And here is what the list was like.

John Lord Fauntleroy, Junior
Twenty years old
High school graduate at Rhodes
Attending Harvard University (that is when he goes to school)
Father—Successful businessman (business especially to do with monkeys)

Every time the list went around, some of the mischievous girls of the Crowning Heights would add their own remarks (in parenthesis) about the boys. They knew these boys from way back when.

Roderick Jonathan Latham, Esquire
Nineteen years old
Student at Rockefeller-on-the-Hudson
He is the only colored one in his class (a funky pot-smoking bushy-haired Black militant, a double agent after dark with his blond-wigged blue-eyed wenches.
He himself wears blue-tinted contact lenses. But he's a "militant!")

Rutherford Van Bismark, the Fifth
Twenty-two years of age
Attended Harvard, Yale, Columbia, Fisk, Oberlin, Antioch (still attending—they had to burn down Jock Strap Prep to get him

out of high school, so maybe there's still hope for him. Baby, burn, baby!)

William Amos Goldberg, the Second
Nineteen years old
Attending Princeton
(sweating it out)
Father—railroad executive
(English translation: Pullman porter, superintendent of the beds and toilets)

And so forth and so on. You could pick one from this impressive list or pick one of your very own choosing, subject, of course, to the Committee's approval. The only requirements by the Committee were that the deserving lad should be of superior family background, first family and all that, second-generation Brooklyn at the very least; doctor's, lawyer's, preacher's son. Heir of teacher, celebrity, athlete, postal clerk, and so on. He should be nice-looking, Nordically speaking, preferably light of skin in coloration, skinny-lipped, soft-headed, on the top, and Heaven forbid, he must not wear a process, he definitely must not conk his hair. Afros are not smiled upon. He must be suave, urbane, presentable, must have a good reputation, regardless of his character. These instructions came down as the gospel according to the Femmes Fatales Committee.

They got into a real hassle over the subject of the men's hairstyles. "To do or not to do," Yoruba whispered to Charlene Robinson. Somehow, from the question of do-rags and Afros the conversation wandered all over the place. "It's a simple question of do-process," the cheeky-tongued Mrs. Brap-bap asserted. Then there was, of course, the Great Debate between integration and Black Power. Mrs. Prissy (P.P.) Patterson came out firmly and unequivocally for integration. "It's what the colored people want. I know those people inside and out. They don't want any power at all, and they are nonviolent to the core. I discussed the whole thing with my cook and she agreed with me."

Are you ready?

Most of the young debutantes-to-be had already chosen their escorts and they had been approved. But the choice of escort had become a real big thing with Yoruba. Should she pick one from the chosen list? From the sons of doctors, lawyers, preachers, teachers and assortments of celebrity? From the so-called colored bourgeoisie? She was tempted to, for, after all, wasn't that what the whole thing was all about?

Like her father said, the whole business of cotillions and debutante balls and whatnot was something the rich white folks learned long ago from cattle farming. "One good bull is half the herd," Matt said. "That's what the whole thing is all about."

Her mother was speechless for a moment, which was like saying the ocean had run dry, or that camel piss was in meager supply at Timbuktu, this woman who was never at a loss for words, of special wisdom. But that her husband should use such blasphemy in speaking of such a sacred shining symbol of Western culture! Even her crosses deserted her somehow. She couldn't even chips this time. She looked up at the ceiling as if she thought the Lord would surely smite them all dead for such a sacrilege. Lightning would suddenly strike this house at any moment. "How-how-how you mean—cattle farming?" They were seated at the kitchen table.

"Ask any cattle rancher," Big Matt said. "One good bull's worth half the herd. Get youself a bull that's good and strong, one of them that can last the whole fifteen rounds, and you naturally in bizness. This ain't no three-round fight. He got to have lasting power, cause them heifers'll damn sure work him overtime. He got to be like John-damn-Henry and Joe Louis combinated."

Daphne looked from him to Yoruba, as if to say, "You usually understand your father's stupidnesses. Translate this abomination for me." She turned to him again. Her café-au-lait had somehow changed to crimson. "What in the devil you talking about? Fifteen rounds—lasting power—bullfighting—prizefighting—cattle ranching—" The color left her cheeks entirely.

He puffed away on his smelly pipe, and refused to upset himself just because she was upset, which drove her further to the brink of temper tantrum. An ignorant Black man like him pretending to intelligence. And had the arrogance to be arrogant about it! He said quietly, "That's the whole trouble with you colored peoples imitating white folks. You try to do everything they do, without even knowing how come they doing what they doing in the first place, or the second place, either one. You like a monkey with straight razor. You cut your damn throat tryna imitate your master."

Out of the corner of her eye Lady Daphne saw Yoruba smiling, encouraging her father in his "nigger" ignorance. "And where did you inherit so much intelligence? Did you graduate from Oxford?"

His soft eyes twinkled. "I graduated from the greatest little old university in all the entire world."

"And you kept it a deep dark secret all these years?" She, now, smiling her sweet smile of contempt.

"I graduated at the top of the class from the University of Hard Knocks and Disappointments. I got my degree in Mother Wit. I took my classes where I found them on the streets of Harlem U. I trickulated at the University of Pennsylvania Station. That oughta qualify me as a expert on white folks and colored peoples. I know the white man cause I done handled all his baggage. I'm a expert on the Negro on accounta I been one all my born days. I know what the white man putting down, cause I been picking it up for almost thirty years, and long before!"

Daphne turned to Yoruba again, then back to Matthew. "Mawn, talk some damn intelligence for once in your stupid life! Make an effort, at least." She was shouting now. "This is the most important moment in your daughter's life and you talking some more of your nigger stupidness!" She turned to Yoruba again. "Now you see your father for what he is. You, his darling doting daughter, come to him with a serious question and he starts talking about cattle ranching and bullfights and whoring around with heifers and a whole lot of other shit!" It was a word she seldom ever used, as if it were a pastime in which queens like herself did not participate.

"Mother, you never understand Father, because you don't ever listen to him."

"Cause he ain't never saying nothing worth listening to. You just heard him and his fifteen-round bullfights."

Matt said, "Let me break it down for you. White folks invented these debitramp balls so that their darling little heifers could git a good shot at the prize bull in the pasture."

"Now we're shooting the bull," Daphne commented sarcastically, pun entirely unintended—she, unaware that she had made a pun.

He chuckled. "But colored folks just do these things cause they see white folks doing them. It ain't no investment like it is with white folks. All the money ends up in Whitey's hands again. To the dance teacher, to the beauty peoples, to Mr. Waldorf. It's just some more white folks' foolishness that don't git Black folks nowheres except in debt. Like Santa Claus and Easter bonnets, it all ends up in Charlie's pockets."

She, the girl, Yoruba, sat there listening to her parents. Listening to the Great Debate and remembering the last Instruction Meeting. At Pattersons. Mrs. Prissy Patterson giving the historical background of the Femmes Fatales in her own inimitable fashion.

"Girls, young ladies, the Grand Cotillion of the Femmes Fatales is in the proud tradition of the Brooklyn upper clawses. Of the Brooklyn upper clawses." She was so proper she didn't understand herself sometimes. Most of the times she spoke as if her slender nostrils were forever clogged. Her thin mouth almost tightly shut, the words came sliding past her teeth like Harvard Yard or Barclay Square. Lumumba had told Yoruba that Englishmen talk the way they do because they keep green peas in their nostrils to keep out the horrific London weather. But what was Miss P.P.'s excuse? "Our club is in the tradition of the Girl Friends, and the Links, and Jack and Jills, but each one of the clubs give their cotillions with their own unique and individualistic style, varying creatively from club to club." Clearing her throat. Her name was Priscilla Patterson. At first, the dear girls named her Prissy Pat. Then they went from Prissy Pat to Miss Pee Pee, affectionately. "From club to club. Now, the Brooklyn Cotillions have a history behind them. We are not fly-by-night. We are not fly-by-night."

"How come she got that broomstick then?" Charlene whispered, loudly whispered.

"Fifty years ago our fathers brought forth—"

"Upon this swampland—" Mrs. Brap-bap interjected.

Miss Prissy stared through her green-tinted contact lenses at her "vulgar" counterpart. She cleared her throat. "Our fathers brought forth, they established an aristocracy."

"An aristocracy of the niggeratti—" was Brap-bap's contribution. Priscilla Patterson stamped her feet. "You will just have to stop these vulgar interruptions. My father was the founding father of the nigger Cotill—I mean we didn't allow any niggers in the Cotillions in the good old days when my father foundered—I mean—"

Yoruba raised her hand and asked, in all her nubile innocence, "Was your floundering father a white man?" Okay, so nobody is entirely innocent. Right?

"Certainly not!" Miss Prissy answered. "Certainly not!"

"What was he then, Mrs. Patterson, if he wasn't a Negro? Was he an Indian?"

"A *West* Indian?" one of the young innocents mumbled out of a corner of her pouting lips. "A monkey chaser!"

Pam Jefferson was cracking up with unladylike laughter.

"Certainly not!" Miss Prissy answered. "Certainly not!" She had heard La-hyphenated-Smythe's aside, and her eagle-beaked nostrils flared with a righteous indignation. Almost exhaling fire. "My father came from Charleston, South Carolina. Came from Charleston, South Carolina."

"He was a Saltwater Geechie," Charlene suggested. "That's a West Indian with a Southern accent."

Miss Prissy was speechless now with rage. She shook her head so hard Yoruba thought her red-haired wig would surely fall off. It was disheveled now, and sliding from east side to west side and all around the crown. Finally she shouted hoarsely, "Not Geechie! Not Geechie!"

Not white, not a Negro, not an Indian, or West Indian, not a Carolina Saltwater Geechie even. "What then, Mrs. Patterson? What then?" A man had to have been something, Yoruba thought.

Miss Prissy said, "He was an aristocrat. That's what my father was. My father was."

Charlene Robinson asked sarcastically, "What race or nation puts out them kind of people?"

"All right," Mrs. Patterson said. "My father was an octoroon."

From Charlene: "What's an octoroon? He's a Negro, isn't he?"

Mrs. Patterson sighed like it was her last breath on this happy earth. "My heavens! No! An octoroon is the offspring of a white person and quadroon."

"All right," Charlene said. "What's a quadroon? I know he's got to be a Negro."

"A quadroon is decidedly not a Negro."

Mrs. Brap-bap gave out with her favorite all-encompassing comment. "Sheee-it!"

"A quadroon is the offspring of a mulatto and a white. Mulatto and a white."

"Okay," Charlene said. "Now please, m'am, tell us what a mulatto is."

Miss Prissy was completely breathless now. Uphill all the way like she was pumping on an English bike. And yet she mustered strength from some unknown source. She whispered, "A mulatto is the offspring of one who's white and the other who is Black."

"In other words," Mrs. Brap-bap said, "an octoroon is a Negro, a quadroon is a Negro, a mulatto is a Negro, a Negro is a Negro is a Negro, and after all your shucking and jiving, your founding father wasn't nothing but a spook whose mother got messed over by a white man."

"Well, anyhow, he had white blood. He had white blood. His blood was whiter than it was Black. And I have whiter blood than anybody in the Femmes Fatales! Than *anybody* in the Femmes Fatales!"

"Okay," Mrs. Brap-bap said. "We'll have a white-blood competition some other time. Right now we're supposed to be concerned with the history of the club."

Prissy Patterson said, "All right, Mrs. Brap-bap. As I was saying, girls, as I was saying, my father lived on Herkimer Street, which was where the elite colored people lived. First families and all that rot. And all that rot."

Mrs. Brap-bap was Mrs. Patterson's unauthorized interpreter. An expert translator, she broke everything down from English into Afro-Americanese. She said, "First Black families to work in the white folks' houses. Cooks, maids, chauffeurs. Redcaps, Pullman porters. Waiting tables at Gage and Tollner's was a status symbol."

"The place where we are now was farmland owned by the Van Nostrand family, who resided on Carroll Street," Mrs. Patterson continued breathlessly. Her voice was trembly now. She closed her eyes, carried away as if she was in a kind of ecstasy of nostalgia. "Oh my dears, those were the good old days of the colored aristocracy. The colored aristocracy. Before they opened up the Eighth Avenue subway and the Black ignorant mawses moved in on us." Her eyes were filling up now and brimming over. "Before the Black ignorant mawses moved in on us. And pushed us upward to the Heights. To the Heights."

"To greater heights, Mrs. Patterson?" Yoruba asked, in all her innocence.

"To Crowning Heights," Miss Prissy answered. "Oh my! What parties they used to give! Money was no object! Money was no object!"

"They out-whited the rich white folks. From Friday through till Sunday evening they partied—" Mrs. Brap-bap said.

"Yes!" Mrs. Patterson exhaled a deep sigh. "Yes!"

"The good times rolled and the whiskey flowed," Brap-bap said.

"Yes!" Mrs. Patterson's eyes were still shut tight, the easier to recreate the images of all those glorious yesteryears, "Yes!" of tinkling glasses, cultured laughter, "Yes!" of loyal servants moving swiftly back and forth, savages-of-the-noble-stripe, softly gliding, "Yes!" on tiptoes, anticipating every whimsical aristocratic desire, "Yes!" lazy, shuffling, white eyeballs bucking, cunning, sly and thieving; sometimes the images collided, and fantasy did mortal combat with reality. "Yes!" Mrs. Patterson was on a trip now into a world with Alice in the Land of Wonder. "The good old days," she said, "before the colored gentlefolk were overrun by the Black hordes on the subway trains."

"And the strong men kept coming on!" Yoruba mumbled.

"Black hordes on the subway trains," Mrs. Patterson repeated. "Not all things concomitant with the Age of the Machine have happened for the best, I fancy."

Mrs. Brap-bap interjected. "From Friday night till Sunday evening they swung their partners, drank their champagne, balled a proper Jack, but then they closed the shutters and kept them closed from Sunday night till the next Friday rolled around, to dodge the pesky bill collectors."

"Yes, my Lord! those were the days," Miss Prissy said, "when all the colored families of the aristocracy had a splendid staff of servants."

"The days when 'cousin clubs' were born," Brap-bap interpolated.

Yoruba said, "Cousin clubs?"

Brap-bap said, "You heard me—'*cousin clubs.*' Migrant workers. They would have them shipped up here from Virginia, Georgia and Barbados and South Carolina, right out the cotton patch and the cane fields, and live with them to help them pay them mortgages. They were paying guests, but since the colored muck-the-mucks were not supposed to let rooms for rent, these people were palmed off to everybody else as first cousins, second cousins, distant cousins. High-yaller families with jet-black cousins."

"Well!" Mrs. Patterson said, coming back to earth, and suddenly. "I never! I just really truly never!"

"Then there were the 'elite cousins' who helped to pay the mortgage, ate with the family and hobnobbed with the Big Shit visitors."

"Well! Ooooh!"

"Then there were the 'domestic cousins' who slept in and did all the housework. And lastly but not leastly, there were the 'slave cousins' who helped with the housework, then went out to work every day and helped to pay the bills, and stayed upstairs when company came. It was all messed up. Sometimes, even the first families couldn't get it straight. Sometimes the 'cousins' were actually servants with no other relationship. Sometimes the servants were actually cousins helping them to hang on to the house. It could really get confusing. If they were really cousins, they were palmed off as servants. If they were really servants they were palmed off as cousins."

She vaguely heard her family now, as she drifted back to the now time of the Great Debate. Her mother was saying, almost screaming, "You ain't got a tuppence worth of intelligence!"

"You mighty damn right! If I'da had any sense I would've put my foot down from the first damn start!" He usually spoke in softer tones, even when upset. "I shoulda said keep that ignorant Cotillion foolishness outa my house and been done with it."

"Every time peoples like the Fem Fatales try to uplift the Colored Race, ignorant niggers like you try to drag them down. That's the trouble with the nigger man—"

"Them Fat Asses ain't tryna lift up no damn Colored Race. They tryna run off and leave the Race and innergrate into the white folks. That's what the Grand-damn-Cotillion is all about—to make little white sissies outa the colored educated boys and girls. Turn the cream of the crap against the poor Black people."

"Fem Fat Tails! Fem Fat Tails!" Miss Daphne screamed. "Not Fat Asses! Not Fat Asses!"

Yoruba was smiling now, unknowingly. Her mother turned to her and demanded, "What in the devil are you laughing at?" She stopped for a moment to catch her breath. She stared up at the ceiling as if she prayed for God's assistance at this trying moment. She slowed down momentarily. She looked back at Yoruba. "Who is going to be your escort?"

"Ma'm?"

"It ain't no laughing matter," her mother told her. "This is one of the most important decisions of our lives. Who's going to be your escort?"

Yoruba swallowed hard, then spoke just above a whisper. Fearful. "I thought I might invite Ben Ali Lumumba." Lightning would really strike this time.

"Who?" her mother asked. Calmer now.

"Ben Ali Lumumba."

"Who is he? Do I know him? What do his father does? Who is his peoples? Was he on the pre-ferrable list?" Almost pleasantly.

"I'm talking about Ernest Billings, Mother. He calls himself Lumumba now."

Her mother stared at her, the enormity of the vicious prank being played on her by these two, her avowed beloveds, sinking into her consciousness. Her eyes were hot with anger, maybe hatred even. These two whom she had given every single iota of her selfdom got no greater pleasure out of life than the delight they had in frustrating her. Every plan she ever had, everything she ever worked for was for advancing them and they got their kicks from her frustration. She mumbled, "Black! Black! Black! Black!" And louder, "Nigger! Nigger! Nigger! Nigger!" She shouted, "No! No! No! You can't do this to me! Eve-lyn! Dearie, how can you hate your mother so? Lord, Saviour, look at my crosses! See my crosses, blessed boychild of the Holy Virgin! After all I went through kissing all them haughty nigger asses to get you into this damn Cotillion!"

"But Mother, Ben Ali is a gentleman. He's—"

"He's a wort'less Black woolly-head nigger, and I should have got me a pistol and blowed his brains out when he was seven or eight years old the first time I saw him grinning in your face."

Lady Daphne sat there now staring from one to the other of her tormentors. "No," she mumbled to herself. "It cannot be—it cannot be—it cannot be!" She shook her head from side to side. "Before I see you marry that wort'less woolly-head nigger man, I blow your brains out, if you got any, and go serenely to the electric chair."

"We are not talking about marriage, Mother. We're talking about an escort to the Cotillion—"

"Why ain't you do like the rest of the young ladies and get yourself a nice boy from the university?"

"I don't know any nice boys from the university, Mother. I—"

"A boy with light skin and with good hair, a doctor or a lawyer's son. That's what I've dreamed of all my life for you. That way your children would be pretty, and would have a chance with white folks." She looked around her at her husband who was smiling grimly now. "Talk to her, Matt. You know what I'm trying to teach her. She'll listen to you."

Matt shook his head. "It's up to Ruba. He ain't gon be taking me to no Cotillion. If she want to invite Lumumba, I don't see harm in it."

Daphne got up and walked the floor. Tears were spilling from her eyes now. She put a wet towel to her forehead. She sat down at the table again. She lowered her voice. "Now," she said, "let us be like sensible people. Let's not get overheated and excited. Can't we discuss this calmly? Now," she said, "he ain't a bad boy. I have nothing against him. But he just wouldn't be comfortable around these other people, the muck-the-mucks, first families and etcetera. He wouldn't fit in."

Big Matt said, "How do you know a key won't fit unless you try it?"

She ignored him, emphatically. "He's a nice boy, Eve-lyn. I ain't doubt it, but he'd be out of place. It's not his fault he hasn't got no culturation."

"Like the white folks say, he'd be happier with his own kind." Matt's own brand of sweet sarcasm.

Yoruba shook her head. "Ben Ali is the most cultured man I ever met. He's read more books than all the boys on the Committee's list put together and multiplied."

"You ain't understand," Daphne told her. "My dear, you just ain't understand."

"No, Mother, it's you who do not understand. Lumumba has rubbed shoulders with more cultures in his young life than most people will in a whole lifetime. He is a very cultured man."

"He's not going to be your escort! Get that through your woolly head!" she shouted. "I'll not stand for it! I'll not stand for it!"

Matt said, "Sit down then. And hold your water."

She sat down and tried to reason with her willful wayward daughter. "He'll make you shame, walking in there with that bushy nappy head of his. White peoples come to these Grand Cotillions to watch the niggers put on airs. What'll they think when they see him coming into a place like the Waldorf looking like King Kong? He'd never make it through the lobby. Ain't you got no pride about you?"

"I'm so proud of myself, Mother, I don't care what white folks think. I know I'm Black and beautiful."

"And besides," Lady Daphne argued, "you got a good opportunity to win the scholarship, to be the Queen of the Ball, Miss Grand Cotillion of this year of our Gracious Lord."

Yoruba smiled. It was a rare kind of smile for Lumumba's Queen of Sheba. A smile of sweet sarcasm almost verging on contempt. "I do not want to be queen of any ball, Mother."

"A thousand dollars ain't nothing to smile at. You be able to go to Smith or Radcliffe in September. All kinda high-class people in them kinda high-class places. Marry excellent and live a splendiferous career as a married lady. I looking out for your future, Eve-lyn darling." The great lady paused to catch her breath. "You're a Black girl, but the ladies of the club ain't holding your color against you. That's cause you Black but comely, like the Holy Bible says. These is Christian ladies. You got a chance to win the grand prize."

"I'm thrilled," the girl said, ironically.

"But to pick that woolly-head Black one for your escort, that's a donkey of another coloration. You wouldn't have a Chinaman's chance to win the scholarship, and I wouldn't blame the judges neither."

"I am Black and beautiful, Mother, and so is Ben Ali Lumumba." Lady Daphne wiped her eyes, and shifted gears again. "Have you thought about the boy? What a burden you'll be putting on him? Associating with all them hi-faluting peoples. It wouldn't be fair to the poor underprivileged feller." She honked her nose.

"You got to be kidding, Mother."

"And besides, he'd have to buy a tuxedo and tails and so forth. And that would be a financial burden on the dear boy. I mean, where would he get the money from? Do he have a job?" Daphne had changed her tactics again, in midstream. Her voice was dripping now with the human milk of kindness, or gentle words to that effect. She had wasted her adult life in an aging tenement in Harlem, when she might have been a great actress. She might have been the first colored queen of celluloid. It was a shame that Oscar Micheaux had not discovered her, or vice versa, take your choice.

Yoruba said, "He is a writer, Mother. And he's going to be a great one one of these days."

"Yes, but meanwhile he has to eat until the world learn about how great he is. Where do he work when he ain't at sea?"

Yoruba said, "The world already knows about him." Proudly she picked up the newspaper. "Look," she said. "His picture is in the *Amsterdam News*. He's already famous." She poured it on. "He's already published in the *Black Page* and the *Harlem Journal* and the *Negro Digest*."

"What do niggers know?" her mother asked. "I mean white folks, they're the ones that count in this world."

"He's very popular, Mother, with the Harlem literati, the avant garde."

"I asked you, where do he work when he is not at sea?"

"He's working on a book, Mother. And his publishers have given him a thousand dollars advance. He's not going to sea anymore. That's what the story in the *Amsterdam* is all about."

Lady Daphne's eyes lit up like glowworms. Against her will she was impressed. White folks did not throw their money around on wort'less no-count vagabunds. Then suspicion filled her face. "How you mean—a thousand dollars? How you know it is for true?"

Yoruba answered, with deep pride mixed up with impatience. "He showed me the letter and the check."

Daphne's voice softened. There must be more to the boy than she suspected. If the white man gave him a thousand dollars, there must be something to the boy, woolly head and all. She said, "If he'd just clean himself up and get a haircut and look like somebody. I've got nothing in my heart against the boy." Meanwhile she would bide her time.

Yoruba went to her mother and put her arms around her neck and kissed her. "I love you too," her mother said. Her father laughed.

Each time she saw Lumumba in the Captain's Quarters his eyes seemed to get redder and redder, and she feared the implications. This night was worse than ever. His eyes were smoky red like lighted lanterns. He took her in his arms and kissed her lightly on the lips. He sailed across the room, poured wine for the two of them, and sat across from her, sipping; and he said all the usual things to her, but it was like going absentmindedly through all the motions, dress-rehearsal time, as if she really did not exist for him in time and space. In this *now* time in *this* place. He was like a man sleepwalking. With his red eyes open. It seemed he had put out to sea. He had set sail, and was sailing. Maybe "flying" was more like it.

He said, "How's the Queen of Sheba?"

She said, "I'm fine." Like she always said.

"I know you're fine. Don't be so arrogant about it." Just like he always said. "I mean, how're you feeling, I mean, what's happening?"

She said, "What's the matter, Ben Ali? You're not here. Your eyes so red like fire—I mean—I mean you seem to be someone somewhere else. I try to reach you but you're not here. You're a thousand miles away at sea. A trip—"

He laughed and came across the room to her and took her into his arms, his body trembling now as if with fever, and there was a great heat in his feverish eyes. "I'm with you, baby, always and forever with my Queen of Sheba. And if I'm on a trip, you can bet it's not from LSD." He fumbled at the buttons of her dress, but she backed away. "What kind of trip?"

"I haven't slept since the day before yesterday. All day all night I've been working on the book." She reached out to him and felt his cheeks and forehead. "Okay," he said. "I got the creative fever. Last night, I started in the Niger Delta and followed the great River Niger off and on and off and on from Calibar, stopped at Enugu and on up through the Northern Region, picked it up again at Yelwa where the vultures walk the streets like people, on and on to the Republic of Niger at Niamey, and further further north to that ancient city, Gao, in the days of old Songhai, then across the back door of the desert where the monkeys romp and play, and the camels and the Tuaregs, all the way to that great pearl of the Sudan all the way to Timbuktu." He went to his typewriter. There was typescript scattered over his desk and cluttering up the floor around his desk. "Look—I've been TCBeeing, baby. Dig it! And it's good. I know it's good. I can feel it's good! I knew it as it flowed from me. It was a beautiful trip, and I wished you'd gone along with me!"

She had never seen him in this state before. He was a different person, red-and-glassy-eyed, like he'd been on stuff for days; he was in a state of creative rapture, and he looked at her now, and she hoped her own eyes told him that she somehow understood, because his eyes told her that he wanted her to understand, to share this moment with him. He poured her another glass of wine and filled his own glass till it spilled over. He picked up part of the typescript from the floor. "Here, share my trip with me."

She started to read his work, tried awfully hard to concentrate (it was good reading, she knew that much), but she could not concentrate, because his mouth would not allow it. Kissing her one moment, talking on and on all the while, reliving the trip he had just come off, was really still on, was where it actually was at. His tongue was like perpetual motion. She looked up from his script and said, "Will you be my escort?" And wished instantly she had not brought up the question.

He said, "Of course. And nobody but you. Believe me when I tell you, little Sheba. O queen of queens, I will be your escort and take you on this trip with me. No one will make this trip with me but you, until it gets to the publishers. And then one day we shall physically make this trip together."

Her voice seemed to have a mind all its own. She heard it say, "I mean, will you be my escort to the Grand Cotillion?" She thought, This is not the time to ask him. But she hoped it was the time. Sometimes she thought there was so little time for anything, and everything got quick-shuffled. All the time there was was right there with them, there was no other time for them, and she felt she was growing old.

He continued talking, as if he had not listened to her. She hoped he had not heard at all. Then he stopped suddenly. "How can you talk about such a trifling thing at a time like this? Here I am opening my heart, baring my beautiful Black soul to you and no one else but you, and you say, will you escort me to some damn bullshit bourgeois Cotillion?"

She sat there now, as quiet as mosquito urine, knowing he was right somehow, but against her will her anger mounted, because she knew how right he was, her eyes becoming hot with tears. She got up and put on her coat and started toward the door. He said, "Where in the hell do you think you're going?"

She stood there crushed, as if a truck had rammed her up against a wall. She wanted desperately to say the things to him that would let him know she understood. And yet she wanted him, her Captain, to be big enough to show a little understanding. She thought of him in pure heroic terms, epic style, stronger than men, larger than life. John Henry. Frederick Douglass. Brother Malcolm. She wanted to say, "I love you, Ben Ali, my Captain! My strong man, please keep coming on. But I am not as strong as you, have not seen the Seven Seas, do not know the world as you do. Show me love and tolerance. Have compassion. Don't call my pitiful happenings bullshit, even if they are. Be mature for both of us. Please don't make me defend the bullshit bourgeois Cotillion!" But instead she said, "I'm going home or somewhere else where people listen to someone else besides themselves." How was it that her mind said one thing and her voice made other noises? Why is it so hard to say, "All right, you're right, I've been a fool?"

He said, "But you just got here."

"I came to ask you a question and now that you have answered it, I'm going home. You are not the only one that has a busy schedule." Grab me! Grab me! Shake some sense into my foolish head.

But he said, "I haven't answered your idiotic question yet."

She stood there saying nothing for a moment and then she began to laugh at the ridiculous irony of everything. She sat down and the laughter issued forth from her as the tears streamed down her face.

He stared at her. How could he explain to her how he felt about the Cotillion? He couldn't even explain it to himself. Was it simply jealousy? He was not the jealous type. Was he running-scared that one of those empty-headed, Cotillion-oriented, glamour-college pretty boys would take his Queen of Sheba from him? Could the hip, sophisticated Ben Ali Lumumba, artist, poet, world traveler, etc., etc., etc., actually be afraid of open competition with those pretty, proper-talking, prissy-assed, high yaller boys from the university? Was he scared he would lose luster in the eyes of his beloved, by comparison? Could that be what was bugging him? He said, "What the hell are you laughing about?"

Mixed up with the laughter she said, "I have this big fight with my mother over inviting you, I fight the Cotillion Committee, and win—I didn't want to ask you till I was sure that you would be accepted—and when I get around to you to tell you of my magnificent victory, you're so caught up with your own importance, you call my efforts bullshit."

He said, "I didn't say that and you know it. I didn't mean it that way at all." Did he fear that the Cotillion would turn her lovely head? Would the beautiful people of the colored social register change his Queen of Sheba?

She said, "I realize it's not as important, I mean, it's not in the league with what you're doing, writing your wonderful book and all, but we little unimportant people have to satisfy ourselves, I mean, we have to get ourselves worked up over small accomplishments." She was crying now without restraint.

He went to her and took her in his arms. He said, "Come on now, my little crybaby. There now, there now—you know I wouldn't say anything to hurt your feelings. Even if I thought you were stupid, would I say so?" he asked teasingly. But she was in no mood for teasing.

"Okay," she said, "you win." And got up to leave again.

"Will you sit still a moment and stop that jumping up and down?" He took her in his arms.

Hell naw, it wasn't fear at all, he told himself. It was just that he saw the Grand Cotillion as some more sophisticated bourgeois shit to mess up the minds of youngbloods. He said, "Can't you see what this Cotillion is all about? It makes no sense for Black people."

"Ben Ali—"

"They helping Whitey to cull off all the Black cream of the crop and churn them into little white toothless harmless bourgeois in black-face. Whitey's using the Fem Fat Asses to do his dirty work for him."

Cream of the crop—cream of the crap. She marveled at how close his words were to her father's when discussing the Cotillion. "Don't you trust me more than that? You think I can be culled off so easily?"

"It's not just you, my queen. It's the whole idea of Cotillion. Monkey see, monkey do. Aping white folks, and them laughing at us. 'Look at them niggers trying to be white.' We are never going to be liberated as long as we mimic the white boy's juju and his cultural symbols. The Grand Cotillion is just another way of conking your head instead of wearing it natural."

"It's hard to imagine," she said sarcastically, "those harmless dear little silly colored ladies of the Femmes Fatales turning out to be dangerous desperadoes in disguise. O Captain mine, it's so hard to keep the faith."

"It's not them!" he said. "They *are* silly, right. They *are* innocent. Yes. They *are* harmless. But they're being used. They're enemy agents without knowing it. It's like they were in the Black neighborhood pushing junk and thought they were selling vitamin pills or blood transfusions. The fact that the Fat Asses may be innocent doesn't do the victims any good. Dig it. You didn't know the gun was loaded. Right? But that don't make me no less dead when you pull the trigger."

She had sat down again, and he was walking back and forth. She said, "Don't you, I mean, really, don't you think you're laying it on kind of heavy? I mean, exaggerating the importance of—"

He stopped and turned to her. "Look. The Black Movement is

going all out to rally our people to a sense of peoplehood. Right?"

She said, "Right, but—"

"The upper class, the middle class, the working class, the workless class. Every living—The word is *Up the Nation*, right? The Black Nation."

"Yes!"

It was as if he were making a speech to the masses. As if he had forgotten it was just him and his Queen of Sheba. He was Malcolm's Second Coming. He was making a speech at One Hundred and Sixteenth Street. "The Grand Cotillion and all that other bourgeois bullshit are pulling Black folks in the opposite direction of peoplehood. The Cotillion says: 'You don't need no power. You don't need no peoplehood. You don't need to be no nation. You going to be integrated. You going to be just like white folks.'"

She said, "Okay, you win. You're the cap'n, Cap'n. Looks like I'll have to get me one of those nice light-skinned boys with good hair from the university, like my mother said I should."

He said, "Why not just forget it? The whole damn thing!"

"It's gone too far for that," she said. "My folks put money in already. And besides"—her voice grew smaller—he could hardly hear her—"there's a scholarship for Miss Grand Cotillion of this year of our Gracious Lord. A thousand dollars."

He took her into his arms, held her tightly. She could feel the awful tensions of his muscles. He said teasingly, "So you'd sell your dear pure sweet Black soul for a thousand lousy bucks."

"Good night, Mr. Lumumba!" She tried to pull away from him, but felt the power of his arms tightening around her pulling her even closer to him. He kissed her fully on the mouth.

She stared up into his face, her eyes gone blank, empty now like Orphan Annie's, her body limp and uncommitted, her lips cold now and impassive. "So you took me in your arms and kissed me. What does that prove?"

"I'm sorry," he said, "I'm terribly sorry. I was rude, thoughtless, insensitive. I'm a brute, a hoodlum. Like I really need to have my head examined. O Queen of Sheba, I should love to be your consort, I mean escort."

She said, "Don't do me any favors. I don't know if the invitation still stands."

"Please! Don't leave me now. I love you. I'll do anything. I'm honored that you asked me. If you'd asked anybody else, I would've been deeply hurt. I would have killed myself." He should have kept his mouth shut. "It was written a million years ago that I would be your escort." She was about to give in when he said, "Please, don't spoil this night for me in a stupid misunderstanding. I feel so good I—"

She exploded. "*Me* spoiling the night for *you*. *You* were feeling good, and *I* spoiled the night! Ben Ali Lumumba, you are the most egotistical, the vainest, the most arrogant, the—"

"Okay, all right, you win, so I'm the spoiler. But have just one more drink with me for the road for old times' sake, and whatnot, for love, for me, for you, for our Black beautiful selves forever always queen and consort for the Grand goddamn Cotillion, for Timbuktu and Harlem too, for all the times I dreamed of my Yoruba while I sailed the seven seas." He went on and on like this for days, it seemed; she was washed away by ocean waves of words, sweet words, meaningless words, which meant nothing to the girl and yet meant everything. Yes, he could turn her on with words, and knew it. Sometimes he could also turn her off. Sometimes he forgot to turn the faucet off in time.

She sat down to have one for the road with him for old times' sake, and especially for whatnot. She said meekly, "It's formal you know, the Cotillion is. You'll have to buy tails or maybe you would rent them."

He laughed. "Tell you what we're going to do. We'll go formal, but we'll go Afro style. I'll wear my gorgeous Yoruba robe. It's so pretty, I have never worn it yet."

She laughed. "It's a formal, not a costume ball. That means black and white for the men and white dresses for the ladies."

"Okay," he said. "You win. I'll get myself a monkey suit."

She laughed, "My mother said, 'I've got nothing against the boy, if he'd just clean himself up and get a haircut and look like something!'"

He said, "Oh she did, honh? Okay, I'll fix her wagon."

She was so happy now. She said, "Don't be so hard on Mother, Ben Ali. She means well, but she does so poorly."

He said, "Anything you say, little Sheba. I'll have that haughty one eating out of my hand, or my name ain't Ben Ali Lumumba."

She said, "You're wonderful! I really mean it!"

He said, "It's just that I love you so much. And I wouldn't hurt your feelings for anything in all the world. You mean everything to me."

She said, "Do I, Ben Ali Lumumba?" Her eyes aglow and shining with the rapture of the moment.

He said, "Sure. I just didn't think you could possibly be so serious about that stupid-ass Cotillion."

And she clouded up and rained again, and left him, and he walked with her all the way home, but she never spoke a word to him, excepting that she said good night. And pecked him on the cheek. Maybe one day he would learn to keep his big mouth shut when he was far out ahead. It was a good thing he was not a salesman. He would always oversell.

CHAPTER NINE

IRRESISTIBLES

She, the girl, Yoruba, wrote:

> The world outside my house is white
> And I am Black
> And God is what?

Kiss—kiss went the soft white fluffy stuff, lisping like the limp-wrist ones against the windowpanes. Last night, at dusk, the sun had given up the ghost in its confrontation with the night, had gone out in a blaze of glory. Then the sky, as she walked westward from the "A" Train, turned a dark and rusty red. And suddenly the heavens, in an over-righteous indignation, began to spit a soft white spit on everything and everybody. All night long the heavens spit, contemptuously. And now the world was white on white. She, the girl, Yoruba, was in a kind of funny sensuous mood this sleep-late Saturday morning. She felt beautiful, and lovable, and in love, and having been loved, and being in love, and loverly. She put her pad and pencil down and went barefoot and woolen-nightgowned to the window and pulled up the shade. All the entire world is white, she thought. And I am Black and comely. Figures dancing stiffly on the clotheslines in the backyards like white and frozen ghosts hanging helplessly in effigy. Dancing their white and rhythmless dance of pure divine virginal death. Cold death is frozen death is white death without rhyme or reason. The few trees out there stood shivering and lonely-looking, all decked out with glistening icicles.

"Dance your cold white dance of death," Yoruba said to the chorus line of stiff-legged dancers doing their lifeless unfelt thing without soul or heart or rhyme or rhythm.

She turned from the window and went and stood before the mirror. She pulled the nightgown over her head and dropped it on the floor beside her. She stared curiously into the mirror, almost as if she had never seen herself before, that is, in her eighteen-year-old birthday suit.

She whispered in a kind of unfamiliar voice:

> "The world outside is white
> And Ben Ali and I are Black
> And beautiful."

She made impish faces at the girl who stared back at her from the mirror. Then seriously she, the girl, Yoruba, took silent inventory. Frowning. She had a neck that tended to be more long than short. "Slim, sweet neck like Fulani women," Lumumba told her. "In the Northern Region of Nigeria." Her breasts were fully blossomed now. "Plump cupcakes with dark sweet rare grapes at the center." She laughed until the cupcakes quivered. "Ben Ali! Benali! Ben-Ahh-lee!" She laughed deliciously. "Honeycombs tipped with wild sweet muscadines." She frowned again. And continued taking inventory. She was short-waisted and long-legged. She smiled. "High Pockets," the boy in junior high had called her. Her hips were round and slim and womanish. "African-ish," Lumumba said. The dark slope of her stomach. The bluish-black mysterious triangle of her pubic hair, which Lumumba said was the loveliest dearest most exquisite hair in all the universe. She felt warm her body over. They should cover up the tophead hair and let the hair of the maidenhead be brought to light, he'd said. There is the beautifulest hair, he said. In jest, she thought, she hoped. She thought she hoped. She smiled. He was the Queen of Sheba's jester. Her knight, her consort, her prince, her escort? The sweet smile left her momentarily. "I love you, Ben Ali Lumumba. Please forgive my foolish childishness, my bourgeois inconsistencies." Then Yoruba smiled again at the Black girl in the mirror.

And now she stood in profile, right, then left. Gazing narrow-wide-eyed at the mirror. She turned her back and stared behind her. Then went into her dance, turning, spinning, pirouetting. I am Black and beautiful, O you daughters of Aunt Hagar. I am Black *and* beautiful. That is why Lumumba loves me. She felt sensual and sexy. She felt loved, loving and lovable. Inside, outside, frontside, backside, I am Black and beautiful. That is why Lumumba loves me. Inside, outside, frontside, backside. She began to giggle at the silly giggling girl who giggled at her from the mirror.

At breakfast, her mother asked her, "When is Ernest coming to pay his respects?"
She said, "Who is Ernest? Oh, you mean Lumumba?"
Her mother said, "Whatever his name is."
"Ben Ali Lumumba—that bushy-headed African will never set foot in no house of mine. I'll take a pistol and blow his few brains out," Yoruba said mischievously, out of her rarest of rare moods. In love with everything and everybody, and especially her mother and especially her father and most particularly her Captain Ben Ali Lumumba. She was a woman all aglow with love. Luxuriating in her love.

Lady Daphne said, "Ask him to come to dinner tomorrow afternoon."

Lady Daphne was finally convinced that there was something to this Black boy, when they did a portrait in the white folks' most prestigious paper. *The New York Times* had covered a reading he had done at the Truth and Consequences Café uptown. The first time *The Times* had tried to cover the poetry happenings at the Truth, it had sent a white reporter and had suffered the consequences, to wit, he was thrown out on his hinderparts. The next time they sent a Black dude who took pictures and interviewed Lumumba, the new bad Black thing and conversational piece of the colored "militant" literati. Yoruba showed *The Times* piece to her mother, who glanced at the news article and stared long at Lumumba, beard and woolly head and all. Her sole comment was "Humph!" And a chips that ended all her chipses. Look at the lady's crosses! It seemed like every day Yoruba came into the house with another Black magazine with a Lumumba poem and face somewhere inside. She would show them to her mother. Lady Daphne got so uptight she hated the sight of the Black and bearded literary vagabond. But she respected him. Especially after the great white folks stamped him with approval.

Yoruba said, "I don't want that common negra in my—" She

stopped. She laughed. And said, "All right, Mother. I love you too."

Her mother's eyes filled instantly with grateful tears. Lady Daphne smiled, and answered, "Do you really?"

Lumumba was an hour late the Sunday that he came for dinner. Yoruba Evelyn was all uptight and strung way out when there came a rapping at the front door. She broke into smiles and almost tripped over the hem of her "African" garment, as she hastened to the door, her eyes and face aglowing now with love and joy and the greatest expectations. When she got there, she stopped before she opened it, to get herself together. She patted her hair, adjusted her dress and this and that and the other thing. She put her hand upon her forehead, patted her cheeks and calmed her wildly beating heart. Keep cool, little Sheba!

She opened the door to greet her lover (she was all grinning smiles again, unknowingly) but her beloved was not there. In his stead there stood a colored dude all decked out in a mucho sharp American suit. Brown, herringbone and truly worsted. White on white shirt, green polka-dot tie, brand-new, gleaming, wing-tipped shoes. So sharp he was almost bleeding. Crew-cut like the Ivy League.

She stood in the door staring at this dude as if he was a Witness for Jehovah or an Adventist of the Seven Days. She said, "Yes?"

He said, "Pardon me, good afternoon, madam. I'm working my way through Harlem, and—"

She was a package of impatience now. Lumumba was already more than an hour late, and she had no time for prettyfaced Sunday salesmen working their way. And especially she had no time for Black white men in their Brooks Brothers Mad Avenue uniformed conformity. She said, "I'm sorry, I don't care for anything today." And she started to close the door, but the dude stepped nimbly, quickly inside. He had fast footwork. She said, "Please! I don't have time!" She said, "Of all the nerve!" And she started to open the door again for him to leave.

The clean-cut fast-footed dude seized her by the shoulders. She pulled away from him. "Take your hands off me! I'll call my father! Ben Ali should be here. He'd—"

The swift dude shouted softly, "Yoruba! Don't you recognize me?"

She stared at him now, hard and fixedly. Suspiciously. Who was this dude?

The voice was strange, yet so familiar and the face—the face—It was him! Her Captain! What had happened to his blessed face? It was naked and obscene. He had shaved away his glorious beard and had trimmed his sacred Afro down to a terrible crew-cut kind of tidiness. He looked more like Harvard Yard than Bamako or Timbuktu. He was so clean-cut it was disgraceful. Like a fugitive from *Esquire* magazine. Like it was ridiculous how pretty he looked. The girl didn't know whether to laugh or cry. "What happened to you?"

"What do you mean what happened to me?"

"I mean—I mean—this ridiculous get-up you got on—I mean—"

He was losing his sense of humor, gradually. "What do you mean—ridiculous?"

She was laughing softly now. "You look like the Americanization of Oooga Booga." She herself had also dressed for the occasion. All day yesterday she had worked on her African dress which reached below her ankles. She looked like the Africanization of Lutiebelle Gussie Mae Jenkins. One of her father's friends—one of Matt's old drinking, checker-playing buddies, from way back—had been at the house when she finished the dress and she had modeled it for both of them.

Wild Will's reaction was: "You ain't gon wear that grand-mammy nightgown out in the streets, is you?"

Matt roared with laughter at first. Then seeing the look on Ruba's face, he said, "Don't pay Uncle Will no never mind, Ruba. He don't know no better. He ain't hip to the African style."

Uncle Wild Will said boisterously, "You ain't no African! You're an American! Git yourself a mini-skirt!"

Her mother said, "Will Branson, that is the first intelligence you have uttered in the last fifteen or twenty years."

Uncle Wild Will was a plainspeaking unpretentious Black man, a man Yoruba had always held in great respect and deep affection. He was possessed of, and by, no bourgeois affectations. A clod of Black-Belt Southern earth, as if he'd grown straight up out of the loamy soil of 'Sippi. The cotton still was with him on his graying sideburns. He was no sophisticated Ben Ali Lumumba; he was Wild Will Branson, Black man, *period*.

She said, "Uncle Will, I'm an African American, and this is a beautiful—" Her voice dropped. "In Africa—"

"You ain't in Africa!" he shouted. "You're an American! Get yourself some mini-skirts. Show them pretty legs of your'n!"

But if Yoruba didn't dig Ben Ali's masquerade (as she characterized his thing this Sunday), her mother dug it the most. The American suit, the British accent, the clean-cut look swept Lady Daphne off her feet. It was as if Lumumba had put his white coat down in the mud for her. No wonder the publishers had given him a thousand dollars. He exuded style and confidence. He was good-looking, that is for a Black man with bad nappy hair. There was snow out on the Harlem streets, and inside the Lovejoys, Ben Ali did a snow job on her Highness, Lady Daphne. And it required a lot of snowing by a champeen snower; the Lady was nobody's fool.

When Yoruba introduced them, he took Miss Daphne's hand and held it with the two of his. "Well, well, I had almost forgotten what an elegant lady your mother was, Yoruba." Then to the mother: "And you haven't changed, and if at all possible, you have become even more majestic. Statuesque is the word for Madame Lovejoy. It's unbelievable. It's just incredible!"

She laughed, conscious of the snow job. And loving it. "Well, I must say, Ernest, you have certainly changed, and, from appearances, it has all been for the better."

He dabbed at the perspiration on his brow with a snow-white handkerchief. "You are very kind, madame, or might I presume to call you Mother Lovejoy?"

She pretended not to hear the question.

At the dinner table, Lumumba let Miss Daphne lead the conversation. It was the case of two irresistible forces. For a time, Matt and Yoruba sat on the sidelines mostly as spectators, leaving the arena to the two combatants who very richly deserved each other.

Lumumba smiled at Lady Daphne admiringly. "I am a gourmet of no mean experience and reputation, madame, but I must say you are not only an exquisite lady of the many graces, but you are also queen of the kitchen ceremonies. I have not partaken of such a splendid cuisine in all my sojourn on this earth."

Yoruba's mother purred like a kitten and giggled like an adolescent. "And you're a flattering vagabund," she said to him, mischievously, more or less in the spirit of "I know you're lying but I love it," or more precisely, in the attitude of "You think you're gilding the lily, but it is not so difficult to gild that which is already golden to the very core."

The conversation went all over the place from one thing to another.

"You have grown into such a cultured young man, Ernest. What university you graduate from?"

He looked quickly across the table at Yoruba, as if to receive a sign from her. Should he put Miss Daphne on? Make up a story for her? After all, he was a storyteller. It was indeed his life's commitment. He got no help from Yoruba. All he got was a blank-faced look. Murderous in its particulars. He said quietly, "I graduated from the University of Hard Knocks, Miss Daphne." His voice a combination of soft pride and feigned humility. They were both consummate actors. "I guess you could call me just a self-made man."

Her father laughed. "The University of Hard Knocks. That's the same damn school I quitcherated from." Matt Lovejoy laughed some more. In the colored way of laughing, like a man was really tickled.

The mother stared down the table at her husband with a look that was as cold and white as the snow outside. She said, "Well, Ernest, I must say you seemed to have gotten a better education from Hard Knocks University than a whole lot of other people. I think a lot of them was educated in the College of Hard Heads instead of Hard Knocks."

"Yes, m'am. It sure is a tough university for a man to get his sheepskin from."

"Then you would advise everybody who can go to a real college and get a real education, to go ahead and take advantage of it?"

"Everybody should get himself a real education, Miss Daphne."

They talked about civil rights. Daphne said, "I'm for the colored man getting his civil rights just like everybody else. I always been on the side of the underdog. It must be my British blood."

Her husband chuckled. "Could be, it's cause you always been one of them dogs that's under."

She stared at him, her cold eyes hot with anger and disdain. If looks could do their intended duty, they would have strung Matt up and quartered him. "I'm for the Blacks," she continued. "But I cannot condone this wort'less looting and burning that's going on in some of our cities. Ain't you agree?"

He turned the question over lightly. "Yes, m'am. And I do not agree with this looting and burning and whatnot. I don't believe it accomplishes anything of significance. After all, burning down the little Jew stores in the Black communities isn't going to rock the boat of the power structure. Is it? Those stores are not the power structure. Right? They burn their own stores down themselves sometimes just to collect the insurance. When we burn the little man's little old store, all we're doing is doing something he didn't have the nerve to do, even though he longed to do it, and we're helping the Establishment in the stated program of urban renewal which we know is really Black removal. What we're really doing is saving them the job of tearing down the neighborhood."

Miss Daphne had started out with him, but somewhere along the road he had lost her with his twists and turns. Notwithstanding, she said, "Exactly so." Not knowing what exactly she was agreeing to. Thinking to herself: He is a tricky clever rascal, intelligent for one so Black, a vagabund for true.

She got him to talk about his trips around the world, to England, and Asia, to Europe and to Africa.

"So you really liked the Mother Country. I would like to make the trip for true." Flirting with him like a girl his age. "Why don't you take me along the next time as your special cook?"

"Oh yes," he answered nostalgically. "I love Mother Africa. I really do. The beautiful people—the Niger Delta—the rain forests —the savannah lands—the bright beige of Sahara—the mountain ranges—" His eyes were closed.

"I mean *the* Mother Country," she corrected him. "I mean *my*, I mean *our* Mother Country. England—England."

"England is quite a mother indeed," he said. He thought, The Last of the Great White Mothers.

"And you've been to those lovely islands in the sun?"

He said, in a kind of singsong, "Lovely islands in the—? Oh yes—those veritable paradises in the West Indies. Sparkling jewels of the Caribbean!"

Lady Daphne beamed. She turned her regal head toward Matt, then toward Yoruba. "You see?" You Southern clods!

"Oh yes," he said dreamily. "Those lovely islands in the sun. Jamaica, Trinidad, Martinique, and most of all, dear old Bimshire, Barbados, remembered fondly as Little England. That glittering pearl of the Caribbean."

Daphne beaming, Yoruba fuming, Matthew chuckling.

"The happiest people in the whole wide world is on that little island," Miss Daphne said. "I try to tell my family what a heaven-on-earth the place of my dear childhood was, but they ain't never listened to me. It must've been the original Garden of Eden, where Adam and Eve-lyn inhabitated."

Yoruba thought, How do you like them forbidden mangos?

"They so damn happy," Matthew said, "they can't wait to get on the boat to make it to New York City. They falling all over each other to leave that happy place."

"It's such a lovely scene." Lady Daphne was ecstatic now. "You ought to write a book about it, Mr. Lumumba. I'll make you a present of a title. Call it 'The Last of the Unspoiled Peoples.' Everybody living the life of Riley in the big mansions with a staff of splendid servants waiting on them hands and feet. Not like these impudent servants here atall. Down there, they know their place. They tip their hats to quality. Clean as a pin, without the servant smell about them. Loyal to their masters and mistresses. It's enough to make you cry at the beautiful relationship. The last of the unspoiled peoples."

"Make you long for the dear old Southern days of slavery," Matt commented with his dry sarcasm. "Way down upon that Swampy River."

"What about the cane workers?" Yoruba asked.

"What about the cane workers indeed—" was Lady Daphne's quick rejoinder. Then to Lumumba. " 'Twould make a splendiferous novel. Make you a million dollars. That should be your second book. 'Twould be an inspiration to the world at large where so much violence is prevailing all over everywhere and prejudice and hatred and rudeness and so on."

Lumumba's comment was, "Yes—" He was uneasy now.

"What about the revolution?" From Yoruba. In the evil mood which was most unusual for this sweet and even-tempered child, who had awakened that morning with so much love in her heart of hearts for the entire human race.

"There'll never be a revolution in Barbados," Miss Daphne asserted with finality. "Ain't you agree?" she demanded of Lumumba.

Ben Ali was aware of the cold white looks being bestowed upon him by his Black-and-comely Queen of Sheba. They were not looks of fond affection. His strategy was foundering. And floundering. The whole expedition had developed swiftly into a question of winning the battle and losing the war. He had better change his tactics, check his compass in midocean. The choppy sea was treacherous, and there were icebergs here beneath the surface. And not another ship in sight. He could feel Yoruba's angry looks hotly on his face and neck and shoulders. He turned Miss Daphne's question over in his mind. "Never is a long long time, Miss Daphne. I will say though, there doesn't seem to be any sign of revolutionary fervor in Barbados at the moment." He mopped his forehead with his handkerchief, shot a quick glance at Yoruba.

"Exactly so!" Miss Daphne shouted softly. "The natives are happy and contented and there never will be a revolution as long as England is an England and rules the waves and just so long as God saves the darling blessed Queen. If the damn wort'less peace-loving cane-cutting natives git some notions in their head we'll show them as long as Britannia rules the waves, after all the dear Queen is done for them, damn their Black contented souls! By Christ, we will not stand for violence. We'll blow that happy little island off the map!"

"Thatta make 'em *good* and happy, and nonviolent," Matt said, and began to laugh and laugh and roar with laughter.

Ben Ali and Yoruba had lost their sense of humor. The shit had hit the air-conditioner. The ship had struck the great iceberg. And the iceberg, with a bit of edge knocked off and a little jagged for the whole experience, stood solid, white and ever awesome. The ship itself was floundering, but was too young and new and strong to founder.

Yoruba said, "Mother, Ben Ali and I are going to the movies. Father?"

"I can't begin to tell you what a splendid afternoon this has been," Lumumba mumbled. "It's really been a revelation."

They walked for blocks quietly along the avenue. Finally he tried to establish new lines of communication. "Which show do you want to see?"

"I already saw a show," she said, "at the dinner table. And it was a terrible performance!"

Another block of silence, then: "Your mother is something else. She really is a character."

She exploded. "My mother is a character? What about my Captain? What about his performance? What about the great Captain Ben Ali Lumumba, pilot of the Black Star Line, poet par excellence of the beautiful Black and militant movement?"

"Aw, come on, Yoruba, now. You don't have to rub it in. After all—"

"After all," she said, "all you did was give an excellent characterization of uncle tom and gunga din rolled into one."

"I was only trying to make an impression. I mean—"

"You succeeded, my Captain. You made an impression all right. Yeah—but it wasn't very impressive."

"I thought you wanted me to—your mother—that is—you know what I mean—I only tried to—"

"I expected you to impress my mother with that rare intelligence of a man of culture and sophistication, a man much traveled, a man with revolution and liberation in his guts. But you—you—made a fool of me, of yourself, and you gunga-dinned and cowtowed to my mother. You're all right with her, but you are nowhere with the lady's daughter."

He stopped and took her by the shoulders. "Aw come on, baby. You know me better than that. You putting me on, aren't you? I mean, you got to be kidding."

"No," she said. "*You* got to be kidding." And she pulled away from him, and they continued walking up the avenue. "Instead of helping me to teach her where the world is going, you catered to her arrogant ignorance."

"Baby—"

A bushy-headed bushy-faced dude walked toward them.

"Lord Blackbeard!" Lumumba softly shouted, and the two men went into their handshake ceremony. "One! Two! Three! Four! Five! Six!" Then Lord Blackbeard stepped backward, almost slipping on the slushy ice. Staring sharply at Lumumba: "Who in the hell? Do I know you?" Then recognition lit his face. He was himself already lit. "Brother! That ain't you! Is it? What happened to you, baby?" he shouted to Lumumba. "You look like an accident going somewhere to make the scene. Look like you lost fifty pounds. You on one of them bourgeois diets?"

"No, I—" Lumumba stammered.

"You on the stuff?" Blackbeard demanded. "Kick it, brother. That's what I had to do. A little grass ain't never kilt nobody. It's like work. It might not ain't never kilt nobody neither. But it's made a many motherfucka sick. I mean, if you on the pot, git off it, baby. And that horse shit brother, will kill you just as dead as you got to meet St. Petey."

Yoruba started laughing uncontrollably. Lumumba stared from her to the bushy one and back to her again, then back to bush man.

He stood slightly bent over in a crouch, as if he were peeking from behind a bush. Blackbeard's face looked like a dilapidated bird nest with the birds gone southward for the winter season. And he was nodding to beat the band, and chanting, mumblingly, to the unheard-by-them beat of a distant drummer. "Stop horsing around and git off the pot, baby! Stop horsing around and git off that darling pot!" His eyes half closed. "Horse that pot, baby, and git off the motherfucking darling—OOooweee! Fly away, Kentucky babe!"

"I am not on pot, or horse, or anything else," Lumumba said, exasperated.

Lord Blackbeard of the Chamber Pot opened his eyes, came in for a ceiling-zero landing, notwithstanding his seat belt remained unfastened.

Undoubtedly, Blackbeard's beard had once been black, hence

his proud nickname. But now his beard looked like a parody of the dirty snowy slush beneath their feet.

"How come you lost so damn much weight then?" he asked. "You ain't eating regular? You need some bread? I ain't got much but I can let a great mother brother like you have—"

"I *am not* broke. I am in good health, have not lost weight." But he had lost his sense of humor.

The man stared at Lumumba long and hard. Peals of laughter gallivanted forth from dear Yoruba now. She could not keep the laughter in. People stopped and stared; she could not help herself. "It's them skinny skimpy-ass clothes you got on," Blackbeard told him, oblivious to Yoruba's laughter and the staring people. "You look like you turning white or something, you look absolutely decadent. I mean, look like you broke into Uncle Jake's pawnshop or something. And man! What happened to your face? It looks like a naked pussy—cat," he added. "I mean, like you tryna pass or something?"

Lumumba said, "Well, my man, I got to be moving along."

Lord Blackbeard said, "Okay. If you sure you don't need nothing. A Salaam Alaikum." And went off down the street. Shaking his bushy head in puzzlement. "Stop potting around and git off that horse, baby darling. Git that potty off the babe!" Laughter bubbling softly from Yoruba like a frisky percolator.

They walked along in silence. Finally he turned on her. "What the hell is so damn funny?"

"Nothing," she said, trying to hold her laughter in, her stomach paining from the effort.

"What the hell are you laughing about? Even Lord Blackbeard of the Chamber Pot is not that funny."

"I'm not laughing—" she began, but could hold the laughter in no longer, and she went off into a laughing jag again. The tears spilled down her cheeks. "You should have seen the look on your face. I mean, you should see it now." Laughing and talking interchangeably. "I'm sorry, Ben Ali, but—but—" and broke off into another gust of loud hawhaws. She, the girl, Yoruba, who had never been the boisterous kind.

He just stood there staring at her with the expression of a half-angry and disgusted sheep dog with his coat shaved from his face and his bare face hanging down and out. "All right," he said. "What movie do you want to see?"

She said, "I don't want to see a movie. I told you, I just wanted to get out of the house, because I was bored with your performance."

They sat in a small café on Seventh Avenue, sipping wine in a roaring silence. Finally he broke the silence. "What's the big deal about me shaving off my beard?"

She said, "Don't ask me. I have said nothing about your beard." Her face wore a serious smile. This time she would not laugh, she told herself. "You should have asked your bearded brother."

"The beard bit," he said, "could be just another copout from our Negritude. If we believe we're Black and beautiful why should we cover up all that beautiful Black skin?"

She smiled. Her Captain was a clever dude. And she had to admit to herself he was a handsome brother, beard or no. She stared at him and smiled, as if she had just told herself a joke and shared it with herself alone.

He demanded, "Why should Black men cover their faces if they really believe that Black is beautiful?"

She kept smiling. "Why did you crop your hair so close? I mean, you look like—"

"All right," he said. "I'm a phony. Now you know. I was playing a game. But it was a question of tactics and not principle. Okay, I thought you would want me to impress your mother." He smiled. "But I'm the same person I was before I went through all these superficial changes. And I'm Ben Ali Lumumba, in a terrible hurt in love with Yoruba. Always was and always will be."

She smiled. "Always is a mighty long time."

He stared across the table at her. Why couldn't she understand that he'd done it all as a joke, a snow job on her mother? Why didn't she understand that he'd done it all for her, his Yoruba? Her father understood. Lumumba felt her father understood. Lumumba remembered the day before, after she had called him, inviting him to dinner. The arguments he'd had with himself, finally deciding that if he and Yoruba understood why he did it, it wouldn't matter what anybody else thought. The bush, the beard, the African garb. He was not a member of an organization that wore them as a uniform. He had not betrayed the cause. The cause was not hair or beard or dashiki. And after all, he was the same person afterward. What else was important?

"Look," he said, "I mean, like you coming out of a freakish bag. You all uptight with me about superficial shit like beards and hair and garbs, dig, but you into the most superficial bag of all, the damn Cotillion. This crew-cut ain't going to mess up my head not one little biddy bit, but them damn cotillions mess up a whole heap of potentially beautiful Black heads, for days, Sheba. Every year some good Black folks, young and future generation folks, get wasted, lost forever to themselves and to the Movement, made over into little Black white boogwuggies, superficial through and through. That's the danger of the Cotillion and no matter how silly and harmless you think the ladies of the Fem Fat Asses are, a madman with a loaded gun might be innocent of bad intentions but he is still a dangerous dude. Not that the Fem Fat Tails are madmen—"

She stared at her beloved and her eyes filled up with tears.

People in the small café were staring at their table now. He paid the check. "Let's get out of here. You need some air."

And they sloshed along the avenue, going nowhere in particular. Ben Ali heard one man say to his ladyfriend, "That's Ben Ali Lumumba. Wonder what happened to the boy?" Another couple walked up to them. "Ben Ali Lumumba!" the man said, like he'd found a long lost brother. Ben Ali said, "Jesus Christ! It's good to see you again!" Wondering what the man's name was, and where they'd met before. "It's been a long time, baby!" The man said, "You ain't never seen me before. I just know your work, and dig it. I heard you blowing at the Truth and Consequences." Ben Ali stared down at the little man, with his wife two inches taller. He sensed that Yoruba had started to laugh again, albeit quietly. He felt like the damndest fool who ever lived. He felt that the man had deliberately set him up, to knock him down. He felt like retaliating in kind, physically, murderously. But he mumbled, "Black blessings" to the man, and took Yoruba by the arm and continued down the avenue. It was not his night. Evil was afoot for him, and he should have stayed in bed. From early morning through the night. He should have consulted some soothsaying cat to say him sooth, then locked the door, secured the windows, pulled down the shades, got his machete, got under the bed, and pulled the world in over him. "It bees that way sometimes."

Now, some Bloods, sixteenish, walked up to them with their bad selves with their bad bad walks in their mucho bad dashikis. One of them said, "You ain't Ben Ali Lumumba! Who you shucking and jiving?"

Ben Ali said, "Really?" He looked around for some place to run and hide.

Youngblood said, "Hell naw! You ain't Lumumba. Who the hell you think you shucking and jiving?"

Yoruba started her giggling jag again. Openly. Helplessly.

Lumumba said, "Okay. Everything's cool. I'm not Lumumba."

Another one of the Bloods said, "We're members of the BBBMF, the Black and Beautiful Bad Mother Fuckahs. We revolutionaries, baby, and you ain't no Ben Ali Lumumba. He is a swinging ass. He lets it all hang out all over every whichawhere."

Lumumba said, "Good. Fine. I dig him too."

"You ain't him though?"

Yoruba was breaking up now, crying, laughing, stomach in an awful hurt.

"Okay. I ain't him though." Heat was creeping into Lumumba's voice.

The first BBBMF got up close and stared at Ben Ali, breathing in his face. "Is you Ben Ali or ain't you?"

"It's a possibility." Getting angry, losing patience now.

The second BBBMF turned to Yoruba. "Is he Ben Ali Lumumba, sister?"

She stopped laughing momentarily. "Ask him," she said. "He ought to know who he is better than anybody else."

They focused on Ben Ali again. "You sure you Ben Ali Lumumba?"

"I thought I was till I met you Black Beautiful Bad Mother Fuckahs."

"That's him!" the first BBBMF shouted. "That's him! That's that soothsaying motherfuckah!"

The third one asked, "What happened to you, I mean your face, I mean—"

"I just felt like taking it off for a while. The damn thing itches like hell, sometimes. Behind which, I wanted everybody to see my beautiful Black skin."

"Yeah! That's him!"

"That's him all right! Ain't nobody talk no shit like that but him."

They spanked the palm of his hand with their hands, they went into the Black-handshake-of-brotherhood, by the numbers and with audibles. They embraced him, laughing, shouting, pounding him on the back.

"You're our main man," Number One BBBMF said. "Any time you need us just give us a blast. We will naturally T.C.B." He gave Ben Ali his card. And now they stood all three of them staring at him in worshipful admiration. Then they gave him the shake again, each in their turn, and strutted off up the avenue in their fifty-dollar alligator boots.

"That wasn't so bad," Yoruba said.

He turned on her. "What's it all about any damn how?" Lumumba said. "When I wore my beard and natural and dashiki, nobody recognized me, nobody stared at me on the streets. Cause I was nobody. But the minute I took them off, every living stops me on the street like I'm some damn big-time celebrity. It's a great big joke, and I don't blame you for laughing."

"Let's face it," Yoruba said. "You are a celebrity, Ben Ali. Modesty will get you everywhere."

"How the hell am I a celebrity?" he shouted. "All I've got is a few jive-ass poems published here and there, and got my picture in the white folks' paper and the I-Be-Damn News. As far as my book is concerned, I'm just getting started good. I mean, reading and rapping all over the place—I mean, I ain't hardly paid no dues in that regard—I'm no hero—"

She stared up into his face, her dark wide eyes all aglow and full of love and adoration. He was more than just her Captain now; beard or no, his was the blessed face God or Allah used when He made man in His own image. He was the Skipper next to God and he could chart her course forever.

He shook his head from side to side. "Don't look at me like that, Yoruba!" He said, jokingly, "There're a half a dozen self-anointed glory-seeking soothsayers to the block in Harlem, every single one of them saying some jive-ass sooth to their own little separate group of desperate people." His voice grew serious. "Well, that ain't me, Yoruba. God hasn't kissed me that I know of. He hasn't given me any holy insights. And I'm not Malcolm's Second Coming. I ain't no soothsayer either, cause I don't know no sooth to say. I'm just a cat who's trying to get his thing together. So when I do say something, it will have some small significance for Black people." He paused. "I mean it. Just last week, I decided, no more rapping for Lumumba till his book has been completed and he gets his thing together."

He was almost out of breath. He looked at his watch. "Damn! I meant to watch Johnny Carson tonight. My main man gon be interviewed. We still got fifteen more minutes."

And so they went straight off to the Captain's Quarters. He served wine and they sat sipping side by side and staring at the idiot box. "My man is the baddest cat that ever said titty mama. He's so bad he's scared of his own self. Jomo Mamadou Zero the Third! How do you like them juicy mangos?"

"I've heard him rap," Yoruba said. Her face quiet, soft and serious, as if she felt a presence in the room. She'd heard him run his fine bad Black thing down in Yankee Stadium last summer before forty thousand screaming Blacks.

Lumumba said, "And like he blows Chuck's natural mind. I mean, he scares his britches off."

She stared silently at the idiot box where Johnny Carson's show was coming on.

"All right," he said, as if she had disputed him. "So it's fun and games. And God bless the child who's got his own. My man got himself a swinging résumé. I want to tell you, it took beaucoup creativity and imagination to put his fine Black thing together. He ain't hardly been in jail them years he was supposed to've been in Ossining, for hustling heroin and prostitutes. He was on a ship with me for months of that time. All right, so he doesn't really scare the Boy that much, cause the Boy don't scare that easily. But it damn sure is good therapy for the souls of Black folks. And he keeps the Boy off balance."

Suddenly she turned to him and laid her head upon his chest. "I'm sorry, Ben Ali! I'm truly sorry!"

"What's with all this being sorry?" he said.

Tears spilling down her face. "I understand! I understand," she said softly. "I was a fool to think my Lumumba had changed. I was just uptight with my mother, and I had looked forward to you educating her. I had my thing going and you had yours, and there was no, I mean, we were not hitting on the same frequency. But I'm sorry, Ben Ali, my Captain! Forgive me, darling! Please forgive me!"

He took her in his arms. "There's nothing to be sorry for, nothing to forgive."

"You did it all for me," she said. "I know it now—I understand."

"What did I do?" he asked. "It was nothing. I didn't give up anything. It'll all grow back in a couple of weeks. It's nothing but superficial superstructure anyhow. It's a symbol of our Black and beautiful selves, and that's a great thing, but it's not the revolution. There ain't no revolution yet. And cats that don't wear Afros are just as Black and beautiful as them that do. I just thought it would be a challenge to see if I could really put your mother on, do a snow job on Lady Daphne. That's all there was to the whole damn thing."

She put her arms around his neck and her mouth reached up for his dear articulate lips. And they kissed long and hard and soft and deep. And the floor moved out from under her.

"Here comes Johnny!" the announcer said. And the people in the audience screamed and screeched and clapped their hands. Johnny was a fresh-faced Brooks Brothered youngish white man. Lumumba and Yoruba came up for air and watched Johnny Carson come on waving his hands like he was the heavyweight champeen of the world. He read a few letters from his ecstatic fans, did a couple of commercials.

"You just watch," Lumumba told her, with excitement in his voice. "They gon be all shook up when my man begins to blow. We shipped out together off and on for fifteen months," he stated proudly. She had never seen him in such a state before. Then he shouted, "My main man! My main man! Jomo Mamadou Zero the Third. Ain't nobody never asked him what the first and second was!" He said, "Quiet now! They're going to introduce him."

She said, "You're the only one that's yapping." She was deliciously happy now.

Lumumba said, "I don't see how they have the nerve to have

him on this show. I mean, this is the primest time on the primest show on the primest network. Boy! They must be really scared!"

Johnny Carson said, "And now, ladies and gentlemen, it is my proud pleasure to introduce to you that greatest revolutionary of all times. He's greater and more dangerous than the late lamented Malcolm X, may he rest in peace and nonviolence, heh heh heh, and with all due respect. When he was two years old, our distinguished guest witnessed his father beat his mother to death with a large hambone. He swore off swine from that day forward. He was raised up by himself in the very jungle wilds of Harlem, hustled heroin and prostitutes since he was eight years old, raped his grandmother at the age of nine. Did five years in Sing Sing. And now he's making plans to overthrow our beloved country and systematically murder all us white folks. Isn't that wonderful? Isn't it truly tremendous? Give him a big hand, fellow Americans. He's gonna kill every white man in this nation. Bring him on with grand applause. Make this great one feel at home."

Johnny Carson began to applaud and scream and squeal, and leap about and up and down, as did the audience, as the camera cut to them, wild-eyed and cheering madly. They gave Lumumba's man a standing ovation, as the great revolutionary one ambled boldly toward the center of the stage into the spotlight, glaring sheepishly from behind his wonderful black beard. "Jomo Mamadou Zero the Third, ladies and gentlemen. Jomo Mamadou Zero the Third! Sit down right here, Jomo, my main man, and tell us how you're going to overthrow the government and kill all the white folks in the world."

Lumumba stared at the scene before him unbelievingly.

"He's everybody's main man," Yoruba said. And began to laugh again. Black folk had to have a sense of humor. Or go out of their minds entirely.

Lumumba sat there silent, lost for words, as he watched the great Black revolutionary one shaking Johnny Carson's hand. Without enthusiasm. He only half heard Yoruba laughing, but he got the full impact of the great big joke, and he started laughing too.

His main man, Jomo Mamadou Zero the Third, in his boss dashiki, with large black glasses covering the upper regions of his face, glared out from behind his bad black beard at the ocean of pink-white faces in the TV audience. He spat across the footlights at them. And they applauded. He growled, "I wished all of you pale-faced pigs a bad damn evening, you swinish cannibalistic motherfuckas! And after them few kind words of salutation, I'm going to say some mean things to you." And the place exploded with applause. Pale-faced Johnny Carson shouted, "Isn't he wonderful, ladies and gentlemen!"

Lumumba shouted, "Can't the damn fools hear him? Don't they dig what he is saying? He didn't come to entertain them! He ain't no court damn jester!"

Lumumba and Yoruba laughed and laughed and laughed and laughed, until their laughter turned to tears. He got up and turned off the television. He turned to his sweet laughing girl. He took her in his arms and held her close to him; so close, so tight, as if he thought that he would lose her then and there, and that they just might lose each other.

"What the hell are *we* laughing at?" Tears spilling down his face. "Another man done gone. These goddamn white folks so sophisticated, if they can't beat you, they don't join you, hell naw, they get you to join them. They kiss your damn Black ass to death." He kissed the laughing tears from his Queen-of-Sheba's eyes. "No matter what we say to Whitey, we always end up as his entertainment."

CHAPTER TEN

"TO BE OR NOT TO BE"

> If at once you don't succeed,
> Keep on sucking
> Till you do suck seed.
> If you can't lick 'em,
> Get 'em to join you.

Brenda Brasswork arrived at her philosophy empirically, independently. Silken-head Brenda with the light-brown hair, she was as high-strung as a cat with brand-new kittens. Her bulging eyes were cold steel-gray, and also catlike. Some of her closest friends said of her that she could see in the blackest darkness. She was known as "Brassy Brenda" to her peers. The dear girl went through changes every time she attended one of the Cotillion preparation happenings. It was like a menopause: hot flashes, cold chills, and the entire bit. Each time she encountered Yoruba, Black and beautiful Yoruba, Brenda always got uptight, even though she had to admit to herself that Yoruba was a fine and foxy chicken, that is for one so swarthy of complexion. Right?

It was bad enough when old Piss Potts, the Prancer, picked out Yoruba to teach the rest of them to do the waltz; it was doubly bad when popular Pamela Jefferson, of the Heights, got real tight and friendly with this Black broad from the "Harlem Jungle"; but when Famous Movie Star chose Yoruba and only Yoruba as his dancing partner at Jeffersons', well, that was when it truly hit the air-conditioner. That was when Brassy Brenda blew her fundamental cool. That fateful evening the dear girl tore her fine plump arse for fair; she drank far more than she was used to drinking, cried a river in the Jeff bathroom, crashed a crystal highball glass in the people's sunken tub.

But it was shortly after Jeffersons' that she got her thing together and decided to change her tactics. From dirty looks for Yoruba to ingratiating smiles. From muscling Yoruba out of the picture as if she were the outsider or the invisible man, she sought Yoruba's company and finally invited her to dinner.

Yoruba's mother jumped up and down like her backside was a nest of frisky hornets. "Huh-hey! Huh-hey!" She had never been overdemonstrative in an energetic manner. "Wool-lah!" She clapped her hands. Yoruba stared at her mother in wonderment at this sudden display of physical fitness. She must've been taking calisthenics when Yoruba's back was turned. "I knew it! I knew it! I knew my child would make the grade!" Lady Daphne shouted upon hearing the news of Yoruba's invitation to the Brassworks' dinner table. It was as if her darling daughter had just been awarded a Rhodes Fellowship at Jolly England's Oxford.

"This is what I wanted for you. Make friends with people like Brenda Brasswork and you'll be getting up in society. You'll go places. You'll be recognized." She threw her arms around Yoruba, and kissed her roughly, clumsily. "The Brassworks is somebody, child! The Brassworks is somebody!"

"Mother!" Yoruba said, moving out of her mother's smothering embrace. "Mother, they are no more somebody than the Lovejoys are somebody."

"You know what I mean," her mother told her. "Brenda's mother's father is a judge. The Brassworks is big niggers, some of the biggest niggers in the Crowning Heights. Don't you understand?"

Yoruba shook her head and laughed a short laugh. "Well, they've really got us there. I have to give them that much. And I don't envy them at all. We Lovejoys sure ain't no big niggers. Neither are we little niggers. We are not niggers at all. We're Black folks and we're damn proud of it."

Her mother said, "You said damn! You said damn! Don't you dare use such language in my presence. Swearing at your own dear mother! You ought to be ashamed of yourself!"

Yoruba laughed. "Oh yes, I dig it now, my own dear mother. It's perfectly nice and proper and Christian-like to call your Black brothers and sisters 'niggers,' right? Cause that's what the white man calls us, okay? And if they say we're niggers I mean, like, that's the way it's got to be. Right, Mother? But to use a naughty word like damn, or hell, that's just plain vulgarity. Obscenity. Blasphemy. Right? I can't dig it, Mother darling, but I sure know where it's coming from."

"I'm not Black!" her mother protested. With a vigor she was not accustomed to. "And you ain't Black neither! You're dark brown-skinned, and you—"

"Would you believe Afro-American, Mother?"

"We ain't Afra-Americans—We got nothing to do with them African savages—"

"But Mother—" Shaking her head and laughing now.

"We ain't Afra-American! You hear me! We ain't Afra-Americans! I'll not stand for us being African-Americans!"

Yoruba went to her mother and took her in her arms. "Poor Mother! Poor Mother dear! She'd rather be a nigger than an African-American. All right, Mother," she said, "you can be a nigger if you want to. Just help yourself. But I'm an African-American, and I'm proud of my African heritage."

Daphne pulled away from Yoruba. "You ain't understand, Evelyn. You ain't understand atall atall. Your grandfather was a Scotchman. A handsome blue-eyed Scotchman. Oh my dear! You should have seen him. Tall and stately and handsome and dignified. Why don't you call yourself a Scotch-American?"

"That's all right, Mother. I can't dig you, but I know exactly where you're coming from. And you can be a nigger if it suits your disposition."

"I'm a Scotch-American," her mother asserted proudly. "I take after my father. I got very little of my mother's nigger blood in me, and thank God for that."

"Yes, Mother. Yes, Mother. Anything that turns you on."

"I'm so happy you making friends with Brenda Brasswork. She's such a lovely girl. Her skin's so smooth."

Yoruba said, "Actually, Brenda's face is as pimply as a pomegranate. She's got a terrible case of acne."

"And she could almost pass for white," her mother said. "And she's got good hair too. It's even better'n mine."

"Good hair, Mother?"

"Yes, she's got good hair. Admit it. Give her credit."

"Everybody's got good hair, Mother, excepting those whose hair is falling out."

"Don't cross-talk me, girl. You know what I mean."

"Okay, I know, Mother. You mean Brenda's got hair like white folks."

"Yes," her mother answered. "That's what I said at first, she's got good stuff up on her head."

Yoruba's large eyes filled with tears. "Okay, Mother, you win. Brassy Brenda is lovely, your daughter is ugly. Brassy Brenda is high yaller, your daughter's Black. Brassy Brenda got good hair, your daughter's hair is evil, bad, and terrible. Brassy Brenda is a big nigger, your daughter is a little biddy nigger. I guess I can dig it."

Notwithstanding the great discourse on Negritude, Yoruba went to dinner at the Brassworks. Maybe she went out of curiosity to see how the "other half," how the "good-haired, big niggers" lived. She was a girl full of healthy curiosity. And the Brassworks were a curious tribe. She had heard enough about them from sources like Pam Jefferson to fill any red-blooded all-American girl with curiosity.

Brenda's mother was a music teacher, as was Brenda's father, who was a tall, slim and genteel gentleman of the old school and fashioned in the olden style. His clothes hung on him like an antiquated hall tree in your grandma's vestibule. Brasswork always seemed as if he had just borrowed some other person's suit to wear on this or that occasion without regard to size or fit or fashion, someone who had lived a hundred years before, or afterward, it didn't matter really. He slouched perpetually, like he was wincing from expected blows. A gay blade for true, he would have been in another time. It seemed he was from the horse and buggy days, and when horses went out, he stopped horsing around. A man born behind his time, many many years too late. His mother got him on the change. People used to call him "old folks' children." But for all that, a pleasant smile always adorned his ordinary face, a face you could as easily forget as struggle valiantly to remember. Mr. and Mrs. Brasswork both taught music at P. S. 1199.5 in the Borough of the Queenly people, although they lived on Union Street in the Crowning Heights of Brooklyn. Also Mr. Brasswork was the conductor of the Men's Glee Club of the Memorable Presbyterian Church of the Mistresses.

She did all the driving (she and Brassy Brenda); he never learned the knack of it. Whenever he went to glee club practice at night, or to any other night affair that she did not attend, she would drop him and come back to pick him up on schedule. Though he was of the middle ages, in longevity and style, she did not trust the darling boy to make it home all by his lonesome. "These are parlous times," she'd say. Sim Brasswork had very little to say for himself; she was their self-appointed spokesman. Some of her friends still said to her sometimes that she should have been a lawyer, what with her gift of gab; others said she should be gagged. And be permanently deprived of free speech, academic freedom and due process, etcetera. But she always pleaded the First and Fifth Amendments. As a matter of fact, she did attempt to follow in her illustrious father's footsteps—he had been a lawyer of renown before he was elevated and went onward and upward to ultimately step upon the throne of judgeship, in his elevated shoes. It was a seat the great man still occupied with dignity and a broadening perspective, his broad backside growing even broader with the years. She went to law school for a time, three law schools, to be exact, and was thrown out of all three of them. She couldn't learn very much because she ran her mouth too much. Therefore, everything went out of her head and very little found its way in. Excepting food, and not the kind for thought. So she did the next best thing, and studied music. Right? Okay, so everything can't make sense for all the people every time, in the words of—Abraham Lincoln?

The Brassworks were the kind of old-fashioned couple who served ice cream and cake (no alcoholic beverages) at their annual Christmas bash. Then puzzled throughout the entire year over the mystery of why nobody ever came back to a second-time Christmas party.

As Yoruba sat there at the Brasswork dinner table, which was plastic-covered (the Brassworks sported a plastic motif similar to the Pattersons), she remembered a story Pam Jefferson had told her about the time Mr. and Mrs. Brasswork came to the Jeffersons to a party. Like white folks, the Brassworks always went everywhere on time, and ahead of time sometimes, even when they went to party. They came to the Jeffersons a full hour before anybody else arrived.

When Pam's mother asked Simeon Brasswork what he'd like to drink, broad-bosomed Antoinette Brasswork spoke right up for him. "He doesn't drink, my dear, but I'll have a bourbon and soda."

"Really?" Pam's mother still directing her question at Sim Brasswork, wondering how anyone could live with Annie Brasswork without being driven to the drink, as well as to the brink.

"He has to stay sober," Mrs. Brasswork explained. "You see, I do all the driving." Understand?

Mrs. Brasswork sat there through the entire party, expounding on Mr. Brasswork's aches and pains; she mouthed a habeas corpus on his maladies, his allergies, his sinuses and such, the sine qua non of his existence. People balling all around them, doing their things and whatnot, dancing, talking, laughing, drinking. What did Antoinette Brasswork do? She picked lint from Mr. Brasswork's jacket all evening long (it could not be properly said that he wore the jacket; it would be more appropriate to say that the jacket wore poor Mr. Brasswork). And the more bourbon the proper Mrs. Brasswork consumed, the more she picked at him and his dashing blazer. From his jacket with the great bright green plaid to his baggy trousers, she was the avid seeker of the lint. Dig it. Before the evening ended she was mashing pimples on his face, talking all the while. As he sat there smiling smugly without a drop to drink.

Now, all through dinner, Brenda and her mother yapped. Yoruba marveled at how they managed to get any food into their mouths at all and chew it, but they somehow managed to put food in and put words out, all at once and simultaneously, as Mr. Brasswork sat there smiling silently.

Double-breasted Annie Brasswork was on the hefty side, portrait of a lady wrestler in her natural prime. Notwithstanding, she worked religiously with a strenuous diet to thwart the vicious scales in her plastic-covered bathroom. And being of a missionary bent, she kept religiously to her diet except on rare and special occasions when company came to dinner, or lunch, or brunch, or snack, or tea (or communion?), whichever, at which time it was anything goes and caution to the hurricane. And said occasions were becoming week by week much more often and ordinary than rare or special. Antoinette was far too clever for an ordinary diet to frustrate her appetite. But on those really rare occasions when it was "just the family," she went strictly by the diet which she kept tacked on the kitchen bulletin board and consulted at each meal and lived by with a fervor that bordered on the fanaticism that is usually associated with missionaries. It was between meals that the damage was done. Those constant innocent little sneaks for snacks during all hours of the day, and night, always on dramatic tippy-toes with her broad rear perspective to the bulletin board as if it had accusing eyes. Nevertheless, Sim Brasswork's wife was on a diet and whenever she was on a diet, he lost three pounds every week.

Now, she, the girl, Yoruba, seated at the Brassworks' dinner table, on this very special occasion, with the plastic-covered chandelier glittering above them, looked from Mrs. to Mr. Brasswork and back again, and remembered an old nursery rhyme. Mr. and Mrs. Brasswork became Mr. and Mrs. Jackson Spratt. And they inspired the dear girl to poetic heights, as she thought: Jack Spratt was never fat, his wife was never lean—She got no further with her inspiration, because Brassy Brenda interrupted her with: "Wherever did you get those beautiful exotic primitive earrings, dear Yoruba?" Out of breath from the sheer overexertion of reaching for helpings, second, third, fourth, and poking food into her face.

"My boyfriend gave them to me." They were a gift from her Lumumba, purchased from Beautique Afrique.

"Isn't Yoruba lovely, Mother? Isn't she a pretty thing?" Brassy Brenda insisted for the umpteenth time.

Each time her mother would say something like "Yes, of course," or "She's pretty as a burnt-black biscuit," or "Cute as a speckled puppy with a bad case of the mumps" or other words of sweet endearment to that effect, as she reached militantly for another helping.

Every now and then, Brenda would stare at Yoruba, admiringly? And she'd say, "I really dig your hair the most. I wish I had your kind of hair. I don't know why I had to be born with this old straight and stringy stuff." Brassy Brenda was a nervous wreck.

When she talked, she was all eyes, mouth, tongue, head, hands, maddening gestures, ever in perpetual motion. Just watching made Yoruba dizzy. But you also had to listen.

Her mother would say, "Cease and desist, Brenda, tootie sweetie." Brenda's mother had always idolized her lawyer-father, and legal terms had rubbed off on her. She was forever speaking quid pro quo and ipso facto and prima facie, and especially ex post facto and sine qua non. She'd sneak them in at every opportunity and relevance was irrelevant as far as Annie was concerned.

Brenda said, "I'll swap hair with you, Yoruba, any day in the week. Oooweee!"

After a while, the subject of hair got boring to Yoruba. She figured the girl was putting her on. But every time she tried to move away from hair, Brenda would bring it right down front again, fait accompli.

Her mother finally said, "Brenda, will you kindly leave Yoruba's hair alone? Cease and desist immediately!"

At which point obedient Brenda left her chair and breezed over to Yoruba and ran her fingers through her hair. "So nice and rough and nappy like a nigger's hair's supposed to be! So nice and rough and nappy! Oooh! I could just run my hand through it forever."

For some unknown reason Yoruba did not appreciate Brenda's slavish admiration for her hair. Each time Brenda ran her hand through Yoruba's hair, Yoruba felt like little devils were dancing on her skull with needles in their shoes.

"Will you cease and discontinue?" her mother ordered. "You're displaying prima facie evidence of bad upbringing and ill manners."

Yoruba kept telling herself that Brenda meant no harm at all. It was just her way of being friendly. Nevertheless it didn't make her feel any better about it. "I wish you wouldn't do that," she finally told the other girl.

But the other girl's eyes were closed now, her head swaying rhythmically from side to side; she seemed to be listening to an orchestra that only she could hear. It must have been a rhapsody, the girl's face was rhapsodic. "I love it!" she murmured, like she was quivering at the brimming brink of sweet orgasm. "If I had your hair I wouldn't let a hot comb come nowhere near it. Ooooweee! How I'd love to just trip barefoot through the jungle of your nappy woolly hair. You ought to wear an Afro, Yoruba, you beautiful Black nigger! You exotic African!"

At which point dear sweet-tempered Yoruba slapped the raving girl clear across the plastic dining room, and split the scene post haste with all deliberate speed. Which just goes to show you, ipso facto, that you can't treat colored people nice, de jure or de facto.

Preparations went apace, even as the seasons altered, trees grew green again in Brooklyn even on the Crowning Heights, windows opened on the world, people thronged the streets of Harlem, Black old-timers went through changes of their long and itchy woollies for the first time since October, strolled along the avenues for the first sunlight of spring. Ashen-faced and eyes ablinking. "Damn, old man! You still alive?" From Miami to Niagara birds and people flew to North. Black folks came alive once more on the streets of Harlem Town. Digging in for the duration of the steamy, long hot summer. Cold wars continued to grow hotter, Vietnam and Lebanon, people dying the world over who had never died before. Blacks laid down their lives for freedom as riots raced throughout the country, especially in the urban centers. Yet with great religious fervor, debutantes in Crowning Heights went ever forward to their goal of the great and Grand Cotillion. A tribute to the Femmes Fatales!

Parties! Parties! Everywhere!

"Oh, my dear!" her mother told her. "This is what I wanted for you! You are in society now!"

"This is what you wanted for me?" She stared, wondering, at her mother, who'd always been a party-pooper when it came to her dear girl. But obviously this was different.

"Yes, my darling, yes! Yes!"

"But Mother?" Some of the parties were pot sessions; sometimes things got really rough.

"Oh my yes!" the mother murmured. "This is what I've waited for!"

"But Mother, please!" Some of the parties got outrageous. Some were never chaperoned.

"Recollects me of back home in dear old Bimshire. Oh my dear, the times we had!"

"Mother!" At a couple of the parties she had barely managed to escape with exactly what she came with.

"Oh, yes! They were such elegant affairs with servants waiting on you hands and feets." Seated at the dinner table were the three Lovejoys that evening.

Yoruba's father said, "Down home we had plenty rats and mouses, but they didn't never turn into no servants or fairy godmothers like they did in Cindyrilla."

"All my father'd have to do was to clap his impressive hands and they would all come arunning, just to do our every biddings, even things we didn't bid. I suspect sometimes we were not as thoughtful for the servants as we might have been. Poor, darling, faithful dears. I suspect sometimes we naughty girls indulged ourselfs at their expenses."

Big Matt laughed his dry sarcastic laugh. "My papa wasn't thoughtful neither. Wait a minute. Come to think of it, he was very thoughtful. I be dog if he didn't make five holes in the bottom of the door for the mice to run out of. My mama asked him how come he made all them holes in the back door. How come all them rats couldn't go out of the same hole? My papa said, 'Cause when I say scat, I mean for ever living ass of 'em to git going in a hurry. I don't mean for them to stand around there, one waiting on the other.' "

Lady Daphne said, "Even when we didn't have parties everything was elegant in my father's house." She sighed very deeply and giggled elegantly. "My father always believed in dressing for the evening meal. Everybody had to dress, or they couldn't sit at his supper table. Every night he'd dress up in his tails. He was stiff shirt all the way. I can see him now. Oh, my dear, he was handsome man, and he wore the grandiosest tails!"

Big Matt commented, "That's cause he was the biggest devil on the island."

She gave Big Matt a cold white look, but she wouldn't let him turn her off. "Now you 'cognize, Eve-lyn darling, all the dreams I dreamt for you. This is what I saved you for. You see, I also have a dream. *I have a dream.* And now you understand it."

Yoruba shook her head. "No, Mother, I do not understand. I really don't."

"Well," Lady Daphne said, "like the negras say in their precious spirituals, you'll 'cognize it better by-and-by."

"But Mother, you don't know what some of these parties are like. I—"

"I never wanted you to go to rowdy parties around here in Harlem with the common Southern negras, but now you with the high-class young people, sons and daughters of the upper-crusting, doctors, lawyers, teachers and all the sellybrites, and I want you to just have yourself a good time, and be carefree and enjoy yourself while you're young and pretty, as if you was free, white and twenty-one, as the saying goes."

Yoruba shook her head in pure amazement. "Free, white and twenty-one!" She didn't think she felt like laughing. "Free, white and twenty-one!" But laughter erupted uncontrolled from her like lava from a wild volcano. She didn't want to laugh at her mother, but she could not help herself. It was just too much! Too much! Too much! Her mother was the everlasting ever-loving mostest of the very most.

Lady Daphne stared askance at her laughing daughter. She looked from her to Matt and back again. "That's what I mean, Eve-lyn. Laugh, sing, dance, enjoy yourself. Be happy as a merry lark." She smiled nostalgically. "You might even marry the son of one of them famous sellybrites."

"Sellybrites?" Big Matt asked. "What kind of country puts out them people? You don't want Ruba to marry no queer or pansy?"

"It's bad enough to be ignorant, Matt Lovejoy," her mother said with great disdain. "But to be proud of it is a magnificent disgrace!"

"Mother means celebrity, Father."

Despite her mother's fondest aspirations, Yoruba didn't get to all of the parties. She never heard of some of them. Only the queens of Crowning Heights were in attendance all the time. After the incident at dinner, Brassy Brenda went back to her old tactics of freezing out the Blacks from Harlem, especially pushy, Black and "unattractive" Yoruba. "Who does she think she is?" She led an anti-Harlem group of Heightsters who responded, "Who indeed?" Yoruba would not have known of most of the parties had it not been for Pam Jefferson. At the rehearsals and all the other happenings, Pam gravitated toward the girls from Uptown more than toward those from the Heights, much to the latter's great frustration.

Then a new thing happened. Ben Ali began to make the scene, at rehearsals, likewise also at the parties. He was a big hit everywhere. The children of the first families knew him from the story of him in *The New York Times*. Some of the Heightsters had dug him at the Uptown Café when they went slumming with the hoi polloi, also at Truth and Consequences. The girls had big eyes for Yoruba's escort, even though her man was Black. He was some kind of half-assed celebrity, the way they figured, and if the white folks dug him enough to put him in the lordly *Times*, they'd better take it easy with him. Overlook for the moment his meager Black beginnings.

Even Pam Jefferson blinked her great black eyes at him, not to mention Brassy Brenda, who was grinning up in his face every time Yoruba looked around. Or wasn't looking.

It puzzled Ruba at first as to why he suddenly became interested in the Cotillion, especially to the extent that he made the scene at all the parties as well as most of the other happenings. She thought, Maybe he's jealous. Hopefully! Maybe he thinks one of these first family dudes will lure his girl away from him. His Queen of Sheba. But she said, no, he knows much better. Unfortunately! There isn't a jealous bone in his body. Dammit! The thing was, he was too cocksure of himself, especially when it came to cats who were his own age. So there had to be another reason.

She was pleased that pretty Pam Jefferson dug her Captain. She really liked Pam. She was one of the few girl Heightsters that was for real, as far as Yoruba was concerned. She and Pam just naturally hit it off together. Direct current, positive vibrations, equal frequency, same wave-length. No strain, no sweat and no pretensions. They were a mutual dig society. But when Pam engaged her Captain in such serious intellectual conversations, with them-there dark eyes flashing bright and full of adoration, at every single one of the happenings, all up in the Captain's face, for days, it seemed, in terms of party time, and the Captain seemingly suffering no pain, enjoying same in fact, well then, after all, Yoruba thought, darling bosom boon pal Pam should just be more unselfish, that's all, and share the Captain with all the other "culturally deprived" of the Crowning Heights.

White girls with Afro wigs made some of the bashes in the Heights, posing as light-skinned soul sisters, spanking the plank and talking that talk, doing varied imitations of the near-white Black bourgeois. Non-Afroed Brassy Brenda went around at one of the parties pointing to girls and whispering out loud, "That one over there in the dungarees with the earrings through her nose is passing for colored," and "That one over there grinning in my boyfriend's face, that one with the brown powder pack on her face and the African robe, she's passing for nigger!" And so forth and so on.

Pam Jefferson said, "They just want to find out if it's true what they say about Sambo."

A group of rip-snorting militants stood in a corner of the basement rec-room, off to themselves, burning incense to the Gods of Pot. They offered potluck to Lumumba, tried to get the Captain to pay a little homage. Casey Bingbop, a long, tall, loosely connected dude from Boston U. with one of those Afros atop so bad and so far-reaching he didn't need a shade tree in the heat of summer, took a long, deep, slow drag from his man-made cucaracha. "Oooooh! One night we had a grass party at my crib up in Boston, we threw up such a smoke screen my next-door neighbor thought the house was on fire. She ran down on the street and turned in the fire alarm. The whole damn motherfucking Boston fire department came down on us. Broke into my pad and started chopping up everything."

Through the comfortable laughter and the coughing and the smoke screen, Rob Stacker said, "You a lying ass!" Rob was a round-faced brown-skinned Blood with a short torso and long sideburns.

Casey Bingbop said, "Dig. We brought charges against the fire department for violation of our civil rights. We accused them of attacking us because we were Black militants. Fifth Amendment, due process, and all that other motherfucking shit."

The cats were nodding and chuckling now, and Lumumba stood

there with them in the middle of the smoke and smell, getting his impressions of how the young and "privileged" Black ones lived, and talked and shucked and jived.

Brassy Brenda integrated the group, took a couple of puffs on somebody's righteous roach, and demanded, "Who in the hell do those white chicks think they fooling with their natural wigs and shit?"

Bingbop said, "Dig, baby, they just love to be around spooks and dig the happenings, and they ain't doing nobody no harm. Imitation is the greatest form of compliment."

Rob Stacker said, "I understand up in Boston some of you so-called Black militants make your white chicks wear Afro wigs and pass them off to the rest of the brothers and sisters as true club members, so as not to blow your image as Black nationalists."

"Man!"

"Wow!"

Casey Bingbop took offense, suddenly lost his sense of humor. "You don't dig Black militants, do you, Stacker?"

Brenda insisted, "If they want to make the scene, why don't they come out in the open instead of under false pretense, which is prima facie evidence that they do not come to equity with clean hands?" Legal terminology had been handed down to her from generation to generation from her great-great-grandfather who was a janitor in the city courthouse, to her great-grandfather who was a chauffeur to Justice Stonehauser of the superior court, to her grandfather who was the judge himself, to her mother who did time in three law schools.

Bingbop said, "Dig, Brenda baby, how come you don't get yourself a natural wig and pass for colored your own self once in a while?"

The dudes cracked up with laughter.

She said, "You know what you can do with your natural wigs." And moved away out of the smoke screen.

"Dig it," Casey Bingbop said. "Some of these Black broads are some evil sisters. Bitches sleep with their fists balled up. You hip to that? They don't never want to give us revolutionary cats no leg, not even for the cause of the glorious Revolution." Speaking all straight-faced and serious, like he was the Second Coming of Franz Fanon. "I mean, like they always psychologically emasculating our Black manhood and whatnot. Yet and still they don't want Miss Bountiful to be giving you no pussy either. But Miss Free-White-and-Twenty-One will give a cat some leg, head, ass, ear. You name it, dads. She aims to please." He paused, regarded his roach, took another long slow drag, blew it back out of his nose, mouth, eyes, ears, he was champeen reefer man, Earl of Pottsville, Prince of Grass. "Pretty soon at these happenings they gon be wig-checking at the door to see who is or ain't for real. They might as well lift up them mini-skirts, Jim, and drop them drawers and check the grass around them pussies. That's foolproof evidence, like Brassy Brenda says, that's prima facie. They can't wear no wigs down there."

The "privileged" ones were laughing now and nodding and clapping their hands and spanking the plank. Rob Stacker said, "Man, some of you so-called militant revolutionary Third World cats ain't made a witness to a nappy cunt in all your life, not since you peeped at baby sister. You wouldn't recognize one if you met one face to face."

Well?

At one of the parties there was a prevalence of African students, crew-cut smooth-faced Brooks Brothers sharp. There was a brief confrontation between them and the natural Black men of the Ivy League contingent. Afroed, bearded and dashikied. It started like this. High-Life music playing in the Jefferson basement, dim lights, dark complexions, grooving in the natural groove. Captain Lumumba was an obvious hybrid of the two contingents, since he wore his bad dashiki but he had not outgrown his cool crew-cut. He had just finished dancing with Yoruba, when an African brother approached him. And asked, "How long have you lived in this country, my brother?"

Lumumba answered, "Off and on and off and on. It's really difficult to say." He was on a tear and feeling good.

"It was rather easy to tell that you were an African. You're a Nigerian, aren't you. Are you of the Yoruba tribe?"

Lumumba said, "My lady friend is Yoruba."

He said, "Then you must be Ibo. You've been to the Lido in Enugu."

The music had stopped and cats were gathering around the dialogue.

Lumumba said, "How could you tell I was African?"

The African said, "A. By the way you did the High-Life like a true West African. B. By the way you wear your hair cut, even though you also wear a dashiki."

One of the American Black brothers with a bad bush atop said, "Dig. How come you cats don't wear Afros like us? I mean you cats are from where it's really at. Y'all from the heritage and shit. Ain't y'all got no Negritude? Don't y'all know that Black is beautiful?"

The African brother smiled deprecatingly. "Certainly, we are knowing that Black is beautiful. And we in Africa are having plenty of Negritude and so on. But we don't wear our hair like you are wearing it, because in the tropical climate lice will have a feast in your head if you wear it so. There will be wild beasts romping in your rain forests."

Understand?

At the same party, Jerry Bundage, a colored fugitive from a white prep school, who had real big eyes for Yoruba, came up to Lumumba; Bundage was up to his very full with alcoholic beverage. He said, "I know you. I saw you at the Truth and Consequences which is not too cool or consequential. Dig it. And I see you got rid of that woolly shit on top of your head. Congratulations."

Lumumba stared long and hard at the lit dude, and answered, "Yeah, brother, for the time being, and like don't worry about it. But I can see you haven't gotten rid of that shit inside of your head. Condolences, baby. Heartfelt sympathies."

Brassy Brenda Brasswork made a play for Lumumba every time a chance afforded. He and Yoruba were leaving one of the parties one night over on the Crowning Heights, and when they reached the door, Brenda breezed up to Lumumba and muscled Yoruba politely out of the way and threw her arms around his neck and pulled his mouth down to her mouth and kissed him soundly on his mouth, with her thick tongue obviously and feverishly at its frantic job.

He, the Captain, took her arms calmly from around his neck. "Well," he said, "you are the demonstrative little bugger, aren't you?" In his terrible terribly British accent, which he assumed upon occasions.

"You don't do so badly, your own damn self, Mr. Big Important Man of Letters."

And the mischievous lads and lassies broke up with raucous laughter which was not genteel or ladylike. Excepting Yoruba, who saw nothing at all to laugh about. All the way home on the filthy subway, mum was the word for Yoruba. Excepting that every now and then she'd say things like, "You sure are enjoying these middle-class bashes." He'd stare at her and away again. "Yeah, they're all right. I mean, if you haven't got anything else to do." And let it go at that. Then the rocking roaring silence of the screaming screeching subway train and the scorchy-smoking smells (the subways always seemed afire), with swirls of dirty bits of newspaper dancing through the train and attacking legs and faces of the uptight passengers. Finally she closed her eyes and pretended to fall asleep on him, with her dear head on his shoulder. She wanted to ask him questions, wanted assurances that he still loved her and was not taken with these empty-headed chicks who made such a big fuss over him, because they thought he was some kind of a Black celebrity. She wanted to ask him did he still love her, but she was too proud to ask him so directly, so she sought to feel his arm around her shoulders which is why she chose to fall "asleep." And he did in fact put his arm around her, and it felt so comfortable and comforting to the dear Yoruba that she closed her eyes and let her head lie on his lap, as if she were the Captain's baby.

And now he looked diagonally across the way from them (he liked to look into other people's faces on trains, to read something about their lives; he had always played these kinds of games since he could remember games), and he stared at a middle-aged Black man, slumped and over-alcoholic, pissy-drunk in fact, immobile, and his dear head greasy-kid-slick and limp and lolling. Lumumba let his mind wander as he wondered about this filthy-clothed, dog-eared, drunken Black man with the neat and greasy process, this human hunk that the society had processed and programmed into obsolescence, as Lumumba verbalized it. His eyes filled up with deep compassion for the man. The train came to a lurching, screeching halt. The Black drunk's head flopped from one side to the other as if his neck would snap, the only motion left in him. Even as he still stared at the drunken Black man Lumumba was aware of the two white nuns in their long black robes, scrub-faced, prim and proper, in their stiffly-collared whiteness, as they came onto the train and started down the aisle. Ben Ali thought, What the hell are they doing out this time of night? It was quite late for precious ones like them to be abroad with so much blackness overhead and underfoot and underground. They came between him and the Black brother across the way, but as they came up to the inebriated one, they stopped and stared, and started again, and stopped again, as if their legs were disobedient.

One of them looked back at Lumumba with a terror in her eyes like a lady in a pure distress. And even though she beckoned desperately, he was not Kid Galahad. The other nun went for the conductor with a righteous indignation, brought the tall Black man back with her. Now in clear view was the obvious reason for the damsels' deep distress. Lord Drunko Blackman sprawled there in all his naked innocence, open to the sea, and unprotected, except for the long, Black, mighty truncheon thrusting nobly from the fly of his proud though ragged trousers, protruding boldly and unsheathed, like a weapon cocked and stripped for action at the everloving ready. Miss Second Nun pointed at Lord Drunko of the bad Black Big Stick Policy. And as he snored so peacefully, he put his hand dreamingly upon his lethal weapon, in a gesture of defiance, or possibly, self-defense. He did not look nonviolent, though nonviolently he slept. The conductor stood chagrined.

"Lady, I mean, Sister, I mean, that ain't my jurisdiction. What I mean, after all—they don't pay me for no odd jobs—"

Meanwhile the awesome ebony instrument stood hard by, objectively and without solicitate, arrogant, erect, burnished-Black, the fierceness of its dignity assumed, assured, quietly asserted. Stately and majestic.

Lumumba thought, Black Power, brother!

They gestured and demanded, did the saintly righteous sisters, for all that they were worth. They cajoled, they threatened excommunication of a cat who was not of their denomination. They called upon the Black conductor's chivalry, his manhood and his racial pride, his Black Consciousness and all. He shook his Black head angrily, but they would not be denied, angry zealots that they were.

They threatened to take matters in their own hands out of the hand of the sleeping brother and put the big bad Black thing in its place. The tall, slim, Black conductor smiled at them benignly, deprecatingly. Finally the sisters threatened that if he signaled the motorman to start the train without first concealing the poor man's murderous weapon, they would pull the emergency cord, so help them the Blessed Virgin.

So in final resignation, he, the pissed-off Black conductor, went grumbling, uttering foul oaths unfit for ears of saintly sisters, and took the Black man's big Black proud and shiny weapon into hand and put it out of sight. And tried to zip the brother, but the brother would not zip, because the zipper wouldn't work.

As they walked from the subway to her house Yoruba asked him, finally, "You're so terribly busy and I know how you don't dig the Cotillion and all and I don't blame you, I'm sorry I got you messed up in it. I just wonder why, I mean, how you find the time to make all these stupid happenings—" She left the question hanging like a dangling participle.

He said, "What's the matter? You don't want me around? I mean, am I cramping your style?" And he thought, Really, why do we always hurt the ones we love? Why are we forever pretending not to understand? Demanding that everything be spelled out for us? Why? Then he said, "Okay, I'll tell you. I didn't want to be in the damn Cotillion, but after I saw it was important to you, I—"

She said, "It wasn't that impor—"

He said, "Hold it. Let me finish. After a while I said to myself, why the hell not? Can it do me any harm? Am I so damn delicate that I'm scared that in rubbing elbows with my Black bourgeoisie brothers and sisters more of them will rub off on me than of me rub off on them? If I'm that insecure, my Black Consciousness must be pretty thin and superficial. I mean, they're part of the Black-and-Beautiful thing as much as anybody else. Every father's child of us has been brainwashed with the whitewash. All of us is trying to make that journey home." He said, "Look, little Sheba, you know your Captain has been out on the turf a long damn time. Right? When I used to come ashore in New York a couple of years ago, I used to hang out at the bar at Wilt's. Me and my shipshape buddy. We'd stand there and dig the chicks standing on the other side of the bar digging us. We were just out for a little old sport. I would say, 'How about that one over there with the green dress on?' He'd say, 'You don't want to mess with her. I know that broad, she ain't no good.' I'd say, 'Hell, baby, I ain't no good either, so what else is new?' "

Yoruba was quiet for a moment, then she laughed, quietly, with him and her. She stopped, he stopped, and they turned toward one another. "Yes!" she said. And then said, "Oh Lumumba, my dear Captain, how did you get so wise in so few years?"

He said modestly, "They do say that travel is the great educator." He cleared his throat. "Together with experience."

She said, "Why do you love me, Lumumba? I mean, I just feel so unworthy sometimes."

He said, "Why is the ocean wet with water? Why is sand in the Sahara?"

She said, "You're so wise and wonderful."

Her Captain said, in all humility, "You're just saying that because it's so damn true."

There was this long silent lull in which she made up her mind and changed it again and again, a thousand times, it seemed. Then she said, finally, "My mother and I are having a great big fight. I—"

His dark eyes were so deeply intense. "Is it about me? I hope it isn't, I mean—"

She shook her head from side to side. "No. It's not about you at all."

"What is it then? All night I felt somehow that there was something on your mind."

Yoruba said, "She wants me to go with her out on the Island to Southampton next week to work at a rich white folks' cotillion."

"And—?"

"You know I told her, No, I wouldn't do it, I didn't care how many tears she shed. I didn't care what kind of argument she put in favor of it. There could be no reason—"

"How did she argue? I mean, what was her reason?"

"She said we could use the extra money toward my college education. But especially, she said, it would be an opportunity to see what a real rich white folks' cotillion was really like."

"Yeah," Lumumba said, "it figures. To see how the rich white folks go at it. That would be the only reason. To dig it at the bloody source."

CHAPTER ELEVEN

THE REALLY REAL THING

>This is the real thing,
>The way it was,
>the way it is,
>the way it always
>will be
>ever,
>as it was in the beginning,
>is now and forevermore.

The Southern "negra" woman across the street from the Lovejoys had told Lady Daphne about the fabulous gig out in Southampton on Long Island. It seems they gave an annual debutante ball out in Southampton during the merry month of May and they made mucho merry, and naturally required additional servants to take care of the mess, the Southern negra woman told her. "You know how nasty and lazy and dirty rich white folks is" . . . No, Lady Daphne thought to herself, she positively did not know how nasty and dirty and lazy rich white folks were, but she did know, decidedly so, how nasty and dirty and shiftless and wort'less Southern negras definitely were, without the shadow of a doubt, amongst people who were reasonable. But she kept her wisdom to herself this time. She didn't want to hurt the negra woman's feelings, and besides she wanted the job, and Black Mrs. Odessa Goodlipt was in charge of organizing the colored wrecking crew.

When Yoruba went to the Captain's Quarters a few nights later she was up real tight and strung way out, and he got loud vibrations from her when she first walked through the door. She drank more of the Captain's wine than usual and sat around closemouthed and unresponsive to the wine, to him, to his mighty word power, to the music of the record player. She would not be turned on, no matter. Most of the time she sat there before him, her legs crossed at the knees, the under leg bouncing up and down, the leg atop swinging to and fro, shaking like she had to make it to the powder room, the fingers of her right hand making like they were typing manuscripts or playing rhythm and blues on a baby grand.

Finally he said, "All right, you can tell the Captain everything."

She stopped bouncing, swinging and twiddling, momentarily. "I have no idea what you mean."

"Okay," he said. "Now I know you have something on your mind to tell me, and I know you want to tell me. It's about that stupid white folks' cotillion. Am I right?"

"Yes," she said, her eyes filling. "It was bad enough for me to let my mother talk me into the stupid colored cotillion, with her weeping bitter tears and crying that nobody loved her and everybody against her and whatnot, and her poor weak heart, and all that, but a person has to draw the line somewhere, and I mean, Ben Ali, this is it, no matter her ranting and raving, but why can't she understand?" She wiped her eyes and blew her nose. "Why can't she understand, Ben Ali? I love my mother! I really love my mother! And I don't like to hurt her, but I have to take a stand. This is where I have to draw the line."

He sipped his wine, reflectively. He looked down at the floor and up into her bleary eyes again. When he spoke, he spoke just above a whisper. "Why?" he asked. "How come?"

She said, "Wha-wha-what do you mean, why, how come?"

He said, "I mean, why? How come? Why do you have to take a stand and draw the line?"

"I-I-I can't compromise any further." Would they never understand each other? The Queen of Sheba and her Captain!

He said, "Who're you compromising with? The white power structure whom you despise? Or your mother who birthed you, all praises to Allah, and Malcolm, and Big Matt, but whom you sometimes strongly disagree with, but whom you also love and respect, because she is your mother and because she is Black and beautiful whether she wants to be or not? I mean, the white establishment is one thing, your mother is a different establishment altogether."

He talked too fast for her sometimes. She had everything pigeonholed in its proper place. Some things were right, some things were wrong, and some things brooked no compromise. Absolutely. Unequivocally. But now he had her all confused. She said, "Sometimes I really don't understand you. I mean, whose side are you on?"

"I'm on your side, my queen. And we're both on the side of Black folks. And your mother is not the enemy. She just truly ain't the enemy. If she is, then we are in a real big hurt. Cause your mother is where a whole heap of the Black and beautiful people of the Black Nation are at. I mean like, she goes overboard, I will admit. Out to lunch indefinitely. Miss Daphne is a caricature of her own dear bourgeois self. I mean, most of the time, she ain't to be believed, okay. But face it, she *is* Black, she *is* of the Nation whether she wants to be or not, she lives in the blackest of Black neighborhoods, she is working class to the core. I mean, she sure ain't middle class. She's just got her head all messed up with bourgeois aspirations. I mean, your mother is the Black masses that we're supposed to be fighting for. If we can't dig what's bugging her, forget it."

He stopped. He slowly smiled. "And besides, look how Mother Daphne and Lumumba hit it off. Who would've predicted it? I mean, have we got the great love affair of the decade going, or haven't we? I mean, who knows? Before long, I might have her wearing a natural before her daughter does. I might have her out in the street throwing Molotov cocktails soon one morning."

She laughed a short laugh. Remembering how her mother had gone around for days after Lumumba's visit. "He's not such a bad young man atall atall—He ain't such a bad young man atall atall—"

Yoruba had said to her, teasingly, "You mean you're not going to add him to your collection of crosses, Mother?"

"He's rather handsome," Lady Daphne said whimsically. "He's intelligent, polite—mannerly—"

"But Mother—he's the same person he was before he got that crew-cut haircut and bought that Brooks Brothers suit. He's your woolly-headed African. He hasn't changed."

"Everybody changes," her mother said surreptitiously, slyly smiling.

"All he has to do, Mother, is grow his hair back and put on his dashiki."

"I know," her mother said. "So I was mistaken about him.

Everybody makes mistakes, queens as well as commoners. And everybody changes." She smiled her sly smile. "And he ain't such a bad young man atall atall—even if he is a vagabund."

And now, here, in the Captain's Quarters, Yoruba said to Lumumba, "But all that was a case of mistaken identity and false pretenses, and neither one of you have really changed, or, maybe one of you has changed, who knows? But which one?"

Lumumba smiled. "Every living human changes. The great ones and the lowly ones. It's the law of the universe."

She laughed, at the similarity of Daphne's and Lumumba's words. And then she said, "But-but-but what's all this got to do with the cotillion on Long Island?"

He said, "I've been thinking about that ever since you mentioned it the other night. Like I say, once I said I'd be your escort, well I mean like I meant I'd be your escort all the way. The implications were not clear to me at first. I thought to myself, I'll just be her escort, cause she's my queen, but that's all I'll be. I ain't about to make the scene at any of those jive rehearsals and all those other bourgeois happenings. But then I began to think, I'm a writer, right? And the whole damn world is my apple. Okay, that means every happening that I experience is grist to my mill, dig? So I decided to make all the cotillion happenings and get me some material for a book. Hey! And call it *The Cotillion*. Dig it. And I've been writing my first novel ever since. I don't mean I've actually been putting it down on paper, but I've been soaking up the experiences."

Yoruba looked into her Captain's face and knew that he was serious. She felt exploited and violated and spied upon. He was a voyeur and had gazed upon her innocence. Her face filled up and the tears stood just out of sight on that other side of her eyes. "So I was just another apple to you, I mean, of your experience and I'm grist to your mill. I'm a literary happening. I'm—I'm—I'm another book you're going to write. Thanks a lot for honesty." The ship was rocky now, the sea was white and foamy and she felt a great seasickness. Her head was swimming around and around, and she could not sit still for fear of sinking. "You—you—you—I feel—Ben Ali—I just don't—" Her voice choked off.

He said roughly, "Stop it, will you?" And came and took her in his arms. "Cut that out! Of course you are an experience to me, the most profound that ever came my way. Lucky me. You are a happening, baby. A tremendous happening. To me, you always were a happening, and always will be. What's wrong with that? Yeah! Go tell it on the mountain, over the hills and everywhere, shout hallelujah, tell them the comforter has come, you're my one and only comforter, and you've brought joy joy joy to my soul." He kissed her eyes wet and salty with her tears, kissing away the tears, her dear eyes wet now with his kisses. "You're the book that I've been writing all my years. You're my one and only masterpiece. You're my first and final inspiration, the greatest novel ever written, sculptured out of purest ebony, written by the natural gods of our fathers and humbly interpreted by the lucky one, Captain Ben Ali Lumumba. I mean when the Black gods got through with you, they fashioned me to glorify you."

She was inundated with the floodtide of Lumumba's words. It was as if he had thrown her out into the deepest part of the great white foam, the Philippine Trench outside of Leyte Gulf; he had thrown her out to sink or swim and then dove in to save her, he, the man, Lumumba, her savior and her only Captain.

"Now," he said, "why not dig the happenings at the stupid rich white folks' cotillion. Let us get it from the horse's mouth, or better, from his hinder parts. I mean, if we're going to write this story of the Grand Cotillion let us put it in the context of the great white thing of which it is a pitiful imitation. I mean, I ain't about to attack the Black bourgeoisie whoever they are and wherever. I ain't about to attack them in a vacuum. I ain't about to overlook the influential white bourgeoisie. Okay, so let us do it in the context of the great white thing itself. Let us dig the source."

He still held her strongly in his arms. She said, "Us?" She was cast adrift again at the total mercy of the sea, where all was organized confusion.

He said, "Yes, *us*. You and me, always and for-goddamn-ever. We will do this thing together. I mean, like see if you can get me a job working the party along with you and Mother Daphne. I want to dig their game so I can blow it. I mean, like I was telling some of my hip Black student brothers and sisters the other night, how you going to beat the Man's system if you do not know his bloody game?" Thinking to himself, Moreover we can teach Miss Daphne a lesson she'll never forget.

"You talk too fast," she said. She had been standing. Now she sat back down again. Get yourself together, girl. When she spoke again, she said again, "You talk too fast."

He said, "Yeah, I'm hip, I talk too fast. But we've been talking too slow too long, as if we ain't never sure what we're talking about, as if we really have to take our time to scratch intelligence out of our lovely naps. One question," he said, "my beloved, can you get me a job working with you and Mama on that stupid white cotillion?"

Okay, he was not easy to keep up with. He was a pace-setter, a long-distance runner with the swiftness of a sprinter, and he would always run way out ahead of the remainder of the pack.

They all worked the cotillion on Long Island, Yoruba, Daphne, and Lumumba, along with other numerous Black brothers and sisters. It was Operation-Overslave, Lumumba thought. There seemed to be a servant for every debutante and even for every escort. I mean, when you arrived at the dinky little old make-do pad out in the disadvantaged, culturally deprived Southampton on Long Island, surrounded by a fence of barbed-wired hedges ten feet high, when you entered the meager little area of twenty-five or thirty acres, in the midst of which was a potluck crib of more than fifty rooms including sitting rooms and living rooms and marble stairways and drawing rooms and back stairs and ballrooms and libraries and dens and especially whatnots of all descriptions, as you drove through the grounds and approached this humble abode to park your car, you were attacked by a team of uniformed men (security agents?) who turned out to be parking attendants, ten of them alert and ever at the ready. Would you believe conspicuous consumption? Were these people ostentatious?

The folks got there before the people came. And were assigned their respective and respectful posts. Then there was the time at the beginning when the most gracious host and hostess, Mr. and Mrs. Von Vundercock, stood near the entrance to the main ballroom in a reception line receiving guests, with two, tall, elegant Black men resplendent in their tails and stuff shirts, taking coats and other outer apparel, and another black-tailed handsome one announcing guests as they arrived and made the scene. It was really a pretty thing to observe, and Lady Daphne did more observing than serving that first hour of her profound enchantment.

"Oh, ain't it too beautiful!" Sighing and sometimes even sobbing with delight, and telling her daughter, "Watch everything. Learn some direct culturation!"

"Congressman and Mrs. Basil Anderson!" See them move now with measured and self-conscious grace toward the great and wealthy Von Vundercocks at the head of the receiving line, the congressman short and chunky seems to be walking around in a perpetual squatting position like a baseball catcher or a man forever in the attitude of a bowel movement, his lady, tall and regal, could put a plate on his head and easily eat therefrom.

"Oh my dear, it almost takes your breath away." From Lady Daphne. "See how they bow, see how they shake hands, see how they curtsey! Now you know why I wanted you to come!" Lady Daphne forgot that she had come there to do an evening's work. "Isn't it thrilling!" She probably would have worked for nothing just to be able to dig the aristocratic happenings. It was cheap at twice the price, a way to go to heaven without paying dying dues.

"Mr. and Mrs. Robert Barren! And their daughter Roberta Barren, Jr.!"

"Mr. and Mrs. William Finkle! And their daughter, Deborah Finkle."

"Ambassador and Mrs. John Vaughn-Johnson!"

And so on.

During the interim between the reception line and the cotillion ceremonial rites, Lady Daphne went around curtseying respectfully and telling everybody (meaning all the nice white people): "My daughter, the pretty dark-skin colored girl over there, she's going to be in the Grand Cotillion at the Waldorf!" They, the white and proper bourgeois, looked at her as if she had just told them that a donkey had been ordained for the ministry by the Presbyterian diocese.

All during the elegant witchcraft of the proper Ceremonial Rites of Cotillion, Miss Daphne strolled around entranced. Indeed, if she but knew it, she strolled with more elegance than any of the debutantes dressed as they were in their long white gowns of virginal purity, aristocracy and dignity personified, the best that money could buy. "Look how they waltz, Eve-lyn, my poor dearest darling! Looka! Looka! Looka!"

"Mother! We're supposed to be doing a gig tonight."

"Dancing the jig?" Her mother looked askance at her, in horror. "Dancing the jig? These genteel peoples doesn't dance no jig! This is a cultural occasion. They doesn't do no nigger dances here!"

"Mother! Please!" the daughter whispered. "I said *we* were supposed to be doing a gig. I mean, we're supposed to be working, not participating in the festivities."

Her mother said. "Oh! Why ain't you speaking plain intelligent king's English then?"

Yoruba smiled softly. "Mother, do you know what Lumumba told me? He said, when the term the 'king's English' came into vogue, Old George, the king of England, was a terrible speaker of the language, spoke English with a guttural German accent."

Her mother looked at her as if she had uttered the last word in blasphemy; it was as if she said that Jesus was a Black man of the Jewish faith. Sometimes truth was horrifying, especially to people who were not accustomed to it. But doing a gig or dancing the jig, whichever, it made no difference to Miss Daphne. Her great spirit remained undaunted, her identification with the glorious happenings totally intact. For truth, it was a most impressive, most splendiferous occasion. Correct, proper, stylish, elegant. It was a thing of unimaginable splendor. A moment when the world took notice. Gentlemen of the fourth estate photographing every matchless minute of it; you almost went blind from flash flares.

Lady Daphne was entranced by the heavenly spectacle, or spectacular, whichever. The fathers, handsome, and of rich-as-creamy faces (some short ugly dumplings but all of them beautiful in her sight), and the daughters, slim and graceful, now they advance regally toward each other, father bows, daughter curtsies in a sweet and queenly fashion. Now as Daphne watched a tall majestic gentleman take his daughter's white-gloved hand, she herself felt so thrilled and uplifted, tears spilled down her cheeks unknowingly, as she conjured up the image of her own father, the years washed away from her, and she became the dear young sweet white thing in the white virginal dress, she got completely carried away, and began to waltz with her imaginary father who watched her smiling from his heavenly perch. Yoruba took her to the kitchen and brought her back to here and now with ice-cold applications. "That's what I want for my little girl! That's what I want for my little girl—for my little girl—for my little girl—" She kept repeating as she sobered up.

It must be said for Daphne that the conduct of the pure and innocent virgins was exemplary, angelic even, somewhat in the tradition of Uncle Tom's Little Eva. You could see the halos around their golden heads, if you had the imagination. "This is what I want for you, Eve-lyn, my dearie. This is how it has to be." You couldn't blame Miss Daphne. No young ladies reaching toward womanhood had ever conducted themselves with such impeccability in the whole recorded history of ladyship and womanhood. Of course, after the ceremonial acts of animal husbandry were concluded, after the press and parents had departed, to do their own thing, or things, whichever and wherever, after the twenty-five-piece orchestra changed their faces from pinkish-white to brownish-black and their repertoire from Lawrence Welk to Raymond Charles, after the dear innocents and their friends and escorts began to sip just a teeny weeny bit of the alcoholic spirits, they sort of naturally got into the spirit of things, Lumumba calling Miss Daphne's attention to the innocent, playful happenings. Little harmless happenings such as fighting over the buffet table, eating with their hands instead of knives and forks ("Look, Miss Daphne!"), grabbing pieces of meat from the platters with their bare hands, using turkey drumsticks as weapons; it was like it must have been more than a thousand years ago at King Arthur's Table Round. One playful young gentleman went around pouring champagne down the fronts of the girlies' party dresses. It was all in the spirit of loosening up and getting to know each other, on more intimate terms, that is. And after that, things began to relax a tiny bit. Over near the bandstand a few of the young socialites began to send up little smoke signals to the holy Gods of Pot.

Meanwhile, Lumumba got his kicks bugging Miss Daphne, pointing out to her the little harmless pranks the cream of the crap were playing on one another. "Look, Miss Daphne, he's goosing her! Isn't this just the really real thing? Look! She's goosing him back! Too much! The really real thing all the way!"

When the party first began to get a little rough, Miss Daphne's reaction was: "Ain't they the most mis-chee-vous ones though? So free, so white, so twenty-one!"

All during the big bash, Lumumba would run into an alcove, off and on, or into an unoccupied room or a pantry or one of the men's rooms, or somewhere else out of sight, and jot down little cultural tidbits of the evening's happenings. He was glad that he had come. He was getting a pocket-sized notebook full of material for his novel. He went into one dark unoccupied room down one of the long corridors that ran off at once in all directions, and fumbled for the switch. When he turned on the lights, he found two young white genteel gentlemen already turned on, and in a serious attitude of mouth-to-mouth resuscitation, cheek to cheek and belly to belly, with no holds barred. Ben Ali said, "Oh, *excuse me.*" But they were not in the least embarrassed, buttressed as they were by the strength of their convictions, or so it seemed, since they very generously invited him to join in the passionate sincere happening. "We believe in integration."

But he left the dear committed lovebirds to their own buggering devices and went in search for another place of solitude. He thought, Miss Daphne should have dug that scene.

After a while, when the atmosphere was filled with alcoholic happenings, like smog over Manhattan Island in the late of afternoon, Lady Daphne, who really never drank a drop, seemed to be affected by the mere proximity of the happy spirits. She went around whispering to the young genteel white people, pointing to Lumumba, "He's a very important person, even if he is a Black man. Ain't a week pass his picture ain't in *The New York Times*. We don't have to do this jigging for a living. We just only merely observing you peoples. We going write a book about you."

With Lady Daphne's kind assistance a few of the young white folks recognized Lumumba from his single *New York Times* notoriety. And bugged him, for days, that night. "You can't fool me. You're somebody. I just know you are. You're somebody in disguise."

One horsey girl insisted, wide-eyed and open-mouthed, "Are

you Sidney Poitier? Harry Belafonte? Cassius Clay? Le Roi Jones? Ralph Bunche? Sammy Davis, Jr.?"

One young dark-eyed woman kept coming over to him with: "Say, I've got my eyes on y'all." She was not fat but she was fully rounded in the proper woman places, amply-assed and double-breasted. She jiggled proudly when she walked. The first time she came over to him, he had looked behind him and around him to see what y'all and how many y'alls the nice little red-headed speckled peach from Georgia was speaking to. He was a champion on accents. Each time she came she would take another highball from his tray and she came with amazing frequency, although, after a while, when she came her legs were not as steady as before. Her jiggle had become a little jagged at the edges. "Say, I've got my eyes on y'all!" And leaning against him to keep from falling. Her eyes so dark and full of seriousness. Once when he went to the men's room to take some notes and to take care of even more urgent business, he was about to close the bathroom door behind him as he entered, when he heard a loud hiccup and somebody say, "Say, I've got my eyes on y'all!" As she started into the bathroom behind him. He let her go in and he closed the door behind her, and went to do his business in another bathroom.

If Lumumba was getting bored with this princess of Southern womanhood, who meant no harm to any man (right?), he was no more bored than her escort who was also from the peachy state. Every time she would go toward Lumumba, he would say, "Penelope, please, y'all embarrassing the po' boy."

Nature and good fortune had been bountiful to Penelope, and she, in her turn, was a generous young woman, it was plain to see, with a heart as enormous as her magnificent tits, which were so large the dear child seemed to be deformed. So liberally furnished were her knockers, men's eyes had been known to permanently cross, even as she engaged in a close-up conversation with them. Full-mouthed, she was, red-lipped, and even-teethed, with an eagerness for eating everything in sight. An appetite for life not easily appeased. Every movement, every gesture told you that life to her was one great feast with no expenses spared and costs no object, and every mother's sister's brother's child should be invited to partake thereof.

The next time she came up to Lumumba, her escort admonished

her. "Y'all making a nuisance out of yourself. That po' boy s'ked to death."

"White peoples is more than a motherfucker," one of the waiters commented dryly to Lumumba. He was a dark brown-skinned, lanky dude nearing six feet tall with most of him in the from-the-waist-up region of him. Short legs like fire plugs, a dog's delight. The Black orchestra was blasting away with rhythm and blues, and the joint was leaping. As much as white folks' joints can ever leap.

"Yeah," Ben Ali answered absently. "They do have a major problem with the Oedipus complex."

Fire Plug said, "Honh?"

Ben Ali said, "After all, Oedipus *was* a motherfucker, wasn't he?"

The girl from Georgia came again, took another drink from Ben Ali. "I'm from Welfare, Georgia, and I just adore y'all alla y'all. I'm a Southern liberal."

Her escort pulled her away again. "Penelope, if that boy don't keep his eyes offa you, I'm just gon have to take him down a peg or two, so you best be careful." Another Southern liberal, obviously.

Miss Georgia Peach turned, undaunted, toward Lumumba. "Say, I've got my eyes on y'all!"

When she came again she said, "We don't know much about New York. We want to go to one of those real hipsy dipsy nightclubs. Could you make us a suggestion? How about the Copah Banana?" Her escort stood there by her side. Glaring, mumbling, grumbling, scowling.

Lumumba said, "You don't want to go to no Copah Banana. That ain't no hipsy dipsy joint. There's a club down in the Village on Bleecker Street known as Decadence Incorporated, where the ofays tear their natural drawers by the numbers."

She swayed from side to side and shouted softly, "Wheeeeee!" And stepped stumbling out of her dress and stood there in her slip and bra. "Do they really tear them by the numbers?"

Lumumba said, "Yes, m'am! By the natural numbers." He saw Miss Daphne watching scowling from a distance. The Georgia peach began to kick up her heels high over her head, her breasts jiggling, flipping and flopping, and then she went into a grinding movement. "Do they do the hoochie koochie?"

Fire Plug and Ben Ali began to clap their hands to give rhythm to the lady's grinding. "Yes, m'am! They really do the hoochie koochie! Believe me when I say so!"

She said, "I believe you!" Sincerely.

Her escort caught up with her again and dragged her away, just as she began to pull the last things she had on off, he mumbling, "Let's git outa here and go to that Decadence place if we going, before I have to whip that nigger's ass."

Meanwhile the party got a little rougher. Like Miss Daphne said, "This was the really real thing!" She wished Lumumba would stop coming up to her and saying, "Look, Miss Daphne! Boys will be boys. Ain't that right? Especially if they're gentlemen of the upper classes." And so on ad infinitum. As if Miss Daphne was blind in one eye and could not see out of the other one.

Some of the young social lions tried to exercise their gentlemanly prerogatives with the colored maiden servants. Hands reached out devilishly accidentally-on-purpose to pinch and pat well-appointed Black backsides and squeeze plump-breasted nipples, and some of the Black women had no more couth and knew no better than to slap the faces of the playful rascals. There was one four-eyed rosy-cheeked dude-of-a-gentleman in particular who kept bugging Yoruba all night long. He stood in her path, surrounded her, breathed on her neck.

"Dance with me, Black beauty," he kept insisting drunkenly.

She told him, "I am not here to dance in the cotillion."

"But the cotillion is over. This is the party."

"I am not here to dance. I came here to work."

"You come on and dance with me," he drunkenly insisted. And took her by the arm. And put his arms around her and tried to pull her up against him.

"Take your hands off her," Lumumba told the rosy-cheeked one, "unless you're tired of living." He roughly pushed the man away from her.

"What business is it of yours, boy?"

"You'll find out what my business is if you don't leave the lady alone," Lumumba told the white boy.

The rosy-cheeked boy said, "You must be one of them bad militant ones."

"Militant what?" Lumumba asked him

Another white lad intervened. "Don't pay him any mind, mister. He's just had too much to drink."

"He'd better not get so drunk that he can't smell my whiskey," Lumumba answered.

Fire Plug walked up. "Yeah," he said, "else St. Peter be checking out his alcoholic content first thing in the morning."

Rosy Cheek's face was afire now with a righteous indignation. He pulled away from his apologetic buddy and moved, stumblingly, toward Lumumba. "No nigger's going to talk to me like—"

It sounded like somebody had blown up a paper bag and burst it with his fist. But what it really was was Lumumba's open hand against the face of Rosy Cheeks. He had gone upside the gentleman's head. Rosy Cheeks stood there rocking and reeling, his hand holding his stinging face. Even so, he couldn't believe a Black man had slapped him, actually. "There must be some mistake," he said.

"Damn right," Lumumba told the reddening dude. "And you're the one that made it, boy. You better believe it."

The rosy-cheeked one bristled with his anger and moved toward Ben Ali again. His buddy pulled him back. "Too many of them out here tonight. They might be planning a race riot and they don't look nonviolent."

Lady Daphne watching everything. The really real thing was really real.

The orchestra was blasting, some Black dude was singing, "Cry Me a River." People all over the ballroom doing their individual thing, dancing, necking, stripteasing. Couples started wandering off all over the house into the bedrooms. Laughing, giggling, moaning, groaning, sighing, screwing, privately and openly. Lumumba came over to Miss Daphne one more time. "Look, Miss Daphne! Look! Look! This is really a cultural evening!"

Cute little harmless happenings began themselves to happen now. And Lumumba never failed to call Miss Daphne's attention to same. He was a very thoughtful lad and wanted his future mother-in-law to miss none of the elegant happenings. A few of the Jacks and Jills began to swing from the delicate glittering

210

chandeliers like Tarzan and Lady Jane. "Aye-oooooohaha!!!" Some sliding down the banister now, and with no hands (some dear girls with no pants on). "Look, Miss Daphne!" Ben Ali was balling back. Some of the little devils were blowing up prophylactics in lieu of toy balloons (boys will be boys, after all, and hopefully). "Look!" Over to the right of the bandstand, a couple of exuberant youngsters of the gentler sex were stripping down to the very nitty gritty of the bare essentials. There they were now in their darling birthday suits, wearing nothing but beautiful smiles. And hair, the long and short of it. Lady Daphne was getting tired of looking and weary of Lumumba pointing things out.

Lumumba and Fire Plug figured they might as well have a little fun. Everybody else was balling back. They started to switching the "Him" and "Her" signs on the seven or fifteen toilet doors, so the boys went in where the girls were doing it, and vice versa. "Mess up their little old white minds," Lumumba told Fire Plug. "They're already beaucoup ambivalent."

"Yeah," Fire Plug responded. "And what about their eeda-pussies and all that complex shit?"

After a while, it didn't matter, the young socialites used the Hims and Hers interchangeably, as if they did not know the difference. Maybe they don't, Lumumba thought. Hopefully. Joyfully.

Some of the toilets were like restrooms, with stand-up urinals and everything, which became quite an interesting and challenging problem for the female of the species. People started to sit on the seats taking care of business with the toilet doors open. Lumumba went into one that was furnished with five urinal stalls. There was one drunken young gentleman leaning tippingly over one of the stalls, trying desperately to get his fly open and his thing unleashed before it was too late. But he was in such an inebriated state he couldn't seem to get the hang of it.

He said to Lumumba, "Hey, old buddy, will you do a pal a favor, old buddy, will you do a pal a real good favor? I mean, will you?"

"What kind of favor?"

"Would you kindly assish me in extricating my noble peenish from this little old prishon here, on account of I definitely have to urinate?"

Lumumba said, "You got to be kidding." And went to take care of his own business.

Meanwhile another young man of the social set came into the restroom. He was more hospitable than Ben Ali. Gentlemen are gentle men. He obliged his drunken fellow man. "Will you zip me down, old buddy?"

Young Old Buddy zipped him down.

"Will you do me just a little bit of another little old favor? Will you take it out for me? Your kindnesh will never be forbliberated."

Lumumba thought, This scene would truly blow Miss Daphne's mind.

Old Buddy, sweating now, and cussing softly to himself in a most ungentlemanly fashion, but nonetheless he was obliging. He did liberate the little pink mousie from its mohair prison.

"Thanks, pal, old buddy of mine. Oowee! It feel so good!" As he spurted forth his little old stream. Then, "I have one more requesh to make. Will you—will you—will you shake it for me?" Old Buddy let flow a stream of oaths that would make a whore's pimp's hair stand on end. But he was obliging. What the hell? Old Buddy shook it for him, gingerly, and put it back where it belonged, and this time zipped him up without the asking. But was the drunken gentleman appreciative? Hardly. Just because Old Buddy spilt a little pee on the gentleman's trousers, said gentleman asked him growlingly, "Who in the hell taught you how to pish?"

Going down the hall, Lumumba heard loud screams from another one of the Him restrooms. "Help! Help! Please! Help me! Help me!"

Lumumba opened the toilet door, and there was this four-eyed rosy-cheeked dude who had been giving Yoruba and him such a bad time, seated on the toilet stool. Apparently he had forgotten his gender, and had sat down to make his water. In any event, he had somehow managed to get his cutest little fellow caught between the toilet seat and the commode. And there he sat in sweat and tears and excruciating pain. "Help me! Help me!" he begged pitifully, as Lumumba slowly closed the door behind him. And locked it. "Help me! Help me! I ain't got nothing against you people!"

Lumumba stood there staring down at the pathetic little bespectacled bugger. Wondering with a weird detachment how in holy hell Rosy Cheeks had managed it.

"I swear to Jesus I love niggers! I'm a member of the Urban League, the N-double-A-C-P, the CORE, Snickers, Panthers and all the rest of it. I'm a Black militant all the way. Please have mercy on me!"

Lumumba pondered the question briefly, held with himself a quick debate, hesitated momentarily. Then he slowly raised his foot and brought it down on the seat with great vigor and enthusiasm. The poor rich white dude's rosy cheeks lost color as he fainted clean away. Shouting "Nigger! Nigger! Nigger!" Even after he lost consciousness, from deep in his unconscious, he kept mumbling "Nigger! Nigger! Nigger! Nigger—Nigger—Nigger—"

Through it all Lumumba faithfully kept record of the little harmless incidents in a notebook he had brought with him for the purpose of note-keeping. Getting material for his novel. Rich material. Later, he would transfer it to his log, where he always made his nightly entries.

Through it all, Daphne Lovejoy kept desperately the faith, even with Lumumba bugging her. "Look! Look, Miss Daphne! So this is the great white upper class, the cream of the crop! Wow!" Well, that is, she almost kept it. But after all is said and done, Miss Daphne was nobody's fool. And she loved her family, though she had a poor way of showing it, sometimes. Would you believe, oftentimes? And now, at this, the "really real thing," the epitome of WASPY culture, a misty veil was slowly lifting from her eyes, even as she struggled valiantly to remain behind the veil of her darling innocence. Just because she believed that these people out here on the Island were the cream of the crop, the most ideal, to-be-emulated people in the world (second to none, excepting, of course, the ladies and gentlemen of the realm of her Britannic Majesty), it did not mean that she did not keep an eye on the young gallant devils when they went toward her Yoruba Evelyn, with their eyes and talk and busy hands. Near the end, she stayed close to her girl, and challenged all the gay young blades with hard black looks from her cold blue eyes which had changed now to the dark consuming fires of her African mother's disposition. Almost against her will, it seemed, her Negritude caught up with her.

"Dance with your own kind," she told one young, tall, drunken gentleman. "My daughter is a colored lady." Near the end, she stood guard against the young, white "cream of the crap," as Matthew Lovejoy called them sometimes. Her husband was not always wrong, she now suspected, as she fought off five or six or seven of the gallant hoodlums of society. She held her daughter as a sacred trust. "Do your thing, Miss Daphne!" Lumumba cheered her from the rooting section. "With your bad self! Olé! Olé! What you say!"

At one point Yoruba escaped the gay (wild?) festivities, going into one of the powder rooms and locking the door behind her. She breathed a deep sigh of deliverance. She would put cold water on her face and get herself together. But as she turned away from the door she became aware that she was not alone. There was this straggly-haired young lady seated on the toilet stool with her skirt up to her elbows. Crying, whimpering, sobbing, talking, interchangeably, from which Yoruba gathered that some cavalier fellow had poured a Texas fifth of Chivas Regal on her head and Scotched the poor dear girl, for days. Dig it, she was all strung out, her blond hair was so stringy it looked like crazy slivers of disintegrated chitterlings. Yoruba's hand went up, unknowingly, and she patted her own hair in place. And moved to the basin with a queenly motion.

The chitterling-haired girl stared up out of her misery. "What the hell are you so smug about? Your hair *should* be in place by now, you spend enough hours at it trying to make it look like mine." And the miserable girl began to laugh hysterically.

Yoruba cupped her hands and doused her face with cold water, wiped it in an awful hurry, and left the laughing girl to her own devices.

Meanwhile things were slowly getting out of hand. Grass fires were breaking out all over the place now as if the joint was burning down. The smell of incensed pot was everywhere. Part of the party had moved out on to the grounds which were more like a campus than a lawn. Dig it, smoking grass out on the grass. Dancing on the dewy breeze and off among the trees in birthday suits with such wild and free abandon like spritely elves of olden times. Wrestling naked in the sweet wet grass. Raucous laughter filled the air, all innocence profound. Love! Love! Love! Love was everywhere. And all was love. And lots of folk were making love. Upstairs. Downstairs. In the bedrooms, in the bathrooms, even on the ballroom floor, it was love, love, love, sometimes even loveless love. If you can dig it.

By now Miss Daphne was sick of the sight of Lumumba, but he kept coming up to her, making sure she missed none of the elegant cultural happenings. "See, Miss Daphne? Over there!"

One young gentleman, doing himself a strange Watusi, came in for a tight-two close-up with his lady dancing partner (surrounded now they were by a band of great admirers who clapped their hands in a kind of off-time rhythm and in profound adoration); he took the fair young lady in his arms, hoisted her delicate skirts like a true stickup man, unshafted his modest weapon and gunned the precious virgin right there on the ballroom floor, to the wild applause of their admirers. "Go! Go! Go! Go!" The cheers came from the rooting section.

Love! Love! Love! So much love was bound to spill over into overlove. Can you dig it? Fights began to break out all over the place, inside, outside, upstairs, downstairs. Whiskey bottles flung, glasses broken. Heads bloodied. All in the name of love, sweet love. Young love, young lovers. Lumumba got into a couple of brawls with some dudes who wanted to carry love too far and get too cozy with Yoruba. Somehow he couldn't get the hang of interracial love-ins. Was he old-fashioned? Miss Daphne was in full agreement.

After all that smoking there was bound to be a fire, and a fire did break out in the west wing of the mansion. Police came to stop the riot, which was not of a racial nature, *The New York Times* reported. Fire engines came replete with firemen and their house-breaking equipment. And they proceded to break up the house. And that broke up the party. Young ladies and gentlemen screaming, police sirens and fire engines blasting the quiet of the cool of the evening.

Finally things went too far, and Lady Daphne had to admit it, even to herself, that is. It started as an uneasy feeling with her that everything was not altogether cricket, but how could that be? She was just letting that vagabund, Lumumba, get on her nerves was what. These were the elite upper classes. The WASPY people. But the feeling inside dear Daphne slowly grew, and by degrees, until finally toward the end, it could no longer be denied. And so, almost against her will, she began to shout, in a manner quite hysterical. Would you believe, unladylike? "It can't be! It can't be! It just can't be! Just can't be! They acting like niggers! Acting like niggers! Just like niggers—just like niggers—"

With disillusion deep in her eyes.

Can you dig her disenchantment?

Daphne made her move before the police and the firemen came. Against her will, she'd got her fill of the high-society people. She started to go into her thing, chipsing away and looking at her blessed crosses. She went in search of Lumumba and when she found him, she said, "Get Yoruba Eve-lyn and let's get out of this Godforsaken den of infidels."

He said, "But how? What happened? I mean, don't we have to go back in the limousines with the rest of the workers?" He could not believe his happy ears.

She said, "How can you stand any more of these white devils? Let's get out of this insane asylum, even if we have to walk all the way to the train station!"

Which is what they had to do.

And they did it.

With no moon or stars above them.

CHAPTER TWELVE

TO WIG OR NOT TO WIG

> everybody goes
> when the wagon comes,
> every living
> with a swinging,
> even them that
> doesn't swing.
> every mother's sister's child,
> every father's darling daughter.

Dig. It was a time for change. Change was in the air you breathed. New York's rainy chilly springtime changing into steamy summer. Springtime of our terrible disenchantment changing into a long hot summer of their sacred violence. It was Shakespeare in the park, it was snakeshit on the avenue. Boys became men, girls stumbled gracefully into blessed ladyhood. Everybody growing old, changing by the second, even babies in their cribs. Dying was a stylish thing from Harlem to Johannesburg. Change, baby, dig it. Life and death. And in between. Everybody's doing it, those who never did before. People made that ultimate change without batting two eyelashes. Everybody went when the wagon came. You cannot teach an old dog new tricks, the wise ones said, in yesteryears of times gone by.

Not that Lady Daphne was any sort of dog, old or new. She was a lady of no mean proportions. A high-class homo sapiens of the female upper-classes. She was Dowager Queen, Mother Superior, above the battle. She was all this, and yet this high-bred (hybrid?) one could not resist the laws of change. You would think a queen like her would not have to go through menopause. Change, brothers, sisters, dig it. Nobody could escape. Missedmenstruals, cold sweat, hot flashes, feelings of unloveliness, the whole damn bit. And other changes. She would never be the same, after the really real thing out on Long Island.

"Yes, I know, I've been a fool," she told Yoruba one evening as they sat at the kitchen table drinking steaming cups of tea. "Somehow I know all along it ain't really true, but I just keep on pretending. I was proud. You young folks talk about dignity now. Well, I wanted dignity bad bad. I saw that the white man had all the pride and dignity in the world. My mother and her folks was the humble people. Wherever my white father walked, Black men bowed and scraped, so I despised the Black in me."

"Mother, we all, I mean, Ben Ali says—"

"Yes," she said, "your Lumumba is a clever boy even though he got the devil in him." She closed her eyes. "I remember when I was a little girl about ten years old, my mother took me to visit one of her sisters. They ain't have the same mother. Her sister lived in Kingston in Jamaica in a big old house with another sister. The house was disrepairing before your very eyes. I can see them now. They were so proud those two, and as haughty as Mrs. Astor's billy goat." She laughed softly to herself. "They lived in genteel poverty. My aunt was blind, and when my mother said to her, this one is Daphne, she wanted to know who I took after, my Black mother or my white father. She didn't know exactly how to go about it. She was as diplomatic as a sly mongoose. She said, 'Come here, dearie, and let me pat your head.' Later, I overhear her say to the sister who lived with her, 'Daphne is the Black one with the woolly head.' I cried, I ran and looked into the looking glass. I was as fair as Goldilocks and I had a bad grade of good hair, or a good grade of bad hair, whichever. And I cried, I wanted to be white. And if I ever had any children I prayed to God they would be white, or I would do everything to make them white."

Yoruba felt like crying now. "But why—I mean—I mean, how come you married Father?"

"Because every white man I met in this country had no respect for me. All of them had one thing in mind. And I swear a long time ago, I kissed the Good Book, that I ain't never be the white man's whore." She paused for breath. "Or his concubine like my mother was, may the dear soul rest in peace. And your father, he respected me. Respected me too much sometimes. And I married him, because he was Black and respected me, and I thought he was beneath me and would bow down to me, his fair queen from Barbados." She paused and wiped her eyes and blew her nose. "But through the years, I learned to love him and respect him."

Almost unknowingly, Yoruba opened her mouth to interrupt.

"I know," Daphne said, "I ain't show it all the time. But I learned his quiet pride and gentle strength." She stopped. She wiped her eyes again. "Give me credit for something, Eve-lyn. If you love both of your parents, me and your father, there must have been some love in the house. You ain't make it up all by yourself. You ain't suck it out your thumb."

She, the girl, Yoruba, sat there smiling through her tears. Just the night before Ben Ali had told her, "There must have been some love in that house, to produce a lovely woman like my Queen of Sheba." It wasn't the same thing her mother was saying, but it was part and parcel of it.

"Oh, I tell you, all my life I live a lie. Kuh-deah! Worshiping the memory of my father, a white man who look upon me as one of his pickaninnies. I got to hold onto something, I keep thinking, even if it ain't real. I know now I been a vain, foolish woman all my life, but I always love my family, you and Matthew, and I going always love you."

Yes, Yoruba thought, not wisely, but you loved us. No thanks to William Shakespeare.

"I'm so happy we go out to that Long Island fete. It was for true the last illusion. I ain't never really loved white people. I was just too respectful of them, cause they got all the power. But the damn thing out on Long Island was the end of the journey for me." Daphne kissed her fingers and threw her hand up toward the Great One Up On High.

Yoruba went to her mother and kissed her and embraced her. She was laughing and crying now and trying to talk at the same time. She felt happy, she felt foolish, her mother crying too. Quietly the tears spilt down. Her mother crying softly, "Yoruba! Yoruba! Yoruba!" Her fingers digging into her daughter's hair. She had never called her Yoruba. It was Eve-lyn, always Eve-lyn. It was silly (right?), foolish, terrible and wonderful, two grown women crying in each other's arms.

Finally, her mother grew ashamed of tears. Felt her awesome

dignity compromised. She pushed gently but firmly away from the girl. "Sit down, Eve-lyn. There ain't nothing to cry about." She went to the stove and came back and poured more tea. She sat across from the girl now, staring at her through the misty fog of steaming tea. The mother said, "Everybody changes, even Lady Daffy." Smiling.

Yoruba blurted out from deep inside her, "Mother, let's do it up right, while we're at it?"

"Hey?"

"Let's make a clean break with the whole stupid idea of Cotillion."

"How you mean?"

"Let's say good-bye to the Femmes Fatales. Let's tell the Grand Cotillion faretheewell. Let's make a clean break with the whole—"

"Stick a pin there," Lady Daphne said. "Your mother ain't changed that radically yet. I'm a gradual changer, dearie. Look how long it take to get me this far."

"But you saw yourself how nowhere the whole thing was out in Long Island."

"It ain't have to be like that with us Black people." Called herself Black for once in life. "We can do it differently—with dignity and elegance. It ain't have to be like these sick white peoples." Her eyes twinkled mischievously, crinkling at the corners. "It can be Black and beautiful."

"Mother!"

"And besides, look at all the money your father is put into it already. Against his will and better judgment, he did it all for you. He already rent his tails and stuff, and I rent the mink stole. We can't go back on him now."

In some ways her mother was like Lumumba, she could turn things into their opposites if it went to suit her purpose. Yoruba stared at her mother now in a kind of unwilling admiration. "Go back on my father! How can you say—"

Lady Daphne said, "Indulge your old foolish mother just once again, Yoruba."

Yoruba said, "Look at my crosses!" Half in truth and half in laughter.

"Stay with it this time, Yoruba. It ain't have to be like them devils does it on Long Island. It could be different. You and Lumumba could make it different."

"All right, Mother. We will make it different. We will make it Black and beautiful."

And there was mischief in her eyes to match the mischief of her mother's.

Yoruba talked to Lumumba about it, and to Pam Jefferson and Charlene. Swore them all to secrecy. They would make this one a Black and Beautiful Cotillion. They would wear their hair *au naturel*, the three ladies and their escorts. Maybe Pamela told her escort, who in turn told somebody, who in turn told somebody, and so forth. Once a thing is established firmly as a secret, it absolutely guarantees a leakage (right?) of sizable proportions. A secret is something that everybody whispers about to everybody else. Maybe Charlene told her mother who told somebody who told somebody, and so on. The blacker the berry the sweeter the juice. The darker the secret the brighter the prospects for the widest circulation. Ordinarily Charlene would tell anybody, "I ain't no refrigerator, I can't keep a damn thing." But this time she took the solemn oath. "Nobody! I mean, not a living ass, so help me Malcolm." Well but it had to be Charlene or Pamela who leaked it, since Yoruba told no one at all, excepting Pam, Charlene and Lumumba, which was a bit much when you come to think of it. Surely, it could not have been Lumumba, the worldly one, the Captain, Master Pilot of all the ships at sea. A hip dude like Lumumba with his international perspective, his savoir faire, his sangfroid, she knew that he had not leaked the secret. As long as he had sailed the seas, he would surely be leakproof. So most likely it was Pam Jefferson, who was a Heightster in her own right, and socialized with them and lived among them, and was more likely, in the natural schedule of her normal events, to have talked with them. It was very likely darling wonderful Pam who accidentally let the secret out, right? Wrong. It was Captain Ben Ali Lumumba, at your service. How did it happen?

It was in part due to his celebrity. Carrying the infamous plot one step further, he went over to the New Generation Clothiers to get those real hip dudes to redo one of his African outfits for the Grand Cotillion. It was one of those fine silkenish robes like the kind Jaja Wachuku of Nigeria used to wear when he favored the New York international scene with his regal presence during his United Nations days. It was a trifle too large for Lumumba, and he wanted everything to be just right. He told one of the bearded New Generation men, "They think I'm going to wear a monkey suit with tails and all that stiff shirt shit." That was all he said. They had a good laugh. "Man!" And Lumumba forgot all about it. After all he didn't tell the dude which cotillion or where cotillion. Right? Okay, but this Black and beautiful dude of the growing middle classes lived up in the Crowning Heights, was in fact himself a part-time Heightster. He told somebody who told somebody who told somebody that Lumumba was going to blow the damn Cotillion thing sky-high and then write a book about it. Who told somebody who told somebody who told somebody and so on till the good news reached dear Brassy Brenda, and by the time it got to her and got translated by her with the benefit of certiorari and free association, which she was famous for, it had grown into a full-scale race riot being plotted by Lumumba and Yoruba and the entire Harlem contingent, in connection with the college militants. Okay?

Well, I mean, my man! The phones began to ring all over the city. I mean, so many phones were ringing at the same time, it caused a sonic incident of soniferous proportions, according to the *Daily News*. Pedestrians' ears were detonated on the streets of New York town. New York Ear, Nose, Eye and Throat Hospital did a booming business that night. A riot at the Waldorf?! What you say?!

And of course, everything was denied out of hand and categorically. Nobody admitted anything. There was nothing to admit. Actually. A case of overcommunication. But nevertheless and notwithstanding, plans and progress went apace toward the day of Grand Cotillion. Friday, which was C-Day, broke bright and pretty for the people, albeit it was a nervous day, clouding up in the late A.M. and raining bitter tears of sweet frustration, then brightening up again with beaming smiles of blessed expectations. In the morning the girls went to the beauty parlors. The Afro-natural thing was a new thing for Yoruba. She had waged a running battle with it for many many months and Sundays. Long, black, shiny velvet cascades of curly stuff spilling down beneath her shoulders. If her mother was possessed with a bad grade of good hair, as the saying goes, then she, Yoruba Evelyn, was surely endowed (?) with a good grade of bad hair, again as the saying goes. During the last two years of her Black and beautiful consciousness, she had vacillated, equivocated, rationalized, hemmed and hawed, and gone through other varied and sundry changes. To be or not to be? Should she or shouldn't she? But now, at this very historic moment, it was a time of great decision.

Now this Friday morning, which she thought of all day long as Saturday, because she did not go to work, this time, she was determined to do her natural thing. And how would she look? Would she become another person? Would she be ugly? Would she be Black and comely? It wasn't the first time she had asked herself these questions. How could she back out? Now that she had discussed it with Lumumba and had reached agreement with him? And with Charlene and with Pamela. But especially Lumumba. But, she asked herself, who shall I get to do it for me? Suppose they mess it up? It would break her mother's heart, in any event. Who would do it for her? Will I be Black and comely like Lumumba says? You had to get the right beautician or you would be out-to-lunch for days. Instead of going to the Beautique Afrique, she made it to the Captain's Quarters.

"I'm scared, Ben Ali. Maybe this is not the time to do it."

"Do what, my Queen?" He was in a fine state of zealous excitement, like the morning before the big game or the champeenship fight. Uptight with enthusiasm. He took a package from his bunk. He undid the package and held the prettiest dress she'd ever seen up against Yoruba. It was a gown of many colors, subtle and melodious, blending one into the other, saying something sweet and gentle, dig it, with all kinds of softly glittering things superimposed and quietly happening, like the gowns the great Makeba wears. He said, "Try it on." He was like an athlete superbly trained, an instrument finely tuned for the occasion, leaping with his happy nerves, whatever the occasion was, or would be. He was with it. She stood there holding the dress, staring at him, her dark eyes wide and full of questions. "It's yours. Try it on—for me." He went to her and started to unzip her from the back. "You shouldn't've—"

He stopped. "You don't like it?" Teasing her. "I love it, but—" He said, "So try it on already."

She went to the bathroom, and when she returned she modeled it for him. He said, "Yes—all right—it'll do."

"It'll do?"

"It'll do to make you the most beautiful woman who ever attended a cotillion since the damn stupidity began. So help me Malcolm, the Queen of Sheba could not possibly have been as beautiful as you!" He went to her and took her into his arms and held her close to him. "I brought this material all the way from Ibadan, capital of Yorubaland. Ever since that fateful first time I met you again at the Café Uptown, I knew that it was meant for only you. I knew that the true gods of our forefathers had sent it to you all the way from Yorubaland, and I was just a humble lucky messenger."

"Ben Ali! Benali! Ben-Ah-lee!"

He said, "Yoruba! Yoruba! Yoruba—Yo-roob-ba—Your-rube-bah!"

"But you shouldn't've! I mean I already have my Cotillion dress. And all the deb dresses are supposed to be white."

He backed away from her, walked around her, inspected her from all angles. "Now you have two to choose from. And I have a good idea what the choice will be."

The way he looked at her now, as he stood there staring at her with love and worshipful adoration in his eyes, she knew her beauty, saw it in reflection in his penetrating eyes, felt her beauty deep in the essence of her, where the quick is ever quickest. She was, in fact, the most beautiful woman in the world, because Lumumba said so, his mouth, his eyes, his face, his voice. She felt herself exuding beauty. She said, "But Ben Ali—I mean—" Her eyes, her cheeks, her face, her entire body beaming with the knowledge of her loveliness. "This is a beautiful dress, but it isn't white, and . . ."

He said, "Hold it—just a second." And he went to his closet for a clothes bag. "Excuse me just a minute." And he went to the bathroom, and when he came out again, he wore his African robe à la Jaja, with one of his shoulders bare. His natural had grown out again. But by now it was more like Stokely's than like Rap's. She stared at him in speechless wonderment.

Lumumba took her by the hand, his queen, like King Jaja of

the olden times. Took her to the mirror. And there they stood side by side staring at the comely couple on the other side, with open admiration. "I mean, let's face it," Lumumba demanded, seriously, but all in fun, "will we, or won't we be the handsomest couple at the ball?"

"What ball?" the Queen of Sheba asked.

"The debutantes' ball. The Grand Cotillion of the Femmes Fat Tails. I mean, what else?"

"But-but-but, I mean, it's beautiful, your robe, but you're not going to wear it to the Cotillion, I mean, are you?"

"Don't you like it?"

"Yes, but, I mean, you promised, you said you were going to wear tails. Remember?"

"It was your idea," he said. "You said we should make it different this time. After all, it was Lady Daphne's own suggestion, wasn't it? Make it Black and beautiful."

"But don't you think you're going a little too far? I mean, you promised me you would wear tails."

"That was before your mother got her soul converted. And if she can be delivered, I mean, like why not every man?"

She laughed nervously; jumpy little bumblebees were buzzing in her stomach. "I just thought you and I and Pam and Charlene and their escorts would, you know, like all wear Afros, I mean naturals—That is the only thing that we agreed to—I mean—"

"Which brings me to the next question. Which is, how even more beautiful you're going to be when you leave the beauty salon. Dig it!"

"Ben Ali, my Captain, I don't know. Which one should I go to? What if they make me look like I'm out-to-lunch and whatnot? Maybe this isn't the time for me to do my natural thing. Maybe after the Cotillion would be better. I mean, after all, it is a grand occasion. And I don't know anybody that I could trust to do a really bang-up job. Do I? And my mother would just—"

He said, "I know the greatest in the USA. And she loves to do a natural. She'll make you so pretty, you'll fall in love with your own self and even make me jealous."

She said, "But—"

He swept her away with words again. A tidal wave of nouns and verbs and adjectives. And finally he said, "Come now, my

Queen of Sheba. Let us make it to the Queen of Stylists, the High Priestess of the Nation." And took her by the arms and led her out of the door, and they had started down the stairs, before she caught herself. And said, "Aren't we a little too dressed up to go to the salon?"

He erupted into laughter, and she joined him. Then they went back to the Captain's Quarters and got themselves together.

From then on it was like walking through a dream for Yoruba. Lumumba made a phone call before they left the house, then took her to the apartment of a famous woman singer, who at this point shall be nameless. Suffice to say she was a beautiful singer, who knew the Blackness of her beauty and the beauty of her Blackness, sang Black songs and wore her hair *au naturel* long before it was in fashion. And before it was commercial. When most folks thought Black Beauty was a horse. Yoruba was uptight with exquisite feelings to meet this great Black lady in the flesh. And this great lady really did her hair. Famous Singer had met Lumumba two years before in West Africa at a concert she had given in Ouagadougou in the Upper Volta. It was just as Lumumba said it would be. Even more than he imagined. When Yoruba stared at herself in the mirror at the lady's house, after the transformation, she fell angrily in love with her reflection. The High Priestess of the Nation had worked her grand Juju, wrought her magic. The dear girl felt she really was the Queen of Sheba. Reincarnation? She'd never believed in anything like that before. But after all, some superstitions were not really superstitions. Right? She felt she really was another person and knew a funny feeling she had never known before, the presence of a new thing taking over where all the old things had left off. A miracle was happening. Her face aglow, a beauty from the inside bursting at the seams now, and beaming on the outside. Before her very eyes, she seemed to grow taller, as if the new person that she was becoming were too majestic for her former being. Then there was a burst of sudden revelation, and she thought, Now I know the truer deeper meaning of Cotillion. Coming out! Yes! Coming out! I am a debutante coming out of my old self into a new society! She felt cotillionized for real. It was her grand debut into the maturation of her Blackness. The true Rites of Cotillion had begun for her. Metamorphosis!

From Famous Beautiful Black Singer and hairstylist, on to home to face the music. Lumumba took her to the house, but she thought it best for her to face her mother's music by herself. Lumumba with his Afro beauty-fully-cropped again would only complicate the musical rendition. She kissed him good-bye till evening and left him downstairs in front of the apartment.

She would just go upstairs and walk right up to her mother and say, "How do you like my hairdo?" And that would be that. And her mother would go into her thing, and she would go into hers, and that would be entirely that. She, the girl, Yoruba, a woman now, a new woman, and she would just stand up to her mother woman-to-woman. No hemming and hawing, no beating about the bush. Even if her mother didn't notice her head, she would call attention to it and get it over with. Right on! And let it all hang out! Get it on, and over with! She was a woman and she must affirm her womanship, and it was now or never! Right?

She came militantly up the stairs and into the house with great determination. This was it! If her mother didn't like it, tough! She'd simply have to lump it. Yoruba closed the door quietly, took off her shoes, and made tracks straight on tiptoe to her bedroom and closed the door behind her.

Her mother had small stingy ears, but she could hear a bedbug pissing on a cup of frozen custard. She called to Yoruba from the kitchen. "That you, Yo-roo-ba?"

There was so much happiness in her mother's voice. It was like a song of joyous jubilee. For the last few days, Miss Daphne had gone around singing calypso. Would you believe, sometimes rhythm and blues? Popping her fingers and doing interpretations of Boogaloo and Funky Broadway. One day Yoruba had come home and her mother had been playing "Brownskin Girl" on the record player, and she had taken her mother's hand and they had danced that dance together. But today, she did not answer her mother. She did not want to face the music, which she knew would be a different kind. She heard her mother calypso-ing toward her room, humming, "It Was Love, Love, Love Alone." And then—
"That you, Yo-roo-ba?"

Yoruba pushed the package with the new dress under her bed. "Yes, Mother," she whispered, not even loud enough for Daphne's radar-equipped ears to pick up. Then she thought, This is ridiculous. "I'm in the bedroom, Mother." Get it over. Get it over with. And she broke into a sweat. I'm a woman. I'm a woman! I am not my mother's child!

"Can I come in?"

The question irritated Yoruba. "Of course, you can come in."

Her mother pushed the door open, and stood there staring at her daughter seated upon the bed. It was as if she truly did not recognize her only child at first. She looked around the room, as if she expected Yoruba to be hiding in a corner.

Yoruba stood up from the bed. "There is no one here but me, Mother. No one here but you and me."

Lady Daphne's face was a mask of consternation now. Her lips moved but no words would come out. Finally she mumbled, "What-what-what happened to you, child? Who did it to you? I'll have she arrested. Lord Jesus, look at my crosses! Look at my blessed crosses!"

"Isn't it beautiful, Mother? Isn't it truly wonderful?" The girl patted at her hair, smiling bravely at her mother. Turning now from side to side.

Daphne looked around the room for the hidden object that was beautiful and wonderful. "How you mean beautiful?"

"Me, Mother. My hairdo—don't you love it?"

"Tell me who did it to you, and I'll have the wort'less vagabund electrocuted!"

"Nobody *did* anything to me, Mother. I wanted it done. I asked them to fix it this way. I am responsible, and I am Black and beautiful."

"You-you-you what?"

"I went to the great lady and asked her to give me a natural. And I love it."

Miss Daphne began to walk the floor. "All that beautiful long hair gone forever!" The tears spilled down her cheeks. She stopped and stared at Yoruba again, as if she thought she might look the hair back on her head. "After all the pains I took to grow it long and pretty, and you cut it all off? You look just like a pickie-head!"

"It's a matter of opinion, Mother." Yoruba's voice was shaky, trembly.

"Rawss!" her mother shouted. "Opinion, rawss!"

Yoruba had a very sneaky suspicion that her mother was upset, because Lady Daphne seldom swore at all, and never ever in the true West Indian fashion. But Yoruba knew that "Rawss" was a West Indian version of "your ass"—"your bloody ass!" And so her mother must be angry. Right?

Miss Daphne sank into a chair, the tears flowing freely. "Kuh-deah! Why you do this to me? Why you hate me so? Look how long it take to grow the hair, and you cut it off like a pickie-head!" She could not sit still. She got up and began to walk the floor again. "When you was a little girl, I would plat your hair with tender care in corn rows and comb it, brush it and put coconut oil on it to make it grow. All the loving tender care and pains I put into all these years to make it grow, and you git it all cut off! Standing there before me with the hair on your head looking like mice titties!"

"But you said, Mother, you said, yourself, we could make this Cotillion different, make it Black and beautiful."

"I didn't say make it Black and ridiculous! You think that boy, Lumumba, is going disgrace hisself by taking you to the Cotillion with you head looking like so? Don't you want to be beautiful, child?"

"I just left Lumumba, Mother," Yoruba answered, with a nervous dignity. "He thinks I'm Black and beautiful."

"I mighta known that Black wort'less devil was behind this. Listen to your mother, dear one! He ain't mean you no good atall atall!"

She said, "Mother—" She said, "Mother, it's done already, and I'm glad it's done. I think I'm beautiful, and I'm sorry that you don't agree, but it's done anyhow, and it can't be undone!"

The mother sat down again. Shaking her head from side to side. "All the plans I ever made, all the dreams gone up in smoke—"

Yoruba laughed a sad and lonely laugh. "Not up in smoke, Mother. Down on the floor your dreams went, along with my blessed tresses, all my curly locks."

Daphne stood up again. She took Yoruba by the hand. "Come,"

she said. "All is not lost yet. Let's go and buy you a wig. Come. Come! I going buy you a lovely wig."

Yoruba pulled away from her mother and stood there staring at her with unbelieving eyes. She had expected her mother to be upset, but not to this extent. She had thought, had hoped, that her mother had truly changed. Not radically, but changed.

"Come. Come, dearie, I going buy you a lovely wig. Come. I forgive you. Come."

"A wig? Forgive me?" She shook her head. What could she say to her mother? What could she do? She could do nothing but stand and stare, and somehow she began to laugh, and could not stop laughing, because she loved her mother, and she laughed and cried because she could not reach her mother who meant well and meant love and glad tidings and beautiful Black blessings for her, and she got no pleasure from making her mother unhappy, but she could not go down this road ever again. No wig for this Black and beautiful child, not even for her mother's sake. She had made her debut into truly Black society. And there was no turning back.

The mother, herself, flowing tears, thought the girl out of her mind standing there like a pickie-head with hair like the titties of a hungry mouse and laughing and crying at the same time. She went to the girl and began to shake her. "Just wait until your father get here. He going talk some sense into your head." They did not have very long to wait, because Matt had gotten off early to get ready for the Grand Cotillion, and when he got home he was almost ready. All ready? All rightie!

When he came through the door, Lady Daphne said, "Come here, Matt, and look at your darling daughter!"

Yoruba wiped her eyes hurriedly and tried to assume a calm appearance for him. He came into the bedroom and took one look at her, and went into his own thing. "Beautiful! Beautiful!" He went and took her in his arms. "A hundred million Queens of Shebas and ten million Cleopatras! Great God from Timbuktu!"

Her eyes filled with tears of rhapsody. She laughed now a happy laugh. "I knowed I named you right," he said, as her nostrils picked up the smell of whiskey on his breath. "You are truly an African beauty. Truly African beauty! So help me Brother Malcolm!" He never ever drank before he made it home from work.

Lady Daphne said, "Are you out of your mind? Ain't you see what she done with she hair?"

He said mockingly, "I see what she done with she hair, and she is more beautifuller than ever she—"

"You was in the plot right from the start, you and that damn smart-ass Lumumba, in it just to spite me, to disgrace me out in high society. After all I done to uplift this family, I get no thanks atall atall. Lord, you see my crosses!" She sniffed the air with her haughty turned-up nose. "You been drinking?"

"Yes," he answered proudly. "And I ain't been drinking tea. How in the hell else can I get myself up to go to this jive-ass Cotillion?"

Daphne turned to Yoruba again, "Let's go now, Eve-lyn, girl. Come. We going get the lovely wig."

She said, quietly and firmly, "No wig, Mother. No wig ever."

"No wig?" the mother asked her.

"I love you, Mother, but no wig, I mean, never."

"No wig—" the mother echoed. "No wig—no wig—no wig—" And sank quietly to the floor. And this time without dignity.

CHAPTER THIRTEEN

YE OLDE PLANTATION

> White dresses
> long white flowing dresses
> like fair ladies wore in olden times,
> the idyllic days of slavery
> in dear old dixieland,
> when life was gay and so carefree,
> and everybody knew their stations,
> ordained by God up in the heavens,
> a time of happy loyal slaves
> and very very kindly masters.

Each year the Grand Cotillion always had a different theme. They were really intellectuals were the darling Femmes Fat Tails. And always gaily chose their theme from some exotic event, historical or literary. One year it was Victorian Days, another was Arabian Knights. And then there was dear Camelot, after that, The King and Us. One year Oklahoma. Last year was their finest hour; Playboy and the Playful Bunnies. Can you dig all those lovely Femmes Fat Tails decked out in the bunny suits? This year the theme was secret like it always was, which was the most delicious aspect of it. Dig it. Each year, no one, but nobody, knew, except the famous Femmes Fat Tails, until the very last moment, what the theme would be that year. Not even the darling debutantes were privy to the deep dark secret.

And they were militant girls, these Femmes Fat Tails, radical right up to their sweet fat asses. This year the theme was cotton, historical and literary. And every other whichaway. A combination of Uncle Tom's Cabin and Gone with the Wind and The Confessions of Willie Styron. Are you ready, brothers, sisters, others?

"Ye Olde Plantation." Slavery in reverse. "Crow Jim," in the immortal words of the one and only Prissy Patterson. "Slavery in reverse—Crow Jim!" Breathing heavy from the inspiration. "Can't you see the wicked irony? White slaves and colored masters! Slaves and colored masters!" She felt militant all over. She sighed and giggled sweetly out of the joy for her dear genius, which she modestly admitted. "Can't you see the wicked irony?" The thing was, Mrs. Brap-bap didn't, couldn't, wouldn't see it. She didn't dig going back to Ye Olde Plantation under any circumstances. It was a stormy session, the night the theme was chosen. A blizzard and a hurricane. A lot of wind was blown, that night, at Brassworks. A few minds were blown too. Hurricane Beverly almost blew the club away. "Talk about generation gap!" Brap-bap shouted. "You funky old broads done gapped so much, you all the way back to the Rock of Ages!" Mrs. Pee-Pee smiled deprecatingly. "You're just too conservative, darling, you're just too conservative." And after the storm subsided, they voted twenty-two to three for Ye Olde Plantation. And all were sworn to secrecy, at the penalty of exorcism and ostracism, and other stuff, which shall forever remain a secret, for the sake of the dignified image of the Femmes Fat Tails, which must forever be maintained. Understand?

And now the moment had arrived toward which they all had worked with tender loving care, and a missionary spirit. The time had come. The stage was set. The Night of Nights was finally upon them, and things would never be the same. 'Twas a night to be remembered. Everything was in readiness. No detail had been forgotten. Therefore nothing could go wrong. After such meticulous preparations, there was no cause to be nervous. Right? Relaxation was the password.

When Yoruba and Lumumba arrived at the Waldorf in the early evening, eight o'clockish, for the really final preparations, the whole damn joint was all uptight. Especially on the lobby level. Security vigilantes and policemen (in plainclothes) all over the place and bumping into one another on the lookout for strange-looking characters and riot-racers, or race-rioters, if it pleases you. The word had gone out, secretly, that the Waldorf would be where the action was, that fatal Friday night of historic infamy. And anybody who came into the lobby with Afros or naturals, or beards, men or women, were guilty until proven very very innocent. Therefore you could not blame these faithful guardians of law and order, who, if not sincere, were definitely serious. Check that. They pounced upon the borough president, a distinguished member of the City Council, a Black leftwing gentleman of the syndicate, a college president, two or three African ambassadors, two and two-thirds Negro leaders, anybody and everybody who wore their hair long, intentionally, or simply needed a haircut, or looked like a colored Abe Lincoln, or looked suspicious, which was the selfsame thing. The conscientious vigilantes even pounced upon each other. The Queen of Sheba and her Captain stood about as much of a chance of making it through the lobby as Mr. H. Rap Brown stood of being elected Supreme Kleagle of the Mississippi Klan.

Earlier, Lumumba had picked Yoruba up at her apartment. By that time, her mother had almost reconciled herself to the terrible fact that her daughter wasn't ugly even with her dear hair in its natural state. Matt, Yoruba, and, finally, Lumumba convinced her that her daughter would be the most beautiful maiden at the ball. Lumumba all dressed up in his Brooks Brothers suit, sharp as a double-edged razor at both edges, with his cool cool Afro-natural à la Stokely Carmichael and his darkly piercing eyes, and talking up a snowstorm in the month of brides and graduates. "Miss Daphne, I have traveled the world over, and I have seen some beautiful women in my time, including one Mrs. Daphne Braithwaite Lovejoy." She said, "Go on, you vagabund." He went on, as she directed. "But you and Mr. Matt have birthed and carefully guided through childhood, and chartered into womanhood the loveliest, most exquisitely beautiful woman on this earth, and I have seen some lovely women in my journeys around the world, believe me when I say so, she will be the talk of the ball, and to put the frosting on the cake, she will be introducing an absolutely new coiffure. Stunning past imagination. Among all those lovely jewels she will gleam and glitter, making the others lose their luster by comparison. This is no ordinary Afro-natural coiffure that adorns your daughter's lovely head." Miss Daphne looked from him to Yoruba who was purring at this point. Unknowingly. "It isn't?" He said, "You can just bet your sweet breadfruit. Her hair was done by a great lady who has done the hair of queens and princesses throughout Africa and Asia and the islands of the seas. She said it was an honor to do the hair of one so beautiful as your Yoruba." Mother Daphne said, "Oh my!" What the innocent woman did not know was that the package Lumumba had with him contained his African robe, and that the package Yoruba took with her contained two dresses. They would redress for the ball down at the Waldorf. Lumumba shook Matt's hand with his fancy Afro-shake-of-brotherhood and he kissed Miss Daphne on her hand like a true gallant. They would meet them later at the ball. He said to Miss Daphne as he and Yoruba went out of the door, "Next week I'm going to take you to the lady for a new coiffure, and then I'll never be able to make up my mind which Lovejoy to marry. You'll both be such a lovely joy divine to look upon and love and marry. Sorry about that, Mr. Matt." She laughed and giggled like a schoolgirl. "Get out of here, you sweet-talking rascal!"

The Vigilantes put Lumumba and Yoruba out of the Waldorf five or six times. Finally, the Queen and Captain sneaked into a side entrance and walked in the midst of a crowd of white folks toward the elevators. Once on the elevators, Lumumba turned to Yoruba, out of breath and puffing like a mountain climber, and said, "I don't know why in the hell we worked so hard to get into this place if they don't want us, when we didn't want to come to the damn thing in the first place." They stared at each other and broke down into hurricanes of wild and raucous laughter, like colored people did when no one else was listening. Apologies to Purlie. Scared the dear white folks all but to death. It was a time when people looked for Black militants and riot-racers under their beds and in their beds and even on their elevators. And, finding none, were gravely disappointed, oftentimes.

Nevertheless and notwithstanding, the stalwart ones made their way to their respective dressing rooms, and got ready for the famous happening.

Meanwhile Matt and Daphne got ready back at the apartment. Daphne had resigned herself (almost) to her daughter's special kind of beauty. Exotic? She didn't really dig it, and she knew not from whence it came, but she could live with it. For a night, at least. And everything would be all right, she told herself, not entirely believing it. Maybe Evelyn would win the prize just because of being different. There was nothing she could do about it at this hour anyhow. And her husband, Matt, whom she dearly loved, truly loved, in her own way, was happy about the whole damn thing. Which made our Lady of Barbados most suspicious. Can you blame her? The fact of the matter, our man from Georgia was getting ready for the Grand Cotillion in his own inimitable way. He had rented a tuxedo, which fitted him like a soldier suit fits a recruit his first day in the army. But it wasn't so bad, after all. Matt had taken his bath, sweating all the time, underneath the shower, singing in the rain, took a shave, in beads of sweat, nipping slyly all the while on a bottle of Four Roses, getting ready for the Grand Cotillion. One swallow of Four Roses, one swift gargle of Listerine, to kill the smell, what else? Another swallow of Four Roses, another gargle of Listerine. And so on. At one point, our man was gargling with Four Roses and drinking Listerine. But when Big Matt was ready, you can believe it, he was ready.

The decor of the Waldorf main ballroom was not to be believed, even though many folks believed it. I mean, religiously. It was dictated by the Ye Olde Plantation, right? The Grand Ballroom was ringed by giant balls of gleaming cotton. The boxes around the dance floor were in the mode of cotton patches. Black men dressed in tails and stiff shirts and the ladies in their elegant gowns and the Femmes Fat Tails in long hoop-skirted dresses of the olden times sitting primly and supremely in the loges like the massas and the missuses of the gone idyllic days, when all the darkies wuzza weeping. Check it. The white waiters were dressed like slaves and houseboys, immaculate in white from head to knee, with white gloves on their hands, yet, and barefooted as yard-dogs, with black cork on their faces. There they go, to and fro, grinning whitely, bless their little old liberal hearts, all got up like Uncle Ben and Old Black Joe and Uncle Tom, to the tune of Swanee Ribber. How do you like them cotton balls? Check it one more time. There were a few false-faced white women got up in Aunt Jemima dresses and grinning all the time like the smiles were frozen on their faces. It was not very clear what their function was. But all had been rehearsed, for days. The Waldorf surely aimed to please.

By the time our main man, Big Matt, and his Lady Daphne arrived at the Grand Cotillion, Big Matt was moon-bound on a bed of Roses Four. Oooooh! They sat in the cotton-patch loge with the famous Pattersons. Mrs. Pee-Pee had insisted that the

Lovejoys be her special guests. The dear lady was a dedicated missionary for sure. She introduced them to her other guests before she went backstage for the final preparations.

"Their daughter is so pretty, Mr. Pat, with her long black hair down to her shoulders . . . down to her shoulders. Prettiest Black girl you will ever lay your eyes on! Ever lay your eyes on!"

Jake Patterson's eyes gleamed with sharp anticipation. He licked his chops, thinking to himself how delightful it would be to lay his hands on one so beautiful. Never mind his eyes. He looked up into Big Matt's face and changed his mind. Let the eyes have it.

Mrs. Patterson leaned in close and lowered her voice, and whispered, secretly, "Their daughter is a perfect angel. She would never in her life take part in any of those horrid militant happenings. There's nothing to worry about on that score. I never believed she was involved a single instant." She stared worriedly at Lady Daphne for instant affirmation. Repeating: "Never take part in any of those horrid militant happenings."

"Never take part," Lady Daphne answered worriedly. Nervously. Mr. Pat had served her a nice sweet harmless drink (she thought), which he had had prepared for those of his distinguished guests who were not accustomed as he was to real hard drinking.

"With her hair down to her shoulders!" Mrs. Patterson repeated. "Oh what charm for one so darkly beautiful! With her hair down to her shoulders!"

Miss Daphne smiling, beaming, like she was letting Yoruba's beauty go to her (dear Daphne's) head. "She is a pretty girl," Daphne admitted, sighing deeply, giggling softly to herself, all ladylike and everything. "But she is a lovely girl, I mean, her hair, I mean, she is pretty with it long or short."

"Oh dear me!" Mrs. Pee-Pee murmured. Worried again. "Don't ever let her cut it off. Cut it off—" she repeated. "Cut it off—cut it off—" When Mrs. Pee-Pee imbibed, she was twice as repetitious as she always was. And Mrs. Pee-Pee was contagious. Lady Daphne murmured after her. "Cut it off—cut it off—Don't ever let her cut it off—" As her eyes began to fill. Mrs. Patterson gracefully excused herself and went backstage where the happenings were about to happen.

Meanwhile, Mr. Pat and Big Matt were hitting it off. "Lapping it up" was a more appropriate description of what was happening to the bottles of Old Grand-Dad. Mr. Pat started to tell dirty jokes, a pastime he was expert at and famous for. And when he told his jokes, I mean he really enjoyed them, much to Lady Daphne's great embarrassment. Between Old Grand-Dad and Mr. Pat's jokes, Big Matt felt no pain whatever and was glad that he had come. It was a gas! A natural gas! Mr. Pat sat in the cotton patch next to Daphne and each time he would tell one of his cute little dirties he would pound her on the back, and slap himself on his knees, and sometimes he would get confused and slap dear Daphne's delicate knees. Sometimes, his horny hand would linger. The Queen of Queens did not know how to handle the situation. Surely he meant no harm, she told herself. He was of the high and Black society. He could not possibly be as uncouth as he obviously was.

Meanwhile Big Matt dug the happenings. As elegant as the colored folks most assuredly were, he thought that, for all that, they really looked like cotton pickers, picking beaucoup bales of cotton, especially when they stirred themselves and moved from patch to patch. The club had hired two white bands. One was like a minstrel show with loud attire and bright banjos. During the getting-ready time they played (supplied?) the incidental music. Tender, heartwarming, nostalgic ballads like "All the Colored Folks Ama Weeping" and "Summertime and the Living Is Easy" and "I Got Plenty of Nothing" "And that is too damn much for you." Big Matt ad-libbing all the while. They played "Carry Me Back to Ol' Virginny." "That's the only way you gon get me there." Go, Big Matt!

With every swallow of the booze, Matt felt more loosened up and free from pain. Likewise he felt freer-wheeling. Now he looked around him at all the lively cotton patches, and bales of cotton on the stage, the whole damn place ass-deep in cotton. "What the hell is this all about?" he said to everybody at once and to no one in particular. "This supposed to be slavery time or something?"

"You are misconscrewing, Matthew," Miss Daphne said, tolerantly, in her most queenly and sophisticated voice.

"I ain't misscrewed nothing," Big Matt asserted. "Don't you see all this slavery-time jive all every whichawhere? I ain't had that much to drink."

"Right!" Jake Patterson heartily agreed. "You ain't had that much to drink!" And poured Matt up another drink of Old Grand-Dad 100 proof bottled in bond, and poured sweet stuff into

Daphne's glass. "This is some weird goddamn shit being put down, you should pardon the expression."

"You gentlemen just don't understand," another lady at the table interjected. She was Anne Goldwig, and elegant.

"I dig," Big Matt disputed, with his uncouth self. "Like Brother Malcolm said, these Negroes don't want no liberation. They tryna sneak back on the old plantation. Look at all this goddamn cotton!"

"Oh dear me!" the exquisite Mrs. Goldwig exclaimed. "You have missed the point completely!"

At which point they came for Big Matt, because the Cotillion ceremonies were beginning to begin. They had to carry him backstage, bodily, almost. Between the Four Roses and the Old Grand-Dad, he had become immobile. Almost.

Meanwhile backstage the excrement had come into sharp contact with the air-conditioner, right? The shit had hit the fan, in all vulgarity. The Femmes Fat Tails were all uptight and strung way out, mucho on the qui vive for anything and everything. How would the trouble come when it came and under what disguise? Just who were the troublemakers? How? When? What? Where? Would there really be a riot? Had any of the riot-racers infiltrated? Filtered through the great dragnet? They stared into the face of each and every lovely maiden. Mrs. Antoinette Brasswork was for searching the fair young innocents' pocketbooks and underwear for weaponry and other items. Maintaining self-righteously, "This is a prima facie, ipso facto case of clear and present danger, and due process is immaterial and totally irrelevant. Search their pocketbooks and panties!" But her darling daughter Brenda argued that mommy-dear was carrying things too far, possibly because Brassy Brenda had a few innocent pep pills and other harmless paraphernalia tucked away on her own person, which might cause some perfectly bigoted persons to draw the wrong conclusions, based on circumstantial evidence. Strong-armed methods were obviously in order now, and why Mrs. Pee-Pee did not go for the stop-and-search routine will forever remain mysterious. Backstage everybody was jumpy. They had every reason to be. Right? After all, riot-racing at the Waldorf would kill the entire image of the Grand Cotillion. The name of the game was vigilance. At stake was the advancement of the entire Colored Race. Don't take anybody else's word for it. Ask Mrs. Prissy P. herself. She'd tell you how significant was the annual Grand Cotillion.

Earlier, three white girls had arrived at the ball, as invited guests, wearing Afro wigs and darkly-tinted contact lenses, and had been refused admission, roughed up, third-degreed, searched for weapons, threatened with arrest, called trouble-making yaller niggers, and so on, until finally they compromised their firm convictions, removed their wigs and declared their whiteness, at which point they were immediately admitted with abject apologies and Southern hospitality. "We thought you all were colored," one of the Fat Tails assured them, curtseying with dignity and deeply felt embarrassment.

Just before the formal rites were about to begin, three debbies arrived at the backstage dressing room strolling with a nervous haughtiness underneath their Afro-naturals. The other dear ones gathered there stared at them as if they all three held hand grenades in one hand, Molotov cocktails in the other. Mistresses Downjohn and Brasswork went screaming toward the troublemakers with fangs bared and claws unsheathed and had to be restrained from committing assault and battery with intent to do extreme bodily harm. Ladies fainted by the thrices. All were weeping bitter tears. You couldn't blame them either. I mean, after all!

"I told you not to let them Harlem niggers in the Grand Cotillion!" Mrs. Downjohn shouted. "I knew they would mess up! I knew it! I knew it! And all my rich white friends are out there watching!" You can understand her feelings.

"Carrying integration too damn far with too much deliberate speed!" was Mrs. Brasswork's contribution.

Mrs. Patterson shouted at the troublemakers. "You can't go on! You can't go on!"

The three naturalized troublemakers had the nerve to act as if they were frightened and surprised. What did they expect from respectable women like the Femmes Fatales? A welcome mat? A red carpet? Flowers maybe? Tolerance was all right, in its place, but temperance in tolerance was sometimes necessary. I mean, set fire to the universities, bomb the police stations, burn down the White House, but don't mess with an institution like the Grand Cotillion.

"I know what you're up to! I know what you're up to! But you won't get away with it! You'll never get away with it! You're a dirty bunch of Communistic reefer-smoking militants!"

Frog-eyed Mrs. Lonestone stood in the middle of the confusion, weeping like a motherless child. "After all our plans and preparations! All our plans and preparations! Why do you inflict this on us, Lord? What did we do wrong, Jesus?"

"Letting them little Black Harlem hoodlums into the Cotillion!" Mrs. Downjohn answered. "That's what the hell we did wrong! I told you niggers from the start! Keep the Black ones out, I told you!"

Now the righteous Christian lady soldiers moved like Carry Nation toward the riot-racing Harlem hoodlums, including Pamela Jefferson who was a Heightster by her birthright, but obviously had been led astray by the hoodlum element. The righteous ones were not deceived by the innocent frightened looks on the faces of the unscrupulous culprits. They knew the devil came with angel faces sometimes.

As uptight and as strung out as Mrs. Prissy Patterson surely was, the tenderhearted woman did not lose perspective. Even through this trying moment, this darkest hour of her illustrious career as a Colored Club woman, she could, notwithstanding, glimpse an ever-shining rainbow over the blue horizon. That rainbow was lovely little angelic Miss Yoruba Evelyn Lovejoy. What a joy and relief not to find her "own Yoruba" among the infamous plotters against all that was American and decent and uplifting! Her faith in underprivileged humanity was vindicated. If out of all those teeming uncultured masses of Harlem, she had redeemed one, just one, like darling Yoruba Evelyn, then her missionary fervor would not have been in vain. With the storm raging around her, she tried to remember one of her favorite Bible quotations. It had something to do with a stray sheep which had lost its way being dearer to the shepherd than all of them already safely in the fold. Or uplifting words to that desired effect. However and unfortunately, not all of her club members were as tolerant or as liberal as Mrs. Prissy Patterson. Nor did they have her broad perspectives.

Ann Brasswork, for example, came into her very own, jumping up and down and shouting, "Search their purses! Tear their dresses off! Investigate their funky drawers! Don't let them plead the First Amendment!"

The troublemakers were cornered now, all three of them. Pamela La-Smythe, Pamela Jefferson and Charlene Johnson. La-Smythe had not been one of the original conspirators, but she heard about the plot through the grapevine and had joined it of her own volition. The troublemakers would have gotten what they so rightfully deserved, had it not been for softhearted Beverly Brap-bap. With all that big bad talk for which she was famous, beneath it all she was a rough-cut diamond, right? Beneath her rugged exterior beat a heart as gentle as a baby kitten with distemper. She appealed to the more human instincts in the members of her club, which they had somehow forgotten, temporarily, and you couldn't blame them, after all. She didn't get any help from Mrs. P. P., who dwelt now momentarily in a kind of romantic daydream fantasy, in which she and angel-Yoruba were the pretty precious heroines. She the missionary, Yoruba the converted heathen.

Brap-bap screamed, "Wait a minute! Wait a goddamn minute!"

She stood between them and the culprits. Pulled off her shoes and brandished them in both hands.

"What the hell you think you are? A lynching mob?"

The ladies hesitated, but only momentarily.

Mrs. Patterson came swiftly back to reality, and immediately wished she hadn't. "Now—now, Beverly, do be careful of your language! There are Christian ladies present. Ladies present. And Mr. Phil Potts." (He had just made his dear entrance. No other men were allowed to enter. It was the backstage ladies' dressing room.) "And don't forget the darling debutantes. Be careful of your language!"

"You're acting like a bunch of goddamn members of the Ku Klux Klan!"

"The Ku Klux Klan!" Mrs. Patterson repeated. "Oh dear me! The Ku Klux Klan!"

"Lynching mob! Lynching mob!" From Beverly Brap-bap.

Repetition was contagious.

"Lynching mob! Lynching mob!"

Which sobered up the Femmes Fatales, and made them gain or lose perspective, but not entirely. Mrs. Patterson said, "We will not be a lynching mob, a lynching mob. Nevertheless they will not be allowed to debut. To debut!" Where is darling Yoruba?

Mrs. Downjohn said, "They will not go out there debutting all over the place looking like wild Africans with all my rich white friends out there watching!"

Mr. Phil Potts was flitting about wonth-two-freeing from debutante to tearful, frightened debutante, adjusting this and fixing that. He flitted up to the naturalized ones. "Magnifique!" he shouted softly. "Beautiful! Exotica!" He closed his eyes and waved his head from side to side.

Mrs. Patterson said, "Beautiful? Magnifique? Exotica?"

Mrs. Brap-bap said, "Of course they're beautiful. What's more they are in the latest style. Mr. P. Potts knows about these things because he's a cultured man of the world, and you girls are old-fashioned slavery-time illiterate provincials. The natural state is chic today and fashionable. We could set the style for years to come this night at this Cotillion."

"Set the style for years to come?" Mrs. Patterson repeated.

"Set the style for years to come!" echoed Mrs. Lonestone.

"We can set the style for years to come!" Mrs. Brasswork advocated, as if the words were her invention.

Meanwhile, there was a fifty-fifty chance that Lumumba and his Queen of Queens would not make the Grand Cotillion, after all the jumping up and down. She had been so imbued with a sense of her own beauty and her Blackness and the rightness of her cause, when Lumumba had left her at the door of the Waldorf suite which she was sharing with the other "super militants"! she had been giving off all kinds of positive vibrations, of majesty and confidence and loveliness, she had been luxuriating in exquisite and delicious feelings of being born again. Conversion! Reincarnation into her blessed Blackness. Yeah!

"I *am* the Queen of Sheba," she told herself. Objectively? "I *am* the Queen of Sheba! I really am the Queen of Sheba?" As she floated into the suite on a carpet of her loveliness.

The other "super militants" were already there when she arrived. And they greeted the late arriver with oohs and aahs and wows! All of them with their new and natural state atop their lovely heads. They hugged her and they kissed her and they spanked the planks of her extended palms. Then each gave her the handshake of their Black and lovely sisterhood. By the numbers. *One! Two! Three! Four!* Wow! Dig! It was a mutual-admiration sisterhood. They, the Black and Beautiful Militant Four, would show the other debutantes and the famous Femmes Fatales the truest meaning of Black beauty. Show all the invited guests. Every mother's brother's child.

"Show them all!" Pam Jefferson shouted softly. "The Black and Beautiful Militant Four will show all those phony black-faced Whiteys a thing or two, or three or four! Maybe even five or six! We'll show the whole nation where it's at!"

"Black and Beautiful Militant Four!" Yoruba repeated. It was a title that Pam Jefferson had just conferred on them. Yoruba tried it on her tongue for sound and taste and magnitude.

"Wow! Yeah! Okay!" Charlene shouted. "Like we going to make ourselves some his-toe-ree too-night! Can you dig it?" She strutted swayingly in the fashion of the truly Black and hip ones over to Pam Jefferson and held her hand out palm up, and Pam slapped it with a Black enthusiasm.

"Pow! The name of the game is Blackness!"

Yoruba thought uneasily, Is that what we're doing? Playing games? Is Blackness just a game we're playing? If it were only a game, was it worth all the pain and anguish they would cause Mrs. Patterson and Mrs. Brap-bap, and, last but far from least, Yoruba's mother? She thought, Was everything in this crazy world only fun and games when you got down to the nitty-gritty?

Pam read the uneasiness in Yoruba's face.

"Is it games?" Yoruba asked her.

Pam came over to her. "No games," she said. "It's life and death. It's the World Serious." Her face broke into a wide and irresistible smile, and she held both hands out toward Yoruba, palms up, and she said, "Give me some to liberate the people!"

Yoruba did not spank the plank at first. She just stared at her good friend from the Crowning Heights. But Pam would not be denied. She kept her hands extended in a kind of put-on attitude of supplication. "Give the liberators some!"

And finally Yoruba spanked the plank. "Pow!" And she said, "Liberate the people!" And they all cracked up with nervous laughter.

Charlene said, "Can you imagine the looks on Mrs. Pee-Pee and Mrs. Downjohn and Mrs. Brassy-ass's faces when they dig our righteous Afros?"

"Man!"

La-Smythe said, uneasily, "You don't reckon they'll be too shook up about it, do you? I mean, they won't lose their cool and have us all arrested, will they? I mean, I told my mother all the girls were wearing Afros."

Yoruba exclaimed, "You told your mother what?"

"Have us arrested?" From Pam Jefferson. The others laughed and whooped and hollered. And they went to her and nervously reassured her with kisses and embraces. "Don't worry about a thing, sugar pie," Charlene said. Charlene loved her Southern accent. "Because there is nothing to worry about," the Queen of Sheba proclaimed with great assurance. And La-Smythe agreed with one and all that there was nothing to worry about. She was just a little kinda sorta almost nervous. Right?

Charlene reminded one and all: "It's party time. Let's get the show on the road."

Yoruba responded in a shaky voice, "Yeah! Put on them party dresses and look pretty for the people!"

The Queen was glad the other girls were in such glorious spirits. It helped greatly to smooth out the little knots of guilt and uneasiness in the bottom of her stomach. Precious Mrs. Patterson had treated Yoruba like her very own daughter ever since she could remember. Yoruba remembered now when she was a little girl and Miss Prissy taught Sunday School at the Cathedral on the Heights. Miss Prissy would walk up to her and place her hand on Yoruba's head and sigh and say, "This one is so darkly beautiful." Speaking to Yoruba's mother. "So darkly beautiful! I'm going to take her home with me. She's my daughter. She's my daughter!" Later, Big Matt would say to Daphne, "Humph! She must think you Mother Hubbard or that other lady in the shoe. And you got so many children you don't know what to do!"

Mrs. Prissy had questioned Yoruba about the Afro-race-riot rumor at their last preparation meeting. And when Yoruba had denied any knowledge of it, the dear lady had sighed a sigh of deep relief and hugged the girl close to her, almost smothering her amongst her silkish hostess gown and her personal assortment of expensive perfumes. And chirping, "I just knew to my heart that my darling sweet Yoruba was not involved in a militant revolution. I told them I would stake my life on it! I would stake my life on it!" Yoruba was not the kind of queen to relish the role of gay deceiver.

There was the sweet and pungent smell of flowers in the suite. Beaucoup bouquets everywhere and of all kinds and sizes. And as the girls began to dress there was the soft scent of perfumes of all accents and denominations. Then there was the faint sweet different smell of alcoholic spirits. La-Smythe had brought along a tiny flask just in case her flagging spirits needed picking up. She had been nipping on the sly ever since she had arrived.

They were all dressed in their cotillion gowns now, and they stood admiring one another. Yeah! And they were truly a boss and beautiful sight for any kind of eyes, sore, well, cross-eyed, cock-eyed. Even a blind man would have sensed their beauty. One at a time they strolled like African models before the Mutual Adoration Sisterhood.

"Oh! How loverly!" Yoruba squealed, as La-Smythe strutted for their deepest admiration.

"What you say!" Pam Jefferson shouted. "Dig that jive from fore to aft!"

"Walk pretty for the people!" came from Charlene in the Amen Corner.

Then Charlene with her bad self strolled pretty for the gasping breathless threesome. Then Pam Jefferson, then Yoruba Evelyn Lovejoy.

Yoruba was so beautiful the other girls were speechless for a moment. Finally from Pam Jefferson: "Wherever did you get that fantastic dress?"

Yoruba said, in a happy trembly voice, "Do you really like it?"

"Like it?" was all Pam Jefferson could answer. "It's-it's-it's—"

"It's out of sight!" Charlene announced enthusiastically.

"Lumumba brought it to me all the way from Africa."

"It's out of sight," La-Smythe agreed. "But where is your cotillion dress? It's getting time for us to make the scene. I mean, like where is your white dress, the symbol of your virginity?"

Yoruba caught the short swift signifying glances that her buddies gave each other. Suddenly, there was this sinking feeling in Yoruba now, from her sweet face all the way down to that bottomless pit where her stomach lived its shaky existence. She swallowed hard. "I have the dress my mother bought me in the box over there, but I promised Lumumba I would wear this one. After all, we did say we were going to make it Black and beautiful, and this is truly a beautiful African garment." She started to say, "Wait till you see what Ben Ali is wearing." But she thought she should save some of the goodies for later on—in the spirit of surprise.

Charlene said, "I guess you figured if you were going to tear your fine Black ass, you might as well tear it good fashion. Wow!"

Pam Jefferson said quietly to Yoruba, "More Black power to you, my favorite sister." Like she was proclaiming benediction.

La-Smythe came on encouragingly with: "I don't think there'll be any signifying just because your dress is different."

They were ready to go now to the backstage dressing room where the others had already gathered. They were running behind time. Actually, Yoruba's colleagues-in-conspiracy were no longer running. They had slowed down to a walk. The Queen's magnificent gown had had a sobering effect. She told them to go ahead without her. "I promised Lumumba I would wait for him. He's going to escort me to the backstage dressing room."

Pam Jefferson asked her, "Are you sure we shouldn't wait?" With a sisterly concern.

Charlene said, "We might as well face the howling mob together. Go down swinging side by side."

Yoruba shook her head. "Please go. I really truly want you to. I'll be along directly as soon as Lumumba comes for me."

And they kissed her on the cheek and left her. And went to meet their fate which was swiftly moving toward them somewhat like a white tornado.

When they left she closed the door behind them, slowly. Then she went and stared at the lovely glittering vision in the mirror. What in the devil was keeping Lumumba? She was beautiful! Truly beautiful. She told herself repeatedly. Queen of Queens! Princess of princesses! But where in the devil was Lumumba? How had she let him talk her into wearing this African gown? She took it off and put on the one her mother bought her. Took that one off hurriedly, before Lumumba arrived for her, and put on the African gown again. She paced the floor. She went to the bathroom. Came back and paced the floor again.

Every single one of Yoruba's firm and militant resolves was melting by the second, now that the actual time had come. It was so much easier to talk militant and act militant than it was to do militant, Yoruba suddenly realized. She did not want to hurt Mrs. Patterson. Or Mrs. Brap-bap. And after what she had gone through with her mother that very same afternoon, her own dearly beloved mother, she was hardly in the mood for more of same, and in triple measure. It didn't take much imagination on Yoruba's part to conjure up the kind of reception she would receive at the hands of the famous Femmes Fatales. Hadn't her African gown already unnerved her colleagues-of-the-militant-conspiracy? By the time Lumumba came for her, she, the girl, Yoruba, was a very shaky revolutionary.

In the suite now with her Captain, she went into his arms. She felt like letting herself go, having a good cry right then and there in the now familiar comfort of his arms. But she wouldn't, couldn't do it. She must not cry now. She must be strong. Must not give in to her feelings. Must be strong for him—for her—for Blackness.

She stood away from him and stared at him, and him at her. He was so handsome in his African robe, he actually looked edible. He said, "My queen!" Like he was uttering a soulful prayer of thanksgiving to the Gods of his forefathers. "You're so beautiful it hurts the heart!" He seemed to suffer from delicious pain.

She shook her head admiringly. "If I'm the Queen of Sheba, you're a Black shining knight of olden times and times to come. You're my handsome prince—you're the King of—"

But he was a sensitive and observant man, and her eyes told him a different story. He said, "Okay, what's the matter, baby?"

She said, "Nothing is the mat—" And her voice broke off. And when she spoke again she said, "How did we get ourselves into this mess, Ben Ali? I mean, I need to have my head examined. We don't need this stupid cotillion, and it surely doesn't need Lumumba and his queen. I know it's all my fault. You told me it was a whole lot of bourgeois stupidness, but I wouldn't listen to you. I mean, it isn't too late though, is it? Let's really be Black and beautiful and walk right out of here this minute and go uptown and have a ball somewhere where Blackness is appreciated."

For once in his young life he was speechless. Momentarily. Then he said, "You really mean it?"

And she answered, "I really mean it." Shaky voice and everything.

He said, "What the hell are we waiting for?"

She felt an overwhelming relief coursing through her entire being, like a cool glass of ice-cold lemonade in the heat of summer, cooling her inside and out, and at the same time giving her a warmish feeling. As he helped her gather up her things. She was trembling with excitement, as they left the suite and double-locked the door. He took her by the hand, and they turned to face each other, and the words formed in their mouth, simultaneously, as in concert they said, "No—"

Then she said softly, "No?"

And he said, "Yes!" In full agreement. Then said, "Let's sit down and talk it over." They went back into the suite.

"Now," he said, as they sat on the sofa, with his arms around her shoulders. "What happened? What's the matter? Why did you suggest we do a cop-out?"

"Nothing, Ben Ali. I don't know what got into me. I just thought maybe we should make a clean break and leave it all behind us."

He said, "Leave Pam and Charlene behind to face the music by their lonesome? That's not like my Queen of Sheba."

Her eyes averted his. "I figured they'd survive. And besides, they're dressed just like the rest of them. They're not wearing colorful African garments."

"And leave Lady Daphne and Mr. Matt behind?"

Her eyes began to fill. "Oh Ben Ali, I just panicked momentarily. I wouldn't've really copped-out on the folks. You know I wouldn't've, don't you, darling? You wouldn't've let me anyhow."

He took her into his arms and kissed away her tears. "I know. It's not easy to make a sharp break with the present-past. I understand. I myself don't like going out there and messing up these people's pretty white cotillion. But look at it this way. We won't be messing it up. We'll be beautifying it. We'll be making it Black and beautiful and significant instead of white and pretty and meaningless." He kissed away her tears again. "Look," he said, "these colored cotillions are aimed against our race pride—against our sense of Black identity—against nationhood and unity. But we can change this thing tonight into its very opposite—and aim the guns the other way. It's the least that we can do."

"I know, Ben Ali, I know, but—" She also knew that she would go with him and take part in the Grand Cotillion. Somehow she'd known it all along, even during those few fleeting moments earlier when they had gone through all those motions of leaving all cotillions, she'd known that they would make the right decisions, because she was his Queen of Sheba and he was the King of Wise Men all the way from Timbuktu. She liked for him to talk things out with her. She knew if she were an Eskimo, he could sell her ice cubes at the North Pole in the dead of winter, if he talked to her long enough. She said, "I know—I'm so silly—crying like a fool. I wasn't going to run out on anybody. I just needed your reassurance was the only thing."

He said he understood. And so they got themselves together and headed backstage, where the storm had raged momentarily, then had quietly blown out to sea. All things considered, it might have been a nobler thing had Yoruba and her captain made tracks up to Harlem instead of backstage to the dressing room. It depended on your point of view.

Entirely on your point of view.

All the maidens and the matrons (including Mr. P. Potts) would have kissed and made up, all would have been forgiven, had not Lumumba brought Yoruba to the door of the backstage dressing room at this particular moment. He was about to leave her and repair, with dignity, to the ballroom floor there to wait along with the other escorts, for her father to deliver her, in the sacrificial ceremony. That was when it really hit the fan. As they stood there underneath their natural hairdos in their African ensembles, he with his right shoulder bare. Both smiling nervously.

When Mrs. Patterson spied them at the door, she jumped up and down like her drawers were full of bumblebees. "No! No! No! No!" As if she were being raped, deliciously, and murdered. The dear nonviolent Christian lady snatched up a vase of flowers and ran toward them. They had not expected such a flowery welcome.

Mrs. Downjohn pulled the fire extinguisher from the wall and ran toward Lumumba at the door. "Get out! Get out! Get out! You naked savage!" Lumumba, with his robe bare at one of the shoulders, would have been bare all over if Mrs. Downjohn had gotten ahold of him. She would have defrocked the dude for sure. He was saved by a couple of vigilantes who were doing sentry duty at the door, and they took him away struggling, to join the other escorts, leaving Yoruba to face the Christian Femmes Fatales who at this point were slightly overwrought. And who could blame them?

Dear overwrought Mrs. Pee-Pee backed Yoruba in a corner, waving a vase over the head of her favorite dubutante, darkly beautiful Yoruba, apple of Mrs. Pee-Pee's blue eyes.

"But Mrs. Patterson!" Yoruba fearfully protested.

"Don't you Missus me!" Mrs. Pee-Pee exclaimed. "You—you—you—you—of all people—you—you—" She fished around desperately in her extensive vocabulary, "You—you—you—you—" for the ugliest word she could utter out of her entire repertoire of ugliness. "You—you—you—Black militant!"

Brap-bap wrested the vase from Patterson. "Wait a minute! Just a damn minute now!"

Mrs. Downjohn said, "Let 'em wear our wigs! Let 'em wear our wigs!" And she pulled hers off and ran toward one of the frightened girls. She had Charlene backed into a corner now. Mrs. Downjohn waved her silver-colored wig at Charlene. Mrs. Downjohn's own natural hair was short and black at the edges and gray at the roots, and God knows what color in between. Charlene warded the dumpy woman off with both hands, shouting, "NO! No! Hell no!" All Mrs. Downjohn was trying to do was to make the dear girl pretty. Right?

The ladies of the Femmes Fatales were all dewigged now and cornering the natural girls, who were putting up a good fight, outnumbered though they definitely were. Mrs. Patterson took her wig off and came toward Yoruba. "Now, dear girl, be reasonable! Be reasona—"

"No!" Yoruba backed away. "I will not be reasonable!"

"I've known your family all these years! All these years—"

"I will not be reasonable!"

Miss Pee-Pee was upon Yoruba now and had her cornered. "Now, Yoruba—now Yoruba—darling dear—dearest darling—"

She tried to put the yellow wig on Yoruba's head and in the scuffle it fell to the floor and got stepped upon. Mrs. Pee-Pee picked up her expensive wig, which was now battered, dirty and discolored. She started to cry as if she had just lost the best friend she had on this earth, weeping anguished tears. She turned and ran out of the dressing room. She made her way back to the Patterson cotton patch, and dragged Lady Daphne with her to the dressing room backstage. By the time they got backstage again, La-Smythe had made her peace and was wearing Mrs. Lonestone's orange-colored store-bought piece, replete with artificial dandruff.

Otherwise, the situation was in a normal state of heavenly uproar. Some of the sweet and innocent Heightsters silently weeping over all their fondest dreams going up in smoke, though no one was smoking grass. Or were they?

Charitable Mrs. Brasswork was trying valiantly to put her famous red wig on Pamela Jefferson's head. Annie Brasswork's natural hair had been dyed so many colors and had died so many deaths, it was multicolored now, and it was impossible to tell what its original color had been. By now, even she did not remember. Then too, the dear girl's hair was spotty, bald in places, like a half-picked row in the cotton patch. Somehow in the scuffle with Pam Jefferson, someone stepped on the bottom of her hoopskirt, and the skirt went to pieces from the bottom to the waist, as did Annie Brasswork, as she stood there defrocked before the world, and with no drawers on. The hair on the dear one's matronhead was a patchy salt-and-pepper coiffure, but looked better than her hair atop. And was better groomed.

Now she stood there in the center of the uproar with her backside and her frontside open to the sea. Fore and aft she was exposed. She began to jump up and down, screaming, "Ipso facto! Certiorari! Sine qua non! Prima facie! Shit! Damn! Hell! Motherfucker! Fifth Amendment!"

Lady Daphne could not believe her eyes or ears. Maybe she had drunk too much of Mr. Patterson's sweetness. These could not be the first Black families, the highest of the high society! And especially this could not be Antoinette Brasswork of the famous Crowning Heights Brassworks! No! No! Miss Daphne had drunk too much. Mr. Pat had played a trick on her. She looked about her and everything and everybody seemed to be on a strange and terrifying trip. She closed her eyes and hoped her ears would also close.

"Ex post facto! Quid pro quo! Res adjudicata! Kiss my ass! With all deliberate speed!" Leaping up and down and all about.

This couldn't be Annie Brasswork? Could it?

Mrs. Brap-bap was shouting now, "Hold it! Hold it!" Her own dear wig perched upon her head lopsided.

Mrs. Patterson dragged Lady Daphne toward her darling daughter. "Look at her!" she screamed. "Look at your daughter! Your daughter! Your daughter!"

"What's the matter with my daughter?" Lady Daphne asked. Then she did a double take. The dress! The dress! Then she knew she'd had too much to drink.

"What's the matter—what's the matter?—You ask me what's the matter—what's the matter—and there she stands with no head on her hair—with no head on her hair—and messing up my Cotillion—my Grand Cotillion—Grand Cotillion—after all I've done for you people—for you people! And look at that horrible dress she's got on!"

"Wait a minute!" Miss Daphne ordered. "You wait just a minute!" She closed her eyes and reopened them, but everything was still the same, even more so.

"After all the trouble I went to take niggers like you Lovejoys out of the gutter, this is all the thanks I get! All the thanks I get!"

"Quiet! Quiet!" Brap-bap was screaming now for quiet. And quiet was finally and quietly maintained, although, even so, you could hear the terrible silent broken-hearted weeping of the disappointed Heightsters, who knew all the while that the Harlem savages had no business in their Grand Cotillion. But you couldn't tell Mrs. Patterson anything once the missionary bug bit her on her skinny bottom.

Mrs. Brap-bap, speaking hoarsely, said, "Now everybody is out there waiting and the show must go on. Now we had a little misunderstanding, but it's time to kiss and make up, so to speak."

"I'll never kiss one of them with hair on their heads!" Mrs. Downjohn firmly stated.

"So to speak!" Brap-bap shouted, quietly, evenly. "I said, so to speak, you emptyheaded, nappyheaded—"

"My head ain't nappy! My head ain't nappy!" Mrs. Downjohn stoutly shouted. "It's just as good as anybody's!"

"All right! All right! Now, I think the girls made a mistake with their Afros and whatnot, but I think we ought to love each other enough to be good sports about it."

"I am not a sporting woman! Am not a sporting woman!"

"This ain't no love-in either!"

Brap-bap continued. "I'm for forgiving and forgetting. Let all the girls participate. It'll be a different kind of cotillion and it'll make history. We'll make good hair bad hair and bad hair good hair. Okay! Just because we're colored we don't have to look on the dark side all the time."

"No! No! No! No!" Mrs. Patterson came back to life, temporarily.

"Let's take a vote," Brap-bap suggested.

You guessed it, sport. She lost the vote.

"Out! Out! You woolly-headed savages!"

Miss Daphne shouted, "No! No! You can't do this to my darling daughter!"

Well, but they would do it to her darling daughter. Right?

The only thing, in all the confusion, they forgot to tell the lady who was calling out the names. The Cotillion had started without the knowledge of some of the Fat Tails. During the first part of the race riot in the dressing room, Brap-bap had sneaked out of the place and told the people to put the show on the road. Which they did, and promptly.

When Yoruba heard them call her name, she walked boldly with a nervous dignity out on the stage. At first there was one loud gasp from the audience, then a murmur went over the ballroom, then wild applause from some. They say a couple of people fainted. It was recorded that Yoruba was the first natural woman to make her grand debut in the annals of cotillions, and when she debuted, it was like the living end—of something. It was supreme cotillion. People did not believe their eyes.

Her own eyes were teary when she walked out on the stage. People seated in the cotton patches near the stage saw the tears and sighed. "Ohh! She's taking her debut to heart. Oh! How sweet!"

Her father walked out from the other side of the stage, straight as a drunk man, to bow and receive his daughter's curtsey and to take her hand and walk her down the steps to the ballroom floor and dance a waltz with her and hand her over to Lumumba. Okay? He walked with dignity and erect as only a truly drunken man can walk. At which point ten or fifteen Fat Tails rushed upon the stage, screaming: "No!"

"No!"

"No!"

"You cannot go on! Cannot go on!"

Mrs. Pee-Pee rushed out on the stage and seized the mike. "This is a mistake!" she screamed. "A horrible mistake! Horrible mistake! Mistake! Mistake! They are rioting the race! They are rioting the race!"

Brap-bap dragged her off the stage.

Big Matt staggered up to the mike and was somehow inspired to spit out poetry(?).

"All you high-society wenches better git up and walk,
Cause Mr. Matthew Lovejoy gonna start some of his nasty talk!"

Lady Daphne shouting from the wings, "My husband is a poet! My dear husband is a poet!" She's had too much to drink. You think?

They pushed Matt away from the mike and he sat heavily down upon a chair that wasn't there. Lumumba leaped up on the stage and helped Big Matt to his feet, and at the same time seized the mike. And shouted, "Black brothers and sisters, come out of the cotton patches! It's time to lay your burden down! Come out of the cotton patch, all you Toms and Aunt Jemimas! Follow us to liberation! Be done with false illusions! Come with us to the real world! Come with us to the real world!" He ended with: "Up the Black Nation!" And gave the proud salute. And took Yoruba by one arm and Big Matt by the other, and walked down the steps to the ballroom floor.

People were jumping up and down in the cotton patches. A few were shouting, "Black Power!" and "Up the Black Nation!" Like they had lost their cotton-picking minds. Can you imagine? At the Waldorf? A very few were actually leaving. Pam Jefferson, La-Smythe and Charlene came out on the stage and followed Yoruba. Even Brassy Brenda came.

Lady Daphne ran out on stage. "Don't leave me! I'm going with you!"

Mrs. Patterson ran after her. Grabbed her by the arm. "You don't have to go! You don't have to go! We know you didn't know about it! Know you didn't know about it! Stay with us, my diamond in the rough! My precious diamond in the rough! You understand! You understand!"

Lady Daphne stood there for an endless moment (seemed a lifetime) torn between the old and new, between illusion and reality. All her life she had lived sincerely in a world of dreams and fancy. Where indeed was the really real world? With Miss Prissy or Lumumba? She should not have had so much to drink of that sweetness of the Pattersons. I need a clear head, she told herself, to find my way to the really real world. Whichever and wherever. She stared out toward where Big Matt and Lumumba were, and darling beautiful short-and-nappy-haired Yoruba. They were beckoning to her frantically. She looked back into Miss Prissy's face. Miss Prissy was a good missionary-hearted woman who meant well to all the world, especially to the underprivileged. A lady of the genteel classes whom Daphne had always looked up to.

"We want you with us!" Miss Prissy shouted. "You understand! Please tell me that you understand." Sincerity oozed from every pore. Daphne saw Matt start to walk back for her.

Then she pulled away from dear Priscilla, and drew herself up to her natural height, which was taller than she'd ever stood. "Yes," she said, "I understand. Finally I understand. And that's exactly why I going with my people." And she went to join the family.

Mrs. Pee-Pee turned to the awestruck orchestra. "Strike up the band! Strike up the band!"

And the startled band played "Dixie."

Which made others leave Ye Olde Plantation.

All things considered, it was the most unusual cotillion in the history of cotillions. By the time Matt and Yoruba and Lumumba and Daphne had walked across the ballroom to the exit, others joined the exodus from Dixieland, even as the band played "Dixie." Jeffersons, Johnsons, Brap-baps, Walkers.

And the famous Femmes Fatales would never ever be the same. Which just goes to show you, you can take democracy and freedom and integration and due process and all them damn amendments too damn far. Particularly when it comes to colored people. Especially them that's truly Black. The kind that's always screaming about Black manhood and dignity, peace and power and liberation and Nationhood. The Black extremist demagogues who can't be bribed, and so you know they can't be trusted. That's the thing you got to watch.

Understand?

/813.54K48C>C1/